A Chance to Say Yes

Books by Tina Murray, PH.D.

Heston Demming Mysteries
A Chance to Say Yes
A Wild Dream of Love
A Big Fan of Yours

A Chance to Say Yes

Tina Murray

SPEAKING VOLUMES, LLC
NAPLES, FLORIDA
2021

A Chance to Say Yes

Cover design by Hannah Linder

ISBN 978-1-64540-553-5

Dedication

To the memory of my beloved parents, who were the most wonderful mother and father and my best friends, and whom I dearly miss.

Acknowledgments

I would like to thank the following people for their assistance in the production and publication of A Chance to Say Yes:

My insightful editor, Vickie DuBois; my dear parents, Leon Benton Murray and Zena Griffith Murray; Gwen Griffith; Irene Griffith; Stephen Lifschitz, Ph.D.; Linda and J.C. Arlington; Judy Hawks; J. Robert Verbesey; John Cooper; Matt Goff; Jordan Hoyt, Mary E. White; Vicki Fillmore, Nancy Burns Rugen; Deborah Angus, Jane Kennedy Sutton, Sandy Lender; M. B. Weston; Prudy Taylor Board, and Cathy and Ed Anderson and Treecie.

Heartfelt thanks, too, to the gifted acting teachers in my past: Robert "Buckets" Lowery, Sherman Marks, and Harry Mastrogeorge. A special word of thanks goes to author Pat Conroy, whom I met at a book signing some years ago at the Miami Book Fair, and who encouraged me to persevere as a writer no matter who said what. I can still feel the "buzz" I felt late that night as I rode home alone on the deserted Miami Metrorail, en route to my parked car—and my future career as a novelist.

Others, too, helped my debut novel on its way by offering me aid, encouragement, good wishes, and opportunities to further my book's success. Please know that I appreciate all of you. I simply am not able to list everyone here.

Tina Murray, Ph.D. Naples, Florida

Chapter One

Standing upon the riprap seawall, Heston Demming surveyed his new domain, an intimate, subtropical waterfront estate—a small paradise, in fact—complete with mansion and manicured lawn, set like a cultured pearl on silvery Naples Bay. *No one could deny it,* Heston assured himself proudly. His new home—six thousand square feet of sumptuous splendor—was spectacular. So was his panoramic view of the bay, and the condo roofs and wild mangroves beyond it. His heart swelled in his chest.

"Awesome!" he cried, euphorically leaping high into the air and returning to earth too soon. Loose-jointed, he landed with innate grace on his sneaker-shod feet in the thick, springy, weed-free, green grass adjacent to the seawall. What he wanted was to soar. What he did, instead, was to launch into modern dance on the spongy, damp, backyard lawn. He had learned some cool moves in his last Broadway role. A few remained part of him.

"Yeah," he whispered fervently as he improvised, not caring what the elite neighbors on either side might think, if they should see or hear him through the box-shaped hedgerows. In his imagination, the morning sun shone like a single spotlight, following him across a dark stage, an invisible audience wildly cheering him on. Breathless, elated, he paused in his impromptu jazz-ballet and closed his eyes. As he stood still, his breathing became slow and rhythmic. Digging his front teeth into his lower lip, he listened, enraptured, to the sloshing sound of waves lapping the seawall. Salt air from the nearby Gulf of Mexico filled his lungs. It was the smell of home. Overhead, a seagull cawed to its mates.

"Tell 'em, man," Heston muttered hoarsely. "Tell 'em all. I'm back and I won." To his surprise, three seagulls cawed in response, and he laughed aloud in delight.

"I rule!" he bellowed, to the elements, fists raised high into the sky. Now he was king, complete with palace, of a luxury neighborhood, *the* luxury neighborhood of his childhood fantasies, Port Royal. The palace was now real—and all his. He owned every grubbing inch of it. He had fought like a mongrel for every coin it took to buy the place. He had compromised, sold out, sold people down the river, bartered his integrity, slaughtered his own soul in the process, and even drunk himself into an endless stupor. He had done whatever it took to get there. Now, at long last, he had arrived.

Now he was in control. He had returned home the conquering hero, and, in his final act of war, he had stormed and taken the last citadel, the bastion of wealth which had excluded him so cruelly in youth. So what if he'd needed a drink to fill the hole in his gut? He had the drinking under control now. He'd been clean and sober for nearly a year. He had gotten his appetite back. At this moment, even his marriage to Malevolent Maude didn't seem so bad. A smile played upon his lips but fell away. Instantly, he beat back the painful memories.

He *needed* this feeling of victory. His heart throbbed in his chest. Breathing deeply, he studied the shimmering bay waters, the brilliant blue sky, the wooden dock that ran from the seawall out into the bay. The dock slip was empty and waiting. Soon his new sailing yacht, *Windswept*, would arrive. Scanning the horizon, he searched for a sign of the vessel. He saw other watercraft—tiny sailfish and motor boats, but no sign yet of his yacht.

As he turned towards the mansion, his gaze followed the row of stately, column-like royal palm trees leading to the south side of the westward-facing British Colonial mansion. He scanned the green asphalt tennis court, and then followed the long lanai which ran the length of the back side of the pale-yellow stucco mansion. Gazing upward, he admired his new home's color scheme.

The three-storied house was trimmed in white and crowned with a white tile roof. Its window shutters were colored the deepest hunter green. *Florida tasteful.* He approved. He couldn't decide which view he liked better, this back side of the house or the front, with its imposing façade, its wide flight of entryway steps, circular stone driveway, tiered fountain, and screen of giant, leafy, multi-trunked banyans on either side of the brass-barred gate.

His gaze lowered as he heard a familiar giggle.

He spotted his tiny, blonde daughter, Winnie, rolling croquet balls across a sliver of manicured lawn. Closing his eyes, he mouthed a silent prayer to the Greater Power. He would remember this moment for the rest of his life. The best part was that he could continue to make reparations, now, to the people in Naples whom he had wronged. Hard as it was, he had to do it. His rehab program demanded it.

"Daddy, watch me!" cried Winnie, throwing down a hard, round ball.

"Attagirl, Winner!" responded Heston, opening his eyes. He shuddered in gratitude.

Now he, Heston Demming, was an international celebrity, acclaimed the world over, and *these people* would clamor for *his* attention, for *his* respect, as he had once clamored for theirs. . He had shown them all, all the rich kids who had lorded it over him in school. He had grown up less than five miles away, on the wrong side of U.S. 41, in a modest but respectable section of town known as Lake Park. Now his servants would live in Lake Park. He would hold court on exclusive Galleon Drive, in a designer-decorated castle secreted at the tip of the premier bight and lodged along a secluded bay-front cul-de-sac.

"We have guests arriving, Heston!" Maude called from pool deck, breaking his reverie. "They just phoned. I hate it when nosy pests drop in uninvited."

Maude Winston Demming—strawberry-blonde, thin, and lanky—was dallying at the outdoor table in the shade of the lanai. Maude, he, and their daughter, four-year-old Winston, had just taken breakfast for the first time in their new home-- egg-white omelets, fresh berries, and hot tea. Darjeeling wasn't Johnny Walker Blue, but this morning it seemed just as heady to him. Even his wife, a former model, had managed to nibble a few bites of solid food.

Today Heston didn't want guests any more than Maude did. He wanted to savor his kill. Swiveling full circle, he raised his hand to block the sun's glare. Gazing out at the bay, he saw light flash on the water's surface. Could it be his yacht approaching?

"Daddy! Daddy!" Winnie scampered towards him across the grass.

As his daughter reached him, he swept her up into his arms and hoisted her onto his left hip. Giggling, she pecked his face with small, dry kisses.

He laughed. "Can you see our big sailboat yet, Ladybug?" he asked her, pointing towards the sparkling water. Rubbing the sunlight from her eyes, Winnie shook her head.

"No, Daddy."

"Me neither. Not yet. But she's coming."

"Can we ride her, Daddy?"

"You betcha," said Heston, chuckling with delight. He couldn't wait to take her out. The change would be good for Win. He had been worried about his daughter lately, especially since returning home from his most recent job, shooting the ribald comedy, *Mars to Earth Men,* in Vancouver. The picture had wrapped a month ago.

What was that? He did a double-take at the bay waters, disappointed when he realized that the flash of light had been only a jet ski, reflecting the sunlight as it skimmed towards Gordon Pass, the waterway leading from Naples Bay into the open Gulf of Mexico. Restlessly, his eyes searched for the sailing ship, until Winnie's small fist pummeled his shoulder.

"Look, Daddy—peoples." Winnie pointed towards the lanai.

Glancing back towards the house, Heston saw, indeed, that visitors had arrived. Maude now stood talking to a man and a woman; whom she was inviting to sit down at the outdoor table.

The svelte woman dressed in resort-casual he recognized as his ex-wife, Inez. *Who could forget that body?* During their four-year marriage, it had almost made up for her relentless willfulness. During the past week, while house-hunting in Naples, he had been keenly aware of Inez's renewed sexual interest in him.

True to form, Inez was bedecked now with gold jewelry, costly bangles which glittered, even in the shadows of the lanai. Heston recognized the dark-haired, panther-like man with her as Danny Vega, Inez's stepson, whom he had met a few times over the years. Like the smooth real-estate professionals they were, Inez and Danny sat down at the patio table and began chatting with Maude. Something—someone—was missing...*Franco.*

Heston heard Inez and Danny declining refreshments as he approached the lanai, daughter Winnie still perched on his hip. Maude waived the maid away imperiously. He hated the way his wife treated the servants, as though they were a subhuman species. He learned the hard way that Maude lacked empathy. It was a hard quality to endure in a mate. He should have realized, early on, that her glittery, powder-blue eyes, and affect-less countenance signaled trouble. Infatuated, and on the rebound once again from Montserrat Flynn, he had seen only vacant bliss in those rocky shallows. *What a joke.*

"Hess! Hello, my handsome ex-husband!" said Inez, rising to air-kiss his cheek. "Hello, again, precious little one," she remarked to Winnie.

Shyly, Winnie buried her face in Heston's shoulder. With a good-natured shrug, Inez sat back down and crossed her lithesome, suntanned legs.

"Good to see you, Inez. Danny." Heston grabbed Danny Vega's outstretched paw and pumped it vigorously. "Where's my son, Inez? Where's Franco?"

"At his middle school, Hess," laughed Inez. Her eyes swept over his body.

Heston knew he was in better shape now than when they'd been married. His trainer kept him in perfect condition.

"Bring him this afternoon," said Heston.

"This afternoon he has soccer practice," whined Inez. "Franco's a devotee. A real soccer fiend. Nothing interferes with his practice, not even his movie-star papa."

"Especially his movie-star papa. I want you to bring the boy around, Inez," Heston demanded sincerely. "I want to spend time with Franco. It's one of the reasons I've moved back to Naples. I want my son to see *this*. I want him to see what he is heir to. Winnie needs to know her big brother, too, don't you, sweetie-pie?"

Winnie nodded, her face still buried. He fingered her fine blonde hair. Inwardly, he hoped his bravado masked his uncertainty. He and Franco had never really *connected*. Franco made him uncomfortable. He felt the boy disliked him.

"Hey, Cuteness," growled Danny Vega to Winnie, who had peeked around cautiously. Teasingly, Danny poked a sausage-like forefinger into the girl's ribs. Winnie flashed a smile at Danny and buried her face again, giggling. Gratified, Danny sank back in his chair and stretched lazily. Slipping into a chair at table, Heston deposited Winnie onto the ground. Instantly, the child sped back onto the lawn and resumed chunking croquet balls into the thick grass.

"Beautiful. Like her mother," Danny said, eyeing Maude cavalierly. Only the faintest smirk crossed Maude's full lips.

Watch out, Vega. Heston had often seen his wife toy with new prey. On the other hand, maybe this cat-like man was up to the game.

"How nice of you to come," said Maude icily to Inez. "This is lovely weather, isn't it? For January, certainly." Maude secured a lock of straight, pink-blonde hair behind her left ear. He could feel Maude's irritation. Everything irritated Maude now. Her powder-blue eyes stared cool and hard as sapphires.

"We came to make sure you'd settled in properly," Inez announced. "I also had a few more papers for you to sign." Inez tapped the zippered portfolio case in her lap.

"We're waiting for my new yacht," he announced proudly. "The delivery crew's bringing her in this morning." He was glad his ex-wife, Inez, was here to see his winnings. It made his triumph even more glorious. *Eat this, Inez.*

Guiltily, Heston rebuked himself in silence. Curious, Danny picked up a slick brochure from the table top. A grand sailing vessel was pictured on the front page.

"*Windswept*," said Heston, pointing to the picture.

"What a beaut" whistled Danny. "She yours?"

"She is now," he replied, his mouth widening, his grin unstoppable.

"My version was custom-built. Do you sail, Vega?"

Danny glanced at him sideways. "My sport is tennis"

Heston expanded, peacock-like. "*Windswept* is a 56-foot cruiser, an aft-cockpit ketch with three staterooms below deck, all polished brass and teak. I based her detailing on a sailing yacht I crewed during high school and college, a ketch called *Lover's Folly*. We roamed the Caribbean Sea like pirates." He laughed, abashed. "Otherwise, she's state-of-the-art."

"There's the smile the world pays to see," observed Inez to Maude.

He stabbed Inez with a petrified grin. *Still the condescending bitch.* "Are you sure you won't have a drink before you leave?" he asked her bluntly.

Danny raised his eyebrows and put down the brochure.

"I was paying you a compliment, Hess," placated Inez.

"Well, it is true, Heston," observed Maude dourly. "The world does pay to see your every move."

"And yours," Danny said to Maude.

"Yes," agreed Maude arrogantly. "But not as much as it pays him. Haven't you heard? Heston is Heaven's Gift to the Women of Earth. Seriously. That's the part he played in the movie he just shot. I'm not joking."

"Enough, Maude," Heston ordered, his jaw locked.

"I can't wait to see it, Hess. I see all your films," said Inez.

"Was it like that before he was a star, Inez?" asked Maude. "Did the girls come crawling out of the woodwork back then, too?"

Inez raised a penciled eyebrow. "The girls and the boys. I couldn't keep rivals away from him. Even at his poorest, they wanted him."

"Unlike you?" Maude said acidly.

"Inez, do you ever see Poppy Craft?" Heston asked quickly, diverting the women's attention from the rancor of their impending cat fight. He heard the sharp intake of breath from Inez as the name registered. Three faces turned towards him.

"Poppy and I were kids together," he explained, raising his eyebrows in feigned innocence. "Do you ever see her?"

"Why, no," Inez said, her earrings shimmering. "Why do you ask, Hess?"

He knew the mention of another woman had hurt Inez. He wished it had hurt Maude, too, but his second wife knew little about his past. He had never trusted her enough to share himself, and she had never cared enough to ask.

Danny snapped to attention. "You mean Poppy Craft-Talbot, the local art dealer?" he asked pointedly. "She's the only Poppy I know."

Inez glared at her stepson, but managed to tame her frown.

8

Amused, Heston sensed that Danny relished his stepmother's discomfort.

"Oh, yes, I know *of* her—but I rarely run across her," Inez lied, admiring her own nails.

Heston's pulse raced. "You talk to Poppy sometimes? Where is she? How can I get in touch with her?" he demanded. He would make peace with himself or die trying. This was just another step on that road.

"Poppy owns a gallery at The Village on Venetian Bay. It's called Poppy Wallace Fine Art. How I know? She's my best-babe Sasha's best girlfriend," Danny explained.

"I need to talk to Poppy," Heston said. "I need to look her up next. For the same reason I looked you up, Inez. To make reparations. Of course, I was also looking for the best real estate agent in Naples. You're good. I'll give you your due."

"I'm damned good," Inez fired back. Cattily, she leaned forward and said in a confidential tone, "Everyone in town knows you treated the Craft girl shabbily, Heston. You do owe the poor dear a few kind words. She's in a loveless marriage, you know, with a humdrum accountant, a great oaf of a Texan. He's long on security, but short on *va-va-voom*."

"I didn't know."

"Worse, she's barren. Life has been less than kind to the poor, homely thing."

"You're all heart, as usual, Inez," he observed wryly, his heart twisting inside him.

"Poppy's okay, Heston. Ignore this blather. So you're on the wagon, eh, man?" Danny asked him, out of the blue. Scandalized, the two women snickered at one another, rolling their eyes. "What? I read it in the Star," Danny glowered hotly.

"The whole world knows my business," grumbled Heston, throwing up his hands.

"Daddy, look!" cried Winnie, pointing, from out on the lawn. "Big boat coming!"

"*Oooh,* Hess!" squealed Inez insincerely as *Windswept* motored into view. "She's divine!"

"Yep! That's the word for her, Inez. Divine," he radiated, as he and Danny charged down to the dock. Taking Winnie reluctantly by the hand, Maude meandered across the grass lawn, while Inez high-stepped prissily behind the two men, the unneeded pouch of papers tucked beneath her arm.

Heston's heart raced at the sight of his yacht's billowing sails. *Windswept* was beautiful—tall, elegant, magnificent in her potential mastery of the sea. Closing his eyes, he recalled the thrill of riding the high seas when he had taken her for a stormy test sail only days earlier in Fort Lauderdale. Now he was welcoming the vessel to her permanent home.

Gathering at water's edge, the spellbound party watched as the gleaming vessel glided towards them, across the bay waters and motored into the slip. *Windswept's* wide deck was white; her long hull, navy blue. Feverishly, Heston watched the delivery crew secure her moorings. He had hired two crew members of his own, both of whom were also on board.

Taking possession of the adventure ship was the culmination of Heston's lifelong fantasy—one of them, at any rate. Only winning the heart of Montserrat Flynn, the Irish-Catalan beauty who had eluded him since youth, could have given him greater satisfaction.

***

Twenty-four hours later, three miles to the north, Poppy Craft-Talbot entered the door of Rainbow's, and her world exploded.

"Hey, Poppy! Have you heard the news?" cried perky Cookie Lee, waving from behind the counter of her popular, upscale coffee shop. Rainbow's on Fifth—known simply as Rainbow's by the affluent year-rounders—was the caffeine hub of downtown Naples.

"What news?" Poppy asked, cocking her head brightly.

"Your old boyfriend—that movie star, Heston Demming—the one you dated in high school, remember? He's moved back to town! Can you believe it? I've been waiting for you come in, just so I could tell you!" Cookie's golden ringlets danced as she chattered. "Want your usual latte, Poppy?"

Instinctively, Poppy nodded 'yes,' but she could not utter a sound. Her mouth was suddenly sandpaper. Her cheeks flamed. Her heart was pounding a hole in her chest. Customers in the coffee bar swirled into pinwheels of color. Melting before her eyes was the life she had built for herself, so painstakingly, over the past twenty years. Heston Demming *couldn't* be coming back into her life again. *He just couldn't be.*

"Fat-free milk, right, Poppy?" she heard Cookie bleat loudly from somewhere. She heard a strange, breathless swooshing noise as Cookie frothed milk in the steamer. Outside, a siren screamed down Fifth Avenue South, the scream echoing in Poppy's ears like past secrets racing back to haunt her.

"Uh-huh," Poppy heard herself utter. Her body felt numb yet bruised, as if the police car tearing past had crashed the window of Rainbow's coffee bar and run her down. Her legs quivered beneath her.

"The sugar's over there. Oh, you don't use sugar. I forgot," beamed Cookie, shoving a hot paper cup filled with espresso and steamed milk under Poppy's nose. Poppy arms wouldn't move, any more than her mouth would form words.

"Say, I like your new hair cut. Chin-length is good on you. Poppy! Hey, girl! Wake up!" snapped Cookie cheerily, setting the cup down on the counter. "I have other customers. That'll be three dollars and 18 cents, please ma'am." A few of the patrons tittered.

"Oh, of course," blurted Poppy, surprised to hear words coming from deep inside her own throat. Her cheeks burned. Somehow, she found her arm and hands. Fumbling through her straw bag, she felt the sharp edge of her plastic debit card. Grasping the card, she tried to swipe it through the machine on the counter but could not locate the slot. The intense odor of old coffee grounds hung heavily in the small shop. Her stomach lurched.

It must be a mistake. Why would Heston move back to Naples? Heston Demming was rich and famous now. He could live anywhere he wanted, anywhere in the world.

"Here, let me," said Cookie, grabbing the card from Poppy. Expertly, Cookie ran the card through the machine, and dropped it back into Poppy's open purse. Poppy's stomach flip-flopped ominously as she watched the simple action.

Fingers trembling, she managed to grasp the paper cup on the counter. She lifted the jiggling cup to her dry mouth. She gagged as the liquid touched her lips. Her fingers slackened. The warm cup slipped from her fingers, plopping onto the floor. Hot, milky, pale-brown liquid splashed across her slim ankles. The shock brought her back to reality.

"I'm sorry, Cookie," she croaked to the server, who quickly rounded the counter and soaked up the spill.

"Forget it, kid," said Cookie, her face worried. "It's my own fault. I upset you. I didn't mean to upset you. I shouldn't have dropped that bombshell on you. I should have warmed you up first. Like a teapot."

Dazed, Poppy watched from on high as Cookie dabbed a paper napkin against her wet ankles. Milky liquid stained her flat taupe sandals.

"Ruined in an instant—like my life," Poppy whispered.

"What's that?" asked Cookie, grabbing hold of the counter's edge and hopping to her feet. "Would you like another latte—on the house?"

"No...no...thank you, Cookie. Caffeine isn't what I need right now."

Cookie nodded her curly head. "Ask me, what you need is a stiff drink, honey," she said compassionately.

"At 10 a.m.?" Poppy eyed the wall clock above the counter. What she needed was to escape the building. *Right away.* Her churning gut urged her towards the front door of the shop. Her skin felt clammy.

"Too early for that apple-tini, eh? Well, you got a credit here any-time," Cookie said kindly.

Somehow, Poppy's feet began to walk Her fingers found the glass front door. Placing her hand on the cool pane, she steadied herself. She had to ask one question.

"Cookie," Poppy ventured, "How do you know Heston is coming?" home? I thought he had settled in California or Aspen or somewhere." Her stomach was a cyclone. But she *had* to know.

Cookie chewed her plump lower lip before answering. "Oh, honey. I saw him. He was in here day before yesterday. I talked to him. See? He autographed this menu for me. I'm gonna have it framed." The spidery black words would not focus. The print ran before Poppy's eyes. Droplets of dew beaded her upper lip.

Cookie continued. "He was here with his new wife. You know, that gorgeous supermodel—she's an actress now—Maude what's-her-name, Winston, that's it, skinny as a rail, and, if you can believe this, they were both in here with Heston's *first* wife, Inez, the one who still lives here in town, that go-getter real-estate broker you can't stand. Both wives at once! Pretty cozy, eh? Oh, honey, I'm sorry. They all ordered cappuccinos. They sat right out there on the sidewalk, at that very table, everybody asking for his autograph. Seems Inez has been showing him—and his new wife—swank homes all over Port Royal. For the past week. They say he bought one."

Bought one? "I thought Inez hated Heston," said Poppy, eyelids flutter-ing involuntarily.

"You know that gal," shrugged Cookie. "Anything for a buck. You look sick, honey. Let me help you sit down."

"No, please!" Poppy was absorbing the truth. He had come back. Her whole being screamed for escape. Thank Heaven it was Monday. Her gal-lery was closed on Mondays. She could go home, crawl into bed, pull the covers over her head, and have a good cry. She might even have that stiff drink Cookie prescribed. James would never know or care or bluster about her lack of responsibility. He had moved out three months ago.

"I'm sorry, Poppy," she heard Cookie say.

Pushing open the front door, Poppy found herself on the sidewalk. The impact of hot, humid air increased her nausea. Clinging to the wall, she edged around the side of the brick building into the back parking lot. Within seconds, she lost her breakfast yogurt into an open trash bin.

***

Heston Demming. Even his name made her weak.

Later that day, alone in her seventh-floor condo at Solarmarina, a high-rise on Vanderbilt Beach, Poppy lay sprawled across her queen-sized bed, her tense muscles relaxing. She had recovered her equilibrium, although the thought of eating still made her queasy. Now sipping a margarita, she savored the salty-sweet lime taste. Maybe the salt was from her tears. Her fingers wiped warm wetness from her eyelashes. Through sliding-glass doors, her raw eyes watched the blue-green Gulf of Mexico. Images of the past flooded her mind.

She saw Heston in the senior class play, a star even then, as he stole the show. She saw Heston, at high-school graduation, tall and handsome and silly-looking in his cap and gown. She saw him, home from college, standing on the beach, the legs of his trousers rolled up, his bare feet deep in wet sand, a loose cotton shirt hanging from his broad shoulders, the warm sun highlighting his wind-tossed brown hair with a golden halo. She saw him, in the dark, shadowy cabin of the sailboat, his muscular young body nude from the waist up, his face ice-hot with the glow of desire, his silver-gray eyes yearning for her touch. She felt him inside her, up against her, his heavy weight across her chest, his thrusting desire, telling her over and over again that she was the only girl he would ever love. She tasted his kiss…

Warm rivulets ran down her cheeks. She heard herself sobbing. Her round chest heaved. She gasped for air to fuel the heaving sobs. Her nose clogged. Placing her glass on the rattan bedside table, she clutched the ball of tissue in her hand and brought it to her nose. She blew her nose between sobs. After a time, her sobs subsided.

Bundling into a fetal position, Poppy laid quietly, her cheek pressed against a tear-soaked pillow. If only she hadn't listened to her Uncle Mel. She would give anything for another chance, a chance to live her life over again, a chance to say yes to Heston Demming's proposal of marriage. *Oh, so many years ago now…*

If only Heston hadn't met Montserrat Flynn that very night, twenty years earlier. Such a hideous quirk of fate. *Whatever happened to Montserrat?* She pondered hazily. *Why hadn't Heston married that girl? Why had he married Inez Greco instead?* Gratefully, Poppy savored the last drops of the lemon-lime liquid. Soon the images swam together, and she sank into the troubled sea of sleep. That night she dreamed Heston had uncovered her long-kept secret. She awoke in a sweat at dawn.

***

At work the next morning, Poppy's head throbbed. Her eyes felt stale and puffy as dried marshmallows. Even wet tea bags had failed to reduce the swelling. In spite of her misery, Poppy located her cell phone and dialed. Morning light had brought new clarity. Maybe Cookie had made a mistake. Maybe it simply wasn't true. Maybe Heston was just here on vacation. She was determined to know the truth about her old flame's return. There was only one way to find out. Go directly to the horse's mare.

A generic receptionist's voice answered the phone. "Good morning. Regal Properties. How may we serve you today?"

Poppy responded. "I'd like to speak to Inez Greco—I mean, Inez Vega, please."

"Whom may I say is calling?"

"Tell her it's Poppy Craft-Talbot. She's known me since high-school. It's a personal call, not business."

"One moment, please." Bland piano music tinkled for a few seconds and then clicked off. A mature woman's voice, sultry and throaty, with the faintest hint of an accent, came through the speaker.

"Poppy, dear. Inez Vega here. How are you? It has been ages." Inez pronounced her name *"EEE-ness,"* even though, legally, she had Anglicized the spelling. Aloud, Poppy responded in kind.

"Hello, Inez. Yes, I'm fine, thank you. I wanted to ask you something. S-Something personal."

"Oh?"

Poppy's throat constricted. She could feel the spite in Inez's tone. Inez knew why she had called. Poppy's whole face heated. She wanted to crawl into a hole and die. But she *had* to be sure.

"Yes. I wanted to ask you about...about..." The words wouldn't form.

"About Heston?" said Inez smugly.

So it is true. "Yes, Inez. It's true? He's moved back home to Naples?" Poppy heard a dainty cough, then a vindictive smile.

"Yes, Poppy, dear, it's true. Heston signed a contract. A few days ago. He's purchased a turnkey mansion in Port Royal—a grand, yellow British-Colonial winter home on Galleon Drive. It has everything—indoor pool, gym, tennis courts, a dock and yacht slip, with Gulf access. An eight-figure deal. Frankly, I'm in heaven," Inez bragged.

"I see," mumbled Poppy, her heart sinking. For years the premiere Naples neighborhood—until newer, outlying developments began to compete for status—bay-front Port Royal was themed on Jamaica's famed port city of the same name. Street names reflected its pirate and British Navy associations: Spyglass Lane, Rum Row, Captain's Walk, Admiralty Parade, Galleon Drive. The Port Royal Club, which fronted the Gulf of

Mexico, was a local social zenith.

"Heston's rich now, Poppy, rich beyond his wildest dreams, blast him! It should have been mine. At least I'll make a big commission on the sale. Frankly, I was shocked when he looked me up last week."

Poppy winced. This was how she remembered Inez, as money-mad. She could just picture Inez—cropped dark hair, svelte body, short skirt, golden earrings—sitting in her plush office. She let Inez ramble on. *It doesn't matter now.* The worst was true. Now what? Poppy's stomach dropped to her feet. Her skin flushed hot and cold. Thank goodness she didn't have to look Inez in the eye.

Inez prattled into her ear. "You just missed him as matter of fact. I could have handed him the phone. You could have chatted directly with your old playmate not ten minutes ago. He and Maude just left my office. Last minute details. You know how it is. Before the purchase, they were staying, along with their *precious* daughter, Winnie, an absolutely stunning child, by the way, as is my Frankie—Anyway, they were staying at the Ritz-Carlton. But the happy family took possession two days ago. As for me, Poppy dear, I ordered a bottle of Dom and carried it home. Rogelio and I celebrated our little hearts out."

Inez's dagger missed her mark. Poppy inhaled deeply and then said evenly, "I already know about Heston's wife and daughter, Inez. I saw Winnie's photo in a fan magazine last month. I was under the drier at the hairdresser's. Otherwise, I never read that trash. Haven't for years."

Inez regrouped. "Who does your hair, dear? Toner will take the brassiness out of red. Of course, the blinding color keeps people from noticing that your eyes are too far apart."

Poppy bridled. "Really, Inez..."

"When I saw you at the Parade of Homes last year, your hair seemed so—vivid"

"At least my hair color is natural," spat Poppy.

"No gray yet? It won't be long now, dear, will it?"

"Oh, Inez, please! I don't want to trade insults with you. I heard a rumor, and I wanted to ask you about it. That's all."

"Poppy, who told you about Heston's return?" Inez quizzed nosily.

"None of your business."

"And why do you care?" Inez grilled.

"I...uh..."stuttered Poppy. "I don't care. I was just curious."

"Don't worry, Poppy, dear. Your secret is safe with me. After all, who could blame you? Carrying a torch for our Hess all these years, even after he dumped you at the altar. He was a hell of a lay. Even I will admit that."

"He didn't dump me at the altar, Inez," retorted Poppy hotly.

"As good as," said Inez snidely. "He never married you. Heston did marry me, Poppy, dear. What's more, I bore him a son."

"How is young Franco?" asked Poppy with exaggerated civility. Her fingernails dug into the chair cushion. Her teeth clenched in her mouth.

"Doing quite well, thank you. Franco's team leads his youth-soccer league—because of Franco. The boy's a genius when it comes to soccer. We hope he'll be tracked to the Olympics, then turn pro. Franco will be 13 next August. We'll be making major decisions about his future then. Heston has promised to come and watch Frankie play. He'll want to be in on the decision-making, naturally."

Poppy's heart leaped into her throat. *Heston's son a professional athlete? What a thought.* "Well, I wish Franco the best of luck," said Poppy earnestly. "I'm sure you and Rogelio—and Heston—are very proud of him." Her heart skipped two beats. This subject came too close to the quick. She wanted to hang up.

"I like your husband, Rogelio," Poppy said to Inez, desperate to change the subject. "He comes in to my gallery every now and then and buys an artwork. He has good taste—in art."

"Some of his tastes are too vulgar for me," said Inez, suddenly frigid. "I prefer the classics."

Poppy understood the dig. Rogelio Vega had made no secret of his attraction to Poppy. Whenever he ventured into the gallery, Rogelio Vega flirted outrageously with her. A married woman, Poppy had fended off Rogelio's advances tactfully—so far. Lately, now that Poppy was separated from James Talbot, her doting husband of ten years, Rogelio had become more persistent in his pursuit.

To needle Inez, Poppy decided on a little payback. "Inez, your stepson Danny is dating my girl friend, Sasha. I'll bet you knew that already since Danny still lives at home. Frankly, I doubt if Danny could keep secrets from you, even if he tried. You seem to know everything about everyone." *Almost.*

"A good saleswoman keeps her ear to the ground," agreed Inez candidly. "Your little friend is too old for my Danny. I've told him so, more than once. He's only 27. She's 35 if she's a day—and paunchy."

"She's 33—and voluptuous," corrected Poppy, fencing. "Anyway, so what? Sasha says Danny prefers older women." *Maybe you're just jealous, Inez.*

Danny's visage quickly flashed into Poppy's mind. Bad-boy Danny Vega was a hunk and a half, a younger, meaner, scarier version of his debonair father, Rogelio. Inez saw Danny every day, at home and at work. No woman could be around Danny Vega for long and *not* be affected by his animal appeal.

Striking back, Inez swung hard. "Older is better? How is *your* husband, the dodderingly dull accountant? Jimbo, isn't it? Jumbo?"

Breath exhaled slowly from Poppy's nostrils. "I believe James is fine, Inez."

Poppy heard the snide smile again. "I heard he left you," said Inez. "Poppy, you should have had children with him. Why on earth didn't you?" The thrust hit home.

"I didn't want children with James, Inez!" cried Poppy defensively, leaping up from her desk "I didn't want children, period. I never, ever wanted children, do you understand me? Like this is any of your business." Pain shot through her arm as the side of her fist hit the desk top.

Inez countered. "But surely your husband wanted children, Poppy, dear. All men do, eventually. If you'd had a family, you wouldn't be trapped in the past, still longing for a man who doesn't love you and never did. Do yourself a favor, dear. Go find your dowdy husband, Jimbo , and make a baby with him. You're still on the good side of 40. Do it before your red hair does go mousy gray."

Poppy sputtered into the phone. "W-where do you get off saying things like that? You know darn well you're the same age as I am. How a nice man like Rogelio Vega puts up with you, Inez, I don't know."

"Rogelio adores me, Poppy. My marriage is ideal. It's everything a woman could wish for."

"In your dreams, Inez." *Be careful.*

"You are barren—aren't you? I told Hess you are," Inez jabbed. "Even if you aren't..."

"You told him *what?*"

"Was I indiscreet? Sorry."

"Be sorry for yourself, Inez, I'm not falling for your sales pitch. And I'm not going to dignify your nastiness with a response. This conversation is over." Poppy threw down the phone. Furious, she drummed her fingers on the desktop. Calming down, she retrieved her cell phone and dialed another number.

"Hello, Sasha?" she cried, as a familiar female voice answered. " I need to talk to you! I need to tell you something really impor...!"

But it was only the answering machine. When the beep sounded, she demanded, "Sasha, pick up. Pick up!" When there was no response, she rang off, dissatisfied.

Collapsing into her desk chair, she waited, lost. The energy drained from her body. Her pale face contorted. She sat at her desk and sobbed for a few moments. Thank goodness her partner, Wallace, hadn't arrived for work yet.

This is foolish. Standing slowly, she smoothed the creases in her flowing gray-silk skirt and hobbled to the front door of the gallery. She exited onto the gray-cement sidewalk outside. Blinking back the sunlight, she gulped a few deep breaths of fresh air. It was beautiful day, cooler than yesterday—another perfect warm, winter day in the wealthy, tucked-away resort city, once known to locals as Naples-On-The-Gulf. The moniker still lingered in local memory as the call letters of radio station, WNOG. No wonder "snowbirds," the year-rounders' term for winter visitors, flocked here from the North in wintertime to escape snow and ice.

Putting a hand to her chest, Poppy tried to focus on the present moment. Warm ripples of sunshine caressed her skin gently. Crisp early-morning air filled her nostrils. Azure skies domed overhead. Giant puffs of white clouds hung aloft, like heavenly mobiles suspended over an earthly crib.

Crib? Why had that image come to mind? She shuddered in spite of the sun's warmth. She needed to talk to Sasha. She needed to talk to someone. She feared she might panic. Alone, she couldn't carry the guilt, the remorse, much longer. Restlessly, her eyes roamed her posh surroundings. Conceivably, she *could* make the twenty-minute drive back down to Fifth Avenue and confide in coffee-maven Cookie Lee; but Cookie was a blabbermouth. Poppy knew she would live to regret such a moment of weakness.

Behind Poppy, as she stood weighing her options, rose the Italianate architecture of The Village on Venetian-Bay. Soaked in sunshine, the mall's thick, multi-colored stucco walls lined the immaculate sidewalk. Its two cupola-topped towers were roofed by undulating coral-colored Spanish tiles. Numerous tall picture windows displayed the expensive wares of the mall's luxury shops, including those of Poppy Wallace Fine Art.

Across the parking lot lay the street, the elegant, palm-lined Gulfshore Boulevard North, and beyond the boulevard stood a row of towering beachfront condominiums. These massive light-colored buildings lined the Park-Shore stretch of Gulf-of-Mexico coastline. Even now Poppy viewed them in amazement. The barrier island had been only partially developed when Poppy and Heston had been children in grade school together.

When Poppy's parents had perished in a crash, she had moved from Lake Park to her prosperous uncle's ranch-style home on Putter Point Court in The Moorings. She had been twelve at the time. She and Heston had ceased to be next-door neighbors then, but they still hung out together every day in middle school. Heston had given her her first cigarette. He had given her her first everything.

People change. Have I changed? Has Heston?

Naples had once been a hamlet haven for the super-rich. However, since Heston had fled his hometown twenty years earlier in search of fortune, fame, and adventure, Naples had grown into a wealthy-man's metropolis. No wonder he felt the need to return home and flaunt his new wealth and celebrity. It was what he had always wanted to do, anyway. What better place to do it? What better time? Naples was Conspicuous Consumption Central.

Truly, Poppy couldn't blame Heston for coming home. She only wanted to avoid him. But could she? In spite of its growth, Naples was still a very small town. Her conversation with Inez Vega had proved that to be true. The question was—could she avoid seeing him, socially or accidentally? She would be afraid to walk the sidewalks. However she might squirm, Poppy felt a net tightening around her.

Chapter Two

S asha Bassett heard the phone ring and heard the answer machine pick up. Hearing her best friend Poppy's voice leaving a message, Sasha rolled back into bed and wrapped her shapely, suntanned arm around Danny Vega's six-pack abs. Snuggling her buxom body against his mass of sleepy, warm muscle, she forgot phones existed. She knew nothing but the nearness of her man.

Danny Vega's musky scent permeated her entire being. She never wanted to be separated from him—never, never, never! She wanted this moment to last for eternity. Hugging Danny tightly, she felt him stirring from sleep. Any moment now the alarm would go off. He would awaken, take her, and then leave her lying alone, in her own bedroom, in her own dreary little apartment in Coco Palms. She would lie there, and the bed would grow cold, and she would start to ache again from missing him. If only they were married, she wouldn't be alone.

For the moment—this one sweet moment—she savored the sound of Danny's deep, regular breathing. If only this man needed her the way she needed him. Softly, she kissed the back of his head. Her lips pressed his silky, dark hair. Her fingers traced the tiger tattoo between his shoulder blades.

The alarm clock buzzed. Groaning, Danny Vega thrust out a hand, slapping the "off" button of the bedside clock. Rolling over, he pulled himself on top of her and engulfed her in a loose embrace. "Hey, baby," he mumbled, gazing down at her sleepily.

She beheld Danny's face with awe. She loved his face. She stroked the bristly black stubble on his square jaw. Still half asleep, Danny kissed her cleft chin and nestled down against her voluminous chest. *Please never let this end*, Sasha begged the Fates. For a moment, Danny's lips toyed with her left nipple. Then, as he dozed again, she softly stroked his hair. Once more, the alarm buzzed.

Jostling her, Danny abruptly sat up in bed. Ripping the electric cord from its socket, he slammed the digital clock against the far wall. Her key-lime-green parrot, Gabby, fluttered fearfully in its ornate white-metal cage. The bird, an Amazon Spectacled Parrot, was six inches tall, with scarlet "spectacle" markings around her alert eyes and a blue-and-white tuft on top of her tiny head.

"Pretty bird," said Gabby, vying for her mistress's attention.

"Son of a bitch," Danny groaned. Pulling one leg from beneath the white eyelet comforter, Danny placed a sock foot down onto the mauve carpet.

"Wait..." Sasha pleaded, reaching out a hand. Danny smiled warmly down at her. "Gotta make it quick," he said. "Meeting clients at ten. Inez'll be pissed as hell if I'm late." With a growl, he scooped her into his muscular arms.

***

Three hours later, Sasha returned Poppy's phone call.

"Hi, Pops," she said dreamily. "It's me. What's up?" She was still languishing in bed, although she was now alone. Satiated, she had been drifting in and out of sleep.

"A lot, Sash," said Poppy nervously.

"Tell me. I've got time. It's my day off," she sighed. "You sound upset," she added, plumping the pillows behind her head.

"I am very upset," replied Poppy through the cell.

"Why?"

"Sasha, I've heard some unbelievable news."

"Oh, yeah? What?"

"I-It's just incredible," stammered Poppy.

"What is it?" she demanded, slapping the mattress with the palm of her diminutive hand.

"Are you alone?"

"Yes, for heaven's sake. Danny's out showing property." She heard Poppy draw air into her lungs.

"Okay, Sasha. Here goes. He's back."

She guessed what was coming. Danny had told her about Inez's big sale. But she let Poppy get it out.

"Sash, Heston Demming is moving back to town."

Clearing her throat, Sasha explained. "Oh, Poppy, I heard already. A couple of days ago, Inez phoned Danny here. She told him she'd sold Heston Demming a waterfront mansion in Port Royal. Danny says Inez hit the jackpot. He says it was a double-dipper. She had the listing, too. Danny's pretty worked up about the sale himself. Even though he won't see any of the commission, their firm will. Poppy, I was going to call you and tell you this morning," she said. "Honest."

21

"Whatever. I believe you. Listen, Sash, you know what's strange? Ever since you started dating Inez's stepson six months ago, I've felt Heston's presence creeping back into my life And now, here he is. And the feeling is growing stronger." She heard the anguish in Poppy's voice.

"Yeah, nothing's more embarrassing than seeing old lovers you want to avoid. Believe me, I know. Oh, maybe it won't be so bad, Poppy. Maybe it won't even matter. You may never even see Heston at all. Unless you want to."

"Of course I don't want to!" cried Poppy.

Was there still feeling there? Most definitely. She tucked this knowledge away for future scrutiny. "I don't understand why you're so upset," she said to Poppy, playing a hunch. "You've never told me the whole story. All I know is what little you've told me. I know you and Heston grew up together here in Naples, and I know he was your boyfriend in high school, and that he went away to college. But that's all I really know. You would never tell me anything else," she prodded. *But I do know you're hiding something. I can feel it.*

"You really want to know?" asked Poppy.

"Yes!" she cried. "Cross my heart, I won't tell a soul. Tell me, Poppy."

A beat of silence. "One night he proposed to me."

Sashes felt her jaw unhinge. "Heston Demming proposed marriage to you? And what exactly did you say?"

"Nothing. That was the whole problem. I said *nothing.*" Poppy confessed.

She sat upright in bed. "Wait a minute, Poppy. Let me get this straight. When you were in high school --"

"And Heston was a freshman in college," added Poppy.

"Heston Demming proposed marriage to you, and you said nothing," she repeated, incredulous.

"That's right," Poppy affirmed sheepishly

"Oh, yeah?" exhaled Sasha, flopping back down in her bed. *What kind of an idiot is this woman?* "So what happened? You just let him get away?" she said aloud.

"Yes." Poppy's voice sounded small and far away.

"Oh, Poppy!"

"I know. I'm an idiot. At my seventeenth birthday party, Heston asked me to marry him—down on one knee, in front of everybody—after I'd graduated high school. Sasha, I was shocked. I hemmed and hawed. You know how I am. I do that when I get nervous."

"Yeah," she acknowledged. She'd seen Poppy tongue-tied over a dinner menu.

"Heston asked me to think about it," Poppy went on. "I nodded. Then he kissed me and went back to the party."

"Kissed you how?"

"Deeply."

"Yeah?"

"Thirty minutes later that hippie heartbreaker, Montserrat Flynn blew in the door on a cloud of reefer smoke. None of us knew her. She was someone's date—a band member, I think."

"What was this chick's name?"

"Montserrat. Montsey, they called her. I think it's a Catalan name."

"A what?"

"It's a part of Spain. She was a foreign-exchange student. For Heston, it was lust at first sight. From that moment on, he was under that girl's spell. I never heard from him again after that night, Sasha. I've never spoken to him since. He went back to college in Miami. Friends told me he was dating Montsey, that they were inseparable. That's the last I heard of Heston, until six years later, when I read in the local newspaper that he'd married Inez Greco in Miami. Even then I never saw him because he and Inez lived on the east coast after they married. Inez only moved back to Naples after she divorced Heston and married Rogelio Vega." Poppy sighed. "Sash, am I telling you more than you wanted to know?"

"Hardly," she breathed. "Rogelio and Inez are my future in-laws, I hope. What can I say?"

"That I'm a fool," said Poppy, tears in her voice.

"Come on now. Pull yourself together, girl. Did you love Heston back then?" she asked carefully. Her open mouth went dry as she waited for Poppy's reply.

"Yes. No. I don't know..." said Poppy, confused.

"You were crazy about Heston Demming, weren't you?" Sasha baited eagerly.

"Maybe I was. But I got over it," said Poppy.

Not likely. For a moment, silence hung heavily. Then she heard Poppy's voice tremble

"There's more, Sasha."

"More? You mean, something else you haven't told me?" she demanded, rising to her knees on the mattress.

"Uh-huh. Something I've never told anyone."

"What is it? Tell me, Poppy!"

"No, I can't!" All of a sudden, Poppy's tone became guarded.

"Why not?"

She heard Poppy whisper into the phone, "Because Wallace just walked in. I'll call you back later, Sash."

"Wait!" She heard the phone go dead. Grasping her cell, her finger jabbed the redial key. Just then, her cell rang.

"Hello?" she cried, thinking Poppy had redialed.

"Hey, Ma-mah," she heard Danny's smooth voice croon. Shifting gears, Sasha dropped back down into the bed and cuddled coyly beneath the bedcovers.

"Hey, yourself, Tiger," she purred. Danny made a growling noise, then chuckled, pleased. "No time for that, babe," he said. "I'm still showing property."

"How's it going?" she asked.

"Ohio Looky-Loos. I'll dump 'em at dinner. But, Babe, I'll be tied up this afternoon. No time for tennis with sexy little you. Hey, did I tell you what I did yesterday? Last night, we got hot and heavy pretty fast, you and me. No chance to talk, you know? So yesterday morning I went over to Heston's new house with Inez. Claimed she had papers for him to sign. My stepmom is no fool. Hey, what a showplace!. The movie-star biz pays good."

"Couldn't she have faxed them?" she asked, her lip curling in irony.

"Sure, but then why visit? Nah, Inez is sticking her nose in, and I'm sticking mine in, too. Wanted to see the great star's new digs—and meet his sexy, supermodel wife. What a knockout Maude Winston is. Just like her magazine covers. Cold as a witch's tit, but who cares."

Incensed, Sasha saw green. "Ooh, she sounds awful. Why did you bother, Danny? You've met Heston before, right? Lots of times?"

"Yeah, sure, babe. Heston Demming is my kid brother's old man. I've met Demming once or twice, over the years. Let me tell you—Demming has not been the ideal father, if you know what I mean. Schmuck ignores Franco. Has for years. Sends the kid birthday presents and Inez child support, but that's it. Don't think he'll be winning Dad of the Year anytime soon."

She made a move. "I agree that being a father is an important job," she said seriously. She heard an intake of breath on Danny's end.

"Don't start that rap with me again, Sasha. I've told you over and over again. I do want to be with you right now. But I am not ready for fatherhood."

She began, "Danny..."

Danny interrupted her. "You took your pill this morning, right? I don't want no surprises coming my way, if you know what I mean. Don't try springing any brats on me, Sasha. I am not ready for marriage. End of story. Got it?"

"Yeah," she said. "I got it. Yeah, I took my pill this morning, Danny."

"As long as we're clear," said Danny, suddenly charming again. "I hurt people who cross me, Sasha. You don't want to be one of those, babe, do you?"

"No. I don't."

"Okay, well, look, I'll call you later. Maybe we can grab a bite or something."

"Okay."

"Ciao, Bella."

"Bye, Danny."

She turned off the phone. She felt her face contort. A wail rose up inside her empty womb. What would she tell her mother?

Portly, post-menopausal Tonya Bassett constantly nagged her daughter about catching a respectable man and producing a grandchild. She was her mother's only hope. However, at 33, Sasha had learned that willing, eligible men didn't grow on trees. If she was ever going to be a mom at all, she knew she must become pregnant—and soon. Unfortunately, marriage was part of Tonya's master plan for her daughter. As far as Tonya was concerned, a sperm bank was out of the question. She had swooned and taken to her bed once when Sasha had brought up the subject.

If only...

As much as she loved Danny Vega, she was forced to face reality. Danny didn't want her. And she didn't want to anger him by insisting. She'd seen Danny ignite once too often. She would have to look elsewhere for a suitable mate. But where? To whom? Most of the men she knew were already taken. There must be *someone*.

Pouting, she rolled over in bed. She watched the sunbeams pouring in through the window panes. Like particles of dust, her thoughts danced dreamily amongst the rays of light.

So Poppy and the movie idol had been a serious item as teenagers. Well, well, well. She wondered if Inez Vega knew that—or Danny, even. She wondered if James Talbot knew it. *I doubt it.*

What else is Poppy hiding? She had long suspected Poppy of nursing a deep, dark secret. Obviously, Heston's proposal was part of that secret. Maybe his return would force Poppy to spill the beans.

Yawning and stretching, Sasha decided to think about it later. Crushing Danny's pillow case against her face, she devoured the lingering scent of her macho lover. She might wear another man's name, she might bear another man's child, but she would never love anyone but wild man Danny Vega. In its nearby cage, the bird, Gabby screamed heartily, still hoping for its owner's attention.

A Chance to Say Yes

***

Entering the art gallery, Wallace noticed his business partner's red-rimmed eyes right away. Tall and bald, Wallace sidled up to Poppy and placed his large hand upon her slim shoulder. He squeezed it to the bone.

"You've been crying, little girl," he said.

She tried to avoid the man's questioning eyes. Today her life seemed foreign to her. So much had changed since yesterday.

"Leave me alone, Wallace," she said, shrugging his hand away.

"Well, I don't have to ask what you did on *your* day off," Wallace quipped, running the hand over his shiny shaved head, then sliding a forefinger under his brush-like moustache. Poppy knew this gesture by heart. She had seen him make it hundreds of times since they had opened Poppy Wallace Fine Art together three years earlier. "Looks like you cried all night long."

"Let's limit our conversation to business, if you don't mind," Poppy pleaded brusquely.

"Not at all, Cruella," said Wallace, feigning huffiness. "If you don't want to tell me what's wrong, don't."

"Stop it, Wally. Please." Poppy placed the palm of her hand against her hot forehead. Hammers were pounding both her temples. She would kill for a pain reliever.

"If you'll stop snapping at me like a sea tortoise, I might even bring you a latte," Wallace offered. The woodsy scent of male cologne now hung in the cool, indoor air. It made her headache worse.

"No thanks," said Poppy, shuffling through the papers on her desk. Just the thought of a latte made her stomach turn. She knew Wally would quiz her until she surrendered. He meant well but nagged doggedly. That very characteristic helped him sell lots of art.

Wallace rose to his feet, stretched, and yawned. "Have it your way, partner. Business-wise, here's what's happening: *Le artiste* Cedric Spicer's paintings will be arriving by van sometime tomorrow morning." Wally reached into his pocket and extracted some folded papers. "Here's the printout for his opening. It's almost ready to be proofed. We may add a couple of pieces. Clear your calendar, girl. Cedric will grace us with his presence at any moment. He text-messaged me. He wants to meet you."

"Where's he staying?" asked Poppy, searching her desk drawers.

"At the Hideaway Bed and Breakfast— that spa in Old Naples—near the city dock."

"He didn't want to stay nearer to us? Somewhere north of town? The Ritz-Carlton? The Naples Grande?"

"He's an artist, Poppy. He seeks bohemian ambience."

"Fine. The Hideaway's about as close as you can get to it in Naples. Sounds like you're on top of things, Wally," said Poppy, downing two headache tablets with leftover diet soda pop.

"Thank you much," smiled Wallace, his eyes raking Poppy's face. "I'm going into the back to check that shipment of glass," he told her.

"Good," agreed Poppy.

"But I'll be back," he said.

"Don't I know it," replied Poppy. The hammering on her temples would soon subside.

"Don't cut your wrists while I'm out back."

"Don't worry, Schmitty."

"The name is Smythe. Long I. Nobody's called me Wally Schmidt since I left Toledo. Not in the three years since you and I opened this junk shop." Wallace's voice faded as he strode out of the main gallery and into the workroom at the rear of the gallery.

"Whoa, Wallace! About face! He's here!" Poppy shouted, only a moment before Cedric Spicer burst through the front door of the art gallery. Wearing his jolly mask, Wallace trotted back into the gallery simultaneously. Without breaking stride, he charged towards Cedric, who was skipping towards him with an outstretched hand.

"Smythe, how are you, my man?" gushed Cedric, grasping Wallace's hand and pulling the larger man to him in a quick hug. "And who's this pretty little thing?" Cedric asked, extending his hand to Poppy. "This little china doll can't be your Poppy?"

"My partner, Poppy Craft-Talbot," Wallace said gallantly.

"Charmed," said Cedric, "Totally." Standing back, he stroked his goateed chin and sized up Poppy from top to toe. "I adore natural redheads. And you're so toned. Do you work out?"

"Two or three times a week. When I can," answered Poppy, surprised at the man's easy familiarity.

"It shows."

"Thanks."

"Do you cream those freckles?"

"I used to."

Poppy had the urge to snarl, but she stifled it. Cedric Spicer, famous painter, was a whirlwind in designer sneakers. The word 'dervish' came to mind. Lean-bodied in a black T-shirt and khaki trousers, Cedric moved with tight flamboyance, not unlike a tipsy Flamenco dancer. Dissipated and unwholesome, he was oddly sexy and very aware of his sexiness. She watched him breeze about the gallery, commenting to Wallace on this or that art object, making plans for the upcoming exhibit of his paintings.

An unusual man, as are many gifted artists. There was something sneaky about Cedric's demeanor, too, an air of gossipy candor which probably tended to focus on whoever had just left the room. The cheeks of his long face were sunken inward, leaving hollows beneath his high cheekbones. A scar zigzagged across his jaw. His straight blonde ponytail was laced with gray.

"Poppy, I'm going to steal Wallace for a few hours, do you mind? I've rented a studio while I'm here, out in the designer district, and I've stuck a few pieces in there. I'd like him to pass judgment on them—you know, for the show," Cedric explained.

"Be my guest," said Poppy gratefully. She wanted nothing more today than to be alone with her emotions.

"Do you have a powder room?" Cedric asked with the delicacy of a sledgehammer.

"In the back," Poppy said with a sweep of her hand. "On the left."

"Thanks ever so." Cedric scampered away out of earshot.

"What a piece of work," Poppy grimaced.

"He's bi, you know," said Wallace, eyebrow raised.

"Bi-sexual? Or bi-polar?" Poppy joked.

"Both, I suppose. I meant bi-sexual. So don't think his come-ons are empty air. He bangs babes with the best of them."

"Thanks for sharing that, Wallace," said Cedric re-entering the room while zipping his khaki trousers. Embarrassed, Poppy burst into laughter. "Get going, you two," she ordered. "Please."

"Ooh, lucky you," Cedric said to Wallace as they left the building. "I like 'em ballsy. 'Bye, Cupcake!" he called back, waving at her.

"'Bye, Cedric," Poppy waved in return. Alone, Poppy gathered her thoughts for a moment. She was interrupted at once by the ringing of her cell.

"Hello?

"Poppy?"

Her heart sank. This was a voice she did not want to hear—her husband, James Talbot.

"When did you get back from Lauderdale, James?" she asked, uninterested in his response.

"Yesterday. I thought I'd check in with you," he said in his Southern monotone. She could envision him in his standard attire, sports shirt and chinos, the iron-gray hair thinning on his domed head, the black-framed spectacles sliding down his bulbous nose.

"Thanks, James. That was thoughtful of you." *How can I get off the*

28

phone? "How's the project going?" she inquired politely.

"Okay. Coming along slowly. Have you thought any more about our conversation last week?" he queried. "I have," he added.

"Um, yes, sort of," stalled Poppy, even though she had thought of nothing but Heston Demming for the past two days.

"My position hasn't changed, honey. I still want kids. I still want kids with you."

"James, my position hasn't changed either. I don't want kids—with you or anyone else."

"Do you know how it hurts me to hear you say that, Poppy?" James said.

"Stop bringing it up, and you won't have to hear me say it anymore," Poppy retorted, cringing.

"Why are you running from motherhood? Maybe you should see a shrink."

"Absolutely not!"

"If you don't change your mind, Poppy, I'm not sure we can stay together."

"We aren't together. Not anymore."

"But I still love you."

"Oh, Jimbo," Poppy moaned. Her head still ached, in spite of the pain pills.

"Please think about it."

"All right," she relented. She felt honor-bound to try to reconcile with her husband. After all, she had made the marriage vow of her own volition. In her wildest dreams, she had never imagined that Heston would reenter her life.

***

The strong, clean smell of chlorine hung in the moist air. Floating in her indoor pool, Inez Vega dangled shapelessly in the still water, feeling her limbs adrift like seaweed greenery. She had taken a morning swim to cleanse her soul of last night's ugly scene with Rogelio. At the moment, the water surrounding her skin felt warm and comforting. Buoyant, she idled for a few more minutes in the pool's deep end.

Using a gentle breast stroke, she began combing the water. In the shallow end, she stood on the pool floor and lifted a terry-cloth towel from pool's edge. She felt the warm water drain down her suit-less body as she climbed the steps to the pool deck. She saw the maid hurrying forward with an elegant towel-robe. The maid slipped the cozy, dry cloth around

Inez's trim nude body.

Ambling across the tiled courtyard of her Mediterranean-style home, Inez mounted the circular staircase to the second floor. Although stylish and elegant, the Vega home was twenty-five hundred feet smaller than Heston's new house, a fact of which she was painfully aware. Entering her spacious bathroom, she doffed the robe, tossing it onto a vanity chair, and slid into the tepid, sudsy bath, prepared earlier by her maid. Luxuriating in the oily, rose-scented water, Inez lay back and let the gentle jet spray massage her limbs.

Head lolling against the rim of the tub, Inez let down her guard. The ugly scene from last night came rushing back. How she wished she were free of Rogelio. They had almost come to blows. She tried to please him sexually, but it was impossible. She could not arouse him anymore. And the things he had said to her were horrible. Horrible. She wouldn't say them to her worst enemy.

Was it her fault she didn't enjoy him anymore? No. It just couldn't be helped, that's all. They had reached a point of no return in their marriage. That's why she had moved out of the downstairs master suite and into a bedroom of her own on the second floor, just across the hall from Danny's bedroom at the top of the stairs. Danny needed watching. She could keep an eye on him now. Oftentimes, Danny stayed out all night, and it bothered her.

A knock at the door and Inez's maid entered, informing her lunch was ready to be served. The pungent fragrance of lobster bisque drifted into the room.

"Leave me. I'll be right down," Inez responded.

The bathroom door closed behind the departing maid. Half an hour later, Inez sat fully dressed in blouse and slacks at the table in the kitchen's breakfast nook. The nook overlooked the loggia and the indoor pool beyond. Inez had declined to eat by herself in the dining room. She hated dining alone, hated it more than anything in the world.

After lunch, she would dress and return to the office. Any type of busy-ness was better than this dull, aching loneliness. Nibbling at her cucumber half-sandwich and lobster-bisque luncheon, she heard the front door slam. Her heart accelerated. *Who was home? Danny? Franco? Not Rogelio?*

It was Franco. As her slender, dark-haired son bounded into the kitchen, Inez was struck once again by his likeness to his father. Not his aquiline facial features, which were more like her Italian family, the Grecos, but rather, his build and his mannerisms. Heston couldn't deny this one. But why had he ignored him for years?

Inez had been shocked when she'd received the phone call from Hess, two weeks earlier, telling her he wanted to view property in Naples. When he'd come to her office and apologized to her for hurting her both during and after their marriage, she had been floored, and smitten, all over again, as if all the fury between them had become so much crumbling dust. Over the years, she had followed his every career move. She had even kept a scrapbook of clippings and a disk of electronic information on Hess. She had told herself these were keepsakes for Franco.

"Hi, Mom," said Franco, opening the refrigerator and peering inside.

"How was soccer practice, Frankie?" she asked, placing her napkin on the table and turning to admire her son.

"Okay," the boy shrugged, fingering the food items on the shelves. "We won."

"Excellent."

"Any *Tres Leches* left over from last night? Or did Rogelio eat it all?" he asked the maid. Quickly, the maid scooped cake-like milk pudding into a bowl and placed it on the breakfast table across from Inez. Hungry, Franco darted over to the table and began devouring the creamy dessert.

"I love this stuff," he said, mouth full. Inez had to chuckle. "Make more," he smiled.

"I saw your father again this morning," she said. "Danny and I visited his new place in Port Royal."

"Sweet," said Franco sarcastically.

"Your father wants you to come visit him. He wants to know you better."

Wolfing the final bite of food, Franco slung his spoon into the empty bowl and leaned back in his chair.

"I don't want to know him," the boy said matter-of-factly. "The Big Star," he sneered. Sighing, Inez studied her son's facial features—the almond-shaped brown eyes, the aquiline nose, the sensual mouth. Already the girls were phoning him daily, and he was only 12 years old. Would he grow up to be like his father, so attractive that he could turn it into millions of dollars? It was possible.

"You must get to know your father, Franco. He's going to be living here in town now, in our midst. It will be the perfect opportunity for you and he to become better acquainted. He could do a lot for your future."

"He doesn't like me. I won't do it," said Franco, standing up and flinging the chair against the small table. "And you can't make me." The impact made a crashing noise. Inez flinched.

"Franco! Of course your father likes you. What about your little half-sister, Winnie? You want to meet her, don't you?" she called sharply, as her son raced from the room and bounded up the staircase, two steps at a time. She heard his bedroom door slam shut. Loud music with a driving beat swelled and filled the vaulted rooms of the courtyard house.

Once more, she sat alone at the breakfast table. She was worried about Franco. She and Rogelio had been summoned three times to the principal's office at Franco's middle school. Three children had accused Franco of bullying. Her son always picked on smaller, younger children. He seemed to possess a streak of weakness that ran counter to his physical prowess. *How would Franco treat Heston's tiny daughter? They'll blame me. Everyone blames the mother.*

Perhaps it was her fault. Where else had this trait come from? The men in her family were not like this. The Greco men were tough but not cruel.

She continued to muse as the maid cleared the dishes and carried them to the sink. Rinsing the dishes, the maid then loaded the dishwasher. Finished, she padded into the laundry room, leaving Inez alone, still worrying.

Where did I go wrong?

She stared through the window at her indoor pool. A black and white soccer ball now floated on the water's surface. Franco must have thrown it there, on his way into the kitchen. The pool tiles were decorated with dolphins, like a Minoan palace. How she had slaved over the details of her home. And now, they didn't seem to matter at all. She hated this house. She hated her marriage. She wanted out. She wanted what should have been hers in the first place. She wanted her youth back.

She wanted Heston Demming and his riches.

Chapter Three

*H*ow *long has he been standing there watching me?*
Poppy's blood pressure rose as she swiveled in her chair. Spellbound, she beheld Heston Demming's tall silhouette framed in the doorway of her art gallery. Backlit by afternoon sunlight, his lean body stood planted in deep shadow, his cool stance unmistakable. One elbow was braced against the door frame.

When she became aware of him, he moved into the light. She could see the boyish features of his photogenic face. A lock of brown hair fringed his fair forehead rakishly.

Like an image in an eight-by-ten glossy, his countenance appeared cocky, self-assured, and every bit the movie actor he was. At the same time, she could sense his reticence. For a moment she thought she was seeing things, as if he were just in her imagination, the way a lost driver might see a mirage on a desert highway. But she could feel his presence. She knew he was real.

"Come in, Heston," she said to him quietly.

Ambling slowly into the large, lighted open space of the gallery entry way, he did not look around at the art objects, on display throughout the gallery. Instead, as his face emerged from shadow, he looked into her eyes.

"Hello, Poppy."

"Hello," she echoed. She was grateful to be sitting down. Usually, at meaningful moments, she tended to trip over her thong sandals or walk into the nearest wall. As she watched him advance, her heart thudded. She was certain he could hear it.

Don't move, stay calm.

Oh, he is beautiful.

He was just as beautiful as her memories of him from all those years ago. No, even more beautiful. At 39, his masculine beauty was at its apex. No wonder he was a box-office sensation around the world. No wonder his DVD's sold millions of copies. Her heart pounded. Blood rushed in her ears. She felt short of breath. She felt her gut clench for the first time in years. She had forgotten how desire felt.

"I can't think of anything to say except some old cliché," he said with that fleeting smile she remembered so vividly. "Like, 'It's been a long time'."

"Twenty years," said Poppy.

"But who counts?" he quipped.

Poppy tried to smile. She wasn't sure her face moved at all. She felt frozen in place like a hosed-down ice sculpture. Heston's silver-blue eyes now flitted back and forth across the room, exploring various works of art.

"This is a nice place you have here. A fine place," he said awkwardly.

"We like it," said Poppy. "We specialize in the work of Florida artists."

"We? Who's we?"

"My business partner, Wallace Smythe, and I. We like it. We bought it together three years ago. Don't you remember? My parents left me some money when they...passed away years ago.

He nodded. "Sure. Old Mel had charge of it, last I heard. Until you came of age."

"I used it, and what Mel left me, to start this business."

"Mel's gone?"

Poppy, nodded numbly. "Wallace was an art historian I met in college. I have a BFA from The Ringling School of Art in Sarasota."

"Really? I didn't know you'd ever left Naples."

"Just once—to study art," she replied. *Can he tell I'm lying?*

"For a moment, I thought *we* meant you and your husband. I heard you have a husband these days."

The man's charm was palpable. It oozed from every pore. *Fight it.* "My husband, James, is a C.P.A. H-he's good at what he does, but he's not all that imaginative. Definitely not artsy. James plays a lot of golf."

"Ah!" Heston commented sagaciously. "You don't play with him?"

Poppy shook her head, mesmerized. As a boy, Heston had been adventurous. Now, as a mature man in his prime, he seemed to embody the very spirit of adventure. His dynamic presence, coupled with such awesome virile beauty, gave him the air of a classic-film swashbuckler come to life. All he lacked was the sword at his hip.

Moving with the grace of a natural athlete, he strolled around the gallery, touching this piece, examining that one, acting authoritatively, as though he had just purchased the business and wanted to familiarize himself with the inventory.

Stumbling backwards as he strode her way, Poppy bumped into a small glove of blown glass. Bounding forward, Heston managed to catch the fragile, hollow orb right before it fell and shattered. Tense, but affecting cool, he grinned at her for the first time.

"Better watch that," he said.

Mortified, Poppy nodded and faked a smile in return. Carefully, she took the piece from his outstretched hands and repositioned it on its pedestal.

"I guess you make me nervous," Poppy admitted softly.

"I'm Heston Demming, Mega-Star. I make everybody nervous." He watched her closely.

"I had heard you'd moved back," she said, attempting a conversational tone.

"Oh? How did you know? Wait. Let me guess," He paced the room. "You heard it from your best friend, who heard it from her boyfriend, who heard it from his stepmother, who just happens to be my ex-wife, Inez Vega."

"Greco Demming Vega," she mumbled, eyes wide.

"I stand corrected," said Heston affably. "Inez Greco-Demming-Vega. My ex-better half."

"You've been talking to Inez."

" Actually, to her shadowy stepson, Danny The Panther."

"Actually," said Poppy, "I heard it from Cookie Lee down at Rainbow's on Fifth. Cookie's the current town crier. Not much happens around here that she doesn't know about."

"Rainbow's on Fifth," mouthed Heston theatrically, posing grandly. *Shakespeare couldn't have staged this blocking better.* "Is that a good place to hang here?"

"If you like coffee—and gossip."

"Oh, I do."

"Don't play innocent, Heston. I know you've been there."

"Would you like to go there with me now, Ms. Craft-Talbot? We could have a cup of adrenaline and chat. I brought shades and a Florida Marlins' cap to confuse my fans. I have some things I need to say to you, Poppy. I didn't come here today just because I like art—although I do. You know I've always wanted to pick up a paint brush."

"Still haven't tried your hand?" she asked him timidly. She looked up into his face. He seemed so...imposing. Where was the boy she had known?

"No." Heston shook his head decidedly.

She licked her lips. "W-We have coffee out back. Already brewed. A little strong maybe, but we can talk alone here. Wallace is out with our up-and-comer, Cedric Spicer. We're showing Cedric's work soon. His opening is a week from tomorrow. Please come. You and..."

"My wife?" he said, following Poppy into the back room of the gallery.

"Yes." In a small kitchen area, a pot of hot coffee stood ready. Poppy took two cups and filled each half way. "Milk? Sugar?" she asked.

"Black is fine. If I don't watch my figure, who will?" Heston remarked glibly.

"Well, I suppose your physique is important to you. Worth millions of dollars, really."

He nodded, silver eyes twinkling

"Please sit," said Poppy, indicating a chair at a small table in the corner. As Heston lowered his slender, muscular body into the chair, Poppy slipped into a chair across the table. For a moment, in the still of the small room, they sipped the strong brew uncertainly. She cleared her throat. He drummed his manicured nails on the table top. The tiny refrigerator hummed. The air conditioning droned. The air blew cold from the vent. Her right shoulder was freezing.

"Well, I won't have to buy that chest wig after all," Heston joked, indicating his cup.

She grimaced. "You are, perhaps, implying that my coffee is strong enough to put hair on your chest ?"

"You always got my jokes, didn't you? Let's just say I have enough chest hair already, thanks. As you well know." He winced comically as he raised his cup and sipped another drop of the tart black brew.

Poppy's cheeks grew hot. She giggled awkwardly. "You're funny, Heston. You were always funny. Remember? In *A Midsummer Night's Dream* you were hilarious as Bottom. Naturally, I thought you should have played one of the romantic leads."

"Ah, but I had to learn my comic timing somewhere," he noted, nose crinkling.

"True."

"My wife has no sense of humor."

"What was it you wanted to say to me?" Poppy asked, cheeks flaming. The hot coffee was warming her soul and clearing her mind, but it—or something—was making her armpits perspire in spite of the air conditioning.

Leaning back in his chair, Heston crossed one long, slender leg, so that his right ankle now rested on his left knee. He stole a glance at her. She met his eyes. She felt her heart leave her body. For a moment, their gaze held. Then Heston looked away and began to speak. Like a maiden under the sword, Poppy had been driven through by Heston's silver-blue gaze.

"I don't know how much you know about me, about my private life," he faltered, then pressed on. "I don't think I'm telling you anything that isn't common knowledge. I don't know how well you've followed my career." He paused here so that she could insert the right words. However, she could not utter them truthfully.

She had never followed his career. She had never seen any of his movies. She had lived the past twenty years in denial, strict denial, of a past mistake too painful to be conjured, even for amusement or old time's sake. When she did not follow his script, Heston improvised.

"What I'm trying to tell you, Poppy, is that *everybody knows* that I'm a recovering alcoholic. My personal life is weekly fodder for the tabloids—here and abroad."

"Oh, Heston!"

"No, wait. Let me finish. Here's the good news. I've been clean and sober for eleven months."

"That's wonderful.

"Here's the not-so-wonderful part. As part of my rehabilitation program, I am obliged to find all the people I once injured and apologize to them. To make reparations to them if I can."

A cloud crossed Poppy's countenance. "So that's why you're here? You came to apologize to me, for..."

"For running out on you twenty years ago. For humiliating you in front of everyone who ever meant anything to you. For publicly asking you to marry me then bolting like a frightened rabbit, when another woman caught my fancy."

In a tender gesture, he took her hand in his. Her flesh throbbed where his fingers pressed. "I'm sorry, Poppy. I've felt like a cad about it for years. Truly sorry, if I hurt you, as I believe I did. I was young, I was stupid. I was a fool. If I can make it up to you now, after all these years, if there is any way, please tell me," he pleaded earnestly.

"I admire your courage, Heston, coming here this way," she responded, trying not to dissolve into a pool of liquid protoplasm. "But I must tell you—it's I who owe you an apology."

"Why?" demanded Heston, surprised. "Why on earth would you say that?"

His jaw line is Michelangelo. His taut, sun-kissed skin is Vermeer. He is finer than any work of art in this gallery. "Because I didn't accept your proposal—not right away, as I should have. Instead, I stammered like an idiot. I'm sure it must have been embarrassing for you. You probably thought I was turning you down."

He arched a tweezed eyebrow. "You mean to say you didn't?"

"No, of course not!" cried Poppy. "I was just shocked when you proposed to me. I was dumbfounded. I couldn't speak. You thought I didn't want to marry you."

His silver-blue eyes shone. "You mean you wanted to...?"

"I never had a chance to say yes—or no. I tried to find you, to talk with you, but you had gone away..."

"With Montsey Flynn."

"Yes. With her. I cried for three days."

Heston sighed heavily. "At the risk of sounding trite: '*Oh, what fools these mortals be*'." Unconsciously dramatic, he rose to his feet as he quoted the Bard. Like a forlorn thespian, he strutted slowly back and forth, hands clasped behind his back.

"You can say that again, Mister," observed Poppy ruefully. It was only then that she remembered her hidden shame. He was unaware of the true state of affairs. What in the world should she do? Tell him? Should she tell him now? Should she wait? She would die if she had to say it to his face. Before she could answer her own silent question, a male voice boomed in the outer room of the gallery. .

"Poppy-girl, where are you? The front door's unlocked! We have customers waiting!"

"We're in the back, Wallace," Poppy called.

"Who's 'we'?" This second voice she recognized as Cedric Spicer's.

Wallace stuck his shiny bald head into the back room. "Hello."

Impishly, Cedric Spicer entered and struck a pose behind Wallace in the doorway.

"What have we here? Oh. My. Garters. ...You're...you're...!" He jiggled a forefinger at Heston. For what may have been the first time in his life, Cedric seemed at a loss for words.

Amused, Poppy said, "Wallace Smythe, my business partner, Cedric Spicer, gifted artist—Heston Demming, international superstar."

Cedric raved, "It is! You are! Heston, honey, I've seen every flick you've ever made. Please forgive me for staring, but you're just so frigging *gorgeous*." With one elbow, Cedric poked Wallace in the ribs. "Fan me, please. My aesthetic sensibilities are in an uproar." To cool his ardor, the artist fanned his face with both hands.

Wallace merely rolled his eyes.

"Calm down, Cedric," laughed Poppy. "He's flesh and blood, not manna from heaven."

"Speak for yourself," said Cedric, eyes bulging.

Even Heston had to laugh at such sincerity. "It's always nice to meet a true fan, Cedric. Thanks for your support," he said, offering his hand. Gawking, Cedric pumped Heston's hand enthusiastically, clinging to the long fingers for just a moment too long.

"Your moving here is all over town. I mean, I guess I knew I'd run into you someday, but not so soon. What are you doing here?" Cedric quizzed. "Poppy, why are you hiding this Adonis in the back room? Does your husband know? Oh, that's right. You're separated. Never mind!" Cedric flailed his hand. "Don't answer that."

Heston threw a glance at Poppy. "You're separated?"

Lowering her eyes, Poppy nodded.

"Do you two know each other well?" Swinging his forefinger back and forth, Cedric was adding one plus one.

Poppy put the brakes on. "We were friends as children, Cedric. Heston and I grew up together in Naples."

"When it was just a sleepy little golfing village," Heston chimed in.

"Well, I'll be a monkey's gay uncle." Cedric's jaw swung on its hinges.

Heston moved towards the outer gallery. "Look, I'd better be off now. My daughter, Winnie, and I have a date for a sail. I have a new yacht."

Poppy nodded her approval as Heston glanced her way. Reaffirmed, he said, "Listen, I'd like you all to attend our housewarming party on Sunday evening. My personal assistant, Andrew Upshaw, will contact you with the details. Bring your husband, too, Poppy, if you're still on good terms with the man."

"Not that good," said Poppy reluctantly.

"I'll be her date!" cried Wallace. She felt Wally's arms encircle her neck. "We'll be there with bells on."

"Me, too!" said Cedric, thrilled.

"You bring a date, too, Cedric, my man," grinned Heston.

"I just might do that. I might even bring a woman. I met this gorgeous creature—no spring chicken, mind you, but with mature allure—at the Hideaway B&B—where I'm staying, Room 3, by the way, Heston, if you're interested," Cedric gushed. "In me, not her."

Heston laughed, nonplussed. "Well, fine. That's great. We'll see you all Sunday, around 6 p.m. Dress is elegant casual. My wife, Maude, will be pleased."

"That's right! Your wife is Maude Winston, the model." Cedric placed a hand over his mouth. "A twofer," he gasped approvingly.

"No doubt she'll be pleased to meet you, too. And you, Wallace."

"Thanks so much," said Wallace, shaking Heston's proffered hand. "Great meeting you."

"Likewise." Heston turned to face Poppy. "*Au revoir*, Brown Eyes." Heston took her hand and pressed it gently. "Thanks for understanding," he said softly.

"You, too," said Poppy. For an instant, her gaze touched his. Then he strode out the front door of the gallery. Rushing to the window, Wallace peered outside.

"Oh, my stars and garters! He drives a red Ferrari. I'm in lust! If I weren't an obsessive-compulsive germ freak, I might never wash this hand again."

"Oh, Cedric, behave," Wallace said snappishly.

What just happened here? Quietly, Poppy slipped away as the two men quibbled. She had felt the lightening pass from Heston into her.

Did I just fall in love all over again? Me and everyone else in the universe. Cringing, she recalled Cedric's ridiculous display. Yet there was one thing she and Heston had in common, one thing no one else could ever share, even if he never learned of it. Only her Uncle Melvin had known. Mel had died eight years ago. *Please, Uncle Mel. You got me into this mess. What should I do now?*

From the top of Wallace's desk, Poppy lifted a pack of cigarettes and a lighter. Escaping the gallery, she trotted to the waterfront railing and sat on a patio bench. She lit a cigarette to steady her nerves. The pungent smoke filled her lungs. She blew the smoke out through her nose. She would have to tell Heston eventually. He had a right to know. *Didn't he?*

***

Later that evening, Poppy lounged alone on the couch in her living room at Solarmarina. Scattered around the room were a few of her own little assemblages, works of art she had created from natural found-objects. Looking at the whimsical art works gave her emotional comfort, which she sorely needed. In the hours since Heston's visit to her gallery, she had bought or rented every movie he had ever made—all the ones she could find. A pile of CD's now sat on the round glass coffee table in front of her. He had made more than 30 films. With the help of the Internet, she had located 18 of them. *Where to begin?*

A white-ceramic bowl of popcorn was standing by. Alongside it stood a plastic beaker of diet soda. Seeking comfort, she eyed the faux-leather recliner beside the couch—the tacky recliner that James had always claimed as his. Getting up from the couch, she dropped down into her estranged husband's easy chair and threw her slipper-shod feet onto the adjacent footstool.

Settling in, she hit the power button on the remote. The screen came alive. Music blared suddenly. Irritated, she turned down the volume and reached for the bowl of popcorn. She grabbed a handful of salty yellow kernels.

"Let's see what you can do, Mr. Demming," she said to herself, munching steadily as the credits rolled.

And then Heston's face came on the screen. But it wasn't the Heston she had spoken with today. No, it was the Heston of fifteen years ago, much closer in time to the teenage Heston she had known. Startled, she clicked the off button on the remote. Swallowing the mush in her mouth, she sipped her diet drink reflectively.

Maybe she wasn't up to this, after all. The moments ticked away. No, she was. Taking a deep breath, Poppy turned the TV back on and nestled back into the recliner. She would watch it—or die. It was time for her to face the reality of who her childhood sweetheart had become. She pressed the forward button.

The first of Heston's films she had chosen to view was *Dragon Claw*. It was a science-fiction thriller, full of savagery, guts and gore. In it, Heston wore a red plastic suit and battled aliens with lasers. It ran only ninety minutes. She watched it through to the end, then slipped a second CD into the player. *One down, seventeen to go.*

The second movie, *Blue Juniper*, had been made more recently. It was a romantic tearjerker, filled with snowy landscapes and roaring wood fires, with a good deal of lovemaking being done in front of a rock-hewn fireplace. This adult Heston was nearly naked in some scenes, and the actress he made love to—starlet Lennox Cordova—was stripped bare. Poppy had long since put down the popcorn bowl and remote. She sat galvanized by the moving images on the screen. Nothing had prepared her for the power of Heston's on-screen sexuality.

All of a sudden, the walls seemed to close in on her. Poppy felt claustrophobic. She couldn't breathe. She needed air. Without stopping to turn off the set, Poppy tore through her bedroom and out the sliding glass doors onto the balcony. In the darkness of night, a steady stream of warm westerly wind was blowing in from the Gulf. She could smell the seaweed and hear the small waves breaking five floors below her. As she looked north, then south, the stretch of coastline in either direction was strung with white electric lights. In front of her stretched the vast blackness of salt water. Faintly, above the ocean's drone, she could hear Heston's voice coming from the TV set.

"I did kill him," said Heston, the actor. "I did it for you, Laurie Jean."

Lennox Cordova's voice answered seductively. "I never knew how much you loved me, Tony, not until today." Then the music rose to a crescendo, and Poppy guessed that Heston was mauling the young actress with kisses. Angrily, she slid the glass door shut. Now the sound from the TV was muffled. On the balcony at midnight, she was free from the terror of her feelings for Heston Demming. But she would never be free of their hidden bond.

Tomorrow she would search out Sasha. She desperately needed advice from her friend. She would tell Sasha the truth and swear her to secrecy. She couldn't go on, not alone like this. Not now. Not after looking into Heston Demming's eyes.

***

Wednesday morning, Sasha Bassett was scarfing donuts at Rainbow's downtown. As she chomped away compulsively, her mother's words were ringing in her ears:

"How long do I have to wait, Chickie? Are you ever going to give me a grand-child? Am I going to die without any kind of legacy? What's it all been for? You've never done anything right in your life. Now you can't even do what comes natural. Get off you lazy duff. Find a man who'll father your child. Forget that Cuban shark. There are other fish in the sea."

Sasha swiveled her head in surprise as James Talbot, Poppy's estranged hubby, strode up to the counter. Swallowing, she watched James exchange words with Cookie Lee. Cookie was laying it on thick. *What a dork he is.* As usual, James was dressed in a sports shirt and trousers. His receding hairline and heavy eyeglasses made him seem older than he was.

Picking up his coffee cup and corn muffin, James turned to scan the seating area. Raising one arm, Sasha waved him to her table. She craved conversation, if only to drown out her mental tapes. Even with her best friend's boring husband.

"Hi, Jimbo!" she smiled. "Join me?"

James shrugged his rounded shoulders. "Don't mind if I do. How's it going, Miss Sa*shay*? You got some powered sugar on that cute little dim-pled chin of yours." There was something so dull about James that it made her teeth hurt. Or maybe it was the powdered sugar.

"Heard you were going to Lauderdale a while back," she said, rubbing her chin with a white paper napkin. "I'm such a pig," she muttered, brush-ing powered sugar from her lap.

"But you're a cute little oinker," grinned James.

What is this? Texas flirtation? She threw him a look of skepticism. Un-nerved, she watched as James carefully unfolded his napkin and laid out his food and drink items on the table. *No wonder he drives Poppy mad. He's such a neat freak.*

"So, James, how's life treating you?" she asked, pushing away her plate of half-eaten donuts and settling down with a toothpick.

"Pretty good. Except for my wife."

"Yeah, that sitch is a bitch," she said sympathetically.

"Have you talked to her lately?" asked James, slurping his decaf.

"She called me yesterday, but we didn't get a chance to talk much."

"Did she say anything about me?" he asked earnestly.

She grimaced sadly. "Not that I can remember. Sorry, guy."

He shrugged. "That's okay. It's not your fault. I doubt if Poppy even thinks about me much anymore." Pouring half-and-half from a small metal pitcher, he laced his decaf generously. Adding three packets of sugar, he meticulously wiped spilled grains from the table top. Inserting a metal spoon into his cup, he stirred methodically, as though counting rotations. Again, he picked up the small pitcher.

"Well, to be honest, you two just don't have that much in common nowadays. She likes the arts and creativity. You like numbers and golf."

"A lot of wives take up golf for their husbands' sake." He began pouring milk into his cup.

"Yeah, and a lot don't. A lot get a divorce. Or a lover." She gasped as soon as the words escaped her mouth. James' gray eyes goggled at her from behind the lenses of his glasses. His puffy, sun-dried skin drained to the color of snow.

"Are you saying my wife has a lover?" Light brown liquid sloshed over the rim of his coffee cup. Befuddled, he set down the pitcher and grabbed a handful of napkins.

"Absolutely not!" Sasha cried. "Here, let me wipe up that spill for you." She dabbed a paper napkin on the table where James had sloshed his milky decaf. "I never meant any such thing. I'm always sticking my foot in my mouth."

"Well, that's a relief. I'd hate to think of Poppy sneaking around behind my back. The one thing she's always been with me is honest. I've always admired my wife for her honesty. It's something I can always count on, like humidity in Florida."

She recovered. "Oh, yeah. She's a peach. I was just trying to emphasize that you and she don't have the same goals in life."

"That's for dang sure," said James. "I want kids. She doesn't. End of story."

"End of story," Sasha echoed, stopping in mid-air and staring at the wall behind James' domed head. "End...of...story." she whispered. She felt as if a great rent had opened in the fabric of consciousness and revealed to her the secret of life. Choirs of angels couldn't have sung out more clearly. Nor her mother's voice: *Go for it!*

"Earth to Miss Sashay," quipped James, waving his stubby fingers in front of her eyes.

"Eh? Oh, James! Sorry. I just thought of something," she said sweetly, sitting up prettily in her seat. Abruptly, she tossed the toothpick into an empty cup. With quick, dainty movements, she adjusted her shirt and shorts and arched her back. She was glad, for the first time, that James couldn't keep his eyes off her bust. *Poppy may not want a kid with you, buddy, but I do.*

"Would you like more milk in your decaf?" she asked James solicitously, picking up the stainless-steel creamer.

He looked at her askance. Then he broke into a smile.

"You mean half-and-half? Why, sure," he said. "Don't mind if I do."

Beaming from ear to ear, she poured a touch of cow juice into Poppy's husband's cup.

"You know, Jamie," she said, eyes wide, "I don't know why Poppy has never wanted children with you. I mean, you're everything a woman could want in a man. You're strong and steadfast. You work hard for a living. You've got that Texas stud thing going on. I guess she doesn't appreciate the life you provide for her."

Face froze in a Mona-Lisa smile, she ruminated. *What the hell are you doing? Shut up and leave me alone. This man wants a baby and so do I. But he's your best friend's husband. Poppy doesn't want him. She's hot for that movie star now.*

The words flashed through her head in an instant. Her smile grew wider.

"Do you realize what an attractive man you are, Jimbo?" she purred, leaning in closer so that her cleavage was even with the table top. From James' expression, she guessed he wanted to dive in. "It wouldn't be hard for a man like you to find female companionship."

"Oh, I don't know..." His nose was suddenly beet red.

"Many a time I've told Poppy what a catch you are," said Sasha.

"Really?"

"Really. Why if I weren't with Danny Vega, I might snap you up myself, you tiger, you!" *Barf me Shut up!.*

"Sasha-girl, do you really feel that way about me?" James seemed enraptured.

"I do indeed." *Shut up and do it. Strike while the iron is hot. Mama, he's got bucks, too.*

"Well, I wish I'd known that all these years." Shaking his head at the ironies of life, James dabbed his cracked lips with his napkin. He then folded the napkin precisely and placed it on the table. With calm, even movements he arranged his empty dishes and soiled utensils, until their positions suited him.

She watched him with leery awe.

"I feel like taking a little stroll down the avenue," he said, suddenly rising. "Care to join me?" His metal chair scraped the floor as he stood.

Sasha grabbed her bulky satchel--which was nearly half as big as she was. "Sure! Sure I would, Jamie. Let's go." Offering James her arm, she allowed him to lead her out the front door. *What if someone sees us? Someone like Danny.*

She knew how violent Danny Vega could be when provoked by jealousy. She feigned ease as James led her down Fifth Avenue South, the smartest shopping street in town. The street was, in fact, the main drag of "downtown" Naples, a classy thoroughfare lined with expensive shops, banks, brokerages, and sidewalk cafes.

Decorated with fancy lampposts and inviting wooden benches, Fifth Avenue South ran east-west for the length of ten full blocks, from US 41 to the public beach. Perpendicular to Fifth Avenue South, the city's public beach ran north-south for miles, from Port Royal, which was south of downtown, to the far north, Vanderbilt Beach.

"I'm right proud to have you on my arm, little girl," James said, dragging Sasha along. "As you well know, I love my wife. And I would do anything for her. But a man gets tired of feeling like there's something wrong with him all the time."

"No doubt," she said in earnest. "No doubt that's true." She turned her face away from passersby.

Chapter Four

"I should never have climbed the stairs to your bedroom, Inez."

Early morning light peeked between the slats of the white Bahamas shutters. Sitting on the sidelines of his wife's full-size bed, Rogelio Vega shoved his stocking feet into his shoes—or tried to. In his anger, he kept entangling his toes. Standing up, the swarthy, barrel-chested man opened the shutter covering the second-story window in his Mediterranean-style courtyard home in Bay Colony. Looking out, he could see dawn breaking over Pelican Bay. His fury was rising with the sun. He must get away. Looking down, he jammed his feet into the troublesome leather loafers.

"Rogelio..." the throaty voice of his wife nagged.

He turned and stared at her. She was sitting hunched on the bed, her arms crossed on her knees, her face buried deep in her forearms. One rose-print sheet was pulled over her knees. Her arched back was bare. She was stripped of jewelry and makeup. He turned away. He could not look at her. She was too pathetic.

"Don't hurt me," she pleaded. "Just don't touch me. Please leave me alone."

Rogelio stood up, his back to her. He stifled the urge to turn and spit. Coldly, he muttered "I'm going out for breakfast. I may not be home until late." Hastily, he buttoned his shirt. He was desperate to escape before it happened, before he lost control again.

Crying out, Inez reached across the bed and grabbed his shirt tail. "No, wait! Don't go! Not like this! Let's talk about it."

Shoving her away, Rogelio glared down at his lithe wife. She now lay sprawled across the bed. Tucking in his shirt, he buckled his belt as he uttered gruffly. "What's done is done, Inez. Words said can't be unsaid. I'm leaving now. I will be back in touch with you later." He clasped his chunky hands to his temples. The vein in his forehead was pounding rhythmically. If the vessel burst, it might be best for all.

Why wasn't Inez a woman like other women, soft and sentimental? She had seemed so when he had married her. Over the years, the truth had come out. It was all an act. It was about the money. All she had wanted was his money. Worse, it was never enough, no matter how much he earned. Inez rode him mercilessly for more money, always more money. She had no more use for him as a man than a whore has for an ascetic. He would not try again. He was finished with her.

"Why can't you be like other women?" he muttered, eyeing her mercilessly.

"What other women?"

"I don't know. Poppy Talbot, for one." It felt good to hurt his wife. At least he could still make her feel something, anything.

"Poppy Tal...?" She was aghast. "You're joking!"

"Am I? She's a lovely woman." He wanted to hurt her more.

"All right, go, then!" She lurched suddenly, climbing awkwardly out of the bed. "See if I care! I have other interests more important than you, Rogelio. So just go along with you. Go along to that little tart, Poppy Craft. See if she'll have you. She won't! She won't even have her own husband. She's lusting for Heston Demming! Go ahead. Go ask her. She'll turn you down, just as she always has."

"How do you know such things, Inez? You are the devil," Rogelio sputtered. Grabbing his wallet from the bureau, he shoved the smooth pouch into his pocket.

"She thinks you're a "nice man." She told me so. She called you a milquetoast. She's an idiot. She can't see behind your mask. Why don't you slap her around a few times? Then she might change her tune!"

Chest tight, Rogelio located his car keys and clutched them in his hand and slipped his sunglasses into his shirt pocket .

"No, she never would! Who wouldn't prefer Hess to you, Rogelio? I can't blame her for that. He's a millionaire a hundred times over. His wealth makes you and your little import-export business seem puny by comparison. If I had it to do over again—"

"You'd have done what, Inez? Stuck with him until he broke the bank? Instead of dumping him when he was a struggling actor, penniless with no prospects? *Bah!* He was lucky to be rid of you. At least he saved his own manhood."

Enraged, Inez came at him. "Go, you failure!" she cried, pushing him towards the bedroom door.

With a mighty thrust, he shoved her back onto the bed. There she lay, writhing and wailing. *A nauseating spectacle.*

"Shut up, you bitch! Never a moment's peace," he snarled. For a second, he thought he might strangle her. He felt the vein pump furiously, swollen, engorged. His breath came in short rasps.

A worried voice called from downstairs. "Mom, are you up yet? I just ate breakfast. I'm going to practice. Mom? Are you okay?"

Rogelio's heart raced. His skin oozed sticky heat. He tore out of the door and onto the second-floor landing, leaving Inez gasping for air.

Half-bathed in morning light, young Franco was standing agape at the bottom of the circular staircase. As Rogelio started down the stairs, Franco started up. The sight of Demming's son made Rogelio's blood boil. He wanted them all out of his life. He wanted to be free of Demming's leavings. Even Poppy Craft-Talbot was tainted now. She was soiled with Demming's stink. There was a quality of guilty innocence about Poppy that Rogelio had loved, so different it had been from his own wife's jaded mindfulness.

"Mom, are you all right?" Franco yelled.

"Out of my way!" Rogelio ran down the staircase towards the boy.

Young Franco shrank back in fear, crying out as his stepfather shoved him back down against the railing and hurried on. Losing his footing, Franco tumbled bumpily down the stairs.

Tripping on the boy, Rogelio felt his feet go out from under him. He heard the boy beneath him shriek in pain and felt the bumpety impact of the hard steps as he hurtled towards the bottom, smacking into both soft flesh and rock-hard muscle as the boy's limbs flailed beneath him. Man and boy landed in a heap on the hardwood first floor. His legs entangled with Franco's, he moaned, feeling searing pain in his back and leg.

Dislodging himself from his stepson's limbs, Rogelio sat up, stunned and in pain. Above him, in a slowly focusing blur, he saw Inez pounding on the door to Danny's room. Her urgency echoed the pounding in his chest. Struggling to his feet, Rogelio looked down at Franco. The boy was struggling to rise.

"What the hell...?" he heard Danny mumble sleepily. "What's going on out here?"

His son appeared at the top of the staircase. Danny's black hair was mussed from sleep. A blue percale bed sheet was wrapped around his naked bronze trunk, his muscular chest and shoulders exposed.

"Danny! Thank Heaven you're here!" Inez cried, now poised next to Danny at the top of the landing. Grasping a flimsy crimson gown to her chest, she pointed frantically towards the foot of the stairs. "Help him, Danny! Help my Frankie!" she wailed, her foundation-free face suntan, crinkly with fine-line wrinkles. "Your father attacked him!"

Dumbstruck, Danny blinked rapidly from his stepmother to his father. "Son of a bitch! What have you done to him, Popi?" he shouted suddenly, clattering down the stairs.

"Nothing!" cried Rogelio. "I've done nothing to the boy. I fell over him, that's all." His veins were pumping full-blast. Danny's rage stoked the fire.

"He tried to kill me!" whined Franco nasally, rolling on the floor. "I hate him. He tried to kill me!"

Tucking the sheet around his waist, Danny extended a hand, yanking the boy into a standing position. Groggily, Franco dusted his wounds.

"I saw him. He tried to kill my baby!" affirmed Inez shrilly, mincing down the staircase as she clung to the railing.

"I did nothing of the sort!" he bellowed, charging towards the front door.

"Dad..." Danny reached out for him, but Rogelio balked, blocking Danny's arm with his own. "Hey! Hey!" he shouted as his father swung at him angrily. "Don't make me, man. Don't make me, man," he warned in a heated chant, bouncing on his heels as he dogged his father's footsteps to the door.

"Get out of my way, *niño!*" Rogelio's fear was driving him towards escape. Scuffling with Danny, Rogelio managed to grab the knob of the front door. The door flew open, socking Danny from behind and knocking him off balance. Staggering backwards, Danny groaned. Behind Danny, Inez now stood hugging Franco in her arms.

Animal instinct on alert, Rogelio bolted through the open front door. Within seconds, he heard pounding footsteps and gasping breaths. His felt his son's energy closing in behind him. As Rogelio grabbed the car-door handle, Danny swung him around and slammed him against the hard metal of the hood. Again, pain seared his back.

"What the hell do you think you are doing?" Danny's hot breath blanketed his face. Gasping for air, Rogelio writhed under his son's grasp, but Danny's superior strength held him pinned. "Are you out of your mind?" demanded Danny, his dark eyes fiery. "What are you doing beating up a twelve-year-old kid? I thought we agreed that wasn't going to happen anymore, Popi."

Rogelio panted. "It didn't happen, son. I swear it. I tripped over the boy. Franco's lying. His mother is lying." The muscles in his chest constricted. He felt Danny's eyes boring into his soul. After a moment, he felt the tight grip loosen.

"You're sure?" Danny asked, wavering. The fire in Danny's dark eyes died down.

Gulping oxygen, Rogelio nodded vigorously. "Absolutely." The muscles in his chest relaxed as Danny let go his grip and stepped back from him. Panting and coughing, Rogelio moved away from the car door. "Can I go now?" he begged, humiliated in defeat but grateful still to be in one piece.

"Go ahead," shrugged Danny in disgust.

Hopping into his black Jaguar, Rogelio careened the car out of the driveway and sped off towards the Bay Colony entry gate.

Waving to the guard at the gate, he turned south on Pelican Bay Boulevard and emitted a gritty sigh of relief. Driving more slowly now, he glanced at his face in the rearview mirror.

I look terrified. He felt ashamed, but he had escaped his son's wrath. He didn't know which was worse—the harridan he had married, or his homicidal progeny.

***

Cedric's art-show opening was less than a week away. At the gallery, Poppy, Wallace, and Cedric were discussing the details while hanging some of Cedric's paintings. A few customers were wandering through the gallery. As Poppy watched Wallace and Cedric directing a man on a ladder, a striking woman approached her, a little girl with blonde braids in tow.

"Are you Poppy Talbot?" the tall beauty inquired. Poppy knew her instantly.

"Yes. May I help you?" Poppy asked, glancing down at the fair child. She recognized the child from her picture in the fan magazine—Heston's daughter, Winston.

"Perhaps. My name is Maude Winston Demming. Heston Demming is my husband. He raved so about your little shop, Winnie and I just had to stop by. Don't mind the bodyguard. For our daughter's safety. My husband insists, when he's not with her." Maude pointed to a large, burly man who had parked himself near the front door. Stupefied, Poppy stared at her old lover's famous wife. Winnie dropped her mother's hand and wandered a feet few away to gaze at a whimsical watercolor. Smirking, Maude strolled casually around the floor of the gallery.

"Mommy, I like this one," cried Winnie impulsively. "A ralligada."

"That's an alligator, honey," said Poppy. Thankful for the diversion, she crouched down to Winnie's eye-level. "You have good taste. That picture was painted by a famous artist named Edd Quested. He painted it for someone just like you to enjoy."

Maude read aloud the legend beneath the work. *"The Chartreuse Alligator.* Quaint."

Old enough to read. Poppy was grappling with the fact that she was ten to fifteen years older than Heston's trophy wife. "Chartreuse is yellow-green," Poppy explained aloud to Winnie. "See how he's not dark green like the other 'gators? He's chartreuse." Fascinated, Poppy drank in Heston's tiny daughter. The child was precious. Poppy felt heartsick. Winnie Demming looked just like Heston, right down to the silver-blue eyes. Her sweetness took Poppy's breath away.

"Chaproose," mouthed Winnie.

Poppy grinned and stood up.

"Would you like to have it in your room, Win?" Maude asked her daughter. Winnie nodded, braids bouncing.

"We'll take it," said Maude.

"Oh, you're buying the Quested," said Cedric, from out of nowhere. Somehow, he had sneaked up on the conversation without Poppy's noticing. "Edd Quested was a gifted watercolorist from backwoods Maine. He used to winter in the Keys. He died a couple of years ago, and the values of his paintings have skyrocketed."

"Good. Then it's not a waste of money," said Maude, handing Poppy her charge card. Incensed, Poppy fumed inwardly. Apparently, for all the woman cared, she could have been a piece of life-sized sculpture. *Why is he married to an abrasive woman like this? Oh, right, her looks.*

"It is definitely not a waste of money. Say, I believe I met your husband the other day. Aren't you Maude Winston, the supermodel?"

"You've caught me," she replied, eyeing Cedric with mild interest. "Who are you? And how did you get that delicious scar on your jaw?"

"I'm Cedric Spicer. I'm a gifted artist, too, but I'm still alive and kicking."

"Oh, yes. My husband mentioned you. And the scar?"

"Too kicking," he replied mysteriously.

"Who did the kicking?" she pressed. Her powder-blue eyes searched for and located her little daughter, who had found the colored chalks. The girl was drawing happily at a children's table in a far corner of the room. The glittery blue eyes returned to Cedric's scar as he spoke.

"I take volunteers," he said pointedly.

Studying him closely, she spoke to Poppy as though she were the gardener. "Have the picture delivered." Then she called to her child. "Kay Winston Demming! Let's go!"

Dropping her chalk, the little girl came running. As she exchanged smiles with Poppy. Winnie's nose crinkled when she smiled. *Just like Heston's.*

"Well trained," observed Cedric, his eyes never leaving Maude.

"You know, I almost like you," Maude said to Cedric.

"Fine and dandy," he said, half-grinning. "We should make a play date."

"Well, aren't you coming to our little soiree? Hubby told me he'd invited the lot of you."

"Well, yes, I'm coming—but not alone. I've invited a guest."

"A date? The more the merrier," said Maude snidely, grasping Winnie by the hand. "I hope the party will liven things up in this burgh. Naples is so boring, I almost miss acting."

"You know you are absolutely, mind-blowingly ravishing, don't you?" Cedric said seductively, as though Winnie were not present. He moved closer to Maude. "Do you tire of hearing it? Maybe I should call you hideous instead? Make you work for it."

Maude snorted. "See you Sunday," she said, amused. Leading Winnie out the door, she left without a parting word to Poppy. The burly bodyguard followed them outdoors.

"You two seemed to hit it off," Poppy said to Cedric.

"Didn't we just," he said quietly, watching Maude's retreating form out the window. Poppy's gaze followed Cedric's. The whole encounter had unnerved her.

Why had Heston's wife really come here? To check me out? Why?

Meeting her old love's daughter had rekindled Poppy's feelings of guilt and fear. Lately, hanging Cedric's show had driven worry from her conscious mind; but she could feel the emotion still smoldering below. *I need to talk. Where's Sasha?* Oddly, for the past forty-eight hours she had missed all phone connections with her. *Maybe there was a reason.* Maybe the Fates wanted her to tell Heston the truth, instead telling of her little friend.

These days Heston was confessing old sins. Why shouldn't she? Surely he would understand, once she explained everything. Mustering her moral courage, Poppy made up her mind. She would tell Heston the truth the next time she saw him—at his and Maude's housewarming party.

***

"Smile, everyone!"

The lone hired photographer snapped a jovial small-group shot. Then the group dispersed into the smart, stylish crowd of seventy-plus people. Members began to mill again, in the enclosed courtyard just off the indoor pool. Poppy felt exhilarated, yet troubled. Paparazzi were gathered outside the solid gate of the Demming's new home. A few minutes earlier, Poppy had heard a helicopter flying over the premises. In the western sky, cool blue was washed warm with coral and salmon pinks. The orange sun, a molten ball of fire, was dripping down the western side of heaven. Soon it would plunge, out of sight, into the Gulf, sizzling as day drowned into night.

Poppy gazed beyond the latticed walls. Around the pool and out on the lawn, lanterns were being lit by servants attired in black trousers and white serving coats. A jazz quartet played gingerly on the long lanai. The low hum of pleasant conversation drifted out over bay waters. Ice tinkled in glasses. Laughter erupted from little pockets of partygoers. The January air was crisp, dry, and fragrant with subtropical foliage. Soon the stars would appear. *And some of them would be human.* Poppy smiled at her own joke. All in all, it promised to be a lovely evening.

However, in spite of the festive atmosphere, she felt anxious. She had been practicing her speech to Heston for two days. She only hoped she would have the courage to go through with it. The first thing she had to do was get him alone. That would be easier said than done. He, as resident lord and master, was the single most in-demand figure at his and Maude's housewarming party. Just for the occasion, Poppy had purchased a strappy teal-colored frock and flat-soled, gold evening slippers. He had always liked her in teal and gold. She hadn't worn the color combination in two decades.

"Here's that drink I promised you," said Wallace, appearing at her elbow. He held a cold, wet glass in hand. Poppy took the cocktail from him. He flung excess moisture from his fingers. "I forgot napkins."

"I have one. Don't worry, Wallace. Thanks." With pleasure, Poppy sipped the tepid margarita and looked around. Wally was dressed to the nines in his most expensive casual wear. His shiny bald pate reflected the flickering lights from the lanterns.

"Seen our host?" Wallace asked her.

"Not yet. Well, once, maybe. I thought I saw him in the middle of a crowd by the piano in the living room. Inside, when we first walked into the house. They probably made him sing. He sings, you know."

Wallace quaffed his imported beer. "Everybody knows. The man has played the lead in at least two Broadway musicals that I know of."

"Oh."

"It must be really strange to grow up with someone and then find he's become a world-wide celebrity. I'm surprised you've never written a book about your experiences with him."

"I've been approached by investigative reporters a couple times," Poppy noted nervously. *Not very good ones.* She must lose Wallace to find Heston. *Too late.*

"Hey, Pretty Poppy!" She heard Danny Vega's voice booming her way.

She saw brawny Danny and little Sasha angling their way through the crowd, as though swimming through a thick school of fish.

"Hi, Wallace," Sasha breathed, as she and Danny squeezed into an empty space in the crowd. "We didn't expect to see you guys here." Danny was holding two mixed drinks, one in either hand, each high above his head. As he squeezed in next to Poppy, he lowered one of the drinks and handed it to his date. The other he lowered to his own thirsty mouth. His dark eyes swept Poppy head to toe.

"Is this great or what?" said Danny above the happy roar of the crowd.

"Great!" said Poppy into his shell-like ear.

"Sash is knocked out by all the celebrities. She can't believe who's here."

"I know! I know what you mean," shouted Poppy. "Plus the Demming's new neighbors and all our old friends from high school. It's an odd mix!" She smiled at Wallace as the music became louder and more lively.

"Poppy, you look beautiful," Sasha cried above the music. "I've never seen you in that color. It really becomes you."

The noise had grown so loud Poppy merely smiled and nodded, as she bopped to the tune played by the jazz band. Sasha looked cute herself, in a sleeveless burgundy pantsuit with a deep, black-lace V-neck and black spike heels, which gave her needed height. Night was falling fast now. The sky was velveteen indigo. Tiny points of light, like natural miniature pearls, appeared miraculously, in a way only an inspired Creator could have crafted.

"Anybody seen our hostess?" Danny yelled. Sasha's eyes threw daggers at her date. Minding her own business, Poppy looked away.

"No!" cried Wallace into Danny's ear. "We haven't exchanged a word with Maude or His Majesty. I'm just assuming we're at the right house party." He swiped his bald head and brushed the perspiration from beneath his bristling moustache.

"Yeah, this is it," chortled Danny. "I was here with Inez a few days ago. They must be around here somewhere."

"I've been trying to call you," Poppy yelled across to Sasha, who stood between Danny and Wallace. "You're never home. You don't return my calls."

"I've been working overtime with Mom's caterers," Sasha called back. "Not this party, though. Mrs. Demming hired some firm from South Beach in Miami."

"Then you can enjoy being a guest for once," Wallace scolded her amiably. With a shrug, she nodded and then raised her glass in a toast to Wallace.

"La dolce vita," said Danny loudly, to no one in particular. "Where's Jimbo?" he said to Poppy suddenly. Sasha was sipping her drink and began coughing.

"I don't know," Poppy called to Danny. "We're separated. Didn't Sash tell you?"

"Yeah, I guess so. But I was hoping you two would make it up."

"W-we might yet," Poppy stammered. Sasha's coughing fit had escalated. Danny pounded the plump flesh between his girlfriend's shoulder blades. "Spit it out, kid," he said smiling at Poppy. "She gets nervous in crowds," he explained, grinning.

"Not a good trait for a caterer," Wallace observed dryly. Settling down, Sasha threw her best friend's business partner a dirty look.

"I'm okay," she said. "I just choked on the olive in the martini."

"Don't do that, babe," Danny teased, pulling her close in an intimate hug. On tiptoe, Sasha swirled her tongue inside his ear. Danny growled. Wallace looked uncomfortable as Danny's teeth nipped the sensuous skin of her exposed neck.

What a good-looking scoundrel Danny Vega is. Purposely ignoring the embarrassing love-in between Danny and her best friend, Poppy scanned the crowd.

"Excuse me for a moment, would you?" she demanded. "I'll be right back." She had spotted her quarry outside. Tall and regal, he had paraded into the crowd on the lanai and was holding court near the bar while ordering a drink. Dodging her way through the throng, Poppy approached him and stood at his elbow.

"Heston?" she said, screwing up her courage. For a moment she feared he was drunk. Then she saw the bartender hand him a ginger ale.

"I love this stuff," Hesston said to her, his silver-blue eyes dancing. "I feel almost happy tonight, Poppy. Are you happy?"

"Heston, I..."

"Come on. Come with me, Red. I want to show you something. Something really cool."

"I've heard *that* line before," Poppy cautioned tongue-in-cheek, as Heston crinkled his nose and grabbed her by the elbow, steering her away from the lanai and down the path towards the seawall and dock. The noise from the crowd lessened as the sound of the music increased. The sky had darkened.

"Aren't the stars beautiful?" he informed her, as he propelled her onto the wooden dock behind the house. She heard water lapping beneath the wooden slats.

"My fantasy yacht," he explained. He presented the sailboat to her as though it were his newest bride, to a disapproving father who must be appeased. *"Windswept."*

"Oh, Heston. She's magnificent!" Then she added. "For a moment, I thought she was *Lover's Folly.*"

His perfect face split in glee. "I knew you'd get it, Poppy. Remember those summer days and nights we spent on board the *Folly*? You hated the sun, but you sailed with us anyhow. You were one big freckle." Heston laughed, enjoying his memory.

"I don't like sunbathing, it's true. But I do love to sail," Poppy confirmed. "You taught me to love it. You let me wear one of your big sweatshirts and a straw hat."

Heston nodded. "I remember like it was yesterday. I remember your bouncing red pigtails. This is the ship I always dreamed of, Poppy," he said in earnest. "I wanted you to see her. I wanted you to know that I finally got her."

"I'm so proud of you, Heston," Poppy breathed into the night air.

"It's important to me for you to know that I did it."

"I know. I know you did it. I'm so very proud of you."

"I truly sorry for the way I treated you, Poppy."

"I know you are."

"I'm a heel. But a successful heel."

"You deserve your success. You earned it with your talent and perseverance." *Not to mention your incredible masculine beauty.*

"Then why am I so lonely?"

The too-candid question shocked Poppy. She had not expected it, coming from the world's number three box-office attraction.

"You're lonely?"

He tossed his remaining ginger ale into the bay. "Forget it. It was a stupid thing to say." He stared down at the rippling water.

"What about your wife?"

"What about her? The Mrs. and I aren't exactly what you'd call close. Just forget it, Poppy. I shouldn't have said anything." A heavy silence hung in the evening air.

"Let's talk about you," he suggested affably.

Maybe now is the time? This might be my only opportunity.

"Heston..." Poppy began. "There *is* something I need to tell..."

"There you are, Hess!" sang the guttural voice of Inez Vega. "I've been looking everywhere for you. Rogelio's at the bar getting us a champagne cocktail. But I told him I just had to find you and congratulate you on this delightful party." A cloud of rose-petal perfume descended as Inez clip-clopped, gold jewelry jingling, onto the dock. Cupping her hand round the back of his neck, she pulled his cheek to her heavily outlined lips. "Smoochy, smoochy," she said before kissing his cheek.

With the back of his hand, Heston wiped his face clean. "You ought to warn a fellow before you have him for dinner, Inez."

"Pshaw." Inez waved away the comment as a jest. "Here comes Rogelio," she said, indicating the figure of a man limping across the lawn, balancing a tippling champagne glass. "Over here, darling!" Inez beckoned, waving her own long-stemmed beaker of bubbly.

"Where's the kid? Where's Franco?" Heston demanded, scanning the lawn party.

"You know boys, Hess. He found the video games. He's inside at the Play Station," Inez sighed. "He's sprained an ankle, by the way. But don't worry. He's okay. Just absorbed in gaming."

"You mean he's avoiding me," Heston acknowledged gloomily. "How'd he sprain his ankle?"

"During practice. It's almost healed," Inez replied, eyes veiled by the night.

All along the seawall, golden lanterns jiggled in the breeze. A dark figure in relief, Rogelio ventured into the light at the dock. "Hello, Poppy," he said, pausing with seemingly unexpected delight.

"Hi, Rogelio!" responded Poppy. She cast a look at her host, but he was now staring at his dream ship. She sensed animosity between Inez and Rogelio.

"You look lovely this evening, Mrs. Craft-Talbot," said Rogelio, handing a cocktail to his splendidly dressed wife.

"He wouldn't notice if I were nude," Inez said venomously, sipping champagne to sterilize the bite.

"Seen my yacht, Rogelio?" queried Heston, his eyes still glued to *Windswept.* The ship lulled mysteriously in the soft, rippling current. A full moon reflected in the dark waters.

"Glorious, my dear fellow," said Rogelio with gallant affectation. Poppy sensed an underlying hostility in Rogelio's regard for Heston, too. Had it always been there? She didn't know. Quite likely, since Inez had once been Heston's spouse. Jealousy was a difficult demon to battle, especially when your competition was Adonis—or was that Bacchus? *A combo, perhaps.*

Moments later, Cedric ran out to the dock, pausing, hands on knees, breathless from his jog. "Too much vodka," he panted. "Maude deployed me to tell you, Mister D., that the buffet's on. So, all of you, don your feedbags and hustle. I'd like to stay and chit the chat, but my date needs me. When I left her at the tiki-bar, she was fighting them off with swizzle sticks. Not my line, by the way. I heard it somewhere." Focusing on Heston, he gasped. "That's not booze you're drinking, is it, gorgeous?"

"It's ginger ale!" cried Heston, Poppy, and Inez in unison. A moment's pause, and the three broke into a gale of silly laughter. Even Rogelio cracked a smile.

"Chill, please. I was merely inquiring," protested Cedric huffily. "*Allons-si*, y'all. It was a direct order from the queen of the hive." Mission accomplished, the artist jogged back to the house, apparently mindful that he was being watched from the rear.

"Let's go, indeed," muttered Heston to himself. As ordered, the party of four proceeded back towards the mansion. Grabbing her ex-husband's arm, Inez dragged him forward, ahead of Poppy and Rogelio, although she frequently looked back at her current husband as he struggled along beside Poppy.

Poppy could sense Heston's lack of comfort as Inez clung to him too closely. *What is she up to?* Poppy strolled slowly to keep up with the newly lame Rogelio.

"Sorry I'm not moving too fast," said Rogelio, limping.

"What happened to your leg?" she asked, concerned.

"I took a spill down the stairs. Nothing serious."

"Did you see a doctor?"

"Yes. It will heal."

She noticed Rogelio watching the two figures in front of them. "You don't like him, do you?" she asked. Ahead of them, Inez and Heston reached the house. Poppy watched the scene as pantomime. Fending off his ex-wife's grasping advances, Heston tore his arm from her grip and excused himself rigidly.

"It's rude to speak ill of one's host," Rogelio replied, his pale brown eyes now on Poppy. "I prefer to talk about people I like. The person I like most is you, Senora Poppy. I feel I've been half in love with you for years, ever since I bought my first piece of pottery."

"Oh, malarkey. Rogelio, you're too, too charming." Poppy tried to laugh off the remark as she and Rogelio entered the brightly lit mansion. Hundreds of small bulbs illuminated the great room, momentarily blinding her. As her eyes adjusted, she saw a sumptuous buffet running the entire length of one wall. The delicious fragrance of gourmet food filled Poppy's nostrils. A plethora of exotic flower arrangements decorated the vaulted space. A tuxedoed trio played chamber music in a corner of the room. Affluent party guests mingled amiably, plates in hand, as waiters wandered among them with trays aloft.

Abandoned by Heston, Inez now dashed back and grabbed Rogelio away from Poppy. "Enjoy your meal," she beamed mechanically. Left alone, Poppy followed Heston through the crowd to the buffet table. She watched as he hesitated, surveying the exquisite feast he had provided for his guests, elite and otherwise.

"Would you like me to make you a plate?" she asked uncertainly at his elbow. *I've got to get his attention somehow.* "I remember you loved shrimp." She *had* to speak with him alone.

"That's *my* job," scolded Maude, approaching her husband possessively. The former supermodel was spectacular in a shimmering ecru hostess gown. A crowd was gathering around Heston.

"Relax, Maudie. Poppy and I are old buddies. Right, Popsicle?"

"Right," said Poppy unconvincingly.

Glaring at Poppy, Maude steered her husband towards an iced tower of cracked crab legs.

Disappointed, Poppy scooped a few sample edibles onto her china plate. Alone in the crowd, she scanned the room for Wallace. Suddenly, Heston, plate in hand, honed in on her position like a GPS monitor. "Come with me," he whispered furtively. "We have a smaller, private lanai around back by the master suite."

Taking her plate, he carried both plates outside as she went with him trustingly around back to the hidden garden.

"Have a seat," he instructed, indicating a table on the deserted screened porch. Placing the plates on the table, he pulled out a chair.

She sat obligingly.

"Drinks," he remembered, snapping his fingers. "And forks. I'll be right back."

As Poppy sat down at the table, she noted the quiet atmosphere of the secluded lanai, which was bordered by lush plant life including robust, electric-green ferns; crotons shrubs, with their gold, green, orange, and maroon leaves; and leafy hibiscus bushes dotted with large pink blossoms. Lulled by alcohol and the faint percussion of the distant jazz band, Poppy was startled when her host, exuding masculine vigor, burst back onto the scene.

"Hope you still like ginger ale," he grinned tentatively, depositing two brimming glasses, one extra unopened bottle, and a couple of cloth-rolls of silverware. Satisfied, he plopped down in the chair across from her. It scraped the floor as he pulled it closer to the table.

"Very much. Thank you, Heston," said Poppy, unrolling her napkin. She was trying to find the right moment to speak out. *Why do I feel at home in his presence? Drink, most likely. I must be drunk.*

"Y-You have a lovely home," she said, managing to engage her brain.

"Thanks. Yeah, I like it best of all my homes. It means the most. You know?" He began to eat with gusto.

Slightly tipsy, Poppy watched him eat. He had always loved food— and never gained an ounce. "I understand. You once vowed you'd own a home in Port Royal someday." Her eyes moistened. "Do you remember, Heston? It was a Friday night. We were sitting in a booth at the Dog 'n Suds. You had a black eye and split lips. Your right wrist was broken. You had a cast on. You were consumed with cold fury. You couldn't even eat your onion rings." She remembered how tightly he had gripped her right hand—with his left hand—all during the movie. Her fingers had felt sore the following day.

Old anger flashed across his face. "How could I forget? That day at school Stewart Adams had called me "poor trash.""

"You punched him out in the cafeteria."

"And got suspended for my trouble." He sighed heavily. "Adams is on my apology list, too. I put him in traction." Heston's eyes narrowed naughtily. "Maybe I'll have him over to my new castle—I mean, house." He grinned maliciously. "Maybe to all my homes. *Heh, heh*."

Sniffing emotionally, she dabbed her eyes dry with her napkin. "How many homes do you own now, Heston?" She dabbed the tip of her nose.

Brows knitted, he pretended to do the mental math. "Let's see, now. Five."

"Five?"

"It would have been six," he shrugged. "But I just sold the log home in Aspen."

Amazed, she stared at him.

He suppressed a grin. "Well, I know guys who have more. It's the crowd I run with. Some of them are here tonight. Want to meet them?"

"Sure. I've never seen so many celebrities in one place." *But I only have eyes for...*

"We get around, us movie star-types. Haven't you heard? We're party animals."

"Where are your other homes located?"

Happily self-conscious, Heston played at modesty. "Well, I maintain a home in Beverly Hills—as my primary residence. Plus I have an apartment in New York. A flat in London. And then there's the place in...Switzerland. I sold my place in the Hamptons to buy it."

"Are you serious?"

"Uh huh. It's cool. Big. Stone. Gray. On a lake." He motioned with his hands for emphasis. "Winnie likes it there. She has an awesome vintage dollhouse."

"You're fabulously rich. Just as Inez said."

"Loaded, Poppy Sue. Beyond my wildest boyhood dreams."

"I'm surprised you didn't buy this house first—before all the others"

He blinked rapidly for a moment. "I couldn't, Red. Too much had happened to me in Naples. Remember, I was drunk for years. I'm just now to the point where I can face any kind of reality. And it sucks, pardon my language. But I'm working on it." He smeared his mouth brusquely with his napkin.

"You've succeeded at everything else," she offered sincerely. "You can succeed at sobriety."

"Not everything, Poppy. I did succeed at the money part. Not so much at the personal part, though." He bowed his head and lowered his eyes, momentarily shutting down the light. She could *feel* his pain. He raised his eyes to meet hers.

"Eat something," he said throatily. "I've come a long way my since onion-ring days."

As ordered, Poppy bit into seafood canapé. He watched her expectantly.

She covered her mouth as she asked the inevitable. "What made you stop drinking?"

Napkin in hand, Heston sat back in his chair. "For your ears only," he said, leveling his gaze at her.

She nodded.

"You've been good about not talking to the press about my past, Poppy. To my knowledge you never have. I want you to know I appreciate it."

Again, she nodded.

"About a year ago, I woke up one morning and didn't know where I was. I was lying on the beach alone. I was sick to death, in and out of delirium. My teeth were chattering. I was wet and freezing. My wallet was missing. My cell phone was missing. I had no car. I didn't know how I'd gotten there. I didn't know who I'd been with or for how long. Turned out I was in Cambria—Central California. I freaked out. I got tested. I'm okay, but it scared some sense into me. I went to my first meeting the next day. That was eleven months ago. The whole thing was weird, like Ray Milland in *The Lost Weekend*. I should do the remake."

Poppy stared down at her plate. She pushed a morsel around with a fork. "Did you ever find out how you got there?"

"No."

She glanced at him sympathetically. "Wow, Sean Heston. That's rough."

He blinked, startled by the old endearment. "Yes. Well, enough of that." Changing the tone, he leaned forward. "Seriously, I hope you like the food," he said graciously. "You were never a big eater."

"It's yummy," she affirmed, swallowing with a smile. Nervously, she forked a section of pineapple and popped it into her mouth. Chewing daintily, she took a sip of ginger ale and dabbed her lips with a napkin. In the soft play of shadow and light, Heston's eyes shone like burning stars.

"Have some more." He forced open a fresh bottle and emptied half its contents into her glass.

As she extended her hand in mock protest, her fingers brushed his hand accidentally. The twin stars met her gaze. She felt her innards contract involuntarily. Alarmed, she gasped. *No! I cannot feel this way.*

Retracting his hand quickly, Heston set the bottle on the table and cleared his throat. "Tell me about your life. Tell me about your husband," he commanded.

She recovered her aplomb. "You already know the main thing. We're separated." Again, she dabbed her lips.

"Too bad. What's he like? What's his name?" With a fork, he picked at his food.

"James. Jamie. Jimbo Talbot. He's older than I am. He's a Texan."

"A tall Texan, ma'am?" he drawled in his best John Wayne voice.

Poppy smiled. "Yes. Big and tall."

"But...?"

"But he's dull and prosaic and fastidious to a fault, and I just don't feel... Oh, I don't know, I just felt that if I watched him fold his napkin into quarters one more time, I would go mad." She put a sweaty palm to her cheek. She could feel Heston watching her breasts. The twin stars seared into her flesh. "Never mind. I guess I still feel some loyalty to him. I am his wife. Legally. He and I just can't communicate."

"Maybe he doesn't understand the big words you use."

"He's a corporate accountant. He's highly educated. Doesn't sound it, but he is." She felt the energy between them ripple. Had she wounded him? *Maybe Heston never finished school.*

He emitted a resigned sigh and scanned the lanai like posing cat. "An educated man." Night sounds filled the silence that fell across the table. "Does he sail?" he asked with quiet intensity.

She remembered that tone. *Always the competitor.* "No," she replied earnestly. Instinctively, she understood that his question was not about sailing. It was about sex. "I haven't sailed in years, Heston." *Twenty years, to be exact.*

He raised the open bottle of ginger ale to his bee-stung lips and drained it. His eyes found her face. "Red, do you remember that Christmas

Eve we spent alone on the beach at Shark River?" he asked, politely stifling a burp. His eyes were searching her inside and out, scouring her soul for buried treasure.

"How could I forget?" she replied softly. Old memories of young lust flashed through her mind. Old feelings of young passion throbbed in her heart. In her memory she felt the cool of that long-ago night, the warmth of the bonfire, the heat of Heston's ardor under the canvas covering. Was the full moon ever so bright as that night long ago? The twin stars of his silver eyes staring down into hers like the firmament come to earth. After that night, she and Heston met regularly at motels, in cars, in Heston's bedroom when his mom was on duty at the hospital. They met wherever they could manage. *Could I ever have been so young?*

"Those were complicated times, Poppy. The time I spent with you was my saving grace as a kid. Everything was happening at home. You didn't have such an easy time with your Uncle Mel, either. The old guy was furious the next day—when we came sneaking back. Remember? He called me libertine. In that heavy Southern accent." Heston mimicked the sound. "I didn't know what that word meant, but I read him loud and clear. Mel hated my guts after that. Tried to keep us apart. Remember, Brown Eyes?" Heston chuckled gloomily. "He had a right to, I guess. I sure as heck gave him cause." He twinkled at Poppy affectionately.

"That was a long time ago."

"It could have been yesterday."

"You've missed sailing, haven't you, Heston?"

"Yes. Have you?"

"You were best captain I ever had." For a moment the magic of the night held them in its spell. Then he cleared his throat and pushed his chair away from the table.

"Let's go down to the dock," he said. "I was going to take you aboard my new toy."

"All right," Poppy said compliantly. Suddenly recalling her mission, she chided herself in silence, vowing to tell Heston the truth as they walked towards the moored sailboat. If she told him while they were walking, she could run away if his response turned ugly. Here on the hidden lanai she would be trapped. Leaving the used dishes on the table and avoiding the crowd as much as possible, Poppy followed him as he sauntered back down to the dock.

Reaching the dock, Heston stopped to admire the evening air. Leaning across the wooden railing, he gazed at the moon's reflection on the surface of the dark water. Then he focused on Poppy face.

"What a blessed sight," he observed. "You really look beautiful tonight. No wonder I was in love with you, Miss Craft."

"Heston, I…"

"Wait, Poppy. Don't say anything, please. Let me just look at you. I think I'm really seeing you tonight for the first time in my life." Quietly, intimately, he began stroking her cheek with the backs of his fingers. Leaning over her, he cupped and tilted her chin to him. She inhaled the old familiar scent, orange blossoms and myrrh mixed with hot male hormones.

Eating food had sobered her head. It wasn't alcohol causing her heart to flutter now.

Does he want to kiss me? Inside she trembled, aching to surrender to his touch. But she knew it was an impossible dream. He felt pity for her, that was all. He was just caught up in the painful memories of his youth. *An hour from now he will have forgotten all about me. He can have any woman in the world, anyone he wants, anytime, anywhere. Why on earth would he want me?*

His hot fingertips tenderly caressed the sensitive skin of her neck. Tall and intent, he stood poised over her. As she looked up into his face, her lips parted involuntarily. In sensory meltdown, she stopped breathing altogether. She closed her eyes. *Can he feel me trembling? What if someone sees us? What if his wife comes looking for him and finds us like this?*

As if reading her thoughts, he suddenly pulled away from her and stepped back.

Her eyelids flew open as she felt the energy dissipate. "Heston…" Her skin grew cold as his fingers withdrew. The chill of the night air assailed her, replacing the pungent warmth of his closeness

No, stay!

Backing away from her, he mumbled apologetically. "The ginger ale must be going to my head. Forgive me. We'll board the yacht another time. My wife is probably wondering where I am." Turning on his heel, he started towards the house.

"Wait!" she cried. "There's something I must tell you."

Abruptly, he halted. Without speaking, he turned to looked at her, his face wary, yet curious. "What's up?"

***

At last, the moment had arrived, but the mood was all wrong. Now she was breathing rapidly from fear. Her heart was palpitating. She felt tiny and insignificant, as though she were shouting into a canyon. "Heston, this is something I should have told you a long time ago…"

Glancing towards the house, he said, "I really should get back to my guests."

"You need to know this," she insisted.

Impatient, he thrust his hands into his pants pockets and adopted a *contraposition* stance.

Her art-conscious mine flashed on the unavoidable. *Michelangelo's David.*

Shrugging and sighing, Heston cocked his head. "What is it, Poppy? What do you want to tell me?"

Like a siren rising from the sea, a woman's lilting voice sang out in the distance. "Heston? Is it really you?"

She turned her head at the sound. So did Heston. They both beheld the impossible. None other than Montserrat Flynn was approaching them from the house. The slender, chic woman—Poppy's nemesis since the night of Heston's proposal twenty years ago—was dogged closely by the mincing steps of Cedric Spicer. Even in Poppy's worst nightmares, she could not have imagined such a scenario. It was as if the earth had split open beneath her and she had plummeted feet first into Hell's inferno. Stunned, she stood speechless, watching her old rival approach.

This is not real.

As if in slow motion, Poppy took in Montserrat's neat and compact figure. Although fashions had changed in the past twenty years, Montsey's sense of style was inborn. Tonight she was clothed in a sparkling lavender designer gown with a slit up one side and fairy-like sandals that laced up her ankles. Now in her late thirties, she seemed every bit as alluring as she had been at eighteen. Long, straight, dark-auburn hair and alabaster skin gave her a dramatic flair. Her poised demeanor belied her bohemian tastes and tendencies.

As Montsey Flynn moved closer, Poppy gleaned that her rival's light eyes were heavy with eyeliner and mascara. Her mouth was wide, her teeth perfect, her upper lip thin, her lower lip protruding. She had an oval-shaped face and a supple, nearly hairless body of classical proportions. Her long nails were the painted the palest of pinks.

Heston seemed as stunned as Poppy to see the dream girl of his youth. Stupefied, he watched Montserrat amble towards him. In his astonishment, he forgot Poppy's existence.

"Montserrat?" he gaped. The name rolled off his tongue like a well-worn hymn.

Melting into Heston's arms, the beaming woman embraced her long-time admirer with intimate affection. Returning her embrace, Heston pressed her body to his, clutching her closely, his eyes tightly shut. Releasing her at last, he stood her back at arm's length and looked down into her face. Coyly, she slipped her diamond-drenched hands into his. In the evening light, the tattoo at her ankle was barely discernible.

"What on earth are you doing here?" Heston demanded. "Where have you been? I searched everywhere for you. For months"

"Africa, mostly. And then in Spain for a while."

***

Grief-stricken, Poppy heard Montsey's words through a terrible rush of emotion.

"Right now, I'm staying at the Hideaway. That's where I met Cedric here. I'm a travel writer now, you know. I'm on assignment for a magazine. The editor knew I once lived in Naples, so he gave me the job."

Inside her mind, Poppy was shrieking. Desperately, she craved escape from this nightmarish event, the repetition of the most traumatic experience of her past. In her mind's eye, she saw herself tearing across the lawn, stumbling in the thick grass, regaining her footing, staggering ahead, gasping for air. She felt herself clutching at her throat as her windpipe constricted. As she ran, the light from the lanterns danced menacingly in the easterly evening breeze. The lanterns seemed to be mocking her, giddy with laughter at her torment.

But, in reality, she did not move an inch or utter a sound. She merely stood, horrified, and watched, once again, as Montserrat Flynn stole Heston from the palm of her hand—and, even more unbelievably, once again prevented her from telling Heston the truth—the truth he needed to know.

I was a fool to have come here tonight.

Quickly, Heston recovered his senses—and his tongue. "Montsey Flynn, you remember my old friend, Poppy Craft? Poppy Craft-Talbot. She's married now."

Montserrat cast a winning smile Poppy's way. "Yes, I believe so. You look vaguely familiar. How do you do, Posy?"

"It's Poppy," Heston admonished skeptically.

"How do you do?" Poppy echoed, abashed. *How do you do it, you witch?* She could not endure this a moment longer. "Heston...Montsey. Will you excuse me, please? I need to find the ladies room...all of a sudden..." Openly hostile, she absorbed the look of compromise on Heston's countenance. *He's racked with guilt, but he doesn't care...about me. He chose her once before. He's choosing her again. I'm out of here.*

"Poppy, please wait," begged Heston as she started walking towards the house.

"Nature calls, Demming," teased Cedric. "Let the lady do her business. Talk to your old lover." Montsey giggled at his witty remarks.

As Poppy lumbered away stoically, the rest of the conversation was lost on the breeze, drowned out by the fluttering sounds of palm fronds on the nearby trees. Once inside the crowded mansion, Poppy searched forlornly for Wallace, in whose car she had ridden to the party. Distraught, but resigned to her fate, she fought the hot, angry tears that singed her lashes. At least she had behaved like an adult, she reassured herself, desperate to tack up the tattered hem of her dignity.

"Are you all right, Poppy?" From out of nowhere, Heston's haughty wife had zeroed in on her pain.

"I...I have a terrible headache, Maude. I need to go home. I need to find my partner, Wallace. I came with him."

"Don't worry. I'll locate him for you. Why don't you wait in here?" Maude suggested, leading Poppy by the arm into another room. Inside what appeared to be a child's playroom, Poppy discerned a brisk, angular young woman poised in front of a flashing TV screen, and young Winnie, clothed in pajamas, sitting in the middle of a twin-sized bed. The young woman on the couch had regular features and a cap of flat, dark hair. "May I present Winston's nanny, Jillian Cady. Jill, Mrs. Craft-Talbot," Maude said perfunctorily.

"Good evening," said Jill Cady, rising, in a clipped tone. Dismissively, Maude turned her attention to Poppy as the nanny resumed her seat. "Jill is such a treasure. Masters from Columbia in Child Development."

Jill smiled. Poppy stared at her glumly.

"I wanted to show you this before you left, so this is the perfect opportunity," Maude said to Poppy. "The painting we bought from you. I hung it here in Winnie's room. I thought you might like to see what we had done with it. Winnie adores it."

Poppy skin prickled. She had feeling Maude was sizing her up, examining her closely, not unlike a bug she was about to strip of its wings.

"Hi!" she heard the child's tiny voice say. The little girl stood up on the bed and bounced. Her flannel pajamas were covered with images of teddy bears.

"Get down, Winnie!" barked Maude, seizing the child's arm and stilling her. "Jill, do your job." Crestfallen, Winnie plunked back down onto the mattress and rubbed her arm. The young nanny rushed forward and took Winnie in her charge. Disgruntled, Maude excused herself.

"I'll find Wallace for you. Please have a seat," she said to Poppy, exiting. Obeying her dictate, Poppy collapsed into an overstuffed yellow chair by the door.

"You the lady with the picture store," said Winnie, pointing to *The Chartreuse Alligator*, now hanging on the wall above the toy chest. The playroom was painted a pastel yellow with accents of pink, as well as pastel greens, and blues. Growing panicky, Poppy tried to control her anxiety for the child's sake.

"Yes," uttered Poppy with difficulty. "I'm glad you like the alligator picture," she said.

"Don't like it. Mommy put it," the child said blankly in her high-pitched little voice. "She say the 'gator will bite me if I bad."

"Honey, that's not true, said Poppy, disturbed. "It's only a picture. It's not real. It can't hurt you."

"Mommy said so."

"Oh, Winston, stop exaggerating. Your mummy said no such thing," the nanny bridled. Politely, Jill Cady smiled in Poppy's direction. However, her eyes remained focused on the quiz program as she guided Winnie back to the couch and dropped down beside her. She turned up the volume on the set. The blaring noise upset Poppy further. Unable to tolerate the atmosphere in the room, and the disquieting presence of the beautiful little child with Heston's face, Poppy stole from the chair and slipped out into the hallway.

Her conflict was intense. She wanted to hold Heston's child, to comfort her, but it wasn't her place to do so, any more than it was her place to fix Heston a plate of food.

"May I help you, Miss?" asked a plump, middle-aged maid in uniform.

"N-no, I-I..." Confused, Poppy recoiled, feeling like a wild thing trapped in a maze.

Darting out among the pool crowd, she spied Wallace talking with Danny and Sasha. Maude spotted him at the same time. Through the thinning throng, she saw Maude beckoning her, while apparently indicating to Wallace that there was a problem with her and that she needed to be taken home. She saw Wallace nod. Putting down his drink, Wallace started towards her. Her knees were giving way beneath her. Running forward, Wallace grabbed her before she hit the tiled terrace floor. She felt herself collapsing against his hard, lean body.

"I've got you," he said, as Danny Vega came around him and took part of Poppy's weight onto his shoulders. "You'd better lie down," Danny said into her ear.

"No!" said Poppy quietly. "Just take me home."

"Okay, okay," said Wallace.

Beside her, she heard Sasha's voice. She caught the drift of sandalwood. "Poppy, what's wrong?" The words were warm breath on her ear.

"I must speak to you, Sasha, alone," she whispered. "I must." *I have to tell someone. I can't keep it locked inside any longer.*

"Not tonight. I'm with Danny."

"Tomorrow night."

"You got it. Seven o'clock? My place?"

Poppy nodded.

"I've already called the valet for your car," she heard Maude's voice say. "Take her out front. It won't be a moment." With Danny's help, Wallace steered Poppy's slumping form out to the front entrance of the home. Seconds later, the valet arrived with Wallace's white Jeep. She felt herself being loaded in. Vaguely, she heard Heston's voice calling from the crowd as the Jeep roared away.

"Poppy?" Heston was calling. "Are you all right? What was it you wanted to tell me?"

Chapter Five

On her bedroom floor, Sasha knelt beside her hope chest, the lid of which stood raised, exposing the interior of the chest to view. Hunched over the side of the large, rectangular, wooden box, she rummaged through its contents. Her mother had presented her with the hope chest on her sixteenth birthday. Seventeen years later, she was still hoping.

Picking up a faded photograph, Sasha crumpled it and flung it into the nearby trash can. In her cage, Gabby squawked excitedly.

"Quiet," she told the bird. "You never liked him anyway."

Lawrence Zimmerman had been her fiancé for three years. That was back when she was in her early twenties, when she'd had a great job with a major corporation and a bright future. Larry had left her two months after she'd been laid off. He had left her for a female attorney with a BMW and a private practice. They were married now with three brats. Larry had become a stay-at-home dad with a BMW all his own.

Yep, it had hurt. It still hurts.

Forget it. Close it up. It's all in the past. When you marry James Talbot, you can buy a whole chest full of new stuff. You can throw out all this old, worn-out crap. You can buy a new Beamer, too, like Poppy's, and drive rings around Larry Zimmerman.

She glanced at the bedside clock. Ten 'til seven. Poppy would be here any minute. The trick would be to keep Poppy from knowing about her and James until it was too late for the silly goose to do anything about it. In spite of her self-confessed contempt, Sasha felt the icky twinge of guilt.

All's fair in love and war. This isn't either one, but the rule surely must apply to biological reproduction.

Sasha let the lid of her hope chest slam shut and sat down on top of it. She wanted a little girl, one that she could dress up in a cornflower-blue satin dress with a white muslin pinafore, and black-patent leather Mary Janes with white, lace-trimmed ankle socks. She wanted a daughter who looked just like that Demming kid. Was James Talbot capable of producing that kind of beauty? Probably not, but she could dream.

Something's wrong with that kid, though. She's, like, slow or something. Sad, maybe. Or scared. When Heston had brought Winnie out in her jimmies, at the party's close, to say goodnight to his guests, the girl had acted weird. Gun shy or something. Maybe she has mental problems. Maybe the ice queen had bad genes. Maybe Heston did.

Oh, well. In this world, the child's looks were all that mattered. Looks and money. Nobody cared about her inner world.

***

Fifteen minutes later, Poppy Craft-Talbot was sitting in her best friend's small living room.

"Brace yourself" Poppy announced calmly, pale-faced. "Tonight I'm going to tell you my whole life story."

"Promises, promises," Sasha joked, adding hopefully, "Need a smoke?"

Unsmiling, Poppy gazed straight ahead. Through the window panes she saw only blackest night. Earlier that day, Heston had left three messages on her voice mail. She had deleted them all. How she had managed the drive to Sasha's place she didn't know.

"You mean pot or tobacco?" queried Poppy, still dazed but trying to focus on matters at hand. "You know I don't smoke pot. I do want nicotine. I just need one cigarette. To calm my nerves."

"Sorry. Guess I've been around Danny too long." Sasha rifled through a drawer in the end table by her sofa. Extracting matches and a pack of menthols, she plunked them on the coffee table.

"Help yourself. Just don't call me an enabler later on," she admonished, procuring an ashtray from somewhere and dropping it onto the mahogany table.

"Okay." Poppy lit up and sank back into the sofa's plump maroon cushions. "Just this one and I'm swearing off again. I've had a bad week."

"Sure you don't want a bite? Some fresh Brie? Glass of wine?"

"Nah." Poppy inhaled and blew out a stream of smoke.

Rising, her hostess opened a window, then plopped back down in the quilted easy chair. Poppy could hear the restless fluttering of Gabby's wings coming from the open bedroom door. Like Sasha herself, the apartment smelled of sandalwood. Poppy had battled her nerves all day, waiting to meet with her closest confidant this evening. Twenty-four hours after Heston's housewarming party, Poppy nerves were still ragged.

"What's this all about, kiddo?" quizzed Sasha, settling in, her tiny feet tucked beneath her in the easy chair. She squashed a burgundy throw pillow behind her head and gazed full-blast at her guest. From the bedroom, Gabby uttered a piercing scream.

"Pipe down!" Sasha yelled to the bird.

"It's about...what I was talking about before," stammered Poppy, disturbed by the outburst.

"Heston?"

"Yes."

"It has something to do with high school, right? When you and he dated? When he proposed to you?"

"Yes."

"Well?"

Poppy sighed and crushed the cigarette into the ashtray. Timidly, she looked at her friend through a thin curtain of gray smoke. "I told you there was something else. Remember?"

"Yes, I remember," acknowledged Sasha.

"Oh, I don't know, I don't know," said Poppy worriedly, rising to pace the floor. *Do I really want to tell her?* Once admitted, it could never be retracted.

"Oh, hell, spit it out, girl! Before we're both too old to care," groaned Sasha.

Poppy stood still and screwed her eyes tightly shut. She said the words quickly, cleanly, just as a surgeon's blade would slice into flesh.

"I had his baby."

Two beats of silence. Then Sasha spoke. *"What?"*

The pent-up words gushed from Poppy's lips. "I had Heston's baby. It was a boy. I gave it up for adoption. I've never told anyone this before, Sasha. Please, please, please don't tell anyone." Poppy felt her whole body quaking. She felt Sasha's hands on her biceps, helping her move to the sofa, lowering her down. She felt the soft body pressing against hers as they sat rocking slowly. She felt her own body shuddering. She felt the small hand rubbing her limbs.

"Holy Jumping Jehosephat," breathed Sasha, rocking her gently back and forth.

"It didn't matter so much before," said Poppy, teeth chattering. "But now he's back. I see him. I talk to him. How can I not tell him the truth?"

Sasha stopped rocking and turned Poppy to face her. "You mean Heston doesn't know?" she gasped, gaping at Poppy in astonishment.

Poppy shook her head. "Nobody knows. I never told him. I never told anyone. The only person who knew was my Uncle Mel—and the people who helped me through the birth, and they don't know it was Heston's baby. Mel's the one who told me. He's the one who advised me not to...not to..."

"Keep the baby?"

"Yes."

"Where is the boy now?" asked Sasha, recovering her composure only to gasp again as Poppy answered ashamedly.

"I don't know."

"You don't know?"

Poppy shook her head. "I'd like that glass of water now, if you don't mind, Sash."

"Surely, honey. Wait here." Hopping up, Sasha disappeared into the cramped kitchen. Returning, she folded the glass of water into Poppy's limp hand. "Drink this. You'll feel better." Gratefully, Poppy sipped the clear liquid. She was calming down. Her volcanic center, after erupting in emotional violence, was now a vast, aching void. She did not feel the relief she had sought by confession. Perhaps only Heston could absolve her of this sin?

No. There is One greater than he. It's time for me to face the music.

Settling back into the easy chair, Sasha frowned. "Poppy, if you were pregnant with Heston's baby, why didn't you just accept him when he proposed?"

"Because...I was afraid."

"Of what?"

"That if I told him I was pregnant, he would leave me."

"Maybe he would have been happy about it. He wanted to marry you."

"Did he? Then why did he dump me for...Montserrat Flynn? In front of everyone..." She could hardly utter the name. She still couldn't believe that woman had returned last night. It was like some terrible repeating nightmare from which she could not awaken. She had had such dreams of not being able to wake up—after giving her baby up for adoption.

"Maybe Heston thought you didn't want to marry him. Did that ever occur to you? Maybe he thought you were turning him down. Young boys can be sensitive about rejection, Poppy. He might have felt you were rejecting him."

"Yes, it occurred to me, years later. In fact, he and I even touched on that subject the other day, when he came to the gallery."

"He came to your art gallery?"

"Yes. Just to talk. Sasha, my whole past was one big mistake. Such a comedy of errors, except that it isn't funny." Poppy began to weep. Sasha rose once again and padded from the room.

"Yeah, that's for sure. Here's the tissues," said Sasha, returning from the bathroom with a flower-printed cardboard box in her hand. Again, she settled into the chair.

"Well, what are we going to do about this?" she asked Poppy. "What do you *want* to do about this?" Poppy blew her nose into a pink tissue. The action relieved the pressure in her sinuses. Nothing mattered now. And yet, nonsensically, everything mattered more.

"Say nothing to anyone. Not yet. I just needed to tell someone, Sasha. Since Uncle Mel died I've had no one to guide me. Not that he was the world's greatest guide."

Sasha's eyes became slits. "Does James know?" she queried casually.

"No. He'd die if he knew. I've always told James I hated kids."

"But you don't?"

Casting raw eyes at Sasha, Poppy shook her head and again burst into tears. "I guess I was traumatized by everything that happened to me that year—Heston publicly dumping me for Montserrat, disappearing on me when I was pregnant, having to face my uncle's fury, having the baby all by myself, loving him...and...wanting my son...and having to give him...away to strangers. All of it—the whole, terrible experience—was too much for me to bear. I've never, ever wanted to go through that—or anything like it—again. I didn't want to remember what I'd done or what I'd been through. I only wanted to forget. I've been hiding from my past for so long. But when Heston came back...it brought everything...up from the depths." She blew her nose and tossed the dirty tissue into a trash can.

"Last night, on the dock, I was about to tell him the truth. And then Montsey Flynn showed up—again. What lousy timing that woman has. It is uncanny."

"Really," agreed Sasha meekly. "You never know about people, do you?"

***

Later that night, Sasha lay snuggled warmly against Danny Vega's back. While Danny slept silently, her mind whirred. She kept thinking about her conversation with Poppy earlier that evening. She had asked Poppy whether or not she still loved Heston Demming. Poppy had said, "Yes, no, I don't know," in her typical fashion. She, however, was now convinced that Poppy adored Heston and always had.

So, the question becomes --How can I use this to my advantage to win Jumbo Jimbo?

In his sleep, Danny Vega snorted and shifted onto his side. Still dreaming, he wound his muscular arm around her neck. She laid her head across his silky chest. He settled down and continued sleeping in deep silence. Lying in Danny's arms, her mind began to imagine.

What if she told James Talbot that his wife had borne the famous star's child? James would be livid. He would hate Poppy. He would despise his wife for deceiving him.

Sasha laughed under her breath. She would see to it. She would plant the idea of betrayal in Jumbo's mind. That would make it easy to pry him away from Poppy. Besides, she would be doing Poppy a favor. Heston might want Poppy, once he found out about his baby.

I will be doing the right thing for everyone concerned if I tell James about Poppy's having Heston's baby. For sure. Such a move would make James Talbot easy prey, although...it might make Poppy furious.

Sasha frowned. She needed to keep the art gallery's business for her mother's catering firm. If she lost their patronage, Tanya might still give her grief. *I'll cross that bridge when I come to it. I'll beg Poppy's forgiveness. She's such a sap. She'll forgive me.*

Could it work? Yes, unless...

What if James doesn't believe me? Poppy might deny the whole thing, call her a liar. That would ruin everything. Sasha's childlike fingers toyed with Danny's black chest hair. As her unsuspecting lover slept into the night, her mind continued to whirr.

***

Adolescent boys sporting bleached white-shorts and crimson jerseys were careening around the open, grassy-green field. Watching from the sidelines, Heston stood aloof, although not incognito, attired in slacks, windbreaker, and sunglasses. When he, Maude, and Winnie had first pulled up to the Pelican Bay County Park, the soccer youths had swarmed his Ferrari. To his son, Franco's dismay, Heston—and wife, Maude—had been besieged by young fans, all of whom were his son's peers. He and Maude had spent thirty minutes signing autographs and posing for shots with the raucous young players. When the coach had called the players back onto the field, peeved at being put to so much trouble, Maude had stalked away from the practice game, shouting at Winnie to follow. Heston now stood watching the activity.

Since arriving at the soccer field, Heston had hardly exchanged five sentences with his disgruntled son. Sulking, the boy had huddled with his companions rather than welcoming his own father to the practice game. Once the game had started, Heston, alone and self-conscious, had hidden behind his designer shades.

Standing alongside him, enjoying glorious sunshine and balmy breezes, were Inez and Rogelio Vega. It was Inez who had issued him the invitation to attend Franco's practice. He had accepted his ex-wife's invitation because he wanted to show an interest—a long overdue interest—in his son, Franco.

Miffed, he sensed that Rogelio was reluctant to exchange words with him. These days the swarthy man almost seemed hostile. Heston wanted to avoid conflict if possible, so he remained remote. Perhaps their relationship was fundamentally adversarial—two men who had possessed the same woman. Tension. Lots of tension there. But not worth a fight. He decided to let it go, if he could, and to concentrate on watching his son play soccer. Occasionally, Heston glanced into the distance, towards his current wife, Maude, and his daughter, Winnie, who had found a bench near the bike path. There the two sat, feeding sesame-seed cracker crumbs to the birds in the shrubbery. A couple of tourists were trying to chat up Maude, who look annoyed.

Soccer wasn't Heston's game. He knew little about it. He preferred baseball. He watched with mild interest as members of Franco's team advanced the black and white ball by kicking it towards the eastern goal. Members of the opposing team, clad in burgundy shorts and gold jerseys, tried diligently to stop them. The air was thick with blossoming testosterone and the fragrance of freshly mown grass.

Fondly, Heston recalled his own youth and the glory of sport. What he wanted was to get Franco on the yacht. He wanted to teach the boy to sail, to let him feel the wind on his face, to know the power of the wind, the majesty of the surging seas, the euphoria of conquering them. Heston *would* teach his son to sail. It would be a first step towards reconciliation— if the boy agreed to go aboard. *Damn. What a fine kick.*

Impressed in spite of himself, Heston noted his son's athletic superiority with pride. Clearly, Franco outshone his team mates. He ran with the speed and grace of a gazelle. He had the kicking power of an angry kangaroo. Heston smiled at his own imagery. He had met a few 'roos while filming *The Diary Key* on location in Sydney.

Franco's stepfather seemed enlivened by the soccer game. Rogelio, cheering on Franco's team, was more animated than Heston had ever seen him. Standing next to Rogelio, wearing a white visor to shade her eyes from the sun's blaze, Inez was her usual self, brazen in support of her darling son. *How tiresome she is. But a good mother.*

Not like Maude, who ran hot and cold with Winnie. The child never knew what to expect from her. Heston knew Maude was only idling with Winnie now because she wanted to avoid Franco and his soccer game. It hurt Heston, *hurt him,* to see how Maude treated his children. What could he do about it? He didn't know what to do. Yelling voices caused him to look alive as a soccer ball soared from out of nowhere and walloped him in the shoulder.

"Hey, watch it!" he bellowed, retrieving the ball and kicking it back to Franco. For a moment, he rubbed the sting in his shoulder. Then, remembering who and where he was, he revived his cool demeanor and macho stance.

"Nice one, Mr. Demming!" cried one of Franco's smiling team mates. Franco's face remained a scowl as he scooped the ball with his foot.

"I bought him new cleats," said Inez to Heston. "I hope they're not pinching his toes. He keeps growing and growing. His feet get bigger every minute. He'll have big feet like you, Heston. My family has small feet and hands, very genteel, we Grecos are."

Don't bite. It's what she wants. Heston knew that needling was Inez's idea of flirtation. She wanted him. He could feel it on every inch of his being—and he wanted none of her. The bad old days were gone forever, as far as he was concerned. He'd made that decision within thirty minutes of their reunion three weeks ago.

He felt a tiny hand tugging at his trouser leg. He looked down.

"Daddy, we out of crackers," said Winnie breathlessly. Glancing around, he saw Maude sauntering reluctantly towards them. "Daddy, put me up high, please, please," begged Winnie, jiggling on her toes.

"Okay, Ladybug," he said, hoisting the child onto his shoulders, wincing as her weight pressed his recent bruise. Prideful lunatic that he was, he pretended it didn't bother him. Maude sauntered up beside him and Winnie. Striking a pose, she sighed heavily.

"I take it you're bored," he said without removing his gaze from the game.

"Excruciatingly," Maude replied under her breath. She and Inez exchanged fake smiles. Each studied the other's attire.

"Do you think you could have the common decency to pretend to be having a good time? For my son's sake? For your daughter's sake?" he seethed quietly. They were arguing again. He could feel the sudden tension in Winnie's limbs. Her little fist pummeled the top of his head.

"Daddy, put me down. Put me down, please."

"Okey-doke," he replied, swinging the child from around his neck and depositing her safely onto the ground. "Stay close," he told her. "Don't wander off." Every now and then he noticed Franco glaring in his direction. To Franco, he did not respond with a smile or wave. Instead, he merely returned his son's glare measure for measure.

Why does he hate me? Why can't this boy and I find a common ground? The boat...

Suddenly, the ball was kicked out of bounds. Flying towards the sidelines, it dropped to the ground and rolled across the grass. Running after it, Winnie stopped the ball and embraced it in her arms. Attempting to throw it, she sent the ball rustling into a thick patch of palmettos which lined the busy roadway adjacent to the field.

Jogging towards his half-sister in his pursuit of the soccer ball, Franco pushed her to the ground. "Now look what you've done, you little geek," he snarled, jogging past her.

Enraged, Heston dashed after Franco and whirled him around.

"What the devil do you think you're doing?" he demanded furiously. "How dare you manhandle your sister that way? Who do you think you are, Big Shot?"

In Heston's mind, a second battle raged. He wanted to punish his son, but, instead, he struggled to reign in his wrath. If he touched the boy, it would be all over Tabloid TV tonight. He could hear the reporter's voice now: *"Out of control, Heston was slapping repeatedly—with both hands—at Franco's face. Cowering, the boy warded off his father's angry blows:"* It would be on the online gossip websites within minutes. His inner voice was warning him. *Chill out.*

With great difficulty, Heston took charge of his own emotions. Instead of slapping the boy senseless, he moved in close and towered about the adolescent, who, though tall, had not yet reached his full height.

Backing away, Franco stumbled into the prickly mesh of palmetto fronds which lined nearby Vanderbilt Beach Road. The spiky fronds dug into his exposed flesh.

"Get away from me, you faggot, you ham actor piece of shit," he croaked, unheard by all but his father. "What do you care? You're so full of yourself you don't have room for anyone else!"

"Heston!" cried Inez, running towards them, followed by her husband.

"Heston, leave him alone!" she cried, pulling Franco from the shrubbery, with Rogelio's help. The game had come to a standstill. From the field, the players and onlookers watched in fascination. The coach came running towards Franco.

"Heston, you're being a jerk," Maude griped, approaching him.

"Damn it, Maude, don't scold me in public! Comfort your child! Don't you care about her well-being? Where's your blessed Mother Love?" spewed Heston, purple with suppressed rage. He pointed to Winnie, who sat crying on the ground.

"She'll recover," Maude said, ambling towards the girl.

In an instant, Heston had scooped his daughter into his arms. Flinging her arms around Heston's neck, Winnie clung to him, wailing. One of Franco's team mates, the boy who had earlier cheered Heston on, sprinted over to Franco and whispered into his ear. Franco, now brushing himself off, in between glares at his father, erupted angrily.

"Shut up, you dumb ass!" he shouted. "Leave me alone." The team mate bowed in laughter. Tears of rage squirted from Franco's eyes. Wildly, he tried kicking at his light-footed teammate until the soccer coach intervened bodily. Half an hour later Heston was leaning against the hood of his red Ferrari, listening, dispirited, to the harangues of both wives, Maude and Inez.

"You think you can just say anything to anybody, Heston, and it's all okay. Well, you can't," griped Maude, bundling Winnie into the car. "You're nothing but an arrogant prick."

She's more concerned about her own embarrassment than she is about her daughter's safety. The woman is a cold-blooded reptile.

"You humiliated Frankie in front of his teammates, Hess," whined Inez. "I don't know if he'll ever forgive you. How could you do that? What were you thinking?"

This one's more concerned about her precious prince's honor than a little girl's injuries. The woman is a selfish shrew.

Rogelio's cigar breath warmed his ear. "Don't tell them I said so, Demming, but for the first moment since I met you, I finally feel a little sympathy for you. The kid is hard to take, even at the best of times." Turning to follow Inez back to the soccer game, Rogelio growled softly, "Even the coach is afraid to discipline him. Franco's spineless, but he retaliates." Rogelio tipped his head towards Heston and sidled away. The rustling fronds of the cabbage palms created the only remaining sound at the soccer field's edge.

"What a frigging disaster," Heston whispered into the balmy breezes. At least, by controlling his temper, he had saved them all from Media Meltdown. What they really owed him was gratitude. Suddenly, the engine beneath him roared. Feeling the car jerk, Heston jumped away. At the wheel, Maude floored the ignition. The car squealed away down Hammock Oak Drive.

"Come back with her, Maude!" he yelled. "Come back with my daughter!"

Frustrated, Heston threw up his hands in disgust. In futility, he swung at empty air until he felt ridiculous. Alone and chagrined, he stood limply at the corner of Vanderbilt Beach Road and Hammock Oak Drive. *What now? Call a cab? A limo service?* More than he needed a ride, he needed a shoulder to cry on. Disgusted with himself, he eyed the EMS firehouse across the road. *Those paramedics' and firemen's lives are worth ten of mine.*

His fingers felt for his cell phone. He dialed 411, the information line.

"Naples, Florida," he replied to the recording. "Poppy Wallace Fine Art." Hearing the phone number, he dialed, but there was no answer. He left no message on the machine. Instead, he again dialed 411.

"Talbot, James, on Vanderbilt Drive," he requested. No response at Poppy's home number either. "Naples, Florida," he said again into his cell phone. "The number for Hideaway Bed and Breakfast, please."

If he couldn't have sympathy, safe sex would do. He'd show Maude—and Inez—just exactly who was in charge.

This time, when he dialed the given number, he met with success. Montserrat Flynn accepted his invitation to dinner at Maxwell's on Venetian Bay. Only then did Heston call for a ride home.

***

Two days later, Maude Demming exited Saks Fifth Avenue, slinking out into the charming waterfall gardens of The Waterside Shops at Pelican Bay. Strolling along the curving interior sidewalk of the pricey shopping mall, Maude drooled greedily over items in designer-shop windows. Deluxe brand names abounded—Cartier, Max Mara, Brooks Brothers, and various others of world renown. How wonderful to know that she could have them all.

Maude adored good clothes. She looked fabulous in them. Then again, she could make a dress bag look elegant, and she knew it. Since age seventeen, she had been paid big bucks for her ability to do just that. Nevertheless, she still relished *owning* the finest of everything. The peignoir she had just purchased at Saks was fit for a queen's boudoir. Too bad it would be wasted on her disinterested hubby.

Who needs him? I'd rather have the peignoir against my flesh.

It was still hard for Maude to accept that she could have any material possession in the world she wanted. As a top model, she had made money on her own. However, as Mrs. Heston Demming, she had become wealthy enough to purchase whatever she desired, cost be damned. If she wanted the bulk of ensembles in Max Mara's window display, all she had to do was tell her assistant to order them.

How trippy—especially for the granddaughter of a Hawthorne trucker. Maude smirked inwardly. Yep, she had 'done good,' as her mother's folks would say.

Pensively, Maude posed for a moment in front of Cartier's storefront. Her shining, strawberry-blonde hair fluttered softly in the dappled sunlight. Lost in thought, she fondled her mother's memory. It had been years since she and her mother had spoken, years since their falling out. Their rift was famous. The tabloids had made a big deal of it a couple of years ago. After that, there was no going back. She'd had to stand her ground, and so, for that matter, had her mother.

Abruptly, Maude moved on, realizing she was attracting gawkers. Often people stared at her. Usually, they found her face familiar but couldn't place her, so they stared. In this regard she was unlike Heston, who was instantly recognizable worldwide. Heston could hardly venture out of the house without a attracting a swarm of human flies.

"Smile," said a familiar female voice behind her. "You look so sad."

Turning, startled, Maude saw the smug countenance of Inez Vega. Instinctively, Maude scrutinized her husband's ex-wife for flaws. Inez was dressed in a loud, but smart scarlet-and-gray ensemble, tight enough to reveal her trim figure. Her gold jewelry was a tad too heavy, *let's face it*, tacky. Early on, Maude had sized Inez up as insecure, an over-compensator. The cropped hair would have made the woman seem dike-y if she hadn't been so small boned. Maude knew all about that, being small boned herself. She was gratified to admit, however, that Inez's finely textured skin was beginning to wrinkle and sag a tad at the jowl. After all, the woman was approaching forty. Maude could recommend a fine treatment for that—but she wouldn't.

"Fabulous shopping," said Maude aloud to Inez.

"Oh, I know. I love it here. I come early and often."

"At least this town has something going on," Maude said, affecting ennui.

"The town is too old for you, Maude. It's a haven for rich retirees, not for bi-coastal beauties in their early thirties."

"Mid-twenties."

"Sorry. Feel like a martini?" Inez invited unexpectedly. "The Starfish Grille is just around the corner. They have a quiet little bar. No one will bother you there. I just held an open house. A really nutty character came in. He gave me a fright, I can tell you. I'm fed up with sitting alone in empty houses. I'm buying a gun. Meanwhile, I need that martini. Coming?"

Curious, Maude agreed, following Inez into the exclusive watering hole. Registering the crack about her age, however, Maude noted it in the debit account. She would make Inez pay later on. Right now, she couldn't help wondering. What tawdry tidbits was Inez angling to plant in her ear? She couldn't wait to find out.

The woman must have some reason for chatting her up. Either that, or Inez just wanted a drinking partner. Secretly, Maude was glad for an opportunity to imbibe. She always had to be so careful around Heston. Plus, today she was shed of the kid. *A little drinky-poo will just hit the spot.* It might enliven her wretched boredom.

The quiet barroom was dark and cool. Tanks filled with exotic fish lined the walls. Afternoon drinkers sat obscurely at scattered tables.

"That was almost a scene at the soccer match," said Inez, sliding into a booth near the wall. "I'll have a martini," she told the server, depositing her Ralph Lauren Polo bag onto the seat. "I bought a little something for Frankie. He needs a lift, poor child," Inez added as an aside.

"A martini for me, as well," Maude informed the server haughtily. "Too bad we're not in South Beach. I worked in Miami as a model. I spent some wild times there. Great fun."

"Sex, drugs, and rock-'n'-roll?"

"Hip-hop, Inez. Time moves on."

"That's where I married Hess, you know. On Key Biscayne at sunrise," remarked Inez, as the server returned and placed martinis on the mahogany tabletop between the two women. In the dim light, Maude discerned a glint in Inez's dark eyes. What was she after?

"He never mentioned it," said Maude aloud.

"You don't talk? I wish Heston and Franco could communicate better," said Inez, taking a sip from her glass. "They've never gotten along. Even when Franco was a baby they were mismatched."

"Odd," said Maude, taking a sip of her own martini. "He dotes on our daughter, Winston. He can't get enough of her." *If I cared, I'd be jealous.*

"Which explains why he went after Frankie the other day," Inez pouted.

"I suppose it does. Face it, Inez. The boy did shove my child." *Heston had not come home that night.*

Flustered, Inez gulped her drink and flagged the server. "Another one," she ordered. Agreeably, the server took the empty glass and departed for the bar.

"You knew Heston before that, didn't you? Didn't you two go to high school together here?"

"Sure did." Inez downed an olive.

"I met some of your class mates at the housewarming. What a crew of Bozos."

"You should have seen them back then. Swamp buggies and swamp cabbage. We've all come a long way, haven't we? We've changed along with the town."

Maude swilled a sip of gin and vermouth. "What about that Poppy woman—that carrot-topped art dealer? She was in your class, wasn't she? She's such a neurotic little slug."

"Oh, yes, in my class. Not in Heston's. He was two years ahead of us in school."

"You were all great buddies?"

"No, not really. I was a cheerleader. Poppy was just sort of 'there.' We didn't run with the same crowd. She dated Heston then. I didn't. Heston was a drama nerd. He and Poppy were artsy. I was dating a fullback on the football team."

Alert, Maude bristled. "So! Heston and Poppy dated in high school."

"Oh, yes. There were a couple."

"For how long?"

"Really, since childhood. They were play pals years before they became lovers." Inez's brow furrowed, reflecting Maude's sudden discomfiture.

"So they aren't just old lovers?"

"They grew up together, best friends who became sweethearts."

Caught off guard, Maude swirled the clear liquid in her glass. "Oh, I see," she enunciated emphatically.

"Heston led you to believe otherwise?" The waiter reappeared with Inez's second drink and a dry cocktail napkin. "Thank you."

"I'm tired," said Maude suddenly. She bolted the remaining liquid in her glass.

"Yes, I know the feeling. You're tired of Heston's half-truths—and his womanizing. How can you stand it, my dear? I know I couldn't, eventually. Divorcing Heston was the best thing I ever did for myself. Believe me, you couldn't give him back to me."

So that was it. Maude narrowed her eyes.

"No, you misunderstand me, Inez. I'm tired of parenting. I'm tired of this conventional role. I need adventure, excitement, people, travel, parties. I'm not cut out for motherhood and apple pie." Maude shuddered.

"You thought marrying Heston would be exciting?" Inez sat back and guffawed. "Oh, my dear! No, I'm afraid our Heston looks fine as crystal but is really sturdy as earthenware." She paused. "Funny, isn't it? I love motherhood. Franco is the most important thing in my life."

"Why did your marriage to Heston end?" said Maude, shifting uncomfortably.

"Heston ignored me. He had caught the theater bug in high school and couldn't shake it. After Franco was born, Heston became involved in theatrical productions around Miami. He was never home. He couldn't keep a regular job because of odd hours, rehearsals and so on. I had no interest in play acting. I grew tired of watching bad performances in run-down theaters. I had a real-estate sales license. So, I made my own life. *Real* life. We grew apart."

83

"Heston left for New York?"

"Once we'd divorced, and I had custody of Franco."

"And the rest is history," Maude smirked snidely. "Well, the world owes you a debt of gratitude, Inez. If you hadn't made Heston Demming miserable, we wouldn't have his star on Hollywood Boulevard today, now would we?"

"A dubious distinction. You seem well-spoken, Maude. Where did you attend school?"

"Cal State, Fullerton. For about a week. I read a lot, Inez. *Shhh*, don't tell anyone." *Anything for a diversion.*

"Were you're parents educated people?"

"My father was. He was an attorney at a prominent law firm in Century City. That's Southern California, to you Floridians. Dad was from an old California family. Laguna area. A ranch in Paso Robles. My mother was a legal secretary, forty years his junior. She was from Hawthorne. It's a working-class suburb of L.A. Her father drove a delivery truck. Mom hooked Dad with bleached-blonde hair and a wicked bikini-tan line. He divorced his wife of thirty years and married Mom. I arrived six months later."

"Are they still married?

That story made her squirm. Watching Inez through slit eyes, Maude twisted a strand of pink-blonde hair between her thumb and forefinger. "My father died at age sixty-three, two years after I was born. My mother inherited everything. But she wouldn't give me a dime. Lucky for me, I was discovered by an agent while working as a meat clerk at Ralph's. He wanted his filet mignon butterflied. I butterflied it for him."

"In Fullerton?"

"Yes. That's when I dropped out of college and went pro."

"And you met Hess when?"

"On Bourbon Street in New Orleans. On set of *Lace And Glory*. I was doing a fashion layout there. I knew the picture's costume designer. He introduced us. Heston was playing a civil war general."

"Oh, I know that film. I own the DVD. Was it love at first sight?"

"On whose part?"

"Either of you?"

"It was something, at first sight, Inez, but not necessarily love. More like greed. We each wanted to own the other." Maude now felt tipsy. Her eyes followed an energetic angelfish. The filmy creature was swimming endless loops in the aquarium tank behind Inez's cropped head.

"And now you both have buyer's remorse?" said Inez watchfully.

"Let's just say I miss the dark side," Maude announced hazily. She, too, was swimming in circles, trapped in a phony world of rosy cheer and cup-cakes and wifely obligations. "But I think Heston is happy enough," Maude added significantly, not too lightheaded to cease protecting her own interests.

Inez waved for the server, who arrived promptly at the table. Handing him plastic, Inez leaned across the table and said to Maude confidentially, "Take my advice, dear. Dump Hess. You won't be sorry. You're young, beautiful, daring. You need excitement in your life. Get it while you still can. Right now, before you're too old to enjoy it. I say dump him and get on with it. No doubt there's someone else you're dying to sleep with. There always is"

"Whom do you want to sleep with, Inez?" Maude teased. "Your step-son?"

Inez met Maude's direct gaze. "Laugh all you want. But I understand you better than you think I do. My family in the old country was dirt poor. We came to the States from a little coastal village, looking for a bet-ter life. I was ten when we emigrated. To this day I can't abide wearing tennis shoes. In the old country, we were so poor I had to wear them to church. I was humiliated. Never again, I swore to myself. When I grow up, I will have fine things and plenty of them." As the server returned with her card, Inez rose from the table. Her eyes glinted again at Maude. "I'm getting there. Thanks for joining me, my dear. Let's do it again sometime. Got to run. I'm showing a villa at four." Gratified, Inez left the bar.

Idly, Maude sat in pensive mode. Her eyes continued to watch the cir-cling angelfish. She knew Inez was after her husband. Yet, the old bag was still right in what she had said.

There is someone I want to sleep with.

"Another martini, Miss?" asked the server. She could tell he was trying to place her.

"Yes, maybe one more," said Maude. *Why not?* Her thin fingers reached into her handbag. She found his business card. She extracted her cell phone and dialed.

"Hello, Cedric?" she said into the cell. "Maude Winston here. Yes, Mrs. H. D. Look, would you like to meet for lunch one day? You would? Groovy."

Why not, indeed?

As she listened to Cedric's voice, Maude's gaze followed the circling angelfish. The fish suddenly broke free from its loop and swam to the sur-face. Maude grinned as she heard Cedric's words.

"Why, yes, we did receive an invitation in the mail. Heston and I would be delighted to come, Cedric!" Maude exclaimed into the cell phone. "I'd love to attend your opening reception tomorrow night."

Chapter Six

Maude was wowed by Cedric's artwork almost as much as she was wowed by his sexual intensity. Already she had found the man oddly tantalizing. Now, as she marveled at his paintings, she was hooked. Primal-colored canvases, large and small, were splashed throughout the high-ceilinged, white-walled room. The mad little gashes of color were vivid, but the subjects were dark.

Punch glass in hand, Maude wandered the crowded room alone, observing. If nothing else, Cedric's art work proved he was passionate, not to mention sexually demented, much to her delight. She knew nothing about art, but, as someone had said, she 'knew what she liked.' She liked this. Her mouth watered hungrily. She wanted a taste of Cedric Spicer. He had grown more fascinating to Maude as a sexual being *because* he was a beat artist.

The slightly creepy feel of Cedric's persona really turned her on, a degenerate unkemptness that would have grossed her out in someone less sexual. Maybe it was the way he moved—slinky but staccato, like a sultry ballroom dancer. His thin arms were sinewy with pronounced veins. Encased in snuggly fitted T-shirts, Cedric's torso looked hot. His midriff seemed extra lean and his shoulders very broad. The high-top sneakers and baggy khakis enveloping sinewy legs sent her over the edge, but it was the jagged scar across his jaw that really drove her wild. So much promise there.

"Like what you see?" asked Poppy Craft-Talbot, suddenly appearing at her side.

"If you're asking me will I buy, the answer is *absolutely*." Condescendingly, Maude gave the slender, thirty-something redhead the once-over. *The little black dress becomes her.* If this simp was what Heston wanted, perhaps let him have her—as long as Poppy didn't go for the money and the title. Maude intended to keep a firm grip on the loving cup.

"Great!" said Poppy. "Please let Wallace or me know when you decide which ones you'd like. But I suggest you make your selection as soon as possible and do let us know. The work is being received quite well." Waving her hand, Poppy indicated the well-to-do patrons, who stood in small pockets scattered around the warmly lit gallery. Others, like Maude, were strolling the room, examining Cedric's latest efforts piece by piece. Maude noticed that Poppy was still wearing a wedding band.

"You're married?" she asked Poppy pointedly.

Poppy nodded evasively. "Separated."

"How convenient," observed Maude, turning a bony shoulder to her hostess.

"Now, now. Mustn't frighten the hand that bleeds you," said Cedric's lilting voice as Poppy moved away. He eased up beside Maude, standing too close. She sensed his bawdy vulnerability. Her blood ran cold at his nearness. She wanted so badly to...

"Maude Winston Demming," said Cedric intimately. "When did you want to do lunch?"

"Whenever."

"Who's going to be lunch?"

"You are."

Cedric's eyes roamed the gallery. "Oh, look. There's your stud of a husband now. Chatting up Our Miss Poppy."

"What?" Maude cried softly, annoyed. She craned her thin neck to see beyond Cedric. *True enough.* She saw Heston and Poppy huddled together alone by the caterer's white-clothed table of hors d'oeuvres. Frowning, Poppy was listening to Heston, whose head was bent low. He was whispering into her ear. Poppy seemed nervous, as if she were trying to pull away. Heston placed an arm on Poppy's wrist. Poppy looked up into his face. *What was happening between them?*

Maude watched as Poppy broke free from Heston and mingled with the crowd. Sipping from his cup of alcohol-free citrus punch, Heston stood alone, for once in his life. As he raised the crystal cup to his mouth, his eyes met Maude's. With disdain, he looked away immediately and moved to speak with the caterer, a short, voluptuous woman with a head of wavy dark hair. Maude had seen the woman at the housewarming but couldn't place her name. Suddenly, Maude realized Cedric had been watching her in amusement.

"Bring your leash?" he asked her, eyebrows raised, eyes laughing.

"Very funny."

"It's Montserrat Flynn you ought to be concerned about, not the China doll," advised Cedric. "Poppy's ancient history."

"Why do you say that?" snapped Maude. "What do you know?"

He peered at her from the corners of his eyes. "I know that Heston stayed all night in Montsey's room. Two nights ago at the Hideaway Bed and Brekkie. Wondering where he was? Now you know, Naughty Maudie.

I saw them through the keyhole."

"You did not."

"As good as. Frankly, I got the lowdown from the goods herself the next day. Montserrat and Heston have been off-again, on-again lovers since youth, did you know? He chased her for years, around the globe. Did you know that?

Yes, you Bozo. Heston married me—and Inez—on the rebound from Montserrat. "Where is the Flynn woman?" Cautiously, Maude again craned her neck.

"Not present, but accounted for. She had to conduct an interview in Everglades City. For the travel article she's writing. Couldn't be here, woe is me."

Angry, Maude glared at Cedric.

"That's the icy hatred I like to see," he whispered. "Pretty please, bony-buns, take it out on little ole me."

She didn't answer. Wallace Smythe was approaching.

"Make any decisions yet?" asked Wallace solicitously. "Fabulous work, eh?" Cedric nudged Wallace gratefully.

"Yes. Several," replied Maude haughtily.

"He means about my paintings." Cedric rolled his eyes knowingly at Wallace.

"Yes," said Maude, indicating the program. "I'll take Numbers 16 and 23."

"Excellent choices. I'll let Poppy know." Wallace bowed obsequiously, backing away, palms pressed together. His bald pate gleamed like a bowling ball.

"Thank you, Maudie," oozed Cedric, rubbing up against her.

"Oh, shut up," she said, discreetly jabbing her bony elbow into his flat belly.

"Make me," Cedric whispered, breathless.

***

I can get this man. I just have to play it smart.

Sunbathing on the public beach in Olde Naples, Sasha schemed inside her mind. She was plotting the best way to take James Talbot away from Poppy. Puzzling, she lay prone on her back, her lush body draped across a fuchsia and orange beach towel with a pineapple motif. Only the most delicate areas of her body were covered with a magenta string bikini. With its finger-like rays, the hot sun massaged the mass of her glistening, voluptuous little form.

She was glad to have the morning off from work. The showing at the gallery last night had been successful for Poppy but time-consuming and tedious for her. She wanted out of the catering business, out of her mother's claw-like grip. Worse, she had freaked out when Heston Demming had started talking to her. It was all she could do not to blurt out Poppy's secret to him.

What an emotional strain. Who needs this? Like an idiot, Poppy had refused to confront him. Last night she had overheard Poppy and Heston's conversation. He had told Poppy he needed to talk to her about that Spanish-Irish chick, the one who had shown up out of the past and messed Poppy up big time. Heston asked Poppy why she hadn't returned his phone calls. He's been leaving her voice mails. But Poppy wasn't having any. She wouldn't respond. She got all gooey-eyed, ran away. The whole situation was really a mess.

Too much to deal with today. She just needed some down time, time to herself, time for herself.

As heat penetrated her pores, Sasha could almost feel her tan growing darker. Her oversized, round sunglasses shielded her vision from mid-morning glare. She felt the perspiration dribbling down her skin onto the damp towel. The beach was sparsely populated this morning. From nearby Naples Pier, she could hear voices or radio static now and then. Once in a while, she heard catcalls coming from the fishermen on the long, wooden pier stretching out into the Gulf. She knew that type—all show and no go.

I wish they would clam up so I could think.

What if she told James about his wife's long-lost child? Poppy could deny the birth—in fact, probably would. She could then accuse Sasha of betraying her trust. Then her mother would lose the art gallery's business. That would be bad. They were good, steady clients.

What if Poppy accused her of lying to steal James? *Which, technically, would be true, and it might turn James against me rather than against Poppy.* A dilemma, for sure. She had to do it right, or it would backfire. *What I need is proof.*

What if she could *prove* to James that Poppy had borne Heston a son? If she could actually *locate* Poppy and Heston's illegitimate child, she could prove to James that Poppy had deceived him for years, from the very beginning. In the face of proof, neither Poppy nor James would be able to deny that Poppy had lied by omission all these years, and that, by lying, Poppy had caused her husband to remain childless.

Then James will turn to me. He will fall into my arms gratefully.

How do you find a child given up for adoption? Hire somebody? A private eye? How do you find a private investigator? The Internet? Sasha's exuberance suddenly burst like a balloon. She hated computers. She owned a handheld, but never used it. It was just for show, so people would think she was up on the latest trends. *What's left? The phone book?*

Maybe—unless she knew somebody who knew somebody who knew somebody. *No, that won't work.* Danny probably knew private detectives, but she couldn't ask him. He would demand to know why she needed a PI. Then she would have to lie to Danny. *Too many lies to keep up with.* If only she had a phone book handy. Another catcall resounded from the fishermen on the pier.

The pier! There is a phone booth up there, a phone with a phone book. I've seen it. Hustling to her feet, Sasha wrapped her moist body in a white-terry beach robe and slipped daisy thongs onto her feet. She noted with pride that her toenails matched her bikini. Grabbing her wallet, she trotted towards the tall, wooden staircase leading up to the pier. Carefully, she climbed each sand-strewn step until she reached the pier's platform walkway itself. Half way down the long pier was a cluster of storefronts. She was sure to find a phone book there. Her sandals slapped the deck loudly and fishermen whistled as she ran.

Yeah! She saw the dog-eared pages flapping in the steady Gulf wind. Below her daisy-sandaled feet, beneath the wooden slats of the pier, the Gulf of Mexico swelled and receded like an immense, undulating slab of jade. Grabbing the phone book, she made a face of disgust. Who knew who had touched it beforehand? *Yecch.*

Driven by curiosity, she fumbled through the yellow pages until she found the list of names. *You can find a private eye in the phone book!* Running her painted fingernail up and down the list, she huffed in frustration. *Which one was good? Which one was bad? Who could tell?* Closing her eyes, Sasha jabbed her nail tip onto the page. Opening her eyes, she stared at a specific name. Depositing coins into the wall phone's slot, she dialed the local number.

"Yello," a thick male voice answered.

"Rick DuBois? Private Investigator?" said Sasha eagerly into the phone. She held the receiver in one hand and, with the other hand, held back the hair blowing into her eyes.

"Depends on who's calling," the mocking voice replied. "Are you in some kind of wind tunnel, Missy?"

"My name is Sasha Bassett. I'm on the pier. I want to hire you for a job."

"What kind of job?"

"To find a baby that was given up for adoption. Nineteen years ago."

"Where?"

"Tampa Hospital."

"Are you the mother?"

"No."

"What's your interest?"

"*Ummm*...I'm calling for my fiancé. He's the mother's husband. Currently."

"Uh-huh. Why didn't he call me himself?"

"He's busy. Look, I can pay. I got lots of dough. I'm a caterer. That's a joke."

"And I'm the proverbial Queen of Sheba. I'll tell you straight out, Missy. It'll be tough. It'll cost money. I may not be successful, but I get paid anyway."

"I have demands, too," Sasha countered. "It's got to be strictly confidential."

"That's what I'm all about," he drawled.

"Then it's a deal."

"Hell, come on down. Let's talk about it. Beggars can't be choosers. And if I don't catch me a fish quick, I'm going to be begging."

As per his instructions, Sasha scribbled the address of the private eye's East Naples office. Hanging up the phone, she exhaled with confidence. She felt pleased with herself. He sounded like a yahoo, but he was available and he was a real PI. *Step One, Accomplished.*

Now she would be able to put the rest of her plan into action. Patience had never been one of her virtues. Danny got mad at her sometimes because she was so impulsive. *Like he should talk.*

***

That same afternoon, within the confines of Cedric Spicer's rented studio in the design district, Maude and Cedric were alone together for the first time. The high-ceilinged, window-filled room was littered with painting materials and canvases, both finished and unfinished. On an antique floral daybed in a secluded corner of the studio, Maude lay still, her long body draped elegantly across the brocade cushions. Aching for release, she stared up at the skylight in the roof and clenched her fingers repeatedly.

Sitting on the floor beside Maude, his back resting against the side of the day bed, his legs stretched out across a ratty oriental rug, Cedric lit a joint and inhaled. Twisting his torso, he offered the marijuana cigarette to Maude. With expert ease, she took the burning paper stub between her fingers and thrust it between her lips. As had Cedric, she inhaled and held the pungent smoke in her lungs before releasing it.

"Why did you marry him?" asked Cedric, mellowing amiably.

Maude pondered the question. "When I first met Heston, I thought I could..."

"Beat him into submission?"

"Something like that. He was a drunkard then. A top-salaried, ascending-star drunkard, mind you. Sober, he's a different man."

"His own man. Why not divorce him? Bad prenuptial agreement?"

"I'll lose everything. That's why I have to get rid of that Poppy person. If Heston divorces me, I'm toast."

"She's not your rival, Maude. Montserrat Flynn is."

"You don't know men as well as you think. I tell you I'm worried about it, Cedric," said Maude. Returning the joint to Cedric, she picked weed particles from her lips. Then her fingers found Cedric's long, blond-gray ponytail. She stroked it gently.

"Forget it, Maude," Cedric said hoarsely, taking the joint from her. "Heston's into Montsey, not Poppy. Montsey's the sexpot. I'm telling you. You should be worried about Montsey. Hell, you should be worried about me. I'm as into him as anyone."

Maude chuckled languidly. "Perhaps you want me to keep Heston away from Montsey because you want her yourself?"

"Or vice versa."

"Because you want Heston? Vice, either way." Around the ponytail, she made a ring of her forefinger and thumb. She rang her finger ring down the length of Cedric's hair.

"Ha, ha. Very droll," he said.

"The grass is always greener..." she joked. "Tough for you middle-of-the-roaders."

"Bitch." Cedric tried to re-light the joint using a platinum cigarette lighter. "Honestly, Maude. I have no real interest in Montserrat Flynn, other than as a portrait model. I might want to paint her one day. You, I adore. You and Heston together? Ah, now, that would be sweet."

"Propping up on one elbow, Maude spoke her thoughts aloud.

"If all you want is kicks, you can have Heston, as far as I'm concerned. Not that I think he'd be interested in you, Cedric. Sorry. No, what I'm worried about is that he may be *serious* about this Poppy person. He *likes* her. That can be a far more dangerous threat than unrequited lust. What kind of a name is that, anyway?"

"It's a red flower," said Cedric, drifting. "One of my favorites."

"No doubt, since it's the source of opium, isn't it? Who names a child after an opium plant?"

"Wally says her real name is Penelope."

"Even worse."

"Poppy? Red hair? Get it?" Cedric lolled lazily.

"The thing is, I really don't love Heston. I really care nothing at all for him. Keep that under your hat, of course. Confidentially, he doesn't give a flip about me, either. I confess. He only married me on the rebound from Montserrat."

"For real?"

Maude grunted assent. "She had dumped him again, for the hundredth time, right before shooting began on *Lace and Glory*. I met Heston on that movie set."

"You caught a rising star?"

"Let's just say I married for love. I love Heston's money. I care deeply for it. I refuse to be parted from it. Anyone who tries to separate me from my husband's earning power will be sorry. Very sorry." Without warning, she yanked Cedric's ponytail, hard and tight.

"*Oooh*! Hurt me, baby," gasped Cedric, wincing. He pulled her down on top of him. "Hurt me, and I'll help you guard your treasure chest."

"It's a deal," whispered Maude disagreeably, digging her nails into his lean flesh.

***

"Thank you for coming, Sasha," said James Talbot. Poppy's dull husband was scrunched into the circular booth. The booth was located in the back corner of the bar in the Starfish Grille. Hunkered down, James was nursing a gin and tonic. In the dark setting, Sasha couldn't see him too well. Some light was coming from the various aquarium tanks, where sleeping schools of fish floated in place in the tank water. Most of the humans in the barroom were seated at the bar or at tables and booths nearer to the front entrance. A low jazz piano tinkled in the background.

"I was surprised to get a call from you so late, James. It's eleven-thirty," she said, sliding into the circular booth. *Thank my lucky stars Danny went to the movies with his little brother tonight. Would he have been mad or what?*

"I know. I apologize. I just didn't want to be alone," said James somberly, in his soft Texas drawl. He glanced at his Rolex.

"Why? What happened?" she asked, slathering on the expression of concern. She was dressed in jeans and a tank top. He had caught her on laundry night.

"I met Poppy for dinner," explained James. "She wants out of our marriage."

"She said that?" asked Sasha, incredulous.

"Not in so many words. But she doesn't want me back right now."

"Right now? Or ever?"

"I'm not sure," said James. "She's not sure. Want a drink?" he asked Sasha, as the waiter approached.

"Whatever you're having," she said, inwardly resigned to the mouth-wash-flavored swill.

"Another gin and tonic," said James. "Make it two." He rattled his empty glass. The waiter nodded and headed for the bar.

"She said she doesn't love me," James blurted out. He blubbered spasmodically. "She said she never did. She said she married me for selfish reasons. She said it wasn't fair to me."

Hot diggety. Eyes wide, Sasha batted her eyelashes and pouted sympathetically.

"At least Poppy's being honest with me. I've always loved Poppy for her honesty. I can't fault her for telling me the truth. Can I, Sasha?" James buried his face in his hands. He took a few deep breaths.

"There, there," she said, patting James on his forearm. *Nice watch.* "Here's a tissue." She handed him a piece of flimsy pink paper from her satchel. The tissues were from the same box as those she had offered to Poppy recently. Rubbing his face vigorously, James sat back in his faux-leather seat and sighed.

"Sorry, Sasha. I'm sorry you had to see me like this." He folded the tissue neatly and set it aside.

She patted his arm. "Don't worry about it, James. Just tell me everything."

"I told Poppy I loved her for her honesty. You know what? She started to cry. What a woman I married."

"Yeah, Poppy's been crying a lot lately," she said under her breath. The waiter returned with two cold cocktails. She smelt the stuffy odor of gin and lime as he placed the drinks onto the tabletop before her.

"You've always been such a good friend to Poppy, Sasha. What do you think she wants?" asked James in an earnest bid for advice. He tossed down half a glass.

Guarding her words carefully, she attempted to answer, "I think Poppy wants out of your marriage but doesn't want to come right out and say so. She doesn't want to hurt you."

Mortified, James let the news sink in. "You really believe she wants out?"

Gently, she placed her hand on his forearm. "Yes, I do. Me, I don't understand why. I told you what kind of man I feel you are. I'd take you in a heartbeat."

"You would?" said James through a gin-and-tonic haze.

"I would," she vowed.

James clasped her hand in his. "Sasha, I..."

Leaning forward, she kissed James quickly on the lips, then pulled away. "I'm sorry," she said, acting flustered.

This time he grabbed her forearms. "Don't be sorry. Look, let's get out of here. Let's go somewhere we can talk. Really talk."

"Well, we could go back to my place," she suggested, as though the idea had occurred to her on impulse. She had been smart to pick up the dirty laundry before leaving home, and to throw it into the hamper. *Preparation meets opportunity.* She was all set. She had even gone off the pill this morning.

"Check, please," called James to the waiter. Grabbing her cocktail glass, she drained it to the dregs. Jittery, James paid the bill. Shaking with anticipation, the gray-haired man guided her out to the parking lot. Forty-five minutes later, she opened the front door to her apartment at Coco Palms. She flicked on the wall light switch to illuminate the darkened interior.

"Let me check Gabby—my parrot," she told James, who tentatively entered the apartment. "I won't be a sec. Make yourself at home." She motioned towards the couch. "Will you drink beer?" It was all she had in the house. Danny had left some Asian brew in the fridge last night.

"Sure, I guess so," said James reticently. After checking on the bird, Sasha reentered the living room and headed into the kitchen. With beer and chips on a tray, she reentered the living room. *Not the greatest spread, but this isn't about that.*

James had positioned himself in the middle of the couch. Both his arms were extended and resting along the top of the couch. His paunch hung over his belt.

"Sit here," he beckoned, patting the sofa cushion to his left.

"Want some music?" She set the tray down on the coffee table and served James a beer.

"Okay," he acquiesced, loosening his collar with his forefinger. Discreetly, out of his sight, she turned off her answering machine. Then she turned on soft music and plopped down beside James in the space he had indicated. She unbuttoned her jeans and smiled at James.

"I just want to get comfortable." She wiggled alluringly. Taking a beer, she raised the foamy glass. "To new adventures," she toasted.

"Bottoms up," said James, and drank lustily. "Want a back rub?"

Sasha looked at James. She saw the paunch, the iron-gray hair, the heavy glasses, the cracked lips. Could she do it? She downed more beer. He probably thought she found him mesmerizing. She couldn't help but stare. It was like going into battle. She had to remember her mission. To catch him. To be impregnated by him. To be legally bound to him. Nothing else mattered at this moment.

Quickly, as James removed his glasses, she tried selling herself on his good traits. *He's a really nice guy. He went to a top Texas university. He works for a big development company. He has money. He's well-connected.*

He's my best friend's husband.

Ex-best friend.

The big accountant lunged at her with the force of a bulldozer.

Chapter Seven

"So, it's the same old song," muttered Heston, head in hands, to siren Montserrat Flynn. In the hidden patio off Montsey's room at The Hideaway, Heston was lounging uncomfortably on a wrought- iron bench. He was still half-clad, having made it only as far as shorts and socks.

Early morning light filtered through the broad, rounded leaves of the tall sea-grape hedge, dappling the stone floor. Raising his head, Heston projected his voice. "You give me what I want, Montserrat—up to a point. Sexually, you give me anything and everything. Emotionally, you give me nothing, nothing but a radiant smile and a kick in the groin."

No response. He wondered whether she had heard him or not. He was so tired of this game. He thought it had ended five years ago, when he and she had agreed to go their separate ways, once and for all. Now, she was in his blood again.

Or was she? Did he really feel the way he once had? He wanted to believe he did. He wanted to keep his dream intact.

Attired in a sheer, lavender teddy and negligee, she stepped from the bedroom out onto the patio stones. Dewy and ladylike, she still stole his breath away. Her figure was classic. Her fair skin glowed. Her dark auburn hair shimmered. He thought he would die just drinking her in. *But is her beauty enough, now?*

"My terms are the same as always, Heston. I give you what you want, as long as it doesn't interfere with what I want," she replied.

"What do you want?" he asked, picking up a stray twig and idly stripping off its leaves. Engrossed in his small task, he waited for her answer. *As if I don't know...*

"I still want what I have always wanted most, Demming—my freedom."

"Your precious freedom," he responded cynically.

"You always say it like it's a disease."

"Your kind is."

"Nothing—no one—in the world is more important than my freedom," she declared hotly.

He loved it when her nostrils flared. She was magnificent. Twenty years ago he would have taken her words so seriously. Twenty years ago he *had* taken them seriously. Not now, however. He was wiser now. Twenty years ago, she had had no fine lines etched around her eyes and mouth. He had learned something about the fleeting nature of reality as well, since their last encounter. *If perfection doesn't last, what does?*

"Will you take breakfast?" she asked him casually.

He shook his head.

"Do you mind if I order a mimosa?"

"Order me a cappuccino, then," he said. It would be a nice change from the tea Maude favored. "You still drink champagne for breakfast?"

"Only on expense account," she hedged. Her tastes had once seemed so exotic to him. Now they seemed banal. What was wrong with him these days? Was it his terrible relationship with Maude? Had it soured him on romance? Nothing felt right; nothing tasted right; nothing seemed right anymore. *Something was missing.*

"Poppy Craft hasn't changed much either, has she?" asked Montserrat tamely, after ordering a continental breakfast for two. "You two seemed pretty wrapped up in one another when I found you on your dock the other night."

"Poppy looks older, sadder, like the rest of us," he replied. "Otherwise, she's still the same sweet person." To his surprise, Montsey seemed rattled by his comment. She cast her eyes at the dresser mirror and put her hands to her face.

"Look," he said, unnerved. "Cancel that cappuccino. I've got to get going. I've got a stack of unread scripts on my desk at home. My agent's after me to pick one. Plus, I'm memorizing lines for the Acapulco shoot." Hastily, he donned his tee shirt and sneakers. His sullen mistress watched him in the mirror.

"I'll call you," he said, quickly kissing the top of her head. He stopped before exiting the door. "Thanks," he said. Their eyes met in the mirror.

"My pleasure," she replied somberly. "Great fun, as always."

He escaped into the lobby and trotted down the front steps. Instead of getting into his sports car however, he turned east and began to jog along the sidewalk leading to the public beach, two blocks away. Jogging felt good. It would work out the kinks. Briskly, he made tracks, crossing Second Street South, which turned into Gordon Drive further south on its way to Port Royal, and then across Gulfshore Boulevard South. Approaching the public beach, he could feel the vast body of water awakening to the day. The damp stillness and the flat calmness of the salt water filled him with the sense that peace was possible.

Fun? That's what I am to Montserrat Flynn? Fun? His mind jogged along with his feet. Why the hell had he gone back to Montsey a second night? She had lured him. He hadn't been able to resist. *Fool.* This was the first time he had broken his marriage vow to Maude. *Liar.*

He swerved northward onto the sugary sand and began jogging north along the shore. Beach-goers were already out, shelling, swimming, setting up umbrellas and lounge chairs. He jogged along, contemplating his current circumstances.

He regretted so much. He regretted that he had left Poppy in the lurch again while he had drooled over Montserrat. *How that must have hurt her.* He felt like a heel. He regretted the way he had treated his son, too, at the soccer game.

Why do I keep doing the same old things?

How he must have embarrassed the boy, right there in front of all of his friends. He should have taken him aside, discussed the matter in private. No wonder Franco hated him. He was glad he would have a second chance with his son. He had accepted Inez's invitation to attend another soccer match. He was becoming good at this 'making-amends' thing. If he could do it with other people, surely he could do it with his own child. He owed the boy an apology for a whole lifetime of neglect, not just for one day of anger—and he knew it.

Just keep running.

He was running now, trying to run off the urge for alcohol. The night after the scene at the soccer game—the first night he had spent with Montsey in five years—he had wanted a drink badly. He had felt so desperate. He had called his sponsor in Los Angeles. The true-blue fellow had helped him through the many ups and downs of his journey to clean sobriety. The man was only a phone call, a text message away, but he wished he were closer.

He could feel himself teetering over the abyss of oblivion. He'd had to escape Montsey's rooms before she started quaffing the bubbly. He hadn't even wanted to taste it on her lips.

Her lips.

He was sweating now. The morning air was humid. The breeze was non-existent, which was why the waves were so small. A lake-like surface was characteristic of the Naples Gulf Coast. He remembered how, as a boy, he and his pals could surf only in the aftermath of hurricanes. The storms actually churned waves big enough to ride. Mid-thought, he hopped over a turtle that was inching its way towards the breaking waves.

He thought about Poppy's lips, the first lips he had ever tasted. He and she had learned lovemaking together.

Why did she keep surfacing in his mind? He thought about the high-school girl she had been. In memory he felt her lean, sturdy, tender body, the playground of his callow youth, the temple of his teenage lust. He pictured her soft, wide-set brown eyes. Soulful and loving, they gave her that endearing dreamy look he still adored. What was it she had been trying to tell him, on the dock during the housewarming party? She'd always had trouble spitting things out. If only *she* hadn't shown up.

He would track Poppy down and make her talk. It would be a good excuse: *Say, what was that thing you meant to tell me the other night?*

To his surprise, he realized he was *searching* for an excuse to make contact with Poppy He still needed someone to talk to. He had tried to unburden his heart to Montserrat. Bored, she had turned the talk towards photojournalism and her own career. She wasn't interested in him as a soul, a heart. She was interested in him only insofar as he gratified the needs of her ego. *Had she always been this way? Fun?*

Doing an about-face, he began jogging southward. The sun was in his face now. The bright heat beat down on him. It was going to be a hot one. Retracing his steps, he jogged down the shoreline. From here, he could see the Naples Pier south of him. He remembered it fondly. He'd spent some of the few happy hours of his boyhood fishing there in the early morning, and rendezvousing with Poppy at night. He would revisit the pier soon, after dark, if necessary, to avoid being mobbed.

He was sprinting now. No one had recognized him. It had been a good run. He loved being in peak condition. He could still pleasure a woman all night and run all day. *How long would that last?* Forever, he hoped, but he doubted it.

At Tenth Avenue South, he turned eastward. Jogging along the sidewalk, he slowed his pace as he approached his Ferrari. The red car was parked along the curb, about half a block from Crayton Cove, site of the Naples City Dock and the Hideaway B&B. Reaching his vehicle, he slowed to a walk. He was dripping sweat. It felt great to rid himself of impurities.

Locating his car keys, he signaled the door opener. About to climb in, he glanced towards the Hideaway, a two-storied tan-stucco building with dark-wood trim in the classic Spanish style. Standing on the front steps, chatting beneath towering bougainvillea shrubs, with its electric-magenta flowers, were Montserrat Flynn and Cedric Spicer. Engaged in humorous banter, they did not notice him. Spicer was animated, gesticulating wildly. Totally engaged, she seemed charmed by him. She was giving the weirdo painter her best airhead facial expression and most spritely giggle, the lilting laughter that sounded like a stream of tiny bubbles breaking, one by one, in mid-air.

Heston's heart skipped a beat. Spicer had brought Montsey to the housewarming. He hadn't been worried then about competition because, after his encounter with Spicer at Poppy's gallery, he'd assumed the painter was gay. Since then, however, he had heard that Spicer was bi-sexual and a notorious libertine.

That word again.

Why the hell do I care? In spite of his new doubts about his mistress, he still felt conflicted. She was like a coveted artifact, for possession of which he had toiled in vain. Worse, he was bound to her by years of intimate sexual knowledge. Wasn't he? *Aren't I?* Could years of jealousy be washed away by a few moments of clarity?

Heston took a step forward. Then, changing his mind, he grabbed a towel from inside the Ferrari and wiped the sweat from his face and body.

What's the point? He needed to sort out his feelings before behaving like an imbecile.

Sliding behind the wheel, he clinched his jaw as he adjusted the rearview mirror. Flooring the foot pedal, he turned the music volume high and sped off towards Port Royal without glancing again at the intimate pair. To a rhythmic beat, he chanted Montserrat's mantra in his mind.

You don't own me, Heston. No one does.

You don't own me, Heston. No one does.

You don't own me, Heston. No one does…

***

The following morning, when he arrived at the Pelican Bay County Park soccer field, he found that a local TV reporter and her cameraman, along with a photojournalist from the local newspaper, had arrived ahead of him. Apparently, word of his and Maude's appearance last week had circulated. He frowned. Dark glasses wouldn't hide him here. Irritated, he resolved to make the best of a bad situation. Although worried, he felt reassured by the presence of bodyguards. *What can happen with these giants around?*

His wife, Maude, was pleased with the attention from the local media. When he proved aloof to their questions, the journalists tackled Maude. Guarding Winnie closely, he moved away from his wife and stood down the sidelines, alongside Inez and Rogelio. Today Inez was sitting in an unfolded lounge chair, her shapely legs positioned at their best viewing angle. Cigar alight, Rogelio was seated on a portable folding stool. The strong odor of the burning cigar disintegrated in the outdoor air.

"We got tired of standing last time, Hess," explained Inez, waving to him and Winnie. "We have other folding chairs in the SUV. If you'd like, Rogelio can fetch a couple." In response, Rogelio half-rose from his stool.

"No, thanks. We'll stand. Rogelio, keep your seat," said Heston, gesturing with one hand, while holding Winnie's hand in the other. "We like to walk up and down the sidelines, don't we, Win?"

Winnie nodded.

A cry rose up from the young players on the field as play intensified. He, Inez, and Rogelio craned their necks to see the action. In the distance, he saw Maude spouting off to the reporter. Heston wished he knew what the devil she was saying. They'd had a fierce row when he'd arrived home yesterday morning. She had been furious about his spending a second night with Montserrat. By nightfall, he'd managed to placate her but he'd had to do it with money and subtle threats. Afterwards, he'd found his daughter huddling in the corner of her bedroom, ears covered as she tried to escape the menacing voices.

Poor Win, always caught in the crossfire. He squeezed the little girl's hand. She squeezed his in reply and his heart flip-flopped. He loved the child, even if Maude didn't.

Over the years he had discovered Maude's Achilles' heel. Her position as his wife and heir was what she most wanted to protect. Now that he knew her weak point, he played it for all it was worth. The threat of divorce usually did the trick. The smartest thing he'd ever done was to make her sign that pre-nuptial agreement. He *was* in charge of his marriage. He would do what he liked and the rest be damned.

A horn honked from the distant road. Traffic noise was faint but steady.

Still, he wondered what bilge she was spewing to the press. Maude was nothing if not vindictive. Her means of retaliation could be subtle but deadly. He might wake up tomorrow morning and find his disgusting bathroom habits, or some such, discussed in the daily newspaper. Then his wife would smile serenely at him and make excuses. "*Hes*-ton, I was just babbling off the top of my head. I didn't *know* they were going to *print* what I said." He could hear it now.

Who told the press I would be here?

He stopped in his tracks. Was it Maude, herself? No, surely not. He was getting paranoid. It must have been the one of the soccer players or his friends or family. Some fan tipped off the newspaper, and now here we are. Well, if they thought they'd catch another outburst of his on tape, they were wrong. He promised himself to mind his *P's* and *Q's* this afternoon.

After all, he was here to make amends with his son. *How could I have been such an idiot as to have humiliated the boy?* He disgusted even himself. At least, he was not behaving the way his own dad had. True, he had felt the urge to belt the kid, but he had restrained himself. There was nothing worse, in his mind, that attacking a child. Even at his most drunk, he had never resorted to such vile behavior. He'd walloped men his own size or bigger, but never an innocent babe—or an adolescent boy.

Memories of his own youth bubbled, trying to surface. Again, he forced them down in favor of the moment. He had embarrassed Franco, and he would have to undo his error.

Oh, hell. His flood of remorse caused his face to color. He was glad the other onlookers were focused on the game. Blushing made him look blotchy.

Still, he couldn't have let Franco get away with hurting Winnie, could he? What was he supposed to have done? Let's face it. The boy was a whiny bully. He needed to be taught a lesson.

My father would have taken a belt to him... Belt?

"Want to sit, Daddy," said Winnie, dangling from his hand as she tried to drop onto the thick green carpet of grass. The pulling sensation on his arm brought him back to reality.

"Sit over here, little one," said Inez, patting the end of the lounge chair. "Come visit your Aunt Inez."

Winnie glanced questioningly at her father. "Go ahead, Ladybug," he told his little girl. "Sit there. It'll be fine. I'll be right here."

Crinkling her nose with pleasure, Winnie dashed over and sat at Inez's feet. Standing alone and tall, he saw his son, Franco, approaching. *Brace up*

Smirking, the darkly handsome youth, clothed in white shorts and a red jersey, slithered up to him.

"Why are you here?" Franco demanded of him.

"Frankie, be nice!" said Inez from the chair, cradling Winnie in her arms. Franco threw a glance at his mother, then back to his father.

"I wanted a second chance," he said. "With you. And I wanted to give you a second chance with me. The two of us need to spend time together, Franco. I thought we'd go yachting. I have a new rig. I could teach you to sail."

"I don't want to learn to sail."

What a nasty vibe the kid has. As though suffering a blow, he had a sudden realization. His son reminded him of his father. The thought stunned him.

Is that where he gets it? From my old man? From me?

"I just wanted you to know—I'm the one who tipped the press you'd be here," said Franco tauntingly. "Let's see you come after me again with the whole world watching, *Daddy*."

"Smart ass," he muttered, feeling his hackles rise as he stared the boy down. Laughing, but retreating, Franco ran back onto the field as play resumed. Every hair on his body bristled. His pulse accelerated like the engine of his Ferrari. His muscles tensed to steely strings of rage. *Damn his impudence.*

The bodyguards were watching closely. So was the reporter. Along with her trusty cameraman, she trod across the green grass towards him.

"Is it true you and your son had a fight here last week?"

"Please, I..." he began.

"We heard reports from several witnesses, including your wife, that you verbally abused your son when he tripped over your daughter. Is that correct?"

He saw Franco watching, laughing, from the field.

"If I did, he deserved it," he mumbled under his breath.

"Excuse me?" said the reporter, excitedly waving the cameraman forward. "Would you please repeat that statement for the camera?"

"I said I have never abused my son, verbally or otherwise," he replied, teeth barred.

Suddenly, the soccer ball flew from the field and rolled near his feet. Franco came loping after it. Instead of returning the ball to Franco, he scooped it up and, with all his strength, kicked it far across the field in the opposite direction. Sailing high into the air, the ball then dropped into the thick row of palmetto bushes lining busy Vanderbilt Beach Road.

"Prick," snarled Franco, turning to chase the ball as it disappeared into the undergrowth of brush. In a few moments, Franco disappeared after the ball. Watching closely, he could see the rustling fronds of the palmetto plants.

"Bad form, Mr. Demming, sir," reprimanded the coach, incredulous. "I teach my boys never to kick a ball in anger." On the soccer field, the players idled hot and sweaty, hands on knees, waiting for play to resume. Rogelio chewed on his cigar stub.

"Did you do that on purpose, Heston?" the reporter gaped, thrusting a microphone under his nose.

Just then a terrible squeal of brakes sounded from behind the hedgerow of palmettos, then a thud, then the sound of one car crashing into another—metal-to-metal impact and shattering glass—and a cry of agony, then the clamor of slamming doors and anxious voices.

"Oh, my ..." he gasped, realizing the worst. Everyone in the vicinity ran towards Vanderbilt Beach Road. Terror gripped him by the throat as he sprinted towards the hideous sounds, bodyguards at his heels.

"Ambulance! Somebody call 911!" cried a man's voice as Heston clawed his way through the prickly palmetto brush and bounded out into the open street. He stopped short at what he saw—his son, Franco's flailing body crushed and bleeding, wedged between two mammoth SUV's crashed together at the busy stoplight intersection.

Behind him, Inez began to scream hysterically.

***

Danny Vega stood at his half-brother's grave site. *Too sunny for a funeral.* Grateful, Danny felt Sasha's hand squeeze his. Dressed in black like the other funeral attendees, she was there for him. He squeezed her little hand in return. Repeatedly, Danny blinked in the bright sunlight. He shifted his weight so that the portable canopy shaded his eyes. It was hard. The whole damn thing was hard. He could feel the muscles in his face quivering. He listened to the priest's final words. Even though the firehouse had been right around the corner, the paramedics hadn't been able to save Frankie.

Poor kid. Poor stupid kid. How many times had he told Franco to be careful crossing the street? Kid wouldn't listen, no matter what. *Life and death.* It was about life and death. Kid was here one minute, gone the next. *Just like that.* Danny felt as if his gut had been hollowed out. With pained eyes, he glanced around at the others who stood silently at Franco's gravesite. *How are they taking it?*

Heston Demming's face looked like a funeral mask. The movie star was taking it hard. He should be. He'd killed the kid. Heston's beautiful wife looked bored, like she'd rather be poolside on a day like this. The pretty baby hadn't come. At home with the help, probably. On the other side of the bronze casket stood dismal Poppy Talbot and that big, gym-rat business partner of hers Wallace Smythe.

Smythe? What kind of sophomoric shit is that? The whole world was phony, including that nutty fruitcake, Spicer, standing next to him. *Guy looks at me like I'm a melting ice-cream cone.* Bet he'd like to comfort Demming through this ordeal. Why else would he be hanging around?

Poppy Talbot looked broken up herself. She was a pretty little thing, getting long in the tooth, but well-maintained, and a still a gen-uine babe. This morning her face looked ragged. *What's eating her?* Poppy couldn't be that moved by Franco's passing. She hadn't even known the kid. Danny mused. The last couple of times he'd seen Poppy she'd acted weird.

Danny eyes followed Poppy's gaze. It led to The Great Celebrity himself. To Danny's surprise, Heston was returning Poppy's stare. Then they both dropped their eyes. *Oh, ho! What's that about?* Danny figured Demming had almost as much woman trouble as he did.

All Demming's women were a similar body build. Proportion, not size. Bodies similar, faces kind of, too. Most guys had a type. Coloring? Come to think of it, Inez's dark hair had been henna-rinsed years ago. He'd seen old snapshots of her when Franco was a kid.

Danny didn't have a type. He liked women–all women, short, tall, fat, thin, old, young–within reason, and even then he'd probably stretch it in a pinch. That's why he hadn't wanted to settle down. *So many delicious dishes at the banquet of love.*

Suddenly, his stepmother moaned and slumped against his biceps. With his right hand, Danny let go of Sasha's small hand and grabbed Inez, who had been standing on his left. On the far side of Inez stood his father, who had grabbed the slumping woman just as Danny had. However, Inez clung to Danny, not his dad. *That has to hurt.*

Cradling Inez in his arm, Danny let her sob. Pressing his cheek against the top of her lace-covered head, Danny rocked his stepmother gently as she sobbed. Inez always smelled like roses. That sachet stuff she kept in all the drawers. Her cries drove a stake through his heart. *This'll kill her. She's not going to make it through this. Kid was her whole life. Said so all the time. Don't cry, Momi.* He felt Inez's hands clutching his lats. He hated that he liked the feel of them.

Guiltily, he glanced towards Sasha. He and she exchanged a look of concern. Supportively, she patted his left shoulder. Danny nodded at her and then glanced at his dad.

He wasn't worried about his father's grief. His only worry there was that Rogelio might act too happy. When he caught his dad's eye, he saw glee. He looked away.

It was good the funeral was private. The memorial service last night had been huge. If that mob had crowded the cemetery, the chaos would have been unmanageable. Looking around the flat grounds of the memorial park, he noted the floral offerings at many of the gravesites scattered around the vast lawn. Here and there, throughout the park, was an occasional marble crypt. A grand, white-marble statue of Jesus, with open arms to welcome the departed, stood beneath a sheltering pine. A new mausoleum had been erected, too.

Death everywhere. Everywhere death.

It was getting hot. Surely this would end soon and they could go back to the house. The empty house. No more kid. No more soccer balls in the pool. Danny felt a cry rising in his own chest. He stifled the pain and hugged Inez more tightly. Regaining control, he cleared his throat and stared at the priest, who was completing his ritual.

Danny hated the thought of facing the paparazzi outside the cemetery entrance on Immokalee Road. Good thing he had his shades. Good thing they lived in a gated community like Bay Colony. Good thing Heston had the bodyguards along.

Heston was watching Inez now. He looked stricken, like a gutted animal. Maybe he loved the kid, after all. At least he feels remorse. Guy like that who has everything. *Hey, Movie Star, real life is hard—you know? If the whole thing hadn't been a freak accident, I'd kill you, you son of a bitch. I may anyhow.*

Shit about Franco's death had been all over the news—in the papers, TV, on the Net, the radio. The whole world was grieving along with The Great Star. Little Winnie will inherit kit and caboodle, Danny speculated. *Now that Franco's dead.*

Cradling his stepmother, whose cries had dwindled to whimpers, Danny looked back at Sasha. Did she ever lust for Demming? Danny wondered. Sash never acted like she cared about celebrity one way or the other. She was a pretty down-to-earth girl.

Danny watched her for a moment. He loved her smallness. She was so cute. Maybe he had been wrong to stall her. Maybe he *should* marry her now. Have a kid of his own right away. Life was short. What if he died tomorrow? *It had happened to Franco.*

Chapter Eight

Heartsick, Heston stood clinging to the handrail of his sailing yacht's bow, as the ship plowed through Gordon's Pass heading for the choppy, gray Gulf of Mexico. Sails rising, the vessel advanced into open sea. Overhead, a thick blanket of rain-laden clouds allowed no patch of blue to break through. To Heston, the whole world felt gray. Even the strong wind powering the sailboat seemed gray and howling as a lonely sea wolf.

What a wicked place this world is.

Sea spray stung his haggard, bearded face. Paralyzed by grief and guilt, he clung to the cold steel rod, the soles of his feet planted firmly upon the yacht's rhythmically undulating deck. Having raised the sails, the new crew of two departed the deck on his orders. In the cockpit, the crew would pilot the ship. For all intents and purposes, he was now alone–alone with his bottle of twelve-year-old Scotch. Lifting the bottle of amber-colored relief to his mouth, he took another gulp and felt warm pleasure trickle down his throat.

Hey, baby. It's been a long time.

Fierce wind whipped his sails and clothes. Distended like a balloon, the mainsail was taut with air. The ship skimmed the waves rapidly. He didn't care anymore. He didn't care if he were swept from the ship and drowned in the deep. It would be a blessing if he were. He couldn't live with it. He couldn't live with what he had done.

He had killed his own son.

What was left for him in this world? *Nothing.* There was nothing left. He had done it. He had committed the heinous act. He could never overcome it. He took another swig of whiskey. Sticky liquid ran down into his beard. He wiped his beard with the sleeve of his windbreaker. He stared at the ever-receding horizon. Few boats were out on such a day. He had counted on that.

All he wanted now was blessed *oblivion.* But would it ever come again?

What a nightmare. How could this hideous thing have happened? If only he could go back and re-live that terrible day, that terrible moment, when, out of vengeance, he had kicked the soccer ball too hard in the wrong direction. Just for one second, one life-altering instant. To be able to change his actions, to be wiser, more loving, more of a father and less of a competitor. His shoulders began to shake. *Oh, Franco, my son I'm so sorry—forgive me forgive me forgive me oh no oh no...*

He beat back the horror with another belt of booze. What was that poem? The one about the nail in the horseshoe and the kingdom being lost for lack of it? It was like that. One second's lapse in judgment had ended his boy's life. *One second.* Turn back the clock. Turn back time. *Please help me to save him. Please help me to do it over again right and not hurt my boy.*

A terrible wail of anguish arose in his throat. He slumped to his knees. His body trembled in the wind. He kept his contorted face turned towards open sea. *No one must see his guilt, his shame.* He would pay the crew well for their silence.

His head ached from crying. He took another drink from the bottle. Somehow, he found himself sitting on the white, fiberglass deck, his elbows locked around the ship's metal railing, his feet dangling over the bow's edge. He could feel the salt spray on his bare ankles. He gloried in the rushing wind. He felt himself soaring into the safety of solitude. Alone at sea, almost, he could become a mere speck in the vast ocean of the universe.

The crew had insisted he don a life preserver before departure. If he fell into the water, he would take it off so he could drown faster. He knew they were worried about him. However, he had given them strict orders to leave him alone. All he wanted in the world was to be alone.

The inquest was behind him, now just a blur in his memory. He had been exonerated, but the media attention had been non-stop. Reporters from all over the globe had converged on him at the courthouse. Trucks with satellite dishes had surrounded the local government complex. Lights, faces, everywhere, yammering at him, assailing him mercilessly.

With their searing questions, the reporters had poked him, prodded him, dissected his motives and his whole damned life and he hated them all. He wanted to kill them all to show them the cruelty of their stupid insensitivity. Franco's friends, his teammates, with their monstrous solicitude, all shaking his hand, wanting a hug, all using the son's death as an excuse to touch the famous father.

In the end, all he had done was to hide behind his sunglasses and weep. *No, I'm not drinking again. Yes, he was my only son. Yes, I will set up a charitable foundation in his name. Leave me alone, oh please, leave me alone, you swirling vultures. My boy is dead. Can't you see that my boy is dead and I killed him?* The headline on the local newspaper had read: *WORLD MOURNS WITH HESTON DEMMING.*

All his frigging manager could say was "Don't ruin your looks." At this moment, Heston hated them all.

If only he had a wife who would support him. But no, he had to have Malevolent Maude, the cavernous mouth from hell, who, behind closed doors, blamed him openly, haranguing him over and over until he was a bloody mess inside. And poor little Win, sitting rigidly on the staircase, her hands covering her ears, her face a blank stare. If only his mother were still alive. She would have helped him, comforted him. She would have known what to say.

Who could he turn to now?

He had loved his mom. She had been a nurse at the local hospital. Often, she had worked extra hours at private nursing homes—anything to put food on the table until he became old enough to work at a local grocery as a bagboy. Only later did he find work crewing ships.

His mom had been a tough cookie, but she had learned to be tough. Like toil-callused hands, she had not been born hard. Most of her wear had come from dealing with his wild-hearted father, the outwardly charming ne'er-do-well. His father had failed at everything he ever tried, and he tried nearly everything. It was the drink, his mother always said, that ruined your father. And so it had been.

In childhood, his psyche had formed around his father's drunken bouts. Many of his early memories were of his father's spells, as his mom had called them, before, during, and after. These episodes often involved screaming fights between his father and his mother. One episode in particular had always stayed with him. Early one evening, when his mother had been at the hospital, Poppy Craft had visited him at home. His father had stumbled home drunk and burst in upon him and Poppy.

Although he and Poppy had been watching TV innocently, merely sitting on the sofa, holding hands, his father had humiliated the teens, accusing them of fornication and other words that Heston hadn't even known. When he had tried to defend Poppy's honor, his father had shamed him in Poppy's eyes, berating him, disgracing him, calling him a loser, a lazy bum, stupid, good-for-nothing. At last, Dad had slapped him across the face, calling him a pretty-boy fairy and telling him to toughen up, even though, during that time, he was getting into at least a fight a month at school. When he had moved to retaliate, Poppy had stopped him, but only with the greatest difficulty.

The next day, sobered up and hung over, his father hadn't even been able to recall the incident, but it had stayed with him into adulthood. He had always believed that Poppy had refused his marriage proposal because of his father's actions that night. Ever since, he had assumed that Poppy was afraid he would turn out the same way—which, right now, he was trying his damnedest to do. Strange that Poppy had claimed she hadn't refused him at all.

How bizarre life is. So twisted.

Why should I be the one who was successful? I did rotten things to other people. Yet they remained peons while I prospered beyond my wildest dreams.

He recalled one typical incident. The thought of it made him flush. His roommate in New York had been a struggling actor, too. The roommate's agent had arranged an interview for his client with a big producer. The agent had left the message on the answering machine in their flea-bitten flat. Hearing the message before his roommate, he had erased the message and kept the interview with the producer, thus acing his roommate out of movie stardom.

That movie role had proved to be his big break, in a teenage horror flick called *Cauldron*. His roommate was now a middle-aged methamphetamine addict somewhere in the Midwest. The roommate's agent had taken him to court for a commission—and lost.

In America, we call that competition, boy.

The sailing ship was flying now across the waters. *I am racing death.* It could not be denied. He was a much worse father than his old man. At least the old man hadn't killed him.

I killed my son.

If only had I been a better father—paid more attention, been more open, been more accepting—just plain been there for my son... If only...if only...if only I hadn't tried to hurt him...

At last, his mind was becoming thick and fuzzy. Not a moment too soon. He peered into the bottle in his hand. It was still nearly a third full. He bolted more Scotch. He thought about the women he had conquered, the men he had used.

He wanted to be held and loved. He wanted warm arms around him and a warm cushion of breast and belly beneath him. He wanted to plunge into the bliss of orgasm. He needed relief and love. There was none to be found anywhere. Except maybe...

Montserrat had wanted no part of his pain. She had even avoided his son's funeral. Poppy had come. Poppy had been there. She had had the guts to show up. Showing up was important. It meant something. Poppy was special.

Hazily, he pondered the many women and girls he had seduced, even the ones he had made love to in films. What quality was it that made Poppy different? It had been a very long time since he had made love to the slender redhead. Yet, in her presence, he could still feel the attraction between them. The thing was still alive inside him and her.

To be able to go back, to start over again...

What was real? What was earnest? He had had his moments. He thought about Lennox Cordova, the supple young actress he had shagged on the set of *Blue Juniper*. That passion had been real. That's why the movie had been a hit. But that passion had been nothing more than a candle flame, a flame which had dwindled as quickly as it had flared. No, it was not sex he needed now. It was *love*.

Or both?

He couldn't bear to think about Inez. He could not contemplate the thought of ever facing his son's mother again. At the funeral, he had not been able to meet her eyes. He and his ex-wife had not even spoken to one another, even in sympathy. She had seemed inconsolable. Later, he had heard she'd become catatonic.

Inez had been hysterical at the crash site. Seeing the light of her life crushed between two massive vehicles had sent her over the edge. He could still hear her screaming. He could still see her running towards the bloody, mangled body of their son. Even now, he heard the sirens from the nearby firehouse. He saw the agony on the faces of the coach, the players, the drivers of the two big SUV's... Inez attacking him, wild with grief... Danny Vega restraining her, Rogelio subduing her until the ambulance arrived... *Everyone avoiding me like I had the plague.*

The doer of the evil deed. Me. Nor would the image of Franco's crushed body ever leave him. What agony the child must have felt in his final moments. Semi-conscious, he cried out in horror

Desperately, he sucked the remaining fluid from the whiskey bottle. Then he tossed the glass bottle into the churning sea. He felt rough hands pulling him away from the watery edge as oblivion became his own.

***

"What do you mean I can't come in?" demanded Danny Vega, bursting through the front door of Sasha's apartment in Coco Palms. The wide front door flew open, thudding against the baseboard doorstop. Danny strode to the middle of the living room. He turned to face Sasha, who was closing the front door quietly. Her eyes were filled with fear. *Good.* Danny liked that. It gave him the upper hand, which he *would* have, no matter what.

"What do you mean you're not playing tennis with me? You and I play tennis every Wednesday afternoon. What's so special about today?"

Something was up. Danny didn't like it. He stood, hands at hips, waiting for her reply. Appropriately, he was dressed in tennis whites, but she was wearing denim. Her satchel sat on the entry table, as though she were about to go out.

Usually, by now, she would have kissed him perkily and snuggled against him, looking for a free feel or giving him one. Not today. Today she kept her distance. Today she circled him like a gelded pony tethered to a post.

She had halted behind the big easy chair. The chair now formed a barrier between him and her. Danny didn't want any barriers between him and his woman. Today he had planned to make everything right between them. He was planning to tell her he wanted her after all. Apparently, his timing was off. He could sense something was wrong.

"What's up, lady?" he barked, watching her steadily. He didn't take his eyes off her face. She looked sheepish, guilty. What the hell was she doing? "Why don't you want to keep our tennis date? I reserved the court, like usual."

She licked her lips. Her eyes shifted in either direction, as if searching for a way out of a bad scene. "Danny, I..."

"You what?" he crowded, moving towards her. As he rounded the back of the chair, she moved into the center of the room. Danny sneered. "What are you doing? You making me chase you? I'll chase you, all right." Irate, he pounced on her, grasping her bodily in his arms.

To his surprise, she kicked and punched at his legs and arms, trying desperately to wrench herself free. Forcing her jaw in place, he arched over her and attempted to kiss her mouth. She fought back hard. He dropped her instantly. She sagged to the floor like a bag of wet mulch. Stepping over her in disgust, Danny collapsed into the easy chair and stared at the woman lying on the hearth rug. This was no tease.

"What the hell do you think you're doing?" he grumbled, hurt, angry.

Wiping her mouth with the back of her wrist, she struggled to her feet.

"I'm going out," she said in a tremulous voice. "I have...a date."

A date? "You have *a date*?" Danny shot from the chair and grabbed her by the shoulders. "You made a date with someone besides me? Who? Who is he? I want to know!" Danny shook her by shoulders until the teeth rattled in her head.

"*Stoop...Danny...please....!*" she uttered, terrified, her dark hair flying wildly about her face. Danny's fingers were gripped tightly round the small muscles of her upper arms. "L-let me go!" she squealed, attempting to pummel his chest with her fists.

"Why should I?" he growled, restraining her.

"Because I have rights!" she spat. "I have a right to a life of my own.

You can't stop me from seeing him. Besides, you're too late. I've already been with him. It's over between you and me, Danny. Over. Do you hear me? I want a real life, with a home and kids and a husband. I want marriage! You can't stop me from grabbing that kind of life, not while I have a chance!"

Loosening his grip, Danny stepped back from her, his hands suspended in mid-air, as though he had just touched a soiled thing. He glared at her, repelled.

"You've been with him? You slept with him? Behind my back?"

"Y-yes." Readying for the coming blow, she shut her eyes. But no blow came. Opening her eyes, she looked up into his face. "I've hurt you," she whispered. "I didn't know..."

"What? That I cared? You bitch! You frigging slut!" He kept up the volume. On some deep level he felt that, if he could keep the rage going, he could hide the hurt. "You slept with him? Oh, shit!" Danny gripped her harder, holding her in place. Suddenly, they heard a scream from the bedroom. Freeing her, Danny bolted through the bedroom door.

"Danny! Don't!" she screamed, following him into the bedroom. She entered just in time to see him tearing open the birdcage door and ripping Gabby from the perch.

"Stop it! Danny!" she screamed, running to claw the parrot from his fist.

"Were you here when they did it, Gabby? Huh? Did you see them make it in this very bed? What else did you see, huh?"

Dancing around the bed, he held the bird aloft, out of her reach. She chased him, clawing at his face. Falling onto the bed, they wrestled, until she wrested the parrot from his hands and the bird flew free. Battered, the creature sped towards the ceiling. Fluttering to land, it perched on the sill of the bedroom's gabled pediment window. Down below, lying on their backs in bed, panting from exertion, he and Sasha watched the stunned parrot for several moments in silence.

Slowly, his fingers found Sasha's and coiled around them. Briefly, her fingers responded. He rolled over on top of her and nuzzled her neck affectionately. Tenderly, she stroked his black hair.

He had her.

Suddenly, he caught a wrist in each hand and, sitting across her midriff pinned her to the bed. "Tell me who he is," he ordered fiercely. Struggling, she shook her head.

"Tell me his name, woman, or, I swear, I'll break your little neck." Something in his tone convinced her. He felt her squirm beneath him.

"Danny, please. I know you're upset about your brother's death. I..."

He squeezed her wrists harder. He bore his weight down upon her until she squealed in pain. "Quit stalling, and spit it out. Who is he?"

"Let me up and I'll tell you," she wheezed. "I can't breathe with you on top of me."

"Tell me now. Then I'll let you up."

"How can I trust you, Danny?" She was struggling. It was his pony ride now.

"How can you not? You have no choice. I'm in the driver's seat here, babe."

"If I tell you, you'll hurt him."

"No, you got it all wrong. If you don't tell me, I'll hurt you."

Reluctantly, she complied. "It's James Talbot."

He relaxed his grip on her wrists. "Poppy's husband?" He was flabbergasted. Out of all the men in the world, James Talbot's was the last name he had expected to hear.

"Let me get up, Danny. You promised you would let me up."

"I promised you nothing, slut," he said, tightening his grip again.

"Are you going to rape me?" Her voice was guttural. He could feel her terror.

"Rape you? I don't even want you anymore," he replied, disgusted. Her pitiful sniffling tore at his heart. Abruptly, he rolled off her body and stood up, looming over her now as she lay spent on the bed.

"How could you do it?" he queried down at her darkly. "You betray not only me, but your best friend, too? You're a pig."

"You don't understand, Danny." Slowly, she peeled herself off the eyelet comforter and stood, shakily, rubbing her bruised wrists. He could tell she was still wary. But he was done with her and wanted only to escape before he lost control totally.

With an angry upwards glance at the parrot, now a mass of ruffled green feathers perched in the high window, he stalked from the bedroom into the living room. He was headed for the front door. Sasha rose and ran after him.

"You didn't want me! What did you expect me to do? Wait forever?" she whined, dogging him closely. He swung around.

"I didn't want you? I didn't want you? What do you know about it, you bitch? What do you know about what I want and don't want? If I ever did want you, I sure as hell don't now."

Grimacing, she recoiled as if slapped.

"Forget about *me!* How could you betray Poppy like that?" he railed, his hand on the front-door knob. "Behind her back. Behind my back. Shit."

"You don't understand, Danny. James wants kids. So do I. He's divorcing Poppy."

"Yeah, right," he smirked, unconvinced.

"He is! Poppy's the one who's deceitful. She's been lying to James all these years. She had a kid she never told him about. Twenty years ago. James doesn't even know. I'm having her kid traced. I hired a private detective. I'm going to prove it to James. James will divorce Poppy and marry me."

"Are you for real?" He felt himself spinning out of control. He wanted out. "What bullshit." He opened the front door. He had to get away before he *did* kill her.

"Danny, don't go! I didn't mean to..."

"To what? Hurt me? Yeah, Sash, you said that." Savagely, he tore at her heart flesh, unable to stop himself. "For your information, I was going to propose marriage to you tonight."

Her mouth flew open. "You...you...?"

That got her. Danny slammed the front door behind him. He stood very still for a moment. Then he dashed out into the night.

***

Just after dawn on the following morning, Poppy Craft-Talbot stood shelling on the sandy beach south of Naples' city pier. Clad in a long-sleeved caftan of yellow-striped cotton, Poppy crouched over a mound of seashells. A white-duck visor shielded her eyes from the newly risen sun, now breaking over the city to the east. In the stillness, on the nearly deserted beach around her, a remnant of early-morning fog hung lightly in the air. To the west, the Gulf of Mexico was still half-slumbering, its sleepy waves nudging the waking shore.

Beneath her bare feet, the grainy sand was cool and damp. With able fingers, she sifted through the natural treasure trove of seashells. Some of the shells were broken, some whole, others crushed utterly. Now and then, finding a specimen to suit her purposes, she wiped excess sand from it and deposited the shell into the large left pocket of her tent-like dress. Behind her back, a tiny white sandpiper scurried along the foamy shoreline. As she shelled, her thoughts roamed the far corners of her life. She was worried about *everything*.

Oh, James, I've already hurt you so badly. She desperately wanted out of her marriage but believed she should stick it out. Her illicit love for her childhood playmate was something she would simply have to tame. Could she do it? It wouldn't be easy. Ashamedly, Poppy admitted a truth to herself. She had come to this beach because it reminded her of bygone days with Heston. She had not been able to sleep last night. Restless, she had found herself walking this lonesome stretch of beach at dawn. If only she had a close friend to confide in, it might help ease her tension. Somehow, she had lost contact with her best friend, Sasha, not long after laying her heart bare about the adoption.

Why won't she return my calls? Normally, she couldn't get rid of Sasha. Now, several days had gone by without a word from the woman. Further, Poppy fretted about Heston's appearance at Franco's funeral and how badly he seemed to be reacting to his son's death. *How guilty he must feel. How devastated Inez Vega looked that day.* Animosity aside, Poppy's heart bled for Inez. *Poor woman.* Rogelio had not called at the gallery since the day of the accident, more than a week ago now. He probably was grief-stricken, too, in his own way. After all, Franco had been his stepson.

After the funeral, Poppy had considered going to Heston, trying to comfort him, but decided it wasn't her place. It was his wife, Maude's, duty. Maude had given her notice that night at the party. When she had tried to fix him a dinner plate, Maude had honed in like a torpedo. The message had been loud and clear: Hands Off My Husband.

Realistically, Poppy felt she wouldn't be able to talk to him again without confronting the truth of her past. Could she do it? Not right now. Her courage had flown. Raising her head, she glanced northward at the pier. A few fishermen were casting off the end of the long wooden structure, their poles now and then flinging optimistically into the mist.

Down the beach, a runner was advancing towards her from the south. Poppy blinked. Were her eyes playing tricks on her? No, it *was* her old heartthrob, jogging up the shore line towards her. Recognizing her, he waved a tentative hand and slowed his pace. For a brief moment, she thought of escape, but, on the open beach, there was nowhere to hide.

As Heston drew close, Poppy was shocked by his disheveled appearance. He was wearing dirty running shoes, a cloth billed cap, a stained gray sweatshirt and scanty running shorts. The cap was stitched in red with the slogan, "Sugar Daddy." His brown hair was greasy and shaggy. His perfect jaw was covered by a beard of several days' growth. His handsome face looked worn with care, his eyes, red and raw. His grief was visible, branded on his facial features by relentless bouts of self-recrimination. Obviously, he was being torn apart by remorse. Alarmed by this drastic change, Poppy tried to hide her concern. She also tried to hide how turned on she was by his rough, cave-man appeal.

"Hello, Heston," she smiled up at him as he came to a stop at her side.

"Hello, Poppy." His manner was grim, but matter-of-fact. He was sweating from his jog.

"How have you been?" she enquired, genuinely interested.

He shrugged. "Drunk."

"Really?"

"For...let's see...about six full days, by my calculations. But let's keep it our little secret, okay?" It was as though they had never been apart.

"Okay. You look exhausted. Did you sleep at all last night?"

"Some call it sleep. Others call it passed out."

"Are you still drinking?"

"Not this morning. I'm trying to shake it off. I feel like she—Excuse me, I feel sick and shaky. Frankly, I'd kill for a Scotch neat about now."

"Your basic healthy breakfast?" Reaching into her right pocket, Poppy drew out a protein bar. "Here. Eat this. It's organic."

He looked at the bar, and then grinned at Poppy. "Thanks," he said, taking the health bar from her hand. She saw that his hand was trembling. Ripping the wrapper open with his teeth, he spat out the shred he'd bitten off. "Don't tell my agent. She worries about my caps."

"I thought your teeth were pearlier than I remembered."

"Straighter, too," he said, gnawing off and chewing a bit of the protein bar. "Bite?" He held the bar up in an offering. Poppy looked at him sympathetically.

"Sure," she said, taking a nibble from the proffered treat. "Thanks."

"Thank you," he said, chewing a mouthful. "Here. You eat the rest. Alcoholics don't like food."

"Honestly..."

"I see your wearing your sexiest outfit this morning. Still protecting your fair skin from the sun, eh? What's all that junk in your pockets?" he asked abruptly, fingering the skirt of her caftan. His hand brushed hers as she reached into her pocket.

"Shells, driftwood, leaves, a broken lure," she explained, following his lead. She wanted to offer condolences but didn't know how. This was the first time she had seen him since Franco's funeral a week ago.

"So, do you still create *assemblages* from found objects?" he asked, half-smiling at the memory. "Proud of me? I remembered the right words to call whatever it is you do."

"Of course I'm proud of you." She opened one pocket of her sundress for his inspection. "Mostly, I use materials from nature now. See?"

"I do see," he said, peering into the pocket to oblige her. He was so close to her that his forehead almost touched hers. She could feel his body heat. She could smell the dried sweat and stale whiskey that mingled with this morning's sweaty orange-myrrh.

"Everyone needs a hobby. You have sailing. I have assemblage," she observed.

"Do you ever sell any of your finished pieces? You could sell them in your gallery."

He seemed determined to keep the conversation light. "No. I keep them or give them away. Each piece is a personal statement," she told him. "I don't need any more for-profit pressure. My assemblages are self-expression."

"Too bad. I'd like to buy one."

"I'll give you one, Heston. I'll give you the one I make from the objects I find today."

"Okay. Cool. I'll put it in my new study. It needs some personal touches. You used to like sailing, Poppy. You made a good crew."

"I still do. I just haven't had the right captain lately. I told you."

"What's with you and James these days? Are you still separated?"

Poppy nodded. "I had dinner with him a few nights ago. I've heard nothing from him since. We're both entrenched in our positions. I doubt if we'll ever resolve our differences."

"What positions would those be?"

"Oh, never mind." Uncomfortable, she scanned the horizon. He persisted.

"Don't want to talk about it?" he asked kindly.

"Oh, it's simple really. James wants children. I don't," she said dismissively in her steeliest voice. *Oh, please, stop now, don't ask me anymore.* Her heart jumped into her throat and was doing the cha-cha.

"Ever?" He seemed alarmed.

Outwardly, she shrugged. "Not with James," she declared. *He's watching me again. Can he tell? Does he know? Can he see it in my face?* She dared not look at him lest her eyes betray her secret—or her hopeless adoration of him. Terrified, she faced the open gulf. A brown pelican was skimming the water's shiny surface.

"May we change the subject?" she asked, heart throbbing.

"Sure. Mind if I go for a quick swim first? I'm pretty rank this morning," he admitted.

"By all means." Tensely, she watched him remove his cap and pull his sweatshirt over his head. His underarm hair was the same brown as the hair on his head. Uncovered, his sweaty upper torso was fit as a gymnast. His gleaming shoulders and upper arms rippled with toned muscle. At a loss, he looked around for a place to toss the cap and sweatshirt. The nearest rocks were fifty feet away.

"Here," she said nostalgically. "I'll hold it."

"Just like old times," he smiled sadly, tossing her the sweatshirt. Then he flung the cap, which she managed to catch as well. "Back in a jiff," he said. With a brave yelp, he plunged into the cool, shallow waves. As he swam, she watched him from the shore. Had Heston a surfboard, she could almost imagine herself back in high school. "A Summer Place" might be playing on the AM radio in his beat-up blue van.

"Want to join me?" He called from the waves.

"No, thanks!" called Poppy, roused from her reverie. "No suit!"

"Don't need one!" he cried. Diving under, he rose out of the water holding his running shorts aloft like a flag. "See what I mean?"

Poppy shrieked with sudden laughter and turned away. "Heston, put your pants back on!" she cried.

"Now if I had a nickel for every time I've heard that...!" he cried. "Okay, you can turn around, Poppy! I put them back on."

"Are you sure?" There was no response. "Sean, are you sure?"

"Only one way to find out," he said right behind her. Again, she shrieked. As he wrapped his slippery, dripping arms around her, she dissolved into giggles but did not push him away.

"You're all wet!" Shyly, she slid her hungry hands up and down his sleek, meaty biceps. She couldn't look him in the face.

"But clothed," he pointed out. Stepping back, she saw that, indeed, he was wearing the running shorts again. Soaking wet, the shorts clung revealingly to his body. He grinned, breathless with pleasure, his silver-blue eyes sparkling momentarily. Poppy felt ridiculous, as usual. Even as a boy, he had teased her mercilessly. It was all coming back to her now. How much she had loved him. And understood him.

Poppy recognized this inane aspect of his personality. She did not judge him harshly for his mirth. This was Heston the Clown. This part of him was silly, juvenile, and, under the right conditions, uproariously funny. This also was the side of him that coped with tragedy when reality became unbearable. Poppy remembered only too well how he had reacted– like some cartoon character from *Mad* or *SNL*–after finding mother's dead body that long-ago sweltering summer. Perhaps this desperate need for denial was what pushed him to become an actor–and an abuser of alcohol and substances.

"Remember my senior prom?" she heard him ask her huskily. Again, she realized he was watching her. The electric, silver-blue stare gave her goose flesh.

"We never got there," she said slyly.

"I know. That's why I remember it so well," he said, lunging for her. Crying out, Poppy dashed away out of his reach. Running down the beach, she was no match for his long legs. Within moments, he caught up with her and swept her into his arms.

"I feel like a kid again," he whispered, spinning her in a loving embrace. In spite of her misgivings, Poppy returned his embrace. The familiar feel of his skin against hers sent a wild thrill through her. She knew that, if she kissed his collarbone openmouthed, she would taste salt from the sea. She had done it many times as a girl, under similar circumstances. It was all she could do to restrain herself. She blurted out the first words that occurred to her.

"If things had been different..."

He pushed her away from him and held her at arm's length. "I'd be a produce manager at the supermarket, and you and I would have six brats together to raise on thirty thousand dollars a year. Spare me."

It was like a knife through her heart. "Maybe we would have been happier."

"Maybe. We'll never know, will we?" Agony flashed across his features, and she knew his denial was again at work. Worried, she studied hid troubled face. "You haven't said a word about Franco."

Dropping his arms, he looked towards the Gulf. "What's left to say? I'm trying to forget." He lowered his head and studied the sand at his feet.

"Here," she said, still clutching his sweatshirt. "Put this on. It's still dry."

"You always took care of me, didn't you, Poppy Craft?" he said, slipping into the warm sweatshirt. She handed him the cap, which he fitted snugly onto his shaggy, wet head. His straggly brown hair and beard were beaded with water droplets. "I could use a little of that caretaking now, for sure." He sank down into the sand and sat facing the gulf.

"That's why you're drinking again. Franco's death, I mean," Poppy stated tenderly, kneeling down beside him and sitting back on her heels. She longed to tell him about their long-lost son, but she had not got the nerve. *He has so many problems. How can I add to them? It's not the right time.* Another excuse, she chided herself. *Coward, coward, coward!* In truth, she had grown afraid of his reaction. For all she knew, he could become violent, or worse, scorn her forever. *Is telling him the truth worth the risk of losing him forever?*

"It's hit me hard, Poppy."

"I understand your feelings. It must be terrible for you."

"Murder always is."

"You didn't murder him, honey."

"You've said that to me before," he said thoughtfully.

Poppy understood the reference to his past. "Franco's death was a freak accident."

"Was it, Poppy? The kid hated me. We didn't get along. There was bad blood between us. Maybe I was trying for revenge. Maybe I wanted to show him who was boss." His voice cracked. "Maybe I kicked the ball too hard on purpose, to hurt the kid, humiliate him, make him bust tail. All because he didn't love me."

Poppy said softly, "He didn't always show you respect. That's not the same thing as not loving you. Remember your dad? Maybe Franco was crying out for you, in his own way. Love and need aren't always expressed through tenderness. Especially in adolescent boys."

He sighed. "I ignored him practically his whole life. No wonder he resented me."

"We all make mistakes. You were concentrating on your career, weren't you?"

"You could call it that. I was moving slick and fast through a world-class jungle. I forgot everything and everybody. I just wanted to win, win, win."

"You won."

"Yes. Only now it all seems meaningless. I lost everything that mattered. The only thing I have now that means anything is Winner. That little angel means the world to me, Poppy. I would die if anything bad happened to her." Fear swept through his eyes.

"Surely nothing will, Heston. Don't look for trouble."

"You don't know Maude."

"You think your wife would hurt her own daughter?"

"I think Maude is capable of cruelty and treachery. I've seen her do things you wouldn't believe. She's asked *me* to do things you wouldn't believe."

"The night of the party," she began, feeling her blood pressure rise as she brought up the night of Montserrat's re-appearance, "Maude took me to your daughter's room. She showed me the Quested painting they'd bought from me—you know, the alligator watercolor?"

He nodded.

"Y-Your daughter told me that her mother had told her the alligator would bite her if she was bad. Then she hung it in the girl's bedroom. It struck me as a vile thing to do to a child. I don't know…"

Sighing heavily, he threw up his hands in disgust. "I had no idea what she was like until after we were married." He put his hands on his hips. "Thanks for letting me know. I'll have the painting removed."

"She's such pretty woman. Maybe she just made a mistake."

"I doubt it. Frankly, I was drunk when I married her. Thank my lucky stars I had a good lawyer by then. The divorce from Inez taught me well."

"Oh, Inez," sighed Poppy.

"I feel horrible about Inez. What I've done. I've ruined her life. I can't imagine what she's going through. I couldn't face her at the funeral."

"You haven't talked with her since?"

He shook his head. "But I'll have to, sooner or later. By the way, Poppy Sue, I noticed you attended the funeral with your business partner. What's the story there? Anything between you two?"

"Hardly," Poppy scoffed. "One meddling husband is enough for me."

Heston inhaled sharply. "May I ask you something? Why did you marry James Talbot?"

"Security, plain and simple. Uncle Melvin died. My folks were gone. You were gone. I was alone. James appeared. Said he loved me. Said he'd help me. Said he'd protect me, support me. Give me whatever I wanted. I accepted. Was that wrong?"

"You weren't in love with him?" he pressed.

"No."

"Are you now?"

"Not the way you mean. And I'm not talking behind his back. I've told James the same things I just told you. He understands. For a long time, he just didn't mind."

"And now he does?"

"Who knows?" Distressed, Poppy made a verbal U-turn. "How's your career going?" Correctly, she guessed he would chat about himself.

"Well, I'm supposed to be reading scripts—and memorizing lines," he replied. "But I can't focus on anything. I'm scheduled to do a new picture in Mexico. We start shooting in a couple of months. I doubt if I'll be ready. I'm too screwed up."

"What part do you play?" Poppy asked.

"I play an American tourist caught up in a drug deal gone sour," he sighed.

"At least it's not a comedy," observed Poppy.

"Actually—it is," he said glibly. Poppy broke into spontaneous laughter. He joined in cynically.

"I'm sorry."

"Don't be. It feels good to laugh. I need it."

"Who's your co-star?" she asked, trying to sound casual. She felt his interest flare.

"What'd you care?" he asked, alerted.

"I don't care," she lied. "I just wondered if it was Lennox Cordova. She's so talented."

"She stacked like a brick pancake house," he declared, eyes gleaming. "Believe me, it's not about her talent."

"Are you and she friends?" Poppy asked, rising to her feet. She brushed the sand from her fanny.

"Does it matter to you if we are?" He stood up beside Poppy.

"I have no right to care, Heston." She glanced up into his face, then looked out to sea.

"You have every right. I'd die if you didn't. You're my best pal."

"Oh, please. Don't say such things to me. It was all so long ago. We're different people now, you and I." She was whispering the words as her eyes followed a passing kayak meandering its way along the surface of the Gulf. "Are we?"

He moved away from her and then looked back, eyes full of pain. "By the way, Poppy. What was the big thing you were going to tell me at the housewarming party? You had just started to make some kind of announcement."

"O-Oh, that," she stuttered.

He looked at her encouragingly.

"Oh, I don't know." She took a few steps away from him. She bent down to examine an odd shell. "Are you going to keep on drinking?"

"For a while." He did not follow her.

"Would it do any good to ask you to stop?"

"It might. Down the line."

"Okay. I'll wait 'til the time is right."

"Thanks for understanding, Poppy—as always."

"Just be careful. Sooner or later, the press will find out. They'll be merciless. Please. I don't want to read about your drinking problems while I'm waiting in the checkout line to buy cereal." She walked back to his side.

He grimaced. "I'll try to keep the drinking under wraps—but I can't promise. I live on a stage, Poppy. On camera. My life is not my own anymore. What little life I still owned died with my son. I'm just a product now, not a man. I'm a brand name, not a human being."

"Oh, Heston..."

"Forget it. It's the life I chose."

"A life of jogging on the beach only when it's deserted."

"You got it. But don't worry. I've been well-compensated for the loss of my soul. But, sometimes, I just have to sneak away without the bodyguards."

Poppy's empathetic eyes found his at last. The pain she absorbed seared her like a hot rod. He had felt her, too. She could tell.

"Look, I've got to go," he announced officially, scanning the shoreline. "The natives are leaving their huts."

"You mean tourists are coming onto the beach. You could be spotted."

"Well, that, too. Hey, I got places to go, people to see, Brown Eyes," he quipped. "Scripts to read, wives to placate, hangers-on to pay, hangovers to squelch." Then he added offhandedly, "I'll be in touch."

"Promise?" she heard herself whispering.

He nodded. The sun was higher now and hotter. He did a few stretches to limber up for his return run up the beach. He began to jog in place, turning to face her.

"I hope you reconsider having kids, Poppy. You'd make a great mom," he said, jogging away from her.

"Thank you, Heston" She wasn't sure if she had spoken the words aloud. She must have said or done something because he turned around, smiled, and waved, before turning back around, and trotting southward down the shoreline. If she were going to die, she wished it would be now, at this very second. The inside of her mouth felt grainy as the sand beneath her feet.

Why can't I tell him? What is wrong with me? At the housewarming party, she had had the bravery born of liquor. Today, face to face with her old lover, here on the beach, in the stark daylight of reality, she hadn't found the courage. It wasn't right. It wasn't fair to him. He had to know. She would have to tell him. That's all there was to it.

Poppy made the decision. He had to know he had fathered another son. She would phone him and make an appointment to speak with him in private. What he did about it after that was his business. She wondered. Perhaps her face would be the one to grace the covers of the tabloid newspapers: *HIGH SCHOOL SWEETHEART CONFESSES ALL—"I BORE SUPERSTAR'S LOVECHILD IN SECRET."*

How awful! Poppy hung her head in abject shame. Even her Uncle Mel could not have imagined a worst-case scenario *this* bad. World-wide notoriety hadn't existed in his day. Poppy desperately needed advice from Sasha, but now even finding her friend seemed hopeless.

Like a smack in the head, a scary thought struck Poppy. Heston had not said a word about Montserrat Flynn. It was a bad sign.

Is he sleeping with her?

Of course he is. He's in love with her, isn't he?

Chapter Nine

That evening at sunset, Montserrat Flynn sipped champagne aboard the floating sea-cloud, *Windswept*. Bobbing offshore, the sailboat rocked gently in the tropical breeze, her crew idling below deck. In the ship's cockpit, Montsey snuggled against Heston's broad hairy chest, her silky knees tucked beneath her.

She flared her dainty nostrils, apparently tickled by the bubbles in her crystal flute glass, or so Heston assumed. His mistress had complained earlier about the fishy smell at sea. He wasn't sure if she were charmed or disgusted by her first outing on his new yacht. Sometimes, with Montserrat, it was hard to tell the difference. Her thick social veneer was hard to crack. Her moods and reactions were unpredictable.

Disappointment tugged at his heartstrings, as so often happened when he was in this woman's company. He had spent years trying to please her. He had never succeeded. He had hoped this trip would prove magical. That was what he had intended late last night when, drunk on Scotch and bravado, he had invited Montserrat to join him for a romantic sunset cruise.

Earlier, on the beach, he had not had the nerve to tell Poppy about his liaisons with Montserrat. Nor had he had the nerve to tell Poppy he was sailing this evening with Montsey aboard *Windswept*. He had not mentioned it to his wife either, but that no longer mattered to him. *Let Maude lump it.* He would deal with her later. Oddly, it was his sin of omission regarding Poppy that troubled him more.

Unfortunately, he was forced to admit another truth to himself. Montserrat Flynn was no sailor. She seemed as uncomfortable on board his yacht as an ostrich on a battleship. First of all, she had no sea legs. She kept barfing. Then, she was bored. Then, she wanted to talk shop. Then, she wanted to lie down. *What next?* Usually, he could count on Montserrat to admire the beauties of nature, if only for a moment. She couldn't stop thinking about herself much longer than that. One thing she never did, he realized forlornly, was show concern for him.

Truth be told, she had barely mentioned Franco's death. Only once did she scrape his cheek with her lacquered lips and whisper, "Poor darling."

That was it. No concern for his feelings. No offers of solace. Nothing, except endless drivel about her world travels, the exotic men she had known, the dangerous situations abroad from which she had escaped with barely a scratch. It wasn't mindless trivia, as some women might spout. Her ramblings were, however, always about herself. *Why have I never noticed this before?*

With her dark-auburn head against his chest, he, too, sipped champagne from a glass. He was drinking again and she knew it. In fact, she encouraged it. Tipsy, this evening he did not bother to follow her conversation. Instead, he let himself be enveloped by the glory of a deepening sunset palette. The whole western sky was a conglomeration of warm liquid pinks.

"What color would you call that?" he asked, interrupting her story about a doomed safari in Kenya. "Out there. " Waving his champagne glass, he indicated the western sky.

"Color?" she asked, visibly disturbed. She looked up, distracted from her tale-telling. "Oh, I don't know. Maybe persimmon?"

"Funny. I would call it something nautical, more sea-related. Like coral. Or salmon."

"Fine. Call it what you like. It's still the same putrid color, regardless."

"Is it?"

"Much too gaudy. You know I favor subtle greens and lavenders. Go figure, you sensitive, artistic types. Most men wouldn't even have asked such a question. Now pay attention, Heston. Let me finish about my trip with the Swedes on the man-eating tiger hunt," she insisted, settling her head, once again, on his chest. As she talked, he fretted silently. Her lilac cologne seemed out of place in the muggy subtropics. And she talked incessantly. In the past, he had never listened to her babble, but he had tolerated it because it had been an aspect of Montserrat Flynn, Dream Woman. Now he found himself bored by her self-centered chatter.

A thought occurred to him from the depths of his being. He had told Poppy she would make a good mother—and she would. Poppy had a nurturing quality about her. Montserrat, on the other hand, was right to have remained childless. She did not have a nurturing bone in her body.

"More champagne?" he asked sitting up abruptly and dislodging Montsey from her position of comfort. She uttered a little cry. Ignoring it, he rose to his feet.

"No, Heston," she pouted, irritated. She tugged at his trousers. "Please, can't we go ashore and have an intimate dinner. Somewhere special, that isn't rocking back and forth. I'd like that very much. Besides, I want to be alone with you, not your hired help." She glanced askance towards the cabin below. "We could order cocktails. I like you better when you're drinking whiskey, Heston. Champagne makes you crabby."

"Fine," he said. "I'll tell the crew to head for port."

"Thank you, kind sir."

"You're welcome, Ms. Persimmon." Clinging to the rigging, he stared, moist-eyed, at the coral/salmon sky. Perhaps Franco was floating up there somewhere now, too, watching down on him, despising him from the heavens, just as his dead father was.

What a nightmare. I still can't believe it happened.

Poppy would have known what color this is. Poppy would have adored this glory.

"Look, Heston!" cried Montsey, pointing. "That cigarette boat has paparazzi! Wave!"

***

Mid-morning the next day, Sasha Bassett's cell phone rang at work while she stood morosely filling canapés. Attired in a hair net and white apron, Sasha answered the cell with one vinyl-gloved hand. In the other she held a spoon. A stainless-steel mixing bowl sat on the granite counter in front of her. Other employees milled about their tasks in the commercial kitchen.

"Sasha? Rick DuBois here—your private eye?"

"Oh. Hi."

"How's life treating you?" he drawled.

"It's been better. Yeah. So, what's going on, Rick?" she whispered, glancing around.

"Got some news," he said. "I found a lead. Looks like that story you heard holds water."

"Yeah?" Her day brightened suddenly. "What did you find?"

"Birth certificate. Same date you suggested. Tampa, Florida. Baby boy born to one Penelope Susan Craft. Father named as Sean H. Demming, address unknown."

"Hot damn." Eagerly, she tapped the end of her spoon on the granite counter top. Dubois cleared his throat expectantly. "Little Miss Sasha, that "H" wouldn't stand for Heston Demming, the movie actor, now would it? Been reading a lot about him in the local papers lately. If so, you neglected to inform me this was a celebrity job."

"Well, I...would it matter?" She played innocent, but intuition kicked in. She had a bad feeling about this.

"Well, as a matter of fact, it might. To me." His sleaze oozed through the cell phone.

"How so, Rick?" She inhaled to do battle.

"Well, I don't know. I'll have to think about it. But I suspect it will involve more money." She could hear his crooked, toothy grin. "Don't you worry, Little Miss. I'll let you know just as soon as I work it out. I'll get back to you." He rang off abruptly.

Rattled, she dropped the spoon into the stainless-steel mixing bowl. She tried to steady herself. This possibility had never occurred to her. She should have realized a private eye would connect the dots. How much would Rick want for his silence? What demands would he make on her? On Heston Demming? Startled, she realized she was wringing her hands.

I've got to get a grip.

Look on the bright side. Rick found the birth certificate. Poppy's story is true. I didn't lose Danny for nothing. I will have a baby with James.

Her cell phone rang again. She leaped from her skin. She grabbed her cell.

"Hello?" Her flesh crawled as he spoke.

"Well, I've thought about it, Little Miss, and, funny thing, I do want more money. A lot more money. To keep silent. About the big star's illegitimate baby. See, I figure I can sell this story to the tabloids for about a hundred thousand dollars, give or take. So, because of my loyalty to you as a valued customer, I'm going to give you first crack at it. If you can come up with a hundred thousand, I'll give the information I find to you solely, as per our deal. If you can't come up with the stated sum, I'm afraid I'll have to go over your head."

"Meaning what?"

"Meaning I go directly to the VIP himself. Or to the tabloids. It's all about the money, sugar."

"You'd go to Heston?"

"I would indeed. Unless you can meet my price. Naturally, I'd rather do business with you, Little Bit. I might even let you take it out in trade. The whole hundred thousand."

She gasped.

"Let me warn you, now," DuBois continued smoothly. "There's more to this than I've told you. I'm on to this kid's whereabouts. I'm good at my job, sugar. Make no mistake about that. So, you see, it won't be just Demming who gets hurt if you don't cough up. It will be everybody involved–the kid, the birth mom, the adoptive family, your 'fiancée, and the Great One... Everybody. Especially you."

"I see," she breathed, mortified.

"I hope you do. Give me a call. By tomorrow noon. Let me know how you plan to proceed. Twenty-four hours should give you enough time to work something out somehow. 'Bye now." The phone went dead.

"Bye," she whispered, disbelieving.

Moments went by. She stood shocked. Around her, the hubbub in the caterer's kitchen went on, but she did not hear it. What to do? Things were going from bad to worse. First, she had alienated the only man she ever loved by sleeping with a man who was a dud. Worse, she now was faced with the prospect of sleeping with a man she found revolting. Unless she could come up with a hundred thousand dollars in twenty-four hours, her goose was cooked.

Fat chance. Unless...

In a flash, she began to scheme. *She* would go to Heston herself. She would spill the beans about his kid herself–*to Heston.* That would knock the wind out of Rick. *She* would ask Heston for the money to pay off Rick. That way, she could convince Heston she was a heroine, a victim who got taken for a ride while trying to help poor Poppy out.

Yeah, by trying to surprise Poppy, that was it. A good deed.

This way, his and Poppy's secret would still be safe from the media. This way, the P.I. would get his hush money–if Heston paid the dough. *Natch, it'll be a shock for him to learn about his and Poppy's kid from me. But I'll make it right, some way or the other. With Poppy, too. Yeah. Wait and see.*

Think, brain. There must be a right way for me to tell Heston he has a bastard son. With renewed vigor, she dug a clean spoon into the bowl of creamy seafood filling.

***

From the balcony off his study, Heston watched uneasily as his wife, Maude, gave daughter, Winston, a swimming lesson in the indoor pool. Little Winnie was sporting a bubble-type life preserver. The flotation device was strapped to her back. Maude was holding Winnie up in the water as the child splashed hands and feet. On the pool deck, looking on, towel in hand, stood Winnie's angular young nanny, Jill Cady.

Steely-jawed, he looked down on the proceedings. Since the death of his only son he now lived in mortal fear of his young daughter's demise. He had to force himself not to run down to the pool deck and pluck the child from the dangerous water.

Be rational. The child can't stop living because her brother died. Better she should learn to swim than not. It might save her life some day.

The problem was he didn't trust Maude to protect Winnie. Nor Jill Cady. In the past weeks Jill had proven to be Maude's pawn. He had caught her in more than one lie about his wife's whereabouts. Desperately, he wished in vain that he had never married Maude. Of course, had he not married her, he would never have had Winner. Truth be known, he doted on his daughter. He would love to have more children—but not with Maude. At this point, it seemed unlikely that Winston would ever have another sibling.

When he had arrived home the previous noon, after spending the night in bed with Montserrat and the morning on the beach with Poppy, he had found the master suite stripped of Maude's belongings. In his absence, his wife had moved out of his bedroom and into a separate suite of rooms upstairs. In what had been her dressing room, just off the master suite, the huge-walk-in closet and built-in drawers now stood open and empty, as though left thus to taunt him. Also, her antique vanity table had been removed from the room and relocated to her new boudoir upstairs. Without a word to him, his wife had established a separate bedroom.

Had Maude been surprised when he hadn't protested? He snickered at the thought. *Perhaps she had been, at that.*

"Miss Bassett has arrived," said a deep, cultured voice. He turned to face the door to the study. A tall, tailored young black man stood waiting.

"Show her in, Andy," he ordered his personal assistant. On cue, Andrew Upshaw ushered a short, dark-haired woman with a voluptuous figure into the study, then exited, quietly closing the door behind him. The curvaceous woman smiled nervously.

"Please, sit down," he said politely. Memory had served him correctly. This *was* the same woman he remembered from the housewarming party and from Franco's funeral. This little girl with the big knockers was Poppy's best friend and the girlfriend of Inez's stepson, Danny Vega. He hadn't been certain this morning, when he had received her frantic phone call, exactly who she was.

Fervently, she had pleaded to see him, telling his assistant that her business was urgent, that it could not wait. Reluctantly, he had agreed to a meeting, and now the time had come. Casting one last worried glance in the direction of the pool, he deposited himself in the overstuffed chair behind his rosewood desk and turned his attention to lovely little Miss Bassett.

"How are you today, young lady?" He knew she was intimidated, but less so than many other women who had entered his presence.

"Fine. I guess. Thank you for seeing me on such short notice, Heston. May I call you Heston?" she inquired, boldly. She had seated herself across from him in a luxurious chair of muted green leather, the chair being a twin of the one beside it. He had selected the chairs himself, against

Maude's wishes.

"Naturally," he replied graciously. Nonchalantly, he watched her breasts as she exhaled and drew in a deep breath. The fleshy woman was dressed seductively in a knit top and ankle-length skirt with a slit up the side. Her breasts were really quite remarkable. She wasn't his type, but he would not kick her out of bed. A hot little minx, she was, perfect for Danny Vega. *A funny little friend for Poppy to pick. More coarse than Poppy, not as fine.* He wondered what the two women had in common. As with love, there was no accounting for the chemistry of friendship.

"Seen Poppy lately?" he enquired, making small talk.

She seemed surprised but recovered quickly. "Yes, as a matter of fact, I have. A few days ago." Anxiously, she scanned the room. "Is that your acting award?" she asked, wide-eyed, pointing towards the gleaming statuette on the fireplace mantle.

"Yes, it is."

"That's awesome! That was a great picture. You were great in it."

"Thank you." He could smell the flattery a foot deep, but, as always, he accepted praise with alacrity. "I'll be returning to work next month," he said, indicating a script, which lay unopened on the desk top between them. Half-rising, she read the title aloud. *"Acapulco Moon.* That sounds great!" she exclaimed.

Pretty smile. "Unfortunately, I haven't felt much like learning my lines," he noted.

"Oh, I'm sorry," she said, resuming her seat and looking back towards him. "I meant to offer my condolences again. On the loss of your son, Franco. The past week must have been terrible for you, Heston. I'm sorry to have to bother you at such a tough time, but, you see, I have no choice. This won't keep."

"So you said on the phone. Yes, thank you for attending the funeral. Well, out with it. What's on your mind?"

She licked her painted lips. "Well, Heston, I have something to tell you. Something you don't know about."

"Oh?"

"It's kind of hard to talk about. There's no other way really but to just come right out and say it," she explained.

"Then, by all means, do so," he encouraged. He was dying to check on Winnie.

"Well, you see, it's like this..."

"Yes?"

Taking a deep breath, she expelled the air rapidly as she spoke. "Franco was not your only son. You have another son, one you don't know about.

I'm here today to tell you about it because, if you don't help me, it could be all over the news by tomorrow night."

"What the devil...?" He felt his pulse rate rise. He had not expected a blackmail attempt from such close quarters. He should have known better. There was no one anymore whom he could trust, not anywhere, not anytime. Everyone and his dog wanted a piece of his fortune, his life, his body, his soul.

"You'll have to excuse me, Miss Bassett," he said, rising. "I didn't expect a cheap extortion trick from a friend of Poppy's. Andy will see you out."

"No, wait!" she cried. "This is no trick. This is for real. You really do have another son, Heston. He's alive today. Right now. And I can prove it."

He snorted. "How? I'll admit I've been with a number of women, but if I had had a son with any one of them, I believe I would already be aware of..."

"Poppy's the mother!" she blurted awkwardly. Gasping, she covered her open mouth with her palm.

"Come again?" he said. His chest imploded. His mouth went dry.

"Poppy Craft-Talbot," said Sasha, cringing. Slowly, she lowered her hand from her mouth "Poppy is the mother of your first-born son," she whispered.

He snorted. "Are you out of your mind?" he demanded self-righteously. Eyes riveted to hers, he lowered himself back onto his seat cushion and gaped at her.

She shook her head. "I wish I was. No, Heston, it's all true. I have solid proof. That's the whole problem. See, I hired this private detective. And he found the birth certificate. And he figured out you were the father, even though I never told him that. See, the birth certificate says 'Sean H. Demming, address unknown,' and now Rick's going to go to the tabloids if I don't pay him a hundred thousand dollars by tomorrow to keep his mouth shut about your bastard son."

Wild-eyed, he goggled across the desk top at the woman sitting opposite him. As the words rushed out of her head, he felt his ears roaring, as if he had been swallowed into the murky deep during a raging hurricane. "You can't be serious," he mumbled unevenly. "Poppy never ...I never...we..."

She cocked her head like a caged bird. "Oh, yes. You did. When Poppy was seventeen."

Reality sunk in like a rock. He swallowed hard. She went on.

"My private eye is on this case like fleas on a dog, and he's tracking down a lead now, and it may not be too long before he finds the boy and exposes your ugly truth to the world, and ruins Poppy's reputation and shocks the hell out of the kid, wherever he is…"

"Stop! Sasha, please." The roaring in his ears had subsided somewhat. His mind struggled to make sense of the data. "You're saying the boy is missing?"

"No! Adopted!"

"Adopted…!" Grasping the situation at last, he collapsed back into his chair. With both hands, he clutched the chair's arms. He stared, bewildered, at her. At last, the wheels were turning. "Poppy had my baby and gave it up for adoption? Is that what you're saying?"

"Exactly!" she cried, appearing relieved. "Twenty years ago."

"Oh, my…" he mumbled to himself. Then his tone grew fierce. "How do I know this is true? Why didn't Poppy tell me herself?"

Sasha shrank back. "You'll have to ask her that yourself."

"I shall." Anger rose in his throat. "Wait a minute!" His palms hit the desktop. "I don't understand this whole situation. How did you even become involved in it? Why are you here telling me this at all? Why not Poppy?"

"Okay, that's a long story…" she sighed, eyes rolling. "I was just trying to help Poppy. I wanted to do her a favor. She came to me last week, all blubbery about you."

"About me?" He felt himself sweating, even in the cool, conditioned air of the study.

"Yeah. I've always known Poppy had some deep, dark secret, but I didn't know what it was. Last week she blurted out the whole story—told me how you and her were teen lovers, how you proposed at the party, not knowing she was pregnant with your kid, how she hesitated, afraid to tell you, and how you turned to that foreign-exchange chick, and then—the real kicker—that you disappeared for good, leaving her high and dry and in the family way."

"Astonishing," he said softly.

She forged ahead. "After you dumped Poppy, her Uncle Mel forced her to leave town during her pregnancy. So, she had the baby in Tampa and then gave it up for adoption and never told a soul. She finished high school up there. The whole thing broke her heart. Trust me, Heston, it really messed with her head. She's been carrying it around like a dead weight all these years. Then, when you became famous, the situation got worse. She couldn't live in denial anymore. Your face was everywhere. When you moved back to town, two weeks ago, and she saw you again, in real life, and spoke with you—well, you can just imagine the rest. She's been nutso."

Yes. "So where do the private dick and the hundred thousand dollars come in?" he asked steadily, his gaze riveted to Sasha's made-up face. He gripped the arm rails of his chair so tightly, he feared the wood might splinter in his hands.

She cleared her throat. "Well, now, that's where it gets interesting. See, I had this bright idea. It was really a good idea. I thought so then. I still think so," she hedged.

His eyes sought hers, in spite of the way she thrust her cleavage forward as distraction. "Answer my question. I want the facts. Who hired the private detective?"

"I did. A few days ago."

"What's his name? Is he local?"

"Rick DuBois. East Naples."

"How did you find him?"

"I–I looked him up in the yellow pages."

"You're not serious," he howled.

"Well, I didn't know what else to do!" she cried lamely.

"Simmer down. Did DuBois search for the child?"

"Yes."

"And what did he find?"

She blinked with defensive rapidity. "I told you. He found the birth certificate. Poppy was listed as the mother. The father was named as 'Sean H. Demming, Address Unknown.' So, Rick put two and two together. He figured out the 'H' was you."

"So you had not told him I was the father?" he demanded, brow furrowed. "Alleged."

"No, of course not. I told you not. Frankly, I wasn't interested in you. I was trying to help my best friend." She pouted.

"Help her? How? By going behind her back to dig up her past?"

"No! By finding her baby and reuniting mother and son. I thought it would help Poppy. I thought it would do her good to face the truth. I didn't think she would ever do it, left to herself. She had too much hurt and shame invested in the situation. Alone she couldn't face it. I thought if she met the kid and got to know him, she could move on with her life. Come to terms with being the mom of a star's kid."

His eyelid twitched. He felt her words bounce off him. He watched her act with disdain. It *was* an act. He had seen better performances at amateur theatricals. Every actor's instinct he had told him something in the woman's manner was false.

"So he hasn't found the boy?" he ventured apprehensively.

"He has a lead. He thinks he will soon. That's why he wants the money now. If he doesn't get a hundred thousand dollars by tomorrow at noon, he says he'll sell the story to the tabloids."

His grip went limp. He slumped back in his chair. "I see," he rasped.

She shrugged, palms up.

"A hundred-thousand is small potatoes," he mused.

"For some of us," she gawked.

"Will it be enough to shut him up permanently?" He pondered pensively.

"I don't know," she replied. "All I know is what he told me. See, he told me that, if I didn't produce the money, he would come to you or the tabloids, depending on who he thought would pay more. Call me a fool, okay? I forgot your celebrity mattered. I forgot you were a target for moneygrubbers. I don't live in your world, Heston. I was trying to help my poor friend, Poppy."

"Ah," he nodded. Rising, he leaned across the desk. " Regardless of how this situation came about, regardless of whether your story is true, my main concern here *is* Poppy. I do not want her name smeared in the press. I'm accustomed to that, but she isn't. Here," he said, reaching into a desk drawer. "Take this. It's my attorney's card. Give it to this man, DuBois. Tell him to phone my attorney and make arrangements for the payment. He must guarantee absolute silence—in writing. Furthermore, I want him to come on board and finish the job. I want him to locate my first-born son—if the boy exists."

The little woman leaped for joy. "Thank you, Heston! You're all class!" She tore the card from his fingertips. Her breasts jiggled as she bounced prettily. He watched, fascinated.

Probably learned that technique at thirteen.

"Some would differ," he noted under his breath in response to her comment. Eyes up, he flashed the billion-dollar smile at her. "Of course, I'll speak with Poppy right away. I need to know the truth of the matter..."

"No!" she cried. "Not yet. See, she doesn't know I hired Rick. You can't tell her. Not yet."

"Why not?"

"*Ummm*...If you go to her unannounced, it will be too much of a shock. I tell you, she's traumatized over this thing. Twenty years is a long time to be bottled up. She might freak out—if she thought you knew. Let me tell her first, okay? I'll break the news to her gently. I'll tell her I told you everything. Okay? That way she's prepared. It won't be a whack in the face with a shovel."

"Picturesque," he observed, rounding his desk. *This little babe is scary.*

"Are you sure you weren't planning to blackmail me–or Poppy–yourself? Sure you aren't planning to share this score with the unscrupulous local dick?"

Instead of moving away as he approached, Sasha stood her ground. "How dare you?" she yipped, staring up into his face.

He felt twice her height. "You think because you are rich, famous, and handsome you can say anything and get away with it!"

"Where have I heard that lately?" He started to laugh. "Won't work on me, baby," he said. "I've seen better acts in burlesque."

"Screw you, Demming," she boiled, stomping her small foot.

With mock gallantry, he opened the office door. "Andrew will see you out, Miss Bassett. I'll give you twenty-four hours to tell Poppy what you've done. After that, I'm going to speak to her myself–and to your man, DuBois . If I really do have a son, I'm damned well going to find it out."

"Twenty-four hours?" Outraged, fuming, she stomped from the room.

He slammed the door behind her and stood stunned. He realized he was shaking all over. Darting to the portable bar, he grabbed a bottle of Scotch whiskey and unplugged the stopper. Changing his mind, he slowly placed the stopper back into the bottle. Clinging to the bar, he stood for a moment, frozen in time and space. Then he stepped out onto the balcony. There, he stared down at his wife and daughter.

What if it's really true? A son! Why did Poppy never tell me? Because I deserted her.

Bloody Mary in hand, Maude was now idling in a chaise lounge and jabbering on the phone. Jill Cady was nowhere to be seen. Winnie appeared to be napping in the nearby hammock. Light and shadow played in deep contrast, as the midday sun shone through vaulted windows. His daughter was safe, still alive–for the moment.

Turning away, he strode back into his study, picked up his cell phone and glanced at the time. He had almost forgotten: Inez had text-messaged him an urgent plea to come by her office. He dreaded the encounter, but it had to be faced. *First things first, however.* He dialed his lawyer's number.

"Miles? The most amazing thing has just happened..."

***

Down on the pool deck, Maude cooed into her cell phone. Through slit eyes, Winnie watched Daddy up on the balcony, until he moved away out of sight. *Come back, Daddy!* He did not reappear. Winnie then watched her mother through the slits. *Mommy is talking soft.*

138

"Cedric, I tell you my plan will work. We have to do something to make Heston feel he's been betrayed by Poppy. This could be it. I'll convince him she's grown selfish and deceitful, can't be trusted, that she's just using him to make money. It's worth a try." Pausing to hear Cedric's response, Maude cast a glance at her dozing daughter. Cuddling a stuffed toy manatee, Winnie lay still as death in the hammock nearby.

"I'm *glad* you told me," Maude said into the cell as Cedric finished his speech. "I *needed* to know that my husband is seeing Freckle-Butt behind my back. If your old buddy, Wallace, hadn't been chatting up fishermen, on the pier at dawn, he wouldn't have seen the two of them embracing on the beach. What a heel Heston is—fondling Poppy, while the Flynn woman's bed is still warm. You did the right thing to pass it along to me. I'll nip this Poppy affair in the bud. I told you 'like' could be more dangerous than 'lust,' when it comes to husbands and mistresses. My mother taught me that one."

Sipping vodka and tomato juice, Maude waited for a response. Eyes tightly shut, Winnie moaned softly and rolled over onto her side. She hugged the toy manatee closer to her chest. Quietly, Winnie began humming a little tune her mother could not hear. In her half-dream Winnie was leading a family of manatee musicians in an underwater parade.

"Yes, Cedric," her mother was saying. "I've looked at the reproduction you sent over. Your artist-friends did a great job. No one could tell that the copy they made is a forgery. The forgery of *The Chartreuse Alligator* looks just like the Edd Quested original. Only an expert could tell it's a fake. I've sent the forgery to the appraiser already. I told my husband I was having it appraised for insurance purposes. Our plan to ruin Poppy Craft-Talbot has been set in motion, Cedric."

Winnie stopped humming. In the hammock, she laid still and quiet, listening to the outdoor sounds. She heard her mother's voice. She heard the droning of the refrigerator at the poolside bar. She heard the low humming of the vacuum cleaner as the plump maid swept the carpet in a distant room. She heard the repetitive slurping of the pool filter. Eyes closed, she frowned, disturbed. Her mother's voice was bad soft today. She could barely hear her words.

"So here's what I'll do, Cedric, once the appraiser discovers it's a forgery. I'll take the reproduction to Poppy's gallery, and I'll accuse her of selling me a fake Quested painting. She'll flip when I show her the appraiser's report. She'll be shocked, aghast, appalled. But it won't matter. I'll accuse her of purposeful fraud. Then I'll inform the press. I'll sick my attorneys on her, sue her in court, and Mrs. Poppy Craft-Talbot will be out of the art business faster than you can say 'Kiss my ass.' The bad publicity alone will shatter her." Pausing briefly to crunch a crisp stalk of celery, Maude continued on, chewing noisily.

"Oh, don't worry about your buddy, Wallace. I'll take care of him later. Set him up in a shop somewhere else—Boca Raton, Palm Beach. He'll come out of the scandal unscathed, I promise you. What? ...No, we cannot include him in the plan. To work, it has to appear real. If he knew our scheme beforehand, he could wreck it for us. He might even tell Poppy what we have in mind. He might feel loyalty to her. No way is he in on it. *Oooh*, this is delicious! Once she's convicted of art fraud, Poppy will topple from Heston's pedestal all by herself. She won't need another push from us.

"You and I will come out clean as a whistle. I'll have my husband's money. You'll have my undivided attention from now on. I'll meet your sickest needs, Cedric, I swear. Poppy will do jail time. And my husband will have to take solace in that aging hippie, Montserrat Flynn, or some other nameless slut who digs candy-coated sex. *Oooh*, this is great!"

For a moment, Mommy's voice disappeared. Opening one eye, Winnie peeped at her mother. Maude's perfect teeth were barred savagely.

Winnie trembled. Clutching the fuzzy toy manatee, she squeezed her eyes tightly shut. Now, the manatee family was having an underwater tea party. The manatee family loved each other. They ate underwater cupcakes together and sang songs with air bubbles coming out and floating up to the surface.

Flinching, Winnie heard the low growl again. The alligator was coming to bite them. He was swimming through the water, but they didn't know it yet.

"Cedric, one more thing. Your friends have stored the original painting in a safe place, right? The one I sneaked out of Winnie's room? Where is it? In storage in Cancun? For real? Fantastic. No, don't tell me where exactly. What I don't know, I can't divulge. No room for slip-ups in this game. *Oooh*, I can't wait to see that bitch Poppy squirm."

The ugly, familiar sound of cackling laughter shattered Winnie's daydream.

"Mommy, be quiet!" she shrieked, opening her eyes fully, hands covering her ears.

"I'll call you back, Cedric," said Maude, tossing down the phone and rising to her feet. Dashing over, she dragged Winnie from the hammock. "Were you listening? All the time you were pretending to sleep? You little monkey! I'll teach you to fake me out. Where do you pick up this shit?" Maude slapped Winnie hard across the face. "Say one word to Daddy about what you've heard and you'll be sorry. You hear me? You know what I mean."

Shielding her face with her arms, Winnie nodded obediently. Lips twisted in disgust, Maude glanced up at the empty balcony above them, and then, satisfied, stalked back to her chaise lounge by the phone.

Winnie, too, looked up at the empty balcony. Then, closing her eyes, she focused on the music playing in her head. Lying back in the hammock, she cradled her stinging cheek with both hands. Her cheek was wet.

Under her breath, Winnie hummed an airy tune. In her daydream, she marched along bravely with the doomed manatee family.

Chapter Ten

Cookie Lee's blonde curls drooped dejectedly. Yawning behind the counter, she poured steaming coffee into a tall paper cup. The afternoon air inside Rainbow's on Fifth was moist and close. The window blinds were drawn. The light in the shop was dim. Only a few fierce sun rays penetrated the retractable, slatted window shields. Standing in front of the counter, waiting to be served, Poppy yawned, too. The whole world wanted a nap. Even the spider plant on the counter top seemed drowsy.

"Sure you don't want a latte?" she asked Poppy glumly. She slid the cup in her friend's direction. "Sure you want it black?"

Poppy yawned at the proprietress.

Definitely not her usual cheerful self.

"Positive, on both counts," she replied aloud, exchanging dollar bills for the hot paper cup. "I just want a cup of plain, decaf coffee to drink at an empty table outside on the shady sidewalk. I just want to sit under your striped awning and watch the world go by without me in it."

"Be my guest," said Cookie scornfully. "*Ow!*" she cried suddenly, accidentally slamming her pinky in the register drawer. Irritated, she shook her fingers loosely in mid-air. "What a crummy day!" she complained. "I wish I were home with my feet up in front of the TV," she muttered. "Or in bed with some manly hunk. You know what? I've been having a lot of first dates lately. I really wish I could meet somebody nice."

Poppy made a sympathetic face but hastened outside to the street-side tables, where she could breathe freely. Finding an empty table, she sat down, alone at last, with her steaming cup of juice-less java. Today was the first day she had visited the coffee shop since learning of Heston's return to Naples.

Although only three weeks had passed, it seemed an eternity. Now, amidst the sophisticated bustle of *Fifth Avenue South*, Poppy meant to take her problems out and sort them mentally, without fear of being overwhelmed by them. Here in public, she wanted to inwardly face the demon of her own deceptions In private, by herself, that evil genie was too strong to combat. She might succumb to its weapons of guilt, doubt, fear—and her growing desire for the man she had most deceived.

She knew she was in the wrong. It was wrong of her to continue deceiving Heston, even if only by omission. Moodily, she ruminated, as Cookie sauntered out the door, a steaming pot of fresh brew in her hand.

"Want a refill?" she asked lackadaisically, swiping at a raspberry stain on her white apron.

Poppy shoved her cup forward. "Just a tad. Thanks."

Cookie poured slowly, and then set the pot down on the table for a moment.

"I had something I've been meaning to tell you," she said, eyes shifting in both directions. "I don't want to upset you or anything—not again. But you ought to know this, Poppy. I feel obliged to tell you. I mean, if the shoe were on the other foot, I'd want you to tell me."

Uh oh. Poppy bristled. Her peace had been violated, and by bad news yet. "Tell me what?" *Here it comes, whatever it is, it's bound to be bad.* She readied herself for a slap in the face.

"Well," said Cookie, easing into an empty chair and pulling it toward, "I thought you ought to know that your husband—James...?"

"Yes, I know who my husband is," Poppy asserted sarcastically. *Uh oh, indeed.*

Cookie's eyes narrowed. "He's been in here two or three times lately with your little friend, Sasha." Using her empty hand, she made hooks of her forefinger and middle finger to indicate quotation marks around the word "friend".

"He's what? Get out!" Poppy scoffed dismissively, fairly barking with laughter at such an absurd implication. "They probably just ran into each other here. Coincidence."

Cookie Lee raised her eyebrows and cocked her head.

"They looked mighty cozy to me last time they were in," she opined significantly. "The first time, they did run into each other here. They left together that day. Since then, they've been meeting here on purpose or coming in together. I'm not kidding, Poppy. I think something is going on between your best friend and your husband," she pronounced. A look of anguish played across her features. "Of course, I don't want to hurt you. I just thought you should know."

"I see." Poppy felt the depth of Cookie's conviction. It flagged her toward further fight. "Surely, you can't be serious. I mean, it *must* be coincidence."

"You know what the fellow said: 'There are no coincidences'." Rising to her feet, Cookie lifted the round glass pot into the air.

"Well, in this case, there is one," admonished Poppy. "Your suggestion is absurd. James is not Sasha's type. Believe me, I know. And she's not his."

"I've always thought James was kind of cute. In a hound-dog kind of way," observed Cookie, moving away to another customer's table.

That's what I once thought. Poppy called to Cookie's receding form, "And James always said Sasha was a flake!"

"Well," Cookie shot back, opening the shop door, "You're separated, anyway, right? So there's no real harm done, right? Guess, if you're separated, you expect your spouse to see other people. Right?"

Not necessarily. Poppy gulped black decaf from her cup. She set the cup down quickly and swallowed hard. The coffee was too hot. *Let it rest for a moment.*

Entering the front door of the shop, Cookie gave Poppy the high sign. Expecting to see James and Sasha coming out the door, Poppy bolted upright in her chair. Instead of her husband and best friend, however, she saw Danny Vega appear in the doorway.

Charmingly, he ushered Cookie through the doorway ahead of him. As the door closed behind her, he caught sight of Poppy at the table under the awning. After a moment's reflection, he strutted over. Automatically, Poppy swept Danny's body with her eyes. *He leads with his crotch.*

He stopped at Poppy's table. In one hand, he carried a tiny white-paper cup. Watching her intently, he drew a sip of liquid from the cup, then flashed a sinister smile.

"Hey, Poppy. Mind if I join you?" he asked.

He's not asking. He was telling her that he was about to sit down.

"Please do, Danny. It's good to see you. I haven't seen you since..."

"Franco's funeral." With ease, he dragged a metal chair from a nearby empty table and planted himself.

"Right."

Danny lifted his cup in a salute. "Café Cubano. Care to join me?"

Poppy shook her head. "Too sweet for my mood today. Another time, perhaps."

"I like the jolt," said Danny, settling in. He was not smiling now. His sensual lips and dark eyes were dangerous. "The sugar-caffeine rush is mother's milk to me," he said. Poppy noticed how his muscles rippled. Accentuated by tennis whites, his suntanned skin glowed like hot copper.

"So, Poppy. How's life?" Danny asked, his nervous energy barely contained.

"Fair to middling," said Poppy sardonically. "How about you, Danny?"

"Been better," he replied, resting a copper ankle on the opposite knee.

His leg hairs were black and silky. There was something magnetic about Danny Vega's skin. She yearned to stroke him. Startled by her feelings, Poppy folded her hands neatly in her lap.

It wasn't the same feeling as with Heston. This feeling was strictly bestial. With Heston, she felt desire and more. She felt earthy. She felt bonded. She felt belonging. She felt enchantment. On the beach with him, she had felt herself on a mystical isle with a mythical being. Heston was every man in the world to her, all in one.

"I didn't see you inside, Danny. I would have waved," she said aloud, apologetically.

"No problem. I was hiding in the corner."

"Hiding? That doesn't sound like you, Danny Vega."

"Yeah, well, I'm not myself these days."

"Oh? What's wrong?" she asked with genuine concern. Tentatively, she took another sip from her cup. Her decaf had cooled slightly, enough to drink. Poppy eyed Danny's face. *His lashes are so black, so long.* Every time she saw him, she had the same reaction: *No wonder Sash is ga-ga over him.* The thought of Sasha brought her back to reality. She remembered Cookie's insinuation about Sasha and James. *It couldn't be true.* The idea was ridiculous. *No way would she ditch this Romeo for James.*

"Poppy, Poppy," said Danny, drumming his fingers on the table top. He seemed to be leading up to something. "Little red Poppy..."

"What's on your mind?" Poppy asked. She wished he would spit it out. She had come here to sort out her problems in safety, although the undivided attention of Danny Vega was not something to be cast aside lightly. Her vanity was not adverse to such rich treats.

"How's your stepmother?" she asked, hoping to draw him out.

"Bad. She took Franco's death hard."

"And you father? He hasn't been into the gallery lately."

"Rogelio's okay. Doing everything he can to help Inez." He seemed uncomfortable. He lowered his leg and stretched both naked legs out in front of him. He jiggled his feet. His bright-white tennis shoes were immaculate.

"Poppy, there's something you ought to know."

Again? What would that be?" she asked hesitantly.

"Sasha and I, we..." Danny turned the palm of his hand up and down.

"Broke up?" Poppy said slowly, disbelieving.

"It's a rocky road right now. See what I mean?"

"Uh-huh," Poppy uttered. Whatever it was, she felt it coming like a boulder rumbling down a mountainside.

Danny leaned forward and spoke throatily into her ear. "The other night Sasha told me something. About you, Poppy."

Warm coffee-breath brushed her cheek.

"Sash told me you had a baby out of wedlock. Heston Demming's baby. She told me you put the baby up for adoption. She also told me she's hired a private detective to find the kid. She didn't tell me the joker's name, but he's working on the case now."

Poppy sat dumfounded.

Satisfied, Danny leaned back in his chair. His eyes scanned the pedestrians on Fifth Avenue South.

Struggling against the quicksand of fear, Poppy's mind clutched at nearby slender reeds of reality.

Cars. Expensive cars. So many expensive cars in Naples. Mechanically, Poppy's gaze followed the automobiles driving up and down the two-lane street. *BMW, Lexus, Jaguar, Porsche, Mercedes-Benz. Rich people from all over the world move here and bring their pricey toys. Sometimes you see Rolls Royce, Bentley, Ferrari, Heston drives a Ferrari, don't think about it, even reworked old classics, usually convertibles. Everyone tools around town in convertibles. The men wear cloth caps and the women wear those brimmed straw hats. Unless the woman is driving. Then she wears a cloth cap herself. The other day I saw that girl driving a red Triumph...red like Heston's Ferrari...*

"Poppy?" Danny's anxious voice interrupted from somewhere. "Did you hear what I said?"

"Yes."

"Are you okay, babe?" His voice resounded in the cavernous depths of her soul.

No.

"Don't take it too hard, kid. You had a right to know. Sasha's a two-timing bitch. She's stabbing you in the back, same way she stabbed me. Little Miss Boobala has gotten uppity. I'm taking her down a notch, don't you worry." Danny's dark eyes were daggers.

"She promised me she wouldn't tell a soul, Danny."

"She lied."

"Why would she hire a detective? Why would she do such a thing?" Poppy's voice sounded distant, even to herself, as though it were being beamed from some faraway satellite, rather than originating within her own chest.

Danny's metal chair scraped the sidewalk as he pushed back from the table and stood up. "That juicy tidbit, you'll have to get from her," he said, standing up. He tossed down the last drop of the Cuban coffee, then crumbled the tiny paper cup and chunked it into a public trash bin. On impulse, he bent down and kissed Poppy on the cheek. He turned to walk away.

"D-Danny, p-please don't you tell anyone!" she cried, jumping to her feet.

"Unlike some people, I don't make promises I can't keep," he said, backing away.

"Danny, please!"

"Got to go. Don't worry, Pretty Redhead. Miss Bassett needs to be taught a lesson. I'm just the man to teach it to her." Turning on his heel, Danny trotted around back to the parking lot. On the way, he waved at Cookie Lee, who was peeking out from between the blind slats. Sick to her soul, Poppy lowered herself down into her chair, and then slumped across the outdoor table in front of her.

***

Two hours later, in her plush office at Regal Properties on Third Street South, Inez Greco Demming Vega glanced repeatedly at the digital clock on her desk. The clock read 5:08 p.m. He would be arriving here any moment.

She felt giddy with anticipation. The little pills had stopped her hysteria, but today they had left her with a slightly out-of-control feeling. Or maybe that was those other pills she'd taken. What were they again? Pulling a face mirror from her desk drawer, Inez primped nervously. Her image in the mirror seemed fuzzy. She couldn't focus.

How is my coiffure?

Patting a stray hair into place, she saw in the mirror that her hands were trembling. She had to stop that. It made her bracelets rattle. How could she stop it? Flinging the mirror back in the drawer, she wrung her shaky hands. She rubbed her lips together to smooth her lipstick. She rubbed her pinky across her front teeth to erase any stray red marks.

He would be here any moment. He had agreed to come at 5:15. He would be punctual. Hess had learned punctuality when he was a struggling actor on the stage, back when they were young and first married.

Oh, why had she been such a fool? She had let him get away, the best thing that had ever happened in her miserable little life, and she hadn't realized it until it was too late, until Hess was rich and famous and lauded around the globe. But that didn't matter now. It wasn't too late. She and Hess could start again. He didn't love that skinny tramp he was married to. Anyone could see that. With a little encouragement, Hess would leave Maude and come back home.

To me.

A knock at the door. Inez gasped. Leaping from her seat onto her high heels, she smoothed her short, tight skirt into place. Was her lip-liner crooked? She needed to see her face in the mirror, but it was too late now. The door was opening. He was entering the room.

"Inez?"

She heard his sweet, rich voice. It was the same voice she had heard in the movies she had been watching, day in and day out. Its deep masculinity held the fecund promise of new life, of fertility, the promise of another son born from their mutual love. It could happen. She and Hess could make another Franco. He only had to be convinced, to be wooed. She could do it. Sales was her game. *I can do it.*

"In here, Hess. Please come in." Had she just said that? She must have. He was standing in front of her, suddenly. Her heart fluttered rapidly. There seemed to be a halo around him. Why hadn't she noticed it years ago? Was it new? His star-aura glowed radiantly. How could she have pushed this angel from her bed? She had been a fool, a fool, *fool, fool, fool, fool, fool...*

"Inez, honey? Are you alright?" She heard the worry in his rapturous voice. She felt his strong hand through her clothing. Heavenly Heston had latched onto her shoulders. He was guiding her into her seat behind the desk. Now he was kneeling on one knee. She was looking up into that beatific face. *Is he going to propose all over again?*

"Inez, would you like some water?" he asked gently. Flustered, Inez's face fell.

"No. You're sweet. I don't need water. I just want to talk to you, Hess. I want to explain how good it can be between us."

Hungrily, with palsied hands, she fingered his shirt collar. His strong fingers found her hands and tenderly enveloped them, holding them in his warm and gentle grip. He did love her. He still had feelings for her. Why wouldn't her heart stop fluttering? She couldn't catch her breath. He was standing up. He was walking around the desk. *No!*

He sat down in the far chair. He silver-blue gazed at her. The look on his face was pity. She didn't want his pity. She wanted his love. She wanted his seed.

"Inez, does Rogelio know you are here at your office?" the smooth voice asked.

"Oh, no, Hess. I didn't tell him. He doesn't let me leave the house."

"Really."

"I had to see you, Hess. We need to talk, you and I." *Sell it.* "Wouldn't you love to have another son like Franco?"

The smile froze on his face. "Oh, Inez, I don't think..."

"Think about it, Hess. Just picture it. Another fine son—tall, strong, handsome—like you. We could make a son, you and I. We made one before. We could do it again. I'm still young enough. I want a baby, Heston. I want your baby. I want another Frankie! What would it take for you to agree? Tell me your objections. I will overcome them. I can find you whatever you want...Don't walk away..."

He was beside her now, stroking her. Again, she felt the heat of his hands through her sleeves. She felt his calm strength as he stroked her hair. Her teeth were chattering. She couldn't speak to him because...because she felt so cold.

"Sit here, honey," he said, leaning towards the phone. "I'm with you. It's okay." Dialing the number, he rested his perfect backside on the desktop. He held the receiver to his ear. His silver eyes magnetized her gaze. She could remember the first time she noticed them—in tenth grade speech class. Then, again, on that day fourteen years ago in Miami.

She had run into him at a boat show in Coconut Grove. He had been working as an announcer. She had recognized him as that handsome boy from her high school days. He'd told her he'd had a TV commercial running on a local station. She had seen it only the night before. She had recognized him then, and the very next day, there he was in person.

She had been impressed. She predicted he was going places. And he did. It just took too long to get there. She had lost hope. *Forgive me, Heston*

"Hello, Rogelio? Heston Demming here. I'm in your wife's office. She's not well. I think you should come over and take her home."

No! No! Inez sprang from the chair and grabbed the receiver from his hand. She flung the receiver into the trash can beneath her desk.

"I don't want him! Don't call him!" She heard her own banshee-like voice. "Rogelio hates me! He's jealous of Danny. Danny wants me! Rogelio can feel it. He hates me!"

Inez felt Heston's muscular arms go round her for support. Giddy, she flung her arms around his torso. Locked in her embrace, he was struggling to free himself, but she clung more tightly to him.

Hess was hers. He belonged to her. By law, she had first claim to him. He would give her another son. He would bring Franco back to her. They would all go on just as if nothing *terrible* had happened to ruin their lives. She didn't hate him for the accident. He hadn't meant to kill Frankie. He needed her forgiveness.

"Inez, turn me loose!" His rich voice boomed in her ear. She felt her arms ratcheted in pain as he tore his body from her. Then there was *blackness.*

Then she was lying on the office couch. Men's voices were murmuring in the background. She heard Rogelio's familiar gargle. She smelt the odor of cigar smoke.

"She's been out of her mind with grief," he said. "I've kept her house-bound. I should have watched her more closely. How did she get here?"

"I have no idea. She texted me and asked me to meet her here." Heston's low, dulcet tones filled Inez's ears with peace. "She said she had to see me on a matter of importance. I agreed to meet her here. I didn't see the harm. I knew she'd been under stress since the accident. I felt she and I needed to talk. It seemed like a good idea to clear the air between us. I found her nearly incoherent. This bottle of pills—what's left of them—was on the floor just there. There are others in her desk drawers. I checked."

Inez moaned, her sense of peace evaporating as consciousness returned. The light from the wall lamp hurt her eyes. She shielded them with her forearm.

"Hess?" she heard herself whimper.

"Here, Inez." Suddenly, he was kneeling at her side. He gripped her hand in his. "Rogelio is here with me. He's going to take you home. You're delirious, honey."

"I've called your doctor, Inez," said Rogelio. "He's sending the para-medics."

No!

"Hold her!" Heston's voice sang far above her. She felt her limbs thrashing. She felt strong hands bind her. Her body writhed mercilessly.

"It is all so damned tragic," she heard Rogelio say through gnashed teeth. "Is it just that she's mixed her medications? Think she's having a nervous breakdown."

"It's all my damned fault," she heard Heston falter.

Oh, how she longed to comfort him. Looking up, she saw the radiant halo round his leonine head. Then his angel face morphed, and she found herself face to face with Franco, only it wasn't a physical Franco, suddenly, it was an ethereal Franco, wispy and see-through like in the movies, and he was smiling at her with that beautiful, Pearly-White-Gates Demming smile and she knew she was doing the right thing to want her first hus-band back. The cloud that was Franco engulfed her in heavenly mist.

Don't worry, Frankie. I'll get your father back—one way or another.

***

Life frigging sucks.

Heston sat weeping behind the wheel of his parked Ferrari. The scene with Inez had been too much for him to bear. He had escaped as soon as the doctor arrived. Now, he wept openly, pressing his forehead against the steering wheel.

He was an alcoholic. He had ruined a lot of lives on his trek to the top. His parents were dead. His son, Franco, was dead. He was responsible. His ex-wife, the boy's mother, was losing her mind to grief. His second marriage was in shambles. His current wife was a greedy degenerate. His mistress didn't love him. His daughter was in danger from abuse and neglect. He himself was nearing middle age. His own looks would fade soon. His career would be over in a few short years. They would all abandon him. Only one thing in this world offered him any promise of hope.

Poppy.

Had the Higher Power brought him full circle?

He wiped his eyes and stared towards the setting sun. Tonight the sky at sunset was uniquely spectacular, an azure ground of sky dotted with tiny, pink puffs of cloud. The ever-changing palette of the Maker astounded him. This was Nature at its most miraculous.

Could it be possible? Had Poppy given him another son?

Without hesitation, he fired the Ferrari engine. Yes, he had told Sasha he would wait before asking Poppy about the birth. But he was tired of life in hell. He was tired of pretending. He needed the truth. He needed a reason to keep on living. Otherwise, he would go the way of his father and mother. Could the Universe be offering him a second chance?

He studied his watch. Poppy's gallery was less than ten minutes away. He placed his hand on the gear shift and shifted the car into drive.

***

Poppy turned out the lights and stood in the darkened, empty art gallery. Outside, the sun was dipping below the horizon. She looked at her watch. Closing time. Wallace had gone home already. He had departed three hours ago, when she had returned to Poppy Wallace Fine Art after her encounter with Danny Vega.

Everything had been done. She knew the closing procedure by rote—money, AC, lights, music, back door, security, front door. Check, double check. Her purse was in hand, along with her briefcase and lunch tote. Her wheat-gold sweater was draped over her arm. It needed cleaning. *Had today really happened? Surely not.*

Standing heavy-laden in the dark, deserted gallery, Poppy felt sad. Yesterday Cedric's garish show had come down, but she'd heard he was hanging around town. She and Wallace were in the middle of hanging other work. Tonight she was surrounded by the surreal shapes of these sculptures, vases, and other *objets d'art.*

In the darkness, she listened sadly to her ghosts. She heard the raspy, Southern voice of Uncle Mel, the chain smoker. He was terrifying her about the shame of unwed motherhood. She heard the weary voice of Heston's good-looking mother, Kay, warning her that Heston had inherited his father's tendency towards drink. She heard the deceptively pone-soft voice of her husband, James, warning her of the dangers of starting her own business. She heard the guttural cries of Inez Vega, wailing for a son who had perished in a violent cataclysm of unexpected death. She heard the youthful voice of Heston Demming thundering urgently at his shaming father. She heard the childlike voice of Sasha Bassett promising to keep the secret of her baby forever

Can it be true? Did Sasha go behind my back and hire a detective to track down Heston's and my child?

Strange as it seemed, the baby boy she had borne, in secret shame in a distant city—and whom she had named Noel because he had been conceived on Christmas Eve at Shark River—that boy was out there somewhere, right this very minute, alive somewhere in this big, wide world. True, the boy might be dead, but more likely, he was alive and thriving somewhere, a handsome, strapping nineteen-year-old youth with movie-star genes.

His friends probably laughed about his resemblance to the world-famous actor. Noel probably would grin and tap his toes like Heston when embarrassed or chew his fingernail. Noel Demming. Their son had once had a name, a name he may never even have heard. *What name do you go by now, little Noel?*

What if Sasha's detective finds Noel somewhere? What then? What if Danny Vega tells Inez or Rogelio or anyone else in the world? The whole sordid story will come out. Heston will hear of it. I'll die. I'll simply die of shame and embarrassment and fright. What on earth will I do if he finds out? Can't face him. I can't. I can't. He'll hate me forever. The baby will hate me, too—if they ever find him. I hate myself, I lied to Heston. I abandoned his child. I abandoned my own son. I don't deserve to live anymore.

Tired and alone, Poppy dropped her guard. All the worries she had tried to deal with objectively at Cookie's that afternoon came spilling forth, as she stood in the tomb-like silence of the darkened gallery. The depth of her feeling for Heston gushed from a source so ancient it could not be named. That day on the beach it all had come flooding back into her heart. *Had it ever really left?* She beat down the panic.

Fight the feeling. Fight it hard. It didn't matter. She didn't really want Heston. Really, she didn't. Who wanted to spend time babysitting a drunk? She wanted her freedom. That's why she had separated from James. She wanted autonomy, not dependency.

Who needs love? It's just another chain around your neck. Bah, Heston Demming, you overrated perpetrator of pork. The only thing worse than a ham actor is a pickled ham actor. She groaned inwardly at her own bad jokes, but she rolled her eyes heavenward in defiance.

I don't need you. Sean Heston. I never did. I don't want to be with you night and day, don't want to share your bed, don't want to feel your muscles envelop me, don't want to feel your mouth against me, don't want to serve your food, launder your clothes, keep your house, bear your children—never again. I don't want you!!!

Those dreams are dead. They died that first night you left me for Montserrat Flynn.

She cried out in despair. If only she could believe her own denials. Unfortunately, she, more than anyone else, knew best what a liar she really was.

Regrouping, she turned and trudged out the front door. Tonight, as usual, her champagne-colored sedan was waiting for her out front, in the parking lot used by the general public when shopping at Venetian Bay Village. For the past two hours, since Wallace's departure from the shop, she, thankfully, had had few customers. She had been able to pull herself together somewhat, at least enough to go through the motions of closing up shop and going home to brood. *Coffee be damned. Nothing in the world sounds better now than a glass of chilled Chardonnay.*

Once outside, Poppy faced the door. Fumbling to secure the lock, she sighed in frustration and then deposited her briefcase on the ground. As she turned back to face the door, she heard the sound of squealing tires. She wheeled around. What she saw sent her heart plummeting to her shoes.

Heston. In his red Ferrari convertible.

Her mouth went dry. Her heart began to thud in her chest. Fight or flight kicked in. She searched for escape. There was none. Even the gallery door was now locked.

The sports car swung erratically into the parking lot and came to a halt along the edge of the curb in front of her gallery, less than six feet from her. Climbing out of the driver's seat, her old sweetheart—tall, lean, muscular, beautiful—stopped in his tracks, suspended in time, like a film in slow motion, as he caught sight of her on the sidewalk. Even from a distance she could feel his emotion. His countenance seemed stern; his demeanor, authoritarian. An image of Heston's tortured father flashed in her mind. Yet the yearning was unmistakable.

He knows.

"Tell me the truth, Poppy!" he commanded, his projected stage voice rich and deep. "I want to know the truth!"

"Heston, I..."

Charging around the hood of the car, he headed straight for her. Terrified, Poppy backed away until her back pressed flat against the gallery door. She could go no further. He was striding towards her. Now, he was upon her, hulking over her. The silver-blue eyes which once undressed her in love were now prying, menacing laser beams boring into her guilty soul. Grabbing her by the wrists, he shook the paraphernalia from her hands. Purse, lunch tote, sweater, all spilled onto the deserted sidewalk.

"Is it true?" he demanded hotly.

"Don't! Please!" she begged breathlessly, struggling to escape.

"Tell me. Is it true, Poppy? Did you have my baby? Did you bear me a son nineteen years ago?"

With the length of his tall body, he flattened her against the gallery door, clamping her wrists in place above her head. His face flamed down at her like an angry idol. There was no escape. The fires of Hell consumed her.

"*Y-Y-Yesss...!*" she screamed in terror. Her scream echoed throughout the concrete canyon. A shock wave rippled through Heston's being.

Suddenly, his hard body went limp. Slowly, his fingers loosened their grip, letting her wrists slip down to her sides. His weight slumped against her. His arms struggled to embrace her. Affectionately, his hands patted her shoulders, her arms. Breathing heavily, he crushed her tentatively in a tender embrace.

Then, in silence, he wrenched himself away. Wavering on loosely hinged knees, he scanned the surrounding buildings with his eyes, looked up at the darkening sky, at last turning his tortured gaze towards Poppy.

"I *do* need a drink," he whispered.

"Heston...!" No further sound escaped Poppy's lips.

Turning on his heel, he stumbled back to the Ferrari. Vaulting over the car door, he slipped into the driver's seat, fired the engine and pressed his foot to the gas pedal. The cars headlights came on as it roared out of the parking lot and headed southward. Little by little, darkness continued to descend on Venetian Bay Village. Dazed in the twilight, Poppy slid to the ground and perched awkwardly on her ankles.

He knows now. He knows now.

The words echoed inside her mind. As she sat, stunned, time seemed to inch along as slowly as the caterpillar on the cement walk in front of her. Poppy's whole world had changed in an instant. She had entered a new reality.

In the eerie twilight, a police car pulled up alongside the curb. A strapping officer emerged from the door of the black-and-white sedan with a flashing red light on its roof.

"Can I help you, ma'am?" The police officer brusquely extended a hand.

"Yes, thank you," breathed Poppy, taking his strong, broad hand and allowing herself to be pulled to a standing position. She felt rocky, shaken to the core.

"What happened here, ma'am?" The officer indicated Poppy's belongings, which were strewn beside her on the sidewalk. Red light flashed rhythmically across the clean-cut officer's serious countenance.

"Nothing, Officer. I'm fine, really. I fell down. I tripped." Poppy wiped her gritty hands on her disheveled silk pantsuit. She smoothed her fly-away hair. Meanwhile, the officer collected the purse and lunch tote and placed them next to the briefcase.

"Do you want to go the Emergency Room?" the strapping man asked in a polite but authoritative voice. From the sidewalk, he scooped together the spilled contents of Poppy's purse and returned her things to the bag.

"There's no need. I'm fine. This is my gallery. I'm the owner. Co-owner." She pointed to the entry door behind her. "Thank you for your help, sir." She wanted him to leave. She wanted to be alone, to digest her astonishing experience with Heston.

"If you need anything later on...," the officer began, his face a mask.

"I'll be fine. Thank you, sir."

Reluctantly, the officer tipped a non-existent cap and climbed back into his car. As the police car drove away, a thought emerged into Poppy's dazed consciousness. *Heston was sober when he arrived.*

There had been no smell of liquor on his breath or body, of that she was certain. Only the beloved scent of orange-myrrh maleness had assailed her nostrils as her old sweetheart had held her close. She savored the memory for a split second. Then the wave of realization crashed through her. *He knows I bore his child.*

How did he find out? Instinct told her. There was only one way he could have found out. Not Danny.

Sasha. But when? And why?

Groping for her possessions, Poppy gathered them to her and then clipped speedily across the parking lot towards her parked BMW. Opening the car's trunk, she hurled her belongings inside, and then edged herself behind the wheel. With rebellious fingers, she started the ignition and turned on the headlights. The sedan lurched forward. Poppy eased the car onto Gulfshore Boulevard North.

She had no idea where to search for him. Was there a bar he frequented? Liquor store he where he shopped regularly? Would he go home to drink in solitude? Poppy had no clue. She knew only *one place* Heston might go to seek solace—the Naples City Pier, the same place she had run into him the other day. Even as a boy he had gone there to brood.

She had to find him. He might do anything. Electric lights guided her way as she flew down Crayton Road, Mooring Line Drive, and then over the bay bridge onto Gulfshore Boulevard South. Driving carelessly as a daredevil racer, she sped her way southward, flying past the multi-storied Naples Grande Hotel, with its brilliant copper-colored roof, past Moorings Beach and Lowdermilk Park, past short, mid-sixties condo buildings and grand beachfront mansions.

By the time she reached Twelfth Street South, night had fallen. Parking her car in the sparsely filled public lot, she scrambled from the vehicle and ran down onto the sandy beach south of the pier entrance. If Heston were here, would she be able to locate him in the darkness? Fainthearted, she wandered among the concrete pilings beneath the pier's slatted floor. Gentle waves sloshed in and out at her feet. Her shoes filled with tepid water. Forlornly, she searched up and down the dark shoreline. He was nowhere to be seen.

Maybe it was better that she hadn't found him tonight. Fatigue was setting in. Fear was rising again in Poppy's soul. She was beginning to feel that facing him tonight was the last thing she wanted to do, especially if he were drunk. He would demand an explanation. How could she explain? She couldn't even justify her actions to herself.

She shuddered. For the first time, she let herself remember what it felt like to hold her baby in her arms. The nurse had brought the child to her for a short time before he had been taken away for adoption. She could let herself feel it now. The wall of fear was crumbling down. The smell of the baby, the tiny feel of him, the way he nestled against her breast...

Lost, Poppy gave herself to the memory. For a long time, she stood contemplating the dark water in front of her. Around her, the moist, fishy gulf breeze gradually increased, blowing stronger and cooler, whipping her hair and clothes. A chill in the night air brought her thoughts round to the present moment.

Heston knows. Now what happens?

The thought of Heston's knowing made her body flash hot, despite the chilly air, as she blushed from crown to toe. Could she face him in earnest? As the mother of his first-born child? Slowly, she accepted the knowledge into her consciousness. She was *a mother*. Perhaps her son was out there somewhere in the vast world, needing her just as badly as she needed him.

Tina Murray

What if Sasha's private eye finds my baby?
What if he doesn't?

Chapter Eleven

From memory, Poppy dialed Sasha's phone number. The line was busy.

I'll wait. I'll try again. Morning fresh, her mind had new clarity.

Five minutes later, Poppy placed a second call. This time, the phone rang repeatedly. Through her living room windows, her eyes caught the fierce glow of sunrise to the east. With the phone at her ear, she sat poised upright on the divan. She was wearing her comfy old standby, a flimsy, sea-green nightgown and chenille robe.

Preoccupied, she ignored a half-eaten bowl of cantaloupe chunks on the coffee table in front of her. Her lips were set in a grim line. All her focus, her energy, her mind was set on pinning down Sasha Bassett like a tournament wrestler. She was determined to know the truth. During the night, her subconscious mind had been putting the pieces together. An ugly picture had started to form.

Why has the woman hired a private detective to find my child? Danny Vega had seemed cock-sure that Sasha had hired someone. But *why* would she do such a thing? Danny wouldn't say.

Has she been dating James behind my back? Cookie Lee said as much. Cookie had seen them together. What in the world would make Sasha dump hunky Danny Vega for frumpy James? If she *had* dumped Danny, it would explain his anger and behavior.

Did Sasha tell Heston about the baby? If *not*, it would be necessary to determine the real source of Heston's sudden knowledge. If *so*, she would demand to know the reason why. And it would be the end of her longtime friendship with Sasha Jean Bassett.

At length, the phone picked up. "Hello?" It was Sasha's voice on the other end.

"Hello!" Poppy tried to sound friendly and festive. If it took an act to reveal the truth, then an act she would play. She would lure Sasha into her lair, and then pounce.

A moment of silence on Sasha's end, then "Poppy! Is that you?"

"With bells on."

"How nice to hear from you." The voice sounded wary.

Not wanting Sasha to discern her true motive, Poppy retained her overt gaiety.

"Sashay, I miss you! It's been so long since I've seen you. Want to come over? I'll make lunch—crab salad, your favorite. Red onions. A few lettuce leaves. A glass of white wine. Lime sorbet. On the balcony. Ocean view. What do you say?"

The caller stammered. "Well, I...don't know, I..."

Poppy laughed gaily. "What's up with you? Usually, I'm the one who can't get the words out. Come on, Sash, please. I miss you. It'll be fun." She could feel Sasha's hesitation.

"Poppy, I..."

"What?"

"Never mind. Sure, I'll come over. What time?"

"Let's see, it's 7:30 now. How about 11 a.m.? We'll call it brunch. Sorry if I woke you, by the way."

"Well, I was sleeping in. I'm prepping a cocktail party at one. How come you're not at work today? Run out of paintings?"

Poppy inhaled sharply. "I phoned in. Wallace is minding the store. He's such a pal."

"You certainly sound more cheerful than the last time I spoke with you. What's going on?"

In danger of overplaying her hand, Poppy changed her tone. "I'm trying to be brave, Sash. Putting on a front, you know? I'm still struggling in my heart. I confess. I need my best friend's shoulder to cry on."

"Meaning me?"

"Who else?"

"I don't know."

Was she buying it? Poppy heard a voice of male timbre in the background.

"I hope I didn't wake Danny?" she asked quickly, the hair rising on the back of her neck. Was James in bed with Sasha now?

"Um, Danny's not here. Want me to bring anything for lunch?" countered Sasha, changing the subject yet again.

Just the truth.

"Just your own sweet, little self, that's all. Come on over when you're ready, Sash. I can't wait to see you. We've got a lot of catching up to do." *Said the spider to the fly.*

"Well, okay, Poppy. Guess I'll see you later on. Look, I've got to go. Nature's calling. Oh, wait a minute." For a second, Sasha's voice disappeared, replaced by a muffling sound, as a hand over the mouthpiece.

Suddenly, her voice was back on line. "Sorry," she said. "I dropped the phone on the floor."

"Was that a man's voice, Sasha? If it's not Danny Vega, who is it?"

Poppy grilled, feigning gossipy girlish interest.

"No one! Just the DJ on satellite radio. Morning program. Sorry to disappoint you," replied Sasha, irritated. "Look, I've got to go."

"See you." Poppy rang off abruptly. Unsmiling, she sat on the divan for a moment, her mind now a swirling vortex of suspicion. Determined to find out the truth, Poppy rose to prepare the luncheon menu for the impending showdown.

At ten minutes past eleven, the doorbell of Poppy's apartment rang. Now dressed in sunny cotton crop-pants and a sleeveless print top, Poppy answered the door. Her manner was subdued but informal as she ushered her guest into the foyer. Tossing her satchel onto the living room couch, Sasha followed Poppy reluctantly through the condo apartment.

"Come on back," Poppy said, leading her out to the balcony. A well-dressed table on the balcony sat waiting invitingly. Poppy had laid the table with her favorite casual china and glassware. The china featured a fish motif. The glassware was a swirling, watery green. As Sasha plopped down at the table, she handed her a half-filled wine glass.

"I can't have much," Sasha grimaced, accepting the glass. "Got to go to work later. Remember?"

"I remember," she smiled, returning with a serving bowl filled with chilled crab salad and placing it on the table. She sat down across from the woman at table. *But I don't care. I want you to talk. Now.*

Clearly uncomfortable, Sasha sipped wine from her glass. Her round, brown eyes scrutinized her surroundings as though seeing the pricey patio furnishings and the ocean view for the first time. A fresh, gentle breeze tossed her dark wavy tresses. She, too, was dressed in pedal pushers and a matching top, but in baby-blue, a color which flattered her nicely.

"That color looks great on you," Poppy said disarmingly, serving the salad into her guest's plate first, then into her own.

"Thanks," said Sasha, watching her hostess nervously.

"So, where was Danny last night? He didn't stay over with you?"

Sasha shook her head. Her eyes avoided Poppy's. She lifted a forkful of crab into her mouth. "Good," she said, chewing mechanically.

"I know it's your favorite," said Poppy, playing idly with the food on her plate. She had framed the questions in her mind, but she wanted her delivery to be right. She watched furtively as Sasha downed the contents of the wine glass, while only nibbling at the food.

"You have a super view," said Sasha. "I've never really looked at your place before. James probably really misses it. He even had an office here, didn't he?"

"Yes," said Poppy conversationally, but her heart skipped a beat as she recalled Cookie Lee's insinuation. "James took most of his things with him when he moved out. Some of it is still there. Some of it is mine. Some is half mine."

"I'd like to see his office," said Sasha.

Is that why you agreed to come over? To scope out James's net worth? Poppy mustered her courage. "His office? Sure," she said compliantly, poising to pounce. "More wine?" She held up a glass carafe.

"Yeah. Okay." Sasha returned to her food as Poppy poured pale gold liquid into the glass and then set down the carafe. As Sasha lifted a crab-filled fork to her mouth, Poppy leaned forward, elbows on the table, her own wine glass in her hands. She turned her gaze on Sasha like a searchlight.

"Did you hire a private detective named Rick DuBois to find my baby?"

Eyes wide, Sasha coughed. Shreds of crab flew from her open mouth. Coughing repeatedly, Sasha raised a linen napkin to her mouth. Swirling her wineglass in her hands, Poppy leaned back smugly in her chair and watched the accused recover. *Caught red-handed.* Her anger began to boil, but she kept a level head.

"Why would you do such a thing, Sasha? Why would you go behind my back? I told you about Heston's baby in confidence. I trusted you to keep my secret," she said.

Still sniffling, but recovered from her coughing fit, Sasha sipped more wine and swallowed hard. Her round face lit up innocently.

"What makes you think I did?" she demanded. "Where did you hear such a thing?"

Poppy narrowed her eyes. "Why, from your lover, Danny Vega. I ran into him at Rainbow's. He told me all about it. Said you had told him about my getting pregnant in high school and having Heston's child in secret. But Danny wouldn't tell me *why* you'd told him. *You* really can't deny it, Sasha. There's no other way Danny could have known about my baby. I haven't told anyone else in nineteen years–only you."

Sasha scoffed. "Well, Danny's just lying, that's all. He can't be trusted. He has some pretty sleazy connections, you know. Maybe he was spying on us that night. Maybe he overheard our conversation. For all I know, he videoed us. He's psycho, you know. He stalks me now."

Poppy watched the guilty woman closely. "Why?"

Sasha gaped. "Why what?"

"Why does Danny stalk you now?"

Sasha flung her napkin onto the table top. "Who knows why? He's nuts!"

"Is it because you're two-timing him?"

Sasha snorted. "Oh, please!" She balled her napkin and tossed it onto the table.

"Have you been seeing James behind my back?"

Jumping from her seat, Sasha grew livid. "What? Where do you get this stuff, Poppy? What a thing to ask me! Hell, I would never...!"

Poppy kept her seat and her cool. "Cookie Lee says you did. She says she's seen you in her shop with my husband several times lately. She thinks you two are dating—or hooked up, as they say nowadays."

Outraged, Sasha walked to the balcony railing and grasped the top rail with both hands. She peered through the thin screen mesh. "I can't believe you would listen to such BS," she said hotly, staring out at the vast, gray-green Gulf of Mexico. "Poppy, you and I have been friends for years. How can you even think I would go behind your back like this?" Eyes averted, the small woman turned and stomped into the kitchen. "Where's my bag?" she demanded, rattled. "I'm going to work."

Rising, Poppy followed her guest through the kitchen and into foyer off the living room. By now, Sasha had located her satchel on the couch. She was swinging the heavy bag over her shoulder and moving towards the front door. Physically, Poppy blocked her path.

"How could you do it to me, girlfriend? That's the real question here. And because I know you so well, I believe I know the answer. You're desperate."

"You're crazy!" said Sasha, trying to dodge her way past her hostess.

"So everybody's crazy but you. Is that your story?" Poppy cried, dancing to stop her.

"Believe what you want, Poppy. If you don't trust me any more than that, we don't have a friendship, anyway," Sasha said huffily, still trying to edge past her. Twice, she glanced towards the front door.

Firmly, Poppy stood her ground. "Here's one last question for you, friend of mine. Did you tell Heston Demming that I had his baby?"

Sasha's mouth flew open. She gaped at Poppy in silent astonishment. "Heston wasn't supposed to..."

"What, Sasha? Tell me? Why not? Everybody else in the universe seems to be in the loop. That's what it sounds like from where I'm sitting!" she cried, indignant. "Why didn't you just post it on the Net?" Tears of ire welled in her eyes. "How could you do this to me, you traitor?"

Exhaling loudly, Sasha slapped her hands against the sides of her thighs. "Yeah, okay," she said. "Look, Poppy, I can explain. Look, sit down for a minute, okay? Hear me out." Doubling back into the living room, she flopped down bodily onto the couch and dropped her satchel onto the clean carpet.

Caught off guard by the sudden change in tactics, Poppy hesitated for a moment and then positioned herself cautiously on the opposite end of the couch.

"All right," Poppy said quietly. "Explain."

Leaning forward into Poppy's space, Sasha began her recital.

"It was an accident," she insisted. "Heston did hear me say it but it was an accident." Sasha paused and looked earnestly at her. "What did he tell you? I'm assuming you spoke with him and he told you he knew about the baby."

Poppy glowered. "He said nothing. Just that he knew. He asked me if it were true. I said yes. Then he left."

Sasha's tension abated. She exhaled, seemingly from the depth of her being. "Yeah, well, here's what really happened. I *was* at Rainbow's. I've been going there a lot lately. Craving powdered donuts. Your hubby, Jimbo, goes there a lot, too. I run into him sometimes. We sit and chat. Have a few laughs. He's pretty depressed, Poppy, in case you didn't know–or care. One day when I was at Rainbow's alone, feeling down, Heston came in. Look, you know how it is with that guy, Poppy. He looks at you with those other-worldly eyes–and you melt." Sasha shrugged, as if to say the situation had been hopeless.

Relentlessly, Poppy stared as Sasha bumbled along.

"I blurted it out. Accidentally. I was just babbling from nerves. I was racking my brain to find a topic of conversation. Heston's a big star, for Pete's sake, and such a hottie. He's scary. He made me nervous, and I shot off my mouth. I wanted to die as soon as I said it. I'm sorry, Poppy. Really, really sorry. I hope you'll be able to forgive me."

Skeptically, Poppy contemplated Sasha's words. "So you're not sleeping with my husband?" she asked.

"*No!*" shouted Sasha, shaking her head as if it were the most ridiculous notion ever.

"And you told Heston about our baby by mistake?" Poppy went on.

"Yes!" said Sasha emphatically, stamping both feet.

"Fine. But that doesn't explain why you hired a private detective to find my lost son. Or why Danny Vega told me so eagerly that you had. Or why you denied all this in the first place."

Sasha stood up. "I denied it at first because I was scared–scared I'd lose your friendship. You're my best friend, Poppy. I care about your feelings."

"It wasn't to keep my gallery's catering business for your mother's firm?"

Sasha picked up her satchel. She turned to face down Poppy, who was still sitting on the couch. "How can you even think such a thing? Good grief. It's your feelings I care about. In fact," she insisted, brown eyes blinking rapidly, "That's why I hired the private eye. Because I do care so much about your feelings. I knew you would never look for the boy. You've been in denial about the baby–and your love for Heston–all these years. I felt I had to help you face the past. I felt if I could find your kid, you could meet him and love him and everything would be alright. Get it?"

Poppy was watching Sasha with trepidation. Now she rose to her feet. As she stood, her guest edged back into the foyer and towards the front door. Following her menacingly, she came to a halt in the foyer. She crossed her arms in front of her and stared at Sasha, who now had one hand on the doorknob.

"So, you see, I did it all for you," Sasha bleated softly, turning the knob. The front door opened a crack.

"So you really have this fellow, Rick DuBois, searching for my son?"

"I do."

"Has he found anything?" Poppy asked, afraid of the answer.

"Not yet. He may never find anything. Those adoption records are kept pretty tight from strangers," said Sasha soothingly. "You might have a better chance of finding out than Rick does." She pushed the door open another inch. She stepped forward on one foot.

"I want you to tell him to stop searching," said Poppy.

"Poppy, you don't mean that."

"I do! I've had a chance to think about it. Disrupting the boy's life would be cruel."

"Heck, it's too late for that now," said Sasha, her brow furrowing. "The cat's out of the bag. Face it, Poppy. Your kid has a famous father. One day soon, the world will find out about Heston's bastard child whether you want it to or not. This way, you can be in control of the situation. You'll be better off knowing the facts, don't you see? The truth will set you free, babe. As far as I'm concerned, Poppy, I did you a favor. Plus, I've saved you the worry of telling Heston. One day you'll thank me for what I've done for you, mark my words."

Poppy glared at her. "Get out of here, you female snake-in-the-grass" she snarled in low fury. "Before I do something we'll both regret."

Without another word, Sasha slipped out the door and made for the elevator. Grasping the doorknob, Poppy slammed the door shut behind her. Flabbergasted, she stood with her back pressed against the cool wood of the heavy door. The feeling of the hard door pressing against her back reminded her of yesterday's scene with her old love.

She began to shudder violently. *What on earth am I supposed to do now?* Stumbling to the couch, she collapsed across the cushions. Sprawling onto her belly, she felt her chest heave. Things simply could not get any worse.

***

On the following morning, at Poppy Wallace Fine Art in Venetian Bay Village, Wallace watched Poppy furtively. Overtly, Wallace chatted charmingly with a middle-aged married couple shopping for specialty glassware. The two art collectors were regular customers whom Wallace knew well. Across the gallery from them, his business partner—that slight, sweet-natured redhead—was sitting despondently at her desk, her brown eyes downcast. One hand clasped the opening of her blouse near the starched collar. The other hand rested, palm up, in her lap. Poppy's countenance was pensive. She had lost weight. Something was definitely wrong with her. He could tell. And he knew what it was.

For weeks now, he had been aware of a new tension in her manner, as though some unnamable anxiety had crept into her life and taken root—and she was desperately trying to hide it. Maybe she could conceal it from others but not from him. He was with her every day, all day long, and had been for three long years. Furthermore, he had seen her at dawn, a few days ago, cavorting with Heston Demming on the beach, embracing the man even. Nobody snuggles that way without meaning it. *Hell, who could blame her?*

As he waved goodbye to the gregarious couple, Wallace toyed with the idea of approaching Poppy on the subject. He could demand to know the truth about her emotional state. Would she confide in him? *Only one way to find out.*

He and she were now alone in the art gallery. It was close to lunch time. This was as good a time as any to approach her. If she rebuffed him, he could scoot down the sidewalk for a Reuben at his favorite deli. Sauntering across the floor, he sighed loudly as he approached her desk.

"I thought they'd never leave," he said in a blasé manner, running the tips of his fingers along the top of Poppy's desk. Idling, he stood with his hand poised on one corner of the desk. He eyed Poppy worriedly. Her expression was wan. She did not look up at him.

"What's wrong, Poppy?" he cajoled.

"Nothing. I feel sick, that's all."

"Think you should see a doctor?"

"No. It wouldn't help."

"It might. I could drive you over."

"No. Thanks, Wallace. That's not it."

"Well, what is it? Have you eaten today?"

"Uh…I don't know. Maybe. Yes, I think so. Earlier." At last, she cast a quick glance his way. Her brown eyes revealed her inner torment. He felt she was fibbing.

Wallace kept his voice low and non-threatening. "Look, whatever it is, you can tell me about it. We've been friends for a long time now, Poppy. By now you ought to know you can trust me. Forgive my asking, but does this spate of nausea have anything to do with Heston Demming? It seems like you've been tangled up inside ever since he first appeared on our doorstep. You were always nervous, but now you're dancing on nails."

Her eyes flew to his and then swept away just as quickly. Silently he congratulated himself. He'd hit the bulls eye. *No doubt about it. She's in agony over the Greek statue.*

"Are you in love with him or something, honey? It would be easy to understand if you were. He's handsome as the devil, after all, and just as unavailable. That's a real turn-on for you women folk, ain't it?" Crouching on one knee, Wallace gently lifted his hand to Poppy's quivering chin. "I'd like to help you if I can."

As Poppy parted her lips to speak, the front door of the art gallery burst open. Through a shop window, Wallace could see a white limo waiting at the curb. But his attention was drawn to a burly bodyguard who entered silently and stood sentinel near the doorway. The bodyguard was followed by an agitated Maude Demming, who stormed into the shop, dragging her small daughter, Winnie, by the hand.

Tucked beneath Maude's rail-thin arm was a small, framed painting, one that looked all too familiar to Wallace. He leaped to his feet as the supermodel charged Poppy's desk like an angry broomstick. Without warning, Maude slammed the painting down on Poppy's desk. Startled, Poppy looked up at Maude perplexedly.

"You're a frigging fraud!" Maude snarled at Poppy, who stared at her, dumbfounded.

Hackles rising, Wallace took charge immediately. "I hate to hear ladies swear. It's so unbecoming." Briefly, he cast a glance down at the small, unhappy child at Maude's side. The girl couldn't be more than five. Her sad silver-blue eyes met his.

"Ladies be damned!" cried Maude. She wagged an index finger at Poppy. "You sold me a fake Quested. This picture is a forgery. I have it on the best authority." Reaching into her purse, Maude pulled out papers and flung them across the desktop. "Read that, if you think I'm kidding.

166

World-class appraisers, who know a hell of a lot more than you two yokels, believe me. How stupid did you think I was, Poppy? Did you really think you could unload this piece of shit on me? Think again."

As Maude spewed venom, Wallace reached for the papers on the desktop. Studying them momentarily, he cast a frightened glance at his partner, who remained sitting, speechless.

"Mommy, Mommy! Let me go! You're hurting me!" Whining vociferously, Winston dangled heavily from her mother's taut arm.

"Let her sit over there. At the art-making station," said Wallace, continuing to read the papers.

"Go on!" said Maude sharply to the nagging child. Escaping, Winnie fled to the corner of the gallery and settled down gratefully with a piece of drawing paper and set of colored oil pastels. Poppy's gaze followed the child. Subconsciously, Wallace made note of Poppy's interest in the girl. Dropping the papers back onto the desk, he turned his attention to Maude.

"So you are accusing us of art fraud?" Wallace demanded of the willowy, irate beauty.

"I'm accusing her, not you!" Maude said brusquely.

"Poppy Craft-Talbot is my business partner. If you accuse her, you accuse me," said Wallace evenly. He was trying not to appear disturbed, even as he tried desperately to remember his attorney's phone number.

"I have no interest in you whatsoever," Maude bristled. "That little bitch tried to cheat me. It's her ass I want to fry." She aimed her words as Poppy. "I'm going to put you out of business, sweetie pie. Just you see if I don't. You'll go to jail before I'm through with you."

Distressed, Wallace waited for Poppy to defend herself. But she did not. He had never seen her so listless. Someone had to do battle with this bitch, even if Poppy wouldn't.

"Mrs. Demming," said Wallace, clearing his throat uneasily. "I'm sure this is some type of misunderstanding. Mrs. Craft-Talbot has an impeccable reputation as an art dealer. *I* have an impeccable reputation as an art dealer. At worst, this is a case of our being buffaloed long before you purchased the painting. As I recall, the provenance of the piece is pristine. However, if you'll give me a moment, I'll check our records and see where we procured the piece." *Anything to buy time.*

"Don't bother," shouted Maude. "And don't try to twist the facts. I know exactly what happened. Poppy tried to screw me out of thousands of dollars. And she nearly succeeded. But she didn't succeed because I wised up in time. I'm going to tell my husband just exactly what kind of a con artist his old *friend* is, and just exactly how much she cares about him and his family. When Heston learns the truth about her, he'll be outraged. He'll call the police, and they'll throw her in the slammer. Count on it."

Wallace threw a glance a Poppy. Ignoring Maude's melodrama, she seemed mesmerized by little Winnie playing quietly in the corner.

"You're overreacting, Mrs. Demming," Wallace commented, returning his gaze to Maude. He swept his eyes over her disparagingly.

"Overreacting?" said Maude, pencil-brows arched. As though on cue, the front door opened, and Cedric floated into the gallery.

"Chill out, y'all!" he cried, scandalized. "I could hear you from the parking lot. Oh, hello, Mrs. D.," he beamed innocently. "What's the problem?"

"Right now, he is." Maude pointed at him.

He objected quickly. "Whatever the problem is, Cedric, it's none of your business!"

"Who says?" cried Maude. "As far as I'm concerned, it's everybody's business. Wait until I tell the news services." She pointed to Poppy. "That lying witch sold me a bogus painting. A fake! A forgery!" She tapped the framed painting on the desk.

Aghast, Cedric examined the painting. "Are you sure?" he said to Maude. Cedric studied the art work closely.

"See for yourself," said Maude, flinging the appraiser's papers at him.

"Oh, my!" he muttered, examining the papers briefly. Looking up, he saw Wallace's worried expression. "Wallace, darling, can this be true?" queried Cedric, not bothering to glance at Poppy, who still sat silently gazing at the play-absorbed child. Again, the flamboyant artist picked up the painting and examined it.

"Oh, yes. I see. Oh, my—it is a forgery!" Gasping, he exchanged glances with Maude. "Oh, Poppy, baby! What were you thinking?" Cedric moaned and rolled his eyes towards the vaulted ceiling. "Another one bites the dust."

"Cut it out, Cedric," growled Wallace, really suspicious now. "Whose side are you on, anyway? If you hurt our rep, you'll end up hurting your own. This whole thing is a mistake."

"Hmmm," said Cedric, pursing his lips. Suddenly, a thought seemed to occur to him. "Madame," he said to Maude. "May I see you in the back room? Believe I may be able to put your mind at rest about this matter."

"No way," said Maude, shaking her pink-blonde head, but she followed the sensual painter as he slinked into the back room of the gallery, beyond the hearing of Wallace and Poppy.

"Watch Winston!" Maude shouted to the bodyguard by the door. The burly man nodded. Closing the door to the backroom, Cedric waved at

Wallace, who returned the wave gratefully, if suspiciously.

Quickly, Wallace dragged Poppy to her feet. Then, searching through her desk, he found her purse. Opening the purse, he fumbled through it until he located a set of car keys. Snapping the purse shut, he thrust it away and the set of keys into Poppy's limp hands.

"Go!" he whispered. "Escape while you can. Ignore the giant. Just walk out the door like you own the place. You do! I'll get to the bottom of this. Don't worry. Just get yourself lost for a while. Ditch the car as soon as you can. Go for a walk on the beach. Clear your head. And turn off your cell! Call me tonight at my place. Okay? Between Cedric and me maybe we can work this thing out. I don't know what he's got in mind, but he may be able to dissuade her from taking legal action."

"Okay, Wallace." Apparently curious, Poppy lifted the painting and examined it. She looked Wallace in the eyes. "This isn't the painting I sold Maude, Wallace. I'm sure of it."

"How can you tell?" demanded Wallace.

"I'll bet Sasha's behind this, too," whispered Poppy dazedly. "She betrayed me, Wally. Who knows what she might try to do to me. I wouldn't put anything past her."

Vehemently, Wallace shook his shiny bald head. Glancing quickly at the behemoth by the door, he whispered, "The caterer? Your little friend with the big boobs? What makes you think that? Whatever else she is, she's not smart enough for this set-up. There's a clever mind at work here. The question is who—and why?" Tearing the painting from her hands, he hustled her towards the front door.

"Go! Hurry! Ignore the limo driver, too. Just get into your car and drive!" he insisted. "She has a doctor's appointment," he smiled to the bodyguard as Poppy darted through the front door. The bodyguard made no reply, nor did he move to stop Poppy. His eyes were glued to little Winston Demming.

Relieved, Wallace watched restlessly through the window until he saw Poppy's sedan safely disappear. His mind now had cleared enough to recall his attorney's e-mail address. However, he decided to wait to make the contact. He would contact his attorney only if Cedric made no headway with Maude in the back room.

What to do in the meantime? His eyes found a focus. In the far corner, at a tiny table, pretty little Winnie sat engrossed in drawing a picture. She seemed to be talking or singing to herself. He could hear faint babbling sounds coming from her direction.

Taking a deep breath, he strolled over to where the child sat in a small cane chair and stood behind her. Feigning interest, he stared down at her chalk drawing. What he saw shocked him. The child's rendering ability was beyond her years. Winnie had drawn two figures on the paper—one huge, one miniscule.

"Who's that?" asked Wallace, pointing to the greater figure in the drawing.

Taken by surprise, Winnie inhaled quickly, and then giggled prettily as she looked up and saw Wallace looming over her.

"Mommy," Winnie explained earnestly. Wallace knelt on the floor beside the child. "Who's that?" he asked pointing to the tiny figure in the drawing.

"Winnie," said Winnie, matter-of-factly, frowning. Suddenly curious, the child stared him directly in the face, flashing a quick smile. Abruptly, she returned to her drawing. Wallace was caught off guard by the child's beauty.

She had inherited her mother's fairness and her father's features—straight blonde hair, porcelain-cream skin, silver-blue eyes, and a nose so perfect that the angels must be jealous. It was Heston Demming's hundred-watt face in feminized miniature. The reason wasn't hard to understand. Beautiful parents make beautiful children. *Them that has, gets.*

Examining Winnie's drawing more closely, he realized the nature of the drawing. Worriedly, he glanced from the drawing to the child's sweet face and back again. With one hand, he brushed a strand of Winnie's blonde hair, securing it behind her fragile ear. From the corner of his eye, he saw the bodyguard stir.

"What's that Mommy's holding in her hand?" Wallace asked gently, backing away from the child. He squatted down, addressing Winnie at her own eye level. A heavy line with many small staccato lines extending from it protruded from the Mommy figure's 'hand.'

"Grop," said Winnie carefully. She continued to draw.

Crop? "Does Mommy ride horses?"

Winnie shook her head. Grimly, he studied the drawing further. The Mommy figure had a big, jagged red circle in the middle of her face.

"Is Mommy screaming?" he asked. The girl nodded, but continued to draw. "What is Winnie doing here?" he asked, pointing to the tiny, huddled figure in the corner.

"She's dead," said Winnie, wagging her head from side to side. "She can't hear Mommy."

He ventured a guess. "Can she feel it when Mommy hits her?"

Winnie sighed in exasperation. "She's *dead.*"

"I see," he replied, stifling his revulsion. "Where's Daddy?"

"Daddy's shooting."

Horrified for a moment, he thought the child meant with a gun. Then he made the connection. "Shooting?" he asked hesitantly. "You mean shooting *a movie?*"

"*Uh-huh,*" nodded Winnie. Using a shred of charcoal, she was now coloring in black sky.

Only slightly relieved, he glanced towards the door to the back room of the gallery. Cedric had been in there with Maude for a long time. *What's going on back there? Is he making any headway with her?*

Noticing his glance towards the door, Winnie reassured him as she drew. "Don't worry," she commented. "Mommy likes Uncle Cedric. It's him you better watch out." She pointed towards the bodyguard, who, hawk-like, had been watching Wallace's every move. Crinkling her perfect nose, Winnie made a face of distaste. Stunned by the child's candor, Wallace sat upright at attention.

"Why do you call him 'Uncle Cedric,' Winnie?" he asked.

"Mommy told me to," said Winnie, patting her own forehead.

"When?" asked Wallace as casually as possible.

"When he come to see Mommy," Winnie replied. "They go away and come back."

The blood was now pounding in Wallace's ears. He felt himself suddenly alive with understanding. "Does Uncle Cedric visit your Mommy often?" he asked, picking up a broken piece of violet oil pastel and toying with it.

"Sometimes he calls her," she offered. "He called her yesterday."

"He did?"

"Yes. He told Mommy the painting was ready," she said.

"The alligator painting?" he asked carefully. He felt as though he were balancing a stack of fine china atop a tall pole.

"Yes. Uncle Cedric made another one. Mommy told him to."

He gaped at the shivering child, who sat drawing, oblivious. "She did?"

Winnie nodded. "Mommy got mad. She told me not to tell Daddy." All at once, Winnie's hand poised in mid-air. Alarmed, she dropped the piece of charcoal from her blackened fingertips. Her face became ashen. At the same moment, the door to the gallery's back room burst open. In a flash of icy heat, Maude strode determinedly out of the back room. Mincing anxiously, Cedric followed, shrugging his shoulders at Wallace, who was now back on his feet and walking towards Maude. Maude's hair was mussed, her blouse askew.

Wallace's heart was beating wildly. He was filled with conflict. On one hand, he did not want to subject the child to further maternal danger.

On the other hand, he now knew he was being conned by both Cedric and Maude, as co-conspirators. What he didn't know was why. He had no time to think, however. He would have to follow his instincts and hope for guidance.

Nervously, he ran one hand over his smooth globe of head. Then he brushed his moustache with his index finger. The familiar action anchored him.

"Well?" he asked Cedric, who glanced at Maude as she was picking up the painting and heading for the front door.

"Come along, Winston." The little girl jumped to her feet and sped towards her mother. "Where's Poppy Talbot?" demanded the young matron looking around the gallery.

As Winnie approached, her mother snatched her hand and yanked her towards the door.

Wallace saw the terror in Winnie's eyes. He longed to reassure her but felt it best, for her sake, to say nothing at the moment. In a fleeting thought, he wondered what would happen to the child when her mother discovered her hands were filthy with charcoal dust.

"Poppy was called away," he said edgily.

"*Hah!*" Maude laughed haughtily, with a withering glance at the bodyguard. "Let her run away, try to hide. It won't do her any good." Her photogenic features seemed sharp as spikes of ice.

"I'm sure the three of us can work this out," he countered, but he noticed Cedric standing by inert, hopelessly shaking his head.

"I'm working out nothing," she said adamantly. "I'm going to my husband with the truth about Poppy Talbot. Then I'm going to the police with this forgery. It's just that simple. I'll see you in court, Mr. Smythe. Shit," she sneered, "Even your name is phony."

"Please be reasonable..." Wallace began, but the haughty woman was having none of it. With the alleged fake tucked under one arm, and her daughter, Winnie, secured at the end of the other, she exited the gallery, followed by her bodyguard. Wallace's heart went with the child. As the limousine departed outside, he, inside the gallery, turned to face Cedric, who shrugged his shoulders and moved to exit himself.

"What can I say, Wallace tried to persuade her. I talked up your good reputation. I tried to convince her not to go to the authorities. It didn't work. Her mind was set. She's really steamed, I can tell you that. You and Poppy have a situation on your hands here. The situation's not all that serious. It's the bad PR that will kill your customer base. Maude Demming will broadcast Poppy's larceny to the solar system. I'll have to disassociate myself from you professionally—just until this little matter is cleared up, of course."

"Of course," he sneered, watching Cedric flee. *The proverbial rat from the sinking ship.* Or was it more sinister that that? He knew it was.

"Sorry I couldn't be more help," said Cedric, his true face veiled by sincerity.

"Why did she even bother to come here? Why didn't she go to the police first?" he asked. His mind was scoping for motives.

"To see Poppy squirm," said Cedric, his customary leer deepening. "She likes that sort of thing. It really blew Maude's mind when she came out, and Poppy was gone."

"Really?" he asked.

"Well, I suppose so," hedged Cedric, walking away casually. "I really don't know what she was feeling. I hardly know her. The only time I've ever met her was at that mansion-warming party. And at my opening, perhaps. Wasn't she there that night?" He had nearly reached the front door.

"Right-oh," said Wallace sardonically, watching him sneak away. "I forgot."

"Well, toodle-loo. Best of luck, Smythe," said Cedric, bolting out the door of the gallery.

Standing alone, Wallace let the emotional dust settle. *What a twerp,* Who'd have believed it? After all he and Poppy had done to further Cedric's career. You never knew with people. They could smile at you one minute and stab you in the back the next.

He remembered what his old grandma used to say: *Life is hard and people are mean.* He just hated it when Granny was proved right. Rural Kentucky and glamorous Naples weren't so different in one respect—human nature. That stayed true to form everywhere.

Sighing, he sat down at his computer terminal. After a moment's searching, he located an unlisted phone number, in the computer's address book, for Heston Demming. Immediately, he placed a call. A man answered the phone and identified himself as Heston's personal assistant, Upshaw.

"I need to speak with Mr. Demming. It's urgent," Wallace told Upshaw.

"May I tell him who is calling, please?" said the cultured male voice.

"Wallace Smythe. I'm calling in reference to Mr. Demming's friend, Poppy Craft-Talbot. This is a matter of great importance. It concerns Mr. Demming's family, as well."

"One moment, please." The line went dead. He waited impatiently. He wanted to beat Maude to Heston, if possible.

Heston's rich voice broke the silence.

"Smythe. What's up, my man?" he demanded. "What's this about Poppy? And my family?"

"Thank you for taking my call, Demming," said Wallace, heaving a sigh of relief. "Look, I can't talk to you about this matter over the phone. We need to meet. Now. Will you meet me at, say, Rainbow's on Fifth in twenty minutes?"

"Smythe, this all sounds obscure. Can't you just say what you need to say right now? Or come here, if you'd like. It's not that easy for me to go out in public, man."

"Listen, wear dark glasses. Wear a beard and an eye patch. I don't care how you manage it. But I've got to see you right away. I can't talk freely over the phone, and I can't come to your house. Please. Do it for Poppy."

"Is Poppy in danger?"

"You might say that. And your wife is brandishing the saber."

"I'll meet you in fifteen minutes," barked Heston, hanging up the phone. Replacing his own phone, Wallace walked to the children's art station and picked up Winnie's drawing from the low table. Shaking his head in disgust, he rolled the drawing into a scroll and secured it with a rubber band.

Chapter Twelve

"There is no easy way to say this to you, Demming," said Wallace, stirring a brimming cup of hot, spicy chai. Around him, the aromas of nutmeg and cinnamon hovered in the air. Facing the doorway, Wallace was seated at the most remote table in the far corner of Rainbow's coffee bar.

Across from him, wearing lens-free, dark-rimmed spectacles and a Marlins baseball cap sat Heston Demming, movie star incognito. He was facing the wall, his privacy protected from probing eyes. Although usually health and weight conscious, he had allowed himself the indulgence of a whole-milk cappuccino while honoring Wallace's urgent request to meet.

Wallace smiled to himself. Heston's disguise was actually fooling people. He had asked Cookie to keep her mouth shut. *So far, so good.* "You're a pretty damned good actor, by the way, to be able to pull off that get-up." *You're a hell of a lot better actor than your wife.*

A fleeting smile crossed Heston's bee-stung lips, but his piercing, silver-blue eyes were all business. "Why did you call me here? Tell me about Poppy. What's wrong? What about my family?"

Wallace slurped one sip of spicy chai and put the cup down. Such close proximity to world-class pulchritude made him feel nervous and clumsy. He didn't want to spill or knock over the cup. Both elbows on the edge of the table, he crossed his arms and leaned forward.

"Your wife is what's wrong. Your wife has openly accused Poppy of art fraud. She's going to the police. She has threatened to take Poppy to court, send her to jail."

"What?" Heston belly-laughed. "That's preposterous."

"It's the damn-straight truth. Not an hour ago, your wife burst into our gallery with an alleged forgery under her arm and started screaming accusations."

"At Poppy?"

Wallace nodded. Heston's nostrils flared in outrage.

"It's the Edd Quested watercolor, remember? *The Chartreuse Alligator,*" Wallace continued. "Your wife had sent the painting to an art appraiser—a good one. He told her—in writing, because she produced the papers—that the painting Poppy had sold her was a forgery. He said the materials—paper, paints—were of recent origin, much too recent to have been used by Quested in 1936. In other words, Heston, it was a *bad* forgery. Believe me, if Poppy or I were going to gouge the public, we would have adequate forgeries made. Maude brought the alleged forgery into our gallery."

With a nod, Heston beckoned Wallace to continue.

"Poppy knew right off it wasn't the same piece she had sold to your wife. How could it have been? The provenance of the work we handled was pristine. It couldn't have been a forgery." Wallace felt himself perspiring. He was too worked up. He took a deep breath and then another, mopping his slick pate with a monogrammed silk handkerchief.

"Where is Poppy now?" asked Heston, his brow furrowed beneath the stiff brim of his Marlins cap.

"I sent her packing, when Maude was in the back room talking with Cedric," answered Wallace. "Cedric was trying to talk sense into her—so he claimed."

"Cedric? You mean that sleazy psycho painter who came to my party?" asked Heston.

"Yea, verily," said Wallace, adding, "Sleazy to you, perhaps, but highly regarded and well-connected in artistic circles."

"He and Maude seemed pretty chummy that night, as I recall," Heston murmured.

"Your daughter was with Maude when she visited the gallery just now," said Wallace knowingly. "Maude was dragging her around by the hand."

"My little Winner?" said Heston, alerted. "Is she all right?"

Wallace pursed his lips. "That depends on what you mean by 'all right.' That's part of what I need to tell you. Look, I'm just going to spill this, if it's okay with you."

"Please do."

"I believe your wife is up to something. Poppy Craft-Talbot would never stoop to art fraud. She has a great reputation as an art dealer. She would never jeopardize our gallery by any shady dealings. She's strictly above-board when it comes to business. No, if you want my opinion, I think your wife has a plan and is working it. What, I don't know. What I'm not sure of—is *why.*"

"What the hell are you getting at, man?" Heston was growing concerned. "Where's Poppy now? Where's my daughter?"

Throat scratchy, Wallace chanced another sip of chai. His cup of the spice-flavored milk-tea beverage had cooled somewhat. "I hurried Poppy out of the gallery. I told her to get in her car and lose herself, to go for a walk on the beach, to turn off her cell. I told her to call me tonight. I'm worried about her, though. She was acting strangely, even before your wife came in."

"Strange? How?"

"Kind of hazy, gloomy—it's hard to describe. When Maude accused her of selling her a forgery, Poppy didn't even blink. That's unusual. Normally, that kind of thing would have her up on hind legs, fighting. Instead, she babbled rubbish about Sasha, her little friend with the big rack."

"Sasha Bassett?" Suddenly, Heston seemed alarmed.

"Is that significant?" quizzed Wallace.

"It could be. So you really don't know where Poppy is?" Heston sounded worried.

Wallace shook his head. "I wanted to get Poppy out of the gallery. I was hoping that Cedric would talk sense into your wife. He didn't. She came out of that back room just as hot as when she went in. Maybe more so. She yelled that she was going to tell *you* about Poppy's treachery. Then she was going to the police. She threatened Poppy with ruin—and me, by association, although she claimed to have no gripe with me. But I told her that what affects Poppy affects me. I have a dog in this fight, Demming."

"Obviously. What about my daughter?" Heston asked, anxiety erupting, no longer subterranean. Reluctantly, Wallace drew the rolled up sheet of paper from his briefcase, which was sitting on the floor beside his chair. Sliding the rubber band from the rolled paper, he unfurled Winston's drawing and handed it to her father, who studied it quizzically. Sighing, Wallace expounded on the drawing's significance.

"While your wife was in the back, talking with Cedric, I spoke with your daughter. Winnie was sitting in our kiddie corner. You know, in our gallery we have a place for children to entertain themselves while their parents browse the merchandise. Well, your daughter was busy drawing. I went over to her, talked to her, very low, so the bodyguard couldn't hear."

"He's history," remarked Heston, eyes glued to Winnie's rendering.

"She was drawing this huge, threatening Mommy figure with screaming red lips. The Mommy figure is brandishing a weapon. Your daughter called it a 'grop.' The thing is bigger even than Mommy. See here? Here she's drawn herself as a tiny figure lying in a sleeping position. She told me she was dead. In other words, she couldn't feel anything Mommy did to her. Mind you, I'm no art therapist. This is strictly my take on the drawing."

Heston's silver-blue glare mirrored the rage still smoldering below. Folding up the drawing, he pocketed it, his furor contained but volatile.

Wallace continued, "Forgive me. I hate to be the bearer of bad news.

But it's something you need to know, for your own sake and for your daughter's sake, too. But I need to tell you what else she told me. And this is hard because I feel like I'm betraying the kid's confidence. I don't want to put her in harm's way. You understand what I'm saying?"

Heston's expression was pained. "I think I'm beginning to," he confessed.

"I wouldn't tell you this if it weren't absolutely necessary. I have to prevent a miscarriage of justice."

"Out with it," commanded Heston. His cappuccino now sat untouched on the table top.

"Okay. Winnie told me—in so many words—that she had overheard her mother talking on the phone yesterday with 'Uncle Cedric'." Wallace felt Heston wince but went on. "Winnie overheard her mommy telling Uncle Cedric to have a copy made of the 'alligator painting'."

Heston sighed heavily. He chewed the nail of an index finger.

Wallace narrowed his eyes. "It gets worse. Winnie told me that Mommy had threatened her with—well, with a beating or worse, I gathered—if she told Daddy what she had overheard. In fact, when Winnie realized that she'd told me, the color drained from her little face and she looked scared to death. Soon after that, your wife dragged her out to the limo." Wallace waited in silence as Heston digested the bitter truth.

"You're saying my wife abuses my daughter behind my back," the beautiful man said, his words more a statement of fact than a question.

"When I asked Winnie where Daddy was during the beatings, she said, 'Shooting'." Wallace looked at him with regret. "Shooting a movie."

A surge of anguish gushed from Heston Demming, but Heston clenched his jaw to stop it.

Wallace now knew that the star had had suspicions of his own. *Poor fellow.*

"Do you know where they are now—my wife and daughter, I mean?"

"No. Only that your wife was on her way to tell you about Poppy's supposed subterfuge. Then to the police. Look, it would be an easy matter for Cedric to arrange for a forgery. What's not so easy to get one's mind around is *why* he would do it."

"Why anything?" said Heston cynically. "Money. Or ..." Heston stopped before saying the word. Across the table, Wallace lowered his eyes and fingered the cold cup of chai. "But you mean why target Poppy specifically." Heston pondered in a half-whisper. "It doesn't make any sense."

Tactfully, Wallace cleared his throat. "It does, if you consider one thing. Perhaps your wife sensed that you were *too fond* of our Poppy. After all, Poppy was your steady girlfriend at one time. Perhaps your wife enlisted Cedric's aid and, between the two of them, they cooked up this scheme to take Poppy out of the picture—if you'll pardon the pun."

Heston grimaced. "It's true. Poppy Craft and I do have a history. Do you believe Maude sees Poppy as my Wife Number Three?" he queried, agape. "As competition for access to my money?"

Wallace cocked his head sideways. *You said it, I didn't.* "It's possible. Your wife seems shrewd to me. Maybe she noticed there was something deep between you and Poppy, something even you aren't aware of. The two of you do act a bit "moony" when you're together. Frankly, I noticed that Poppy began behaving oddly right around the time you first showed up here again."

"You think?" Unconsciously, Heston removed his lens-free spectacles, rubbed the bridge of his nose between thumb and forefinger, and then pinned Wallace with his gaze. "Wallace, I don't want the police involved in this matter at all. I will handle it myself," he said decisively. "The first thing—the thing I *must* do—is to find Maude and Winnie." Abruptly, he rose to his feet and handed Wallace a card from his wallet.

"Here's my cell number. Give me yours. I'll contact you as soon as I've cornered my wife. Your job is to locate Poppy ASAP. I'll search for her, too, after I've dealt with Maude. All clear?"

"Absolutely," said Wallace, complying. "As long as you realize it's my butt, too."

"I understand full well. And I'm grateful that you came to me first. Listen, if you talk to Poppy before I do, please tell her how sorry I am for this situation. And tell her not to worry." Sliding his spectacles back across his nose, Heston began to move away. Staring upward from his seat, Wallace marveled at the film idol's tall, slim physique.

"Oh, one more thing," Wallace clamped a hand on the actor's muscle-hard arm, stopping him briefly. "A word of advice—I'd beware of Cedric Spicer, regardless. He's a real stinker."

"Got it," muttered Heston fiercely, easing his arm away. As the actor trod briskly away, Wallace fanned himself with his handkerchief. Relieved, he scrubbed his shiny scalp and then, using his right forefinger, fluffed his moustache.

What comes next? Telling the man his wife is a cheating sadist? More fun than a root canal. But not until I'm sure.

That evening, alone at the gallery, Wallace paced the floor. Nearly five hours had elapsed since he had hustled Poppy out the front door of the art gallery. Three and a half hours since he and the hunk had parted company at Cookie's.

Wallace was worried. Indeed, he was growing frantic. He had searched for Poppy everywhere. He had called all the numbers. She was nowhere to be found, not even in the emergency room of the Naples Central Hospital. He was up in the air about everything. As yet, he had heard nothing from Heston. On the other hand, he had had no contact from the police, either.

No new is good news? Easy to say when you're not the one sweating it out.

Suddenly, his cell phone rang. His heart leapt. He grabbed the cell with gusto.

"Hello?" he squeaked, then cleared his throat.

"Wally?"

Wallace clutched his chest. "Heston? Yes, 'tis I. What's happening on your end?

The rich voice came back loud, clear, and confident. "Before I fill you in, any word from Poppy? I've tried to phone her. IM her. Even tried to e-mail her. I get no response."

"Nothing here, either. It's still early. Only six p.m. or thereabouts. She may yet call," Wallace said doubtfully. He wouldn't be so worried if she hadn't been lackadaisical. A random thought occurred to him. *What if she had been on drugs?*

"I'll look for her myself," Heston assured him over the phone. "I know where she sometimes goes. On the beach. A place we used to meet in high school. I ran into her there the other morning."

A secret rendezvous spot? At least Wallace knew that his instincts had been right on. But, worried as he was about Poppy, his mind was aching to know about the relationship between Cedric and Maude.

"Heston!" he barked. "Did you speak with your wife yet?"

"Yes. We had it out, she and I—a terrific row."

"What happened? What did she say?"

"Don't worry, Wally. You're in the clear. Poppy's in the clear. Everything is taken care of—well, almost everything. It's my daughter I'm worried about now. I don't want to say too much on the phone. I'm on a land line right now, but you're probably on a cell. A man in my position can't be too careful."

"No, I'm not using a cell. I'm on a land line, too. Please give me the scoop," Wallace begged eagerly. The full story broke from Heston's lips like water from a dam.

"Suffice it to say that I drove home and found my wife's limo just pulling into the driveway. Real quick, I grabbed Winnie and carried her into the house. Once alone, I asked Winnie to repeat her story, which she did, very reluctantly, wailing, howling, poor little kid. I had to lock the door to keep Maude out. She kept pounding on the door and rattling the knob. But Winnie told me what I needed to know.

"Then I handed Winnie over to Lissette, our maid, with strict instructions to keep the child away from Mrs. Demming. Then I confronted Maude about the forgery. That's when we had the big fight. The upshot was, I threatened her with the police if she didn't recant her story about Poppy's selling her a fake.

"I told Maude I would personally see to it that Poppy pressed charges against her and Spicer for attempt to defraud. I don't know if that's possible, but it sure scared the dickens out of the woman." Heston chuckled bitterly. "I've had Winnie sent to an undisclosed location. Maude is furious. She's tearing through the house like a tornado. She's threatening me with court proceedings if I keep the child away from her. Let her shriek and tear her hair. I wouldn't let Winnie near her now if she were dying."

In the gallery, Wallace was still clutching at his chest. He felt faint with exhaustion and relief. "Good job Demming," he said, breathing heavily.

"So our only problem now is Poppy's whereabouts.".

"And how best to put the screws to Cedric," grinned Wallace maliciously. "In a manner of speaking." He heard the movie star snort.

"That, too. Listen, if I don't find Poppy, or don't hear from you later tonight, I'll come by the gallery in the morning. She might show up there. There's a lot Poppy and I have get straight between us. Not just this situation."

"I know you've had a rough time lately, Heston. Your only son dying and all. The odious inquest. All that nasty publicity. I hated to, but I *had* bring you on board with this abuse situation. You understand?"

"Of course I do, Wallace. Listen, get some rest, my friend—if you can."

"Call me if you hear anything, guy. No matter what the time."

"Same here, buddy. And thanks."

***

Three hours later, Heston squinted irritably into the darkness at his illuminated Swiss wrist watch: Nine. He had missed his dinner, and Poppy was nowhere to be found

What to do? Hunched over the steering wheel of his red Ferrari, he stared through the windshield, out into the blackness of night. No stars shone. A cloud blanketed the sky. In the distance, the surf was pounding. He could smell the salt air. After an exhausting search for Poppy, in every place he could think of to look, he had driven, despondent, to the beach at Seventh Avenue North and parked his car.

He was frantic about Poppy. At the same time, he was driven by his protective feelings for her. The knowledge that she had borne his son, so many years ago, had revolutionized his emotional life. *Everything had changed.* And now, here she was missing and possibly lost. If anything ever happened to her because of Maude—because of his bringing Maude here—he would never forgive himself.

In the darkness, his cell phone rang. Reaching into his breast pocket, Heston extracted the cell. "Hello?" he said hopefully, a frog in his throat.

"Good news, my man," said the now-familiar voice of Wallace Smythe. "I've located Poppy. She's at home now. She phoned. She's okay. I gave her your message, and she said to tell you she will see you tomorrow morning at the gallery."

"Fantastic, Wallace! Thanks so very, very much for letting me know. Where was she? Did she say?" he yelped.

"Haven't a clue, dear boy," Wallace replied. "All I know is that she's safe and sound now."

He closed his eyes in swift, silent prayer. "Thanks, again, Smythe," he said. "I owe you one."

"Relax. She's safe. Goodnight, Heston." The cell phone went dead.

For a few moments, he sat in silence, soaking in the precious information given him by his caller. He felt the relief from worry break over him like soothing rain from an ominous cloud. He had been much too worried about Poppy. He could admit it now.

Tomorrow he would see her, talk to her, confront her about their son. He felt warm blood rush into his cheeks as he remembered how he had behaved the last time he had seen her. But he had been so stunned, so embarrassed, so overcome by her revelation. Tomorrow he would talk to her about their son. Tomorrow he would formulate words. He clenched his jaw in anticipation. He chewed a nail.

He felt his empty stomach rumble. *Dinner time.* Starting the car's ignition, he began to drive away from the beach, and then poised his foot on the brake. Again he extracted the cell phone and pressed a key. He heard three rings. Then a female voice answered.

"Montserrat?" he said into the phone.

"Heston?" she answered, seemingly pleased to hear from him. "Where have you been these past few days? It's good to hear from you."

"I know this is spur-of-the-moment, but would you like to grab some dinner?" he asked.

"I've already had dinner, silly boy. It's late."

"Then meet me for a drink. Half and hour. The Starfish Grille."

"Well..."

"Give me a break, Montsey. Just be there. We need to talk." Exasperated, he rang off abruptly. He was in no mood for her catch-and-release games tonight.

***

Driving steadily through the dark, damp streets of Naples, Heston examined his options. He could give his mistress an ultimatum—become his, exclusively and permanently, or forget about a relationship with him altogether. Or, he could tell her about his son with Poppy and ask her to share only a slice of his life, however best she chose, since he was not a free man, even less so now. Or, he could be blatant, tell her he was in love with someone else, someone not his current wife.

Did I just say that? What a frigging mess. I don't even know what I want.

Raindrops plopped onto the windshield, as he drove past the Naples Central Hospital. Seeing the pink, box-shaped building brought back painful memories of his mother, who had worked there as a nurse. Remembering, he rested his auto at the red light on the corner if Seventh Avenue North and the Tamiami Trail. Unconsciously, he revved the car's engine, and then idled it. Mindlessly, he turned on the wipers and then turned them off again.

Rain, damn it, don't rain. Make up your frigging mind.

In the rear-view mirror, he saw sheet lightening flash in the big, black clouds over the Gulf. Bitterly, his roaming thoughts settled on his two wives. Maude, he could not even contemplate without fury; Inez, without guilt. Tomorrow he would see Winnie safely out of Maude's clutches for good. Inez's agony was more difficult to resolve. Would she ever recover from their son Franco's death? *Will I ever recover?* Warm, stinging liquid filled his eyes. The red and then green of the changing traffic light blurred in his vision. Flooring the accelerator, he turned northward onto the Trail. Speeding along US 41, he wiped his eyes with the back of his wrist, and then wiped his wrists on his slacks. He had forgotten he was wearing leather driving gloves.

Like a shooting star, he realized all at once what he wanted right now, this very night. He wanted to know, once and for all, how Montserrat Flynn really felt about him. He wanted to know where he stood with her. What's more, he wanted to know where she stood with him. Because he wasn't sure anymore. Poppy had turned his world upside down.

Thirty-minutes later, he found himself seated in a booth at the seafood restaurant. Sipping a vodka gimlet, Montserrat Flynn was seated across the table from him. In the dim evening light, she seemed slinky and elegant. Wearing a low-cut, sleeveless, black cocktail dress, she had floated in, a few minutes earlier, on a cloud of his favorite perfume. Now she smiled at him engagingly, her wide mouth a slash of vivid scarlet promise. No matter what else happened in his life, he would always remember her beauty, even after–especially after–it had faded forever.

A server approached the table. Looking embarrassed, the wiry man bent low and spoke into Heston's ear. "Excuse me, Mr. Demming. The ladies at the bar would like your autograph. Plus, they'd like to buy you a drink–non-alcoholic, of course, sir."

Swiveling his head, Heston beheld a gaggle of middle-aged females seated around the granite-faced bar. When he looked their way, the women giggled and waved. Beckoning the server, he spoke into the wiry man's ear. "Tell the ladies 'no thank you' to the drink. Tell them I'm buying them a drink. But here, give them this first." Quickly, he slashed his autograph across a loose page from the menu. Handing the signed page to the server, then added, "Then bring me a tonic water on the rocks with lime–and put it on my tab." He made a circling motion with his hand.

"Good for you, Mr. Demming," grinned the wiry server. Bowing, the server took the autographed menu page from Heston and delivered it, along with Heston's message, to the eager, swarm of matronly barflies.

"Thank you, Heston!" the ladies cried loudly, waving.

"Damn it," growled Heston. "Everybody knows my personal business, even runty waiters in seafood restaurants."

"They know I'm not your wife," observed Montserrat, glancing coolly at his giddy fans. "Think I'll make the tabloids? Last time you and I slept together–five years ago–you weren't quite the news fodder you are today, Heston."

He grunted. At the moment, he did not care what the world thought. He did not care about propriety or publicity. He now cared only about nourishing his starving soul.

Across the table, Montsey sat gloating. "Still it's nice," she purred, "to be out with the most desirable man in the world."

"Third most desirable," he noted sardonically.

Ignoring his comment, she frowned. "Nice, but not so nice, too. A girl can never relax." Eyes lowered, she swilled her drink. She smiled mysteriously to herself

"What do you mean, relax?" he snorted. "You're the chase-ee. I'm the chaser, remember? I'm the one who's done all the work all these years."

"Maybe, I've changed," Montserrat said, out of nowhere.

"Excuse me?" he demanded, widening his eyes in disbelief.

With a bejeweled finger, his mistress traced a drop of moisture on the table top. "Heston, sweetheart, what if I said I had changed my mind about you? Suppose I said I want to marry you at last? How would you feel? Would you divorce your wife?" She cocked her head prettily, auburn hair draping her alabaster shoulders in thick waves.

To his own surprise, he balked. *Why?* Wasn't this the moment he had prayed for all his life? Yet, now he didn't want it. He stammered a reply.

"*Uh*, well, *um*, I guess I...Listen, Montsey, let's not go there right now. Things are too intense. I just want to talk. I need a sounding board. A lot has been happening to me, and I can't confide in my wife. Hell, it's about my wife. Would you mind if I just get a few things off my chest? Be my friend."

Her wide, red mouth drooped into a sensual pout. "If you must," she acquiesced laconically, adjusting her seat for the long haul. Bracing her back against the wall, she stretched one leg along the cushioned seat of the booth.

Damn it. As usual, he had slammed up against the roadblock of her careless heart. How desperately he had tried, over the years, to engage her in his life's interests. But she would have none of it. For years, Monsey's lack of interest in his affairs had not mattered to him. It had hurt him, yes, but all he had really needed was to be close to her. Now, suddenly, that wasn't enough anymore.

Now I need to communicate.

Staring at the middle-aged woman across the table from him, he had an epiphany. He would *never* be able to communicate with Montserrat Flynn. It was as simple as that.

He could let go now. Montserrat Flynn was a fantasy he had been dragging around all these years, but she was just that–a fantasy. It was the fantasy he had loved, not the real woman. In truth, he did not even like the real woman very much.

Montserrat Flynn was egotistical and arrogant, shallow and self-absorbed. The real Montserrat was in love with herself. Worse, the sex, for him, had become mechanical. *Without fire in the soul, what is the point?* He felt the desperation go out of him. He felt himself sinking into the peace of acceptance.

Altering his strategy, he reclined in the booth and accepted a lime tonic from the wiry server. "Want to tell me about your day, Montserrat?"

Her oval face brightened. "Absolutely. I want to tell you about the interview I conducted today. I had lunch with one of the biggest real-estate developers in the area. He was really a fascinating man. Do you know what type of huge project he's developing next?"

"No. And, frankly, I don't care," he said resignedly, and then bolted tonic water from his cocktail glass. "I hope he gets his ass kicked by Mother Nature."

"You're always so rude, Heston, whenever I want to talk," she whined petulantly, sitting up straight.

"And you're always so critical, Montserrat, about every blasted thing I do or say." His empty glass rattled as he dropped it onto the table top. Exhaling forcefully, he stood up and flung down his napkin. He signaled the server for the check. "I'm sorry, Montsey. It's just not working for me anymore. I have to go."

"Go?"

"Listen, can you get yourself home all right? I'm sorry to leave you hanging like this, but...hey... 'Turnabout is fair play.' Who said that, anyway?" he smiled without humor. "You've got your car here, right?"

She nodded slowly. "Yes, but..."

"Okay. Great. I'll see you." He bent and kissed her gently on the crown of her head.

"Will you call me?" she asked, aghast, watching him walk backwards down the aisle on his way out of the restaurant. The nearby gaggle of barflies watched his movement raptly. Others patrons, suddenly cognizant that a movie star was in their midst, spun around agog at the sound of the world-famous voice.

"I don't know," he called to Montserrat across the restaurant. He raised his hands, palms up, in uncertainty.

"You never answered my question!" she called in return.

"I'm answering it now," he cried sadly, voice breaking. "As usual, Montserrat, you're just not hearing me." Spinning on his heel, he rapidly exited the Starfish for the safety of his favorite Ferrari.

Jumping into the front seat and firing the engine, he congratulated himself. Now he knew one thing for certain. He would make no plans for his future—not until he had talked to Poppy, tomorrow morning, and to the Bassett woman's private investigator tomorrow afternoon. Andrew Upshaw had scheduled the appointment with the private dick for 2:00 p.m.

Roaring out of the parking lot, he felt a twinge of guilt. Unquestionably, it was lousy of him to leave Montsey in the lurch, but he had no major qualms. She had led him on a merry chase for twenty years. *Time's up, baby.*

Sliding his hands, one by one, into the leather driving gloves, he drove slowly towards his mansion in Port Royal. The night sky was clear now. The storm had passed at last.

Chapter Thirteen

"Here he comes!" Wallace hissed to Poppy, darting away from the front window of the gallery. "The Ferrari just pulled up in the parking lot."

Poppy felt the breath go out of her. She couldn't move. Her limbs felt heavy. Approaching, Wallace took her by the elbow and guided her to her desk chair.

"Okay, girl, chill. Take deep breaths. That's right," he prompted paternally.

Breathing slowly and deeply, Poppy struggled for emotional control. She wished she were more prepared for this meeting with Heston, but she wasn't. The biggest moment in her life, next to giving birth, and she was in danger of passing out. Her heart was fluttering. Her palms were sweaty. Her mind was racing. What would she say to him? What would he say to her?

No matter what happened, she knew she looked good. She had dressed carefully before arriving for work, and she had primped all morning between customers. At home, she had decided upon a teal-colored day-dress with spaghetti straps. Her beaded shoes were open-toed French heels. Once at work, Wallace had teased her about dolling up for her boyfriend.

Let him. An off-hand comment Heston had made more than twenty years ago had surfaced in her brain. "I know high heels are uncomfortable," he had remarked, "but they sure make women's legs look great."

As a teenager, to please then-boyfriend Heston, she had compromised and worn short French heels to the junior prom. Wallace realized she hadn't worn shoes other than flats in all the years he'd known her, and he had been vocal about the fact all morning.

She had been forced to laugh at herself. She felt grateful to Wally. He had been trying to help ease her tension. If he hadn't distracted her, sheer panic would have seized her.

Now, through the big glass window pane, she peered, spellbound. She watched Heston's tall, lean figure striding through the parking lot, crossing the thoroughfare, and stepping up onto the sidewalk. He was coming closer. His hand was reaching for the door handle. He was opening the shop door. He walked into the gallery.

His eyes met hers and held.

There are magical moments, heightened moments in time which become solidified in memory, as psychic energy becomes solidified in art. For Poppy, this moment of psychic union with Heston instantly became substance. It became part of her, a part which would never leave her. This sudden feeling of linking, of bonding, would stay with her forever, a treasured thing to be taken out and caressed tenderly in her waning years. She had borne his son. He knew it. And he loved her for it. Of that, she was suddenly certain.

"Come in, sir. Welcome," said Wallace graciously. "We've been expecting you." Trotting up to the tall, handsome actor, he ushered him into the large room. Across the room a few customers, evidently tourists, were browsing, but none appeared to be a serious buyer. Even so, Wallace excused himself, after politely ushering Heston into Poppy's presence, and departed to speak with the shoppers. In silent reverie, Heston stood warmly contemplating Poppy in strappy teal.

Her mind had gone blank. She could think of nothing to say, nothing befitting the momentousness of the occasion. Shoving his hands into his pants pockets, Heston struck a casual pose. For a moment, his eyes left her and roamed the room. Then they found her again. Despite his suave manner, his eyes grew apprehensive. He licked his lips.

"Hi," he said, at last.

"H-hi," she responded softly. Strangely, she felt awkward, yet completely at home. She grinned shyly. "I tried to find you," she ventured. "Did you have that drink?"

"No, I didn't, actually. But I sure could use one now" he joked, shifting his weight.

"You and me both," she giggled. Charmed, Heston laughed aloud. "W-w-would you like to go in the back?" she asked him, tossing her eyes at the annoying tourists.

"Sure," he said, biting his lower lip in anticipation. Removing his hands from his trouser pockets, he followed her to the back of the shop. Entering the backroom, she closed the door behind him. As she turned back to face him, he came forward and took her in his embrace. With infinite tenderness, he held her to him, and she melted into his being, enveloped in the orange-myrrh maleness that had haunted her dreams for twenty years.

He was everything and more, everything she had ever wanted, everything she had ever had, everything she had ever lost. He was her childhood playmate, her natural soul mate, her star-destined lover. There could be no other answer—not in this lifetime. Legally, he belonged to someone else;

but even if he would never be hers in the eyes of society, he *was* hers in the only way that mattered.

Pushing her away gently, he touched his fingers to her chin. Searching her eyes, he lifted her mouth to his. Then, he kissed her softly on the lips, then again, then, as she yielded, he kissed her deeply and profoundly, in a kiss that claimed her for his own, at last.

Memories came flooding back to her as she tasted the kiss of her teen-aged lover. All the old passion, the wild desire, now coupled with a strange, new mature yearning, a desperate yearning born of need, sorrow, suffering, and experience. It wasn't over. What was between her and Heston would never be over, not so long as she had breath in her body, and beyond. She knew she would feel this away into eternity.

At last, his kisses spent, he held her fast. "I had to know," he said. "How you felt."

"Now you know," she mumbled, burying her face in his shoulder.

"I tried to find you last night," he whispered. She felt his hand on the back of her head. "I looked everywhere, even on the beach. Where were you?"

Embarrassed, she pressed her forehead to his chest. "I was at home, with the lights turned out and the cell turned off. I was watching your movies." She began to weep.

"Oh, honey," he said, pushing her back and smoothing her hair. "No, don't. Don't cry. It's okay. Everything is okay now. You don't have to worry about Maude and her BS anymore. I've taken care of it. She won't bother you again, I promise. Honestly, if I didn't think it would be all over the tabloids, I'd punch her lights out."

"No, Heston!" Poppy wept, protesting sloppily.

"Oh, not really. But how I want to. I can't tell you," he laughed, bitter and hostile.

"And you're not angry at me?" Poppy said in the smallest of voices.

"About what?"

"About our…baby?"

"Oh, no, my sweet, no, no, not at all, far from it," he exhaled, wrapping his arms around her and kissing the top of her head. "No, it's wonderful."

"You're not angry that I didn't tell you about it? Back then, when it happened."

"Angry? No. Saddened. That's what. Oh, how I wish I had known. I wish you had told me then. Why didn't you tell me, Poppy?" He had drawn her to him tightly and was holding her fast. She felt nearly crushed by the strength in his muscular arms. She wanted to be crushed. She ached to be crushed.

"I wanted to, but Uncle Mel said no. He became furious. He started raving when he found out. He found out by accident. I tried to make an appointment at a free clinic. There were no pregnancy tests for sale in stores back then. Uncle Mel heard me on the phone. He slapped me. He demanded to know why I thought I was pregnant. He forced me to tell him I'd missed my cycle. He demanded to know who the father was. I wouldn't tell him. He guessed, but I never confirmed it. Not until the day of Noel's birth. By then, Uncle Mel had calmed down. He was still cold towards me, but he was past violence. And by then, you were long gone, Heston. You had moved away." Poppy's tears had ceased flowing as she told her story.

Cradling her in his arms. Heston rested his cheek upon the crown of her head. "Noel?" he asked tentatively. Her body flinched at the name. He held her tighter.

"I gave him a name. Our baby was a boy. Noel. I named him Noel because he had been conceived at Christmastime."

"Christmas time?" Heston whispered. "Oh, yes. The night you and I spent together in the captain's berth. On *Lover's Folly,* when we put in at Shark River. That *was* the night before Christmas Eve, wasn't it?"

"Yes. Later on, up on deck, we watched the sun come up together. All alone."

"I remember. That day Captain Mackay had let me take her out for a joy ride. You made a fine first mate. Late that afternoon, the weather turned foul." His eyebrows met as he reminisced.

Poppy sighed. "We had to wait out the storm, alone on that sailboat, miles from civilization, surrounded by the Everglades and the Gulf." The old feelings and images seemed all too real. Poppy shivered. "It was frightening–but wonderful."

"By the early morning hours, the sky had cleared," he said. "We put out to sea. Remember how magical it was just before dawn? No lights anywhere." The silver-blues sparkled.

"'Just starlight on saltwater,' you said, Heston, 'like the dawn of creation'."

He squeezed her arm to end the fancy. "Noel Demming, eh? Did you know there is a private eye searching for our child now? Little Miss Bassett hired him."

"She told me," said Poppy, anger in her voice. *I forced it out of her.*

"I doubt if the boy goes by that name now. If he's still alive. You should be prepared for the worst, Poppy. Anything could have happened to Noel. It's been twenty years."

"Yes. I know."

"I have an appointment with the detective this afternoon. I'm taking charge of the investigation. I want it all to be hush-hush."

Gently, Poppy pushed him away. She looked up into his famous face. "You do?"

"It will be better for everyone concerned, Poppy. For now, at any rate. Had you given any thought to going to the adoption agency yourself?"

Startled, Poppy inhaled. "No."

"Just as well. I'd rather keep this quiet, as long as possible." He threw his arms around her and hugged her once more for good measure. "Good Ole Uncle Mel," he rasped in a faux Southern accent while holding her protectively. Releasing her, he added. "I told you, he hated my guts. I'm surprised he didn't come after me with a shotgun."

"Mel had his first heart attack not long after I gave birth," explained Poppy. "He wasn't in the best of shape. Hadn't been for years. At the end, he became an invalid."

"Really?"

"He went into a nursing home in Tampa. Melvin died eight years ago. That's when I married James Talbot."

"A rebound of sorts. Been there, done that. What about you? If you attended the Ringling School, you must have finished high school first."

"In Tampa."

"Oh. So you came back to Naples after college?"

"Yes. I was hired by a gallery on Third Street South. And met James one night at an opening reception. You forget that I'm still a married woman."

"I haven't forgotten. Not for a moment. How's your marriage going?" asked Heston pointedly. "What's your current status?"

"Still separated. I want out, but I feel so guilty about it. I vowed a lifetime of fidelity. James doesn't want out, so far as I know."

Heston moved away from her. As always, his absence left a void around her. Her knees felt weak. To stay upright, she clung to the marble counter top which held the coffee maker and small refrigerator. She could hear the refrigerator humming. Her eyes swept the length of Heston's tall, sinewy form. His sport clothes were expensive and elegant. His grooming was now immaculate, except for the pair of favorite scruffy deck shoes on his feet.

Too handsome to be real. Am I still dreaming? Poppy pinched her own inner forearm.

"This thing with Maude—I hate it that it happened," He said with his back to her. Then he wheeled around, his face twisted in bitterness. "I've told Maude I won't stand for any more, Poppy. I threatened her with the police if she ever tries to hurt you again." His gaze fell to the floor. An amused little smile lit his lips. He looked at her. "Silly woman. She got it into her head that I am in love with you."

Poppy flushed. "With me? Not with Montserrat Flynn?"

His face grew serious. "No, not with Montserrat. My wife, Maude, isn't a total fool. She was shrewd enough to realize my true feelings before I did."

"You're not in love with Montsey anymore?" Poppy said in her smallest voice.

Virility so potent it has a life of its own.

Assertively, he drew her to him. He held her hands in his. "I never was," he confessed. "I only thought I was. Infatuation," he quipped theatrically, "the cruel sister of true love. No, it's over between me and The Lady Flynn. I won't be seeing her again."

Poppy was aghast. "Ever?"

"Ever."

His words were more than Poppy could take in. *This is too good to be true. I must be dreaming.* "What about your first wife–Inez?" she asked, pushing the envelope. His strong fingers were like points of lightning on her skin.

"All my fault," he muttered, fondling her hands in his. "I've destroyed her life. I owe her something."

"Inez destroyed yours years ago," she noted defensively. "You bounced back." Dropping her hands, he stepped back in consternation "I'm morally responsible for the death of her son, Poppy–and mine. That's not a small matter."

Chagrined, she conceded the truth. "I didn't mean it that way. I'm sorry. I understand how you must feel about Franco's death. I only meant that, well, Inez didn't want you when you were a starving actor."

"Ouch."

"Inez cut you loose, Heston. Once you became rich and famous, she changed her tune. Now she brags about you. Years ago she scorned you. I know. I heard her. I remember how she was and how she talked about you." *Inez laughed at you.*

"For real?"

"Back in the day, whenever I ran into Inez socially or on business, she always made sure to remind me that you had dumped me, but that you weren't good enough for her. It's not that I don't have compassion for her loss now. I do. I just don't want you getting false notions of debts owed. Do you understand me?"

He pursed his lips. "Yes." Stepping towards her, he embraced her again, tenderly, this time. "You're good for me," he said, inhaling the fragrance of her hair. "I *would* have married you, Poppy. I *would* have been a father to our son. At any rate, I like to believe I would have. I wanted you for my wife when I was just a boy."

Drawing her near again, he nuzzled her neck. "What's that they say? Trust your first instincts? I wish I came home to you every night, instead of to Malevolent Maude." He winced at his own words. "Does that sound like betrayal? You have no idea how many times I've had to rescue the woman from her own evil deeds—just in the five short years since we wed."

"Poor Heston."

"Talk about bait and switch. Once she and I married, Maude let her true nature shine forth. I had no idea I'd married a female version of the Marquis de Sade."

"No!" gasped Poppy with a giggle.

He nodded, less than amused. "Maude kept the whips and chains in the cellar. She only brought them out after the ring was on her finger and the preacher had been paid. And that's just the tip of the iceberg. My wife has what they call a 'checkered past.' Her PR guy's a genius. He's kept it all mum."

"Incredible." Her amusement had faded.

"Critics call my wife a bad actress. But she sure fooled me."

"Poor little Winnie," muttered Poppy. She rested tenuously in his arms.

"Damn straight," he said, worried. "I don't know what the hell to do about it. I have Winnie under wraps right now. I've been an oblivious fool for too long. Listen, Red," he said earnestly. "I've told Maude to shape up or I'll divorce her. I don't know where things stand right now. I have my daughter to consider. Do you understand me, Poppy? Can you handle this—working things out, I mean? Letting it ride? I'm still trying to figure out how—and where—Maude and Cedric Spicer had the forged painting made. I don't like it that my daughter's mother was involved in a criminal conspiracy. Once I find that ambidextrous sewer rat, Spicer, I'll..."

"Yes, I can handle it," said Poppy demurely, putting her index finger to his lips. Then, cupping his jaw in her hands, she rose on tiptoe and drew his face down to hers. A deep, open-mouthed kiss sealed the bargain.

"Like starlight on salt water," whispered Heston huskily, coming up for air. "I don't know where we're headed, Poppy, but there's no turning back now."

"I don't want to turn back."

"Good." He bent to kiss her again.

"Heston?"

"What?"

"I'm glad you didn't have that drink. I'm proud of you."

"Me, too, Red. Thanks. "

***

That afternoon Wallace sat idly in Rainbow's on Fifth. After a late lunch alone, he now was waiting for Heston to arrive as planned. When his cell phone rang, he answered it.

"Hey, Wallace. Demming here. I just buzzed the place. Too many people in Rainbow's today. A mob on the sidewalk, too. I'd rather talk alone. Can you meet me in the parking lot? I'm not in the Ferrari. I'm in the Lexus. Camouflage car," he explained. "I wised up."

"Are you out back now?" said Wallace, sitting up and locating his sunglasses.

"Check. Come on back. We can talk in the car."

"Okay. See you in a sec," he said, rising and heading towards the door. Less than a minute later he spotted Heston, who was seated in the front seat of a non-descript white sedan. Half the autos in Naples were white sedans. *If Heston wants to blend, he's found the right vehicle.* Bending down and peering inside, he rapped sharply on the car window.

From inside the car, Heston pushed open the passenger-side door, and he slid into the front seat. The coolness of the air-conditioned car interior was in stark contrast to the turgid outdoor air.

Closing the car door, he faced Heston intimately. "Quite a come-down from the Ferrari," he commented snidely. "What gives? Being pursued by too many wildly adoring fans?"

"No. I mean, yes, but that's not the reason for the car. I was on my way to see a private eye. But he just called and cancelled. The man had to go out of town—he said. Said he was "on" to something. Said he'd call me by tomorrow afternoon at the latest."

"Sounds intriguing," he coaxed invitingly. "Am I in the loop?"

Heston looked at him sideways and pursed his lips. "Frankly, no. Sorry, old man." Reaching into his shirt pocket, he pulled out a check. "Thanks for your help," he said quietly, thrusting the check at him.

"What? No, I don't want that," he said.

"No? You deserve it. You saved Poppy's honor,' said Heston, waving the check.

"I saved my own butt from a lawsuit," he scoffed. "Don't paint me the hero."

Shrugging his broad shoulders, Heston tucked the check into his own shirt pocket. "I'd like to do something for you, Smythe. To show my appreciation. Name it."

He laughed, too loudly. "What I want from you, I ain't gonna get," he said crudely.

"Uh, oh," said Heston, staring across the steering wheel at the forest-green SUV parked in front of him. He placed his hands on the wheel to brace for the latest confession of ardor.

"Okay," Wallace gulped quickly. "I'm just going to say this once–and fast. I've had a thing for you for years. It's not a crush. I don't think it becomes a crush unless you know the person. So, I've had a thing for you for years and a crush on you for weeks. Okay. There. I've said it." He, too, was staring straight ahead, not daring to look at Heston.

Heston chewed his lower lip. After a moment of silence, he said, "Thank you for the compliment, Wallace."

"*But...*" he sighed.

"But I'm not available," said Heston with finality.

"I know," he sighed again. "And, truth be told, although I wouldn't have a moment's qualms stealing from Maude, I'd never steal you from Poppy, even if I could."

Heston shuddered. "You can't," he said. He seemed embarrassed, yet amused by the irony of the situation.

"I'm sure this happens to you all the time," he groaned in comic humiliation.

He nodded, his sad eyes dancing. "From time to time," he allowed. "Look, I made up my mind years ago on this question. It's nothing personal."

"Guess you had to learn how to fight early."

"Guess I did."

"Poppy and I go way back, too," Wallace said thoughtfully. He felt embarrassed but not foolish, as he had been afraid he might. "She's been a good pal. She gave me a leg up when no one else would. I owe her a lot."

"Yes, she's a fine person," agreed Heston.

"Not like that Gorgon you're married to, Heston. Please forgive my rudeness, but I'm going to set you straight–if you'll pardon the expression–before we part company for keeps."

"Shoot," said Heston, his embarrassment seeming to subside.

"I like you. I'm *encrushed* on you, if there is such a word, which I doubt. I wish the best for you. And I want you to know the truth," he said. "Then I'm out of here." He glanced out at the bright afternoon sky.

"What's the truth, friend?" asked Heston, watching him wipe his moustaches with a pointed index finger.

He wanted to speak, but he feared Heston's anger. *Just don't kill the bearer of bad news.*

"Go on. Say it," ordered Heston unequivocally.

"All right," he said, plunging in. "The truth is—your wife, Maude, and that horny bitch, Cedric Spicer, are more than just co-conspirators." Wallace raised his eyebrows meaningfully. "Follow me? Those two are L-O-V-E-R-S, Heston—if you can call what they do to each other 'love'."

Heston's eyes narrowed menacingly. "I know you said Spicer was bisexual..."

Wallace shook his head. "Not just bisexual, my friend. He's also a well-traveled masochist. Get my drift?"

"Got it," said Heston, his face suddenly a frozen mask.

Wallace felt the temperature inside the car drop ten degrees. Heston's rigid jaw was pulsing. "I know Cedric pretty well. If I know my old friend—my ex-friend, that is—as well as I think I do, he was just using Maude to get to you, anyway, Heston. Cedric's a real piece of work. A real mischief-maker, that one. What'd you call 'em? An imp? A sprite?"

"A troll?" said Heston frigidly. "An ogre?"

"A finagler. Cedric finagles his way through life, never caring whom he hurts. He takes what he wants and be damned." He put his hand on the door handle and pulled it. "Forgive me, if I've hurt you too badly. I like you, man. And I respect you. I didn't want you to be the last to know." He climbed out of the car and stood peering in at the handsome star. A blast of hot, damp air filled the Lexus. The smell of exhaust fumes floated in heavily.

"Wallace, how do you know this? Are you sure?" said Heston.

He sighed. "Cedric and I were an item at one time. Back in the glory days in South Beach. What an idiot I was, eh? Now we're just friends, but I know him pretty well. He confided to me that he was schooling your wife. What he forgot to mention was that he was planning to have me thrown in jail for fraud. Oops."

Heston shook his head in sympathetic ire. "Does Poppy know you're gay?" he asked.

"I'm not gay," he countered. "To coin a phrase: I'm not homosexual. I'm not heterosexual. I'm not bisexual. I'm just sexual."

"Ah," acknowledged Heston.

"What I really am, Demming, is a lover of beauty. A connoisseur of great beauty. That's how I fell into the art game." He stole a sly glance from the corner of his eye. "You, Heston Demming, are a thing of great beauty."

Heston stared straight ahead. "But for how much longer? I need something real in my life, Wallace. Before it's too late."

He nodded. "You already know what you need. You need Poppy. Poppy is an angel. She doesn't judge what I am or what I do. She's just my friend," he said, choking up. Embarrassed, he put his hand on the door handle. "See you around, Heston. It's been a rough last couple of days. I'm going to The Dock for a Mai Tai. Or maybe to the River Walk at Tin City. Here's a hot tip. You can always find me at the nearest watering hole."

"Thanks again for your help, Wallace," said Heston sincerely. "And your candor. You've helped me make an important decision. Please take the check. I'm paying a private dick for information. Why shouldn't I pay you?"

He looked away and thought for a moment. "Okay," he said, disappointed in himself. "If it'll make you feel better." He nipped the check from Heston's outthrust hand. "You know, his whole thing may be my fault. I was cruising the pier one morning. Saw you and Poppy on the beach—embracing. I told Cedric. No doubt he told Maude."

Heston shrugged. Dejected, Wallace shut the door and slinked away, waving.

It was worth a try. If Heston decides to murder Cedric—and Maude—it wouldn't surprise me.

***

In the netherworld of dusk, Inez Vega sat, hunched in grief, on a marble bench overlooking her son Franco's grave. Her demeanor was calm, dream-like, but not to the point of stupor. She was conscious of her surroundings. She knew where she was. Hadn't she visited her son's gravesite every day? Today, however, was different. Today was special. She had lingered longer than usual, and she had been rewarded. Today was becoming tonight. Tonight Franco had come to visit her.

Alone with Franco in the vast field of tombstones and plastic flowers, in a graveyard separated from the Gulf by only a strip of sand dunes and high-rises, Inez uttered a few soft words now and then, words caught up by warm wind, words that disappeared into the ether. Behind her, the western sky was a graying blaze of pink and tangerine clouds, its vivid colors slowly fading into night. Beside the bench on which she sat stood a tall cabbage-palm. The westerly wind whispered through its rustling fronds. That whisper was Franco voice speaking to her. She listened closely to the precious vapor.

You loved me. He never loved me. See what he did to me. Do you see, Mami?

Inez listened closely to her son's angry words. Franco was helpless now. He could not avenge his own death, but she could avenge it for him. He wanted her to. He was asking her to take matters into her own hands. It was all Heston's fault. Everything bad that had ever happened to her was Hess's fault. Every mistake she had made was over Hess. Now he scorned her and had cast her off. Franco realized the injustice of this. Franco wanted justice for her, as well as for himself. Franco wanted vengeance.

Please, Mami. For me. For you.

The wind grew cool and steady as darkness fell. Franco's words grew cold and bold. Beyond his gravesite stood a gnarled pine tree, its pliant limbs wafting in the wind. In the descending darkness, Inez heard the tree rather than saw it. She listened closely.

On the road beyond, blinding headlights swerved into view. She shielded her eyes with the back of her hand. The black Jaguar screeched to a halt. Danny Vega was at her side.

"Inez, get up," said Danny's deep voice, above the gentle stirrings of palm fronds and pine needles. "Please get up, my love."

Somehow she found herself lying in the thick, wet grass next to Franco's grave. How had she gotten there? She felt strong young hands on the small of her back. The stars were now bright in the heavens. With Danny's help, she sat upright in the grass. Danny's face was close to hers, a contrast of light and dark. She could see only half his features. As though she were a little child, he took her in his strong arms and lifted her to her feet.

Don't forget, Mami.

I won't forget, Frankie. Yes, Poppy, too. She's the one who turned him against me.

Danny stood in the wet grass. He held her upright. "How did you get here, Inez? How long have you been here? We've been going crazy. Rogelio is combing the streets for you."

"I come here every day," she said, head lolling forward.

"No, you don't," he said, as she flung her arms around his neck and collapsed against his hard chest. "How did you get out of the house again? From now on, I'm giving orders to the guard—to stop you at the gate." Alarmed, he worked to pry his stepmother's arms away.

"Kiss me, Danny," she whispered, snuggling against him. "I need you to."

"No, Inez. It's not right."

Her svelte form grew limp. Danny removed her thin arms from around his neck and scooped her bodily into his arms. Dutifully, he carried the limp woman back to the black Jaguar. After phoning his father with the news that his wife had been found, he drove the unconscious woman from Vanderbilt Beach to her courtyard home in Bay Colony. A full moon rose as he journeyed through the night.

One thought played over and over in his mind. He had to get away from Inez. With Sasha out of the picture, there was no longer a barrier between him and his stepmother's seductive come-ons—except, of course, filial loyalty to his father, something he did not want to put to a test.

Chapter Fourteen

"**N**o, Daddy! Don't come in!" wailed Winnie, terrified. "Go 'way! Go 'way! I can't talk you! Mommy knows!"

"It's all right, Ladybug," Heston assured her, easing his way into the small bedroom. In the blink of an eye, he took in his surroundings. A single lamp lit the close, dim room, a tiny ballerina lamp with a lacy pink lampshade. The lamp stood on a painted white nightstand between two twin beds. Against the wall, a white, wooden window seat held five or six elaborate dolls in frilly dresses. Above the window seat, dusty rose-colored curtains were tightly drawn. The hard, speckled terrazzo floor was worn but clean. The toy-cluttered bedroom smelled of Play-Doh and fabric softener. The twin beds were fitted with pink sheets.

Ensconced in one of the twin beds, his daughter huddled beneath a threadbare bedspread. In the twin bed next to hers, lay a cute, pudgy girl with thick black hair. The girl's brown eyes were wide open and searching. The girl's big eyes followed Heston closely as he moved into the room and sat down on the edge of Winnie's bed.

"Winston, honey," he said soothingly. Placing a hand tentatively on Winnie's shoulder, he felt the child shudder in fright. "It's me. Daddy. It's all right. Everything is all right, Win."

"No! Mommy kill me! She said! I told! I told!" The child's fear was palpable. His heart ached in sorrow, even as it throbbed with rage. *How had it come to this?*

"No, she won't. I promise," he said evenly, stroking the flank of the huddled child. "You did the right thing to tell me, honey. I'm your father. I love you. I'll protect you."

Finally.

"It's okay, sir?" asked Lissette Garcia, the Demming household's plump, middle-aged maid, from the open doorway. From down a short hallway, the sounds of a Spanish-language television program floated into the room.

"Yes, Lissette, thanks," he answered, still stroking his trembling daughter lovingly. "Thanks for bringing Winnie here, to your own home.

Thanks for keeping her safe."

"I tried to tell you, sir. More than once."

"I know that now. By the way, I fired Jill Cady. She was my wife's dupe. Dowdy girl tried to seduce me in front of the refrigerator at 2:00 a.m. I don't think so."

"Ooh, that's bad." The maternal woman nodded in understanding.

"I'll be hiring a temporary nanny soon—once Mrs. Demming is gone for good."

"Bravo, *senor*."

Heston almost smiled. "I can take it from here, Lissette." Tenderly, he touched his hand to Winnie's fine blonde hair and smoothed the fragile wisps. "You have my deepest gratitude."

If I am the guardian, Winnie's the angel. And I am the guardian, damn it.

"Our pleasure, sir," the maid said. "We were glad to keep her safe for you." She fired a parting word at her own daughter in the next bed. "Felicia Garcia! Go to sleep!" The girl shut her big eyes instantly. Lying tensely, Felicia feigned slumber.

"I've come to take you home, Winner," Heston said softly to his daughter, who had begun to relax until he spoke the word "home."

"No!" Winnie howled in terror. Clawing at the sheets, she rolled away from him. Hearing the outburst, Felicia opened her eyes, but his focus was on his distressed daughter. Filled with deep remorse, he gathered Winnie in his arms and rocked her gently until, at last, the child stopped squirming and relaxed in his embrace. Hoarse with compassion, he crooned, in a low, reassuring tone, into Winnie's delicate ear. "Don't cry, Ladybug. Don't be afraid. You're coming home with me now. Everything's all right. It's Mommy who's leaving this time."

"Really?" asked Winnie, torn. Her little heart was palpitating against his chest.

"I promise. You'll never have to be afraid of Mommy again. Come on, Ladybug." He pecked her damp cheek.

Coyly, Winnie giggled and pecked his cheek in return. Then her joy morphed into concern. "Where Mommy go?"

Heston's gut wrenched as he wiped her wet cheek with his thumb.

Courage, man.

Rising to his feet, he hoisted his daughter into his arms. He felt her legs go round him. Clutching his precious cargo protectively, he padded to the bedroom door.

"Goodnight, *nina bonita*," he whispered on the way out of the bedroom. "Thanks for your hospitality"

The brown eyes smiled. "Goodnight, Mr. Heston," Felicia's sweet voice whispered in return. "Bye-bye, Winnie!" Balanced on her father's broad shoulder, Winnie waved a sad goodbye to her new playmate.

Determinedly, Heston carried his daughter through the cramped living room, where Lissette's husband and son sat watching the blaring TV. Both father and son waved, and he returned their salute. Nervously, Lissette gave each male relative a farewell kiss. Then, following Heston and Winnie out the door and onto the front lawn, she handed him a small Louis Vuitton suitcase.

"Miss Winston's clothes," she said in a low voice, glancing furtively towards the neighboring house. Like hers, the neighbor's house was a small, rectangular, flat-roofed stucco home, one built in mid-1960s modern style. The neighbor's house was painted avocado green, while the Garcia home was pink with white trim. Moved, Heston listened to the sounds of the night. The streets of his old neighborhood seemed filled with ghosts.

"I grew up in the house three doors down from here," he said, accepting the suitcase from his housemaid and flinging it into his car.

"It's a fine neighborhood," she observed. "Good for children. A good place to grow up."

"Yes," he admitted hoarsely, looking around. "It was–although I didn't realize it at the time. I wanted bigger things, brighter things."

"You found them," she said philosophically.

The corners of his mouth rose.

"Yes, so I did. Get in, Lissette." He held the car door open for her. Above his heads, a lone streetlight blinked erratically. A full moon hovered in the star-sprinkled indigo sky.

"Are you sure she'll be all right?" Lissette looked worried as she settled into the car seat.

Outside the car, Heston deposited Winnie in her lap and strapped both females in securely. Then he rounded the car and opened the driver's side door.

"My wife is history," he said, piling into the driver's seat. "As soon as we arrive home, Maude is out the door. Gonzo—Right, Win?"

Winnie nodded once, sharply, but she glanced at him uncertainly from beneath heavy lids.

"Wouldn't it be better–safer–for Winnie to spend one more night with my Felicia?" asked Lissette, her heavy brows knitted together. She cast a wistful glance towards her home.

"No," he said decisively. "I want Winston with me. From now on."

"Mommy! Where are you going?" called black-haired Felicia, suddenly appearing the front porch of the Garcia family home.

"Go back to bed, Niña," She called to the girl. "Mind your father."

Just then Mr. Garcia, a round-bellied construction worker, appeared and stood behind Felicia on the front porch. He called to Heston.

"Okay, Mr. Demming, sir! Good luck, Winnie!" Waving, Felicia's father took his daughter by the hand beneath the porch light and led her into the house.

"*Hasta la manana, Corazon,*" Lissette called bravely, waving goodbye as the Land Rover—Heston's latest camouflage vehicle—crept stealthily down the dark residential street. By the time the SUV reached Port Royal, Winnie was asleep on Lissette's broad lap. Passing the gate of his own home and steering the car up the drive, Heston girded his loins, psychologically, for the coming bout with his wife. Obviously, Maude was wide awake and stoking the fire. The mansion was ablaze with electric lights. Parking the car, he got out and then leaned inside the passenger-side window.

"Stay put," he told Lissette. "No matter what Mrs. Demming says or does, do not let her have Winnie. Don't let her *near* Winnie. Understood? Keep the doors locked."

Face pinched, Lissette nodded, her strong arms hugging the sleeping child. "In five minutes, my wife will be in that Lexus and out of here," he vowed emphatically, pointing to a car in the drive. "Or I'll be a dead man"

"Good luck, *senor,*" whispered Lissette making the sign of the cross. Licking his lips anxiously, he marched to the front door and disarmed the alarm. With a swift backward glance at the Land Rover, he deliberately shook out his limbs, dragged his fingers through his thick hair, mouthed a silent prayer, and then, drawing a deep breath, entered the mansion authoritatively, master of his domain. He was tired of the whole damn mess, tired of the fiasco his marriage had become. He was about to give his finest performance. He hoped the security camera was rolling.

Maude was waiting for him, eyes aflame. Whirling around, she confronted him boldly as he crossed the foyer and strode into the living room. A gray haze of smoke filled the room's crisp, frigid air. The air reeked of cigarettes. Maude had been chain-smoking, instead of eating, and drinking heavily, too, unless he missed his guess, and alone, at that. He saw no sign of Spicer. "So, the prodigal returns!" She cried gutturally from her flat belly. "Or make that the prostitute. That's what you are. You're not a prodigal, you're a prostitute. You sell body and soul to the highest bidder." She was weaving with drink.

"And you don't?" he said *voce sotto.* "What's a model if not a whore?"

"Bite me," sneered Maude, waving her cigarette freely. Dead ash dropped to the carpet. "What's this about your firing Winston's nanny?"

Heston kept his cool. "I'm asking the questions here, Maude, not answering them. I only want to know two things from you. One is this: Have you been sleeping with that mangy bag of vermin, Cedric Spicer?"

Maude froze, her shrewd eyes slits. Then, recovering her aplomb, she drew deeply on her cigarette and exhaled. "What of it?" she said brazenly. "Where've you been tonight, stud? Out with your hot, but aging, mistress? Or was it your coy little childhood s-s-sweetheart this time?" Mocking Poppy, she minced her words for emphasis. "Are you banging her, too? Good for you. Maybe we should have a contest. Who can be more unfaithful?"

He felt hot blood flush his face. Blood pounded in his ears, but he wasn't ready to act. Not yet. *Keep an even keel. You have to know one more thing.*

"The second question I have is this: Have you been harming Winnie behind my back?" he demanded, teeth gritted, fingers clenching sporadically.

Her bravado faltered. Her glittering, powder-blue eyes fell to the plush beige carpet.

"Who told you that? Surely not Jill Cady," she bluffed. "The brat? That figures." She circled the room commandingly, as though on a runway. "I've disciplined Winston, that's all. As any normal parent would. Unlike you, you coddling son of a bitch."

"You're anything but normal, Maude," he said. "You've terrified the child."

"Good. Maybe she'll obey me now."

"Then you *are* beating her? When you're alone with her? You're torturing her? Is that what you're telling me?"

"I swear, Heston, you are such a sap." Maude gargled a laugh. "You're a sniveling alcoholic, an emotional weakling, and worst of all, *worst of all*, Heston, you're a damned lousy actor!" Spitefully, she sneaked a peak to see whether her arrow had pierced the mark, and then added, "Who are you to judge me, anyway? You killed your own son. Deliberately, I might add. I know you kicked that ball into the street on purpose, Heston. You can't fool me. You're a lousy ham, remember?"

"Get out," he said, his voice low and fierce.

"Yeah, right!" she jeered, unaware that her makeup had smeared when she wiped her perspiring face with the back of her wrist. Plopping resolutely on the sofa, she kicked her bare feet across the marble-topped coffee table. Flicking ashes onto the carpet, she crossed her hands behind her head and laughed.

"Get out of my house, Maude," he reiterated, tensed rigidly. "I'll give you five minutes to collect your things and go of your own volition. If you don't go willingly, I will pick you up and throw you out bodily."

"Bug off," Maude said caustically but her powder-blue eyes had narrowed. She stubbed the butt end in an ashtray. Abruptly, she leaped up from the sofa and wheeled around to face him. "Say, where *is* the kid? I want to see my kid. Where you hiding her? You've got no right..."

"I have every right, you vicious, two-timing psychopath! I have a duty to my child, to protect her from the sorry likes of you!" he exploded, charging her.

Gasping, Maude backed away out of his path. She clung to the wall for support as he moved forward menacingly. "You now have four minutes. Four minutes and you're out the door. You will not darken my doorstep again, woman. Do you understand me? Tomorrow morning you will hear from my lawyer. I want a divorce. I will *have* a divorce—*and* custody of my daughter *and* control of my intact fortune. And you, harlot, will have zip." He was face to face with her now. He could smell the booze on her breath.

"In your dreams, jerk-off," she snarled, cornered. His lips twisted into a wicked leer. Panic flared in Maude's eyes.

Seizing her, he dragged his wife across the carpet and into the foyer. Flailing wildly, she beat her bony fists against his ribs. Jaws snapping, she tried to bite him, but he deftly slid his elbow around her throat and scooted her, shrieking and thrashing, out the door and down the marble steps leading to the driveway.

In the brightly lit driveway, Lissette and Winnie were waiting inside the Land Rover. Winnie was now wide awake. Horrified, the young child pressed her face to the windshield pane, ogling the action, as her father forced her screeching mother down the steps. From inside the house, the Demming's wizened, gray-haired, live-in housekeeper, in bathrobe and slippers, suddenly appeared in the open doorway, a look of scandalized awe on her face.

"Mr. Demming!" Lissette cried anxiously.

"Stay back!" commanded Heston, funneling Maude, arms behind her back, into the white Lexus and jamming the keys into the ignition.

"Call the pol..." Maude started to yell, but Heston clamped his hand across her mouth.

"Start it up," he growled. Dazed and breathing through her heavily insured nose, Maude sat noncompliant.

"Start it up, damn it!" he yelled, raising his hand to backhand her.

Inside the locked SUV, Winnie was crying and screaming. The maid was attempting to restrain her. On the front steps of the mansion, the wizened housekeeper watched the whole scene in disbelief. Inside the Lexus,

Maude lifted a shaky hand to the ignition and placed a bare foot on the gas pedal. The sedan leaped to life. Backing away, Heston slammed the car door and peered in at Maude's smeared features. The car engine hummed excitedly.

"Now, drive," he commanded. "And never come back."

Seething with rage, Maude pressed her foot to the gas pedal. Jerkily, the car jaunted down the driveway. Boldly, she poked her scraggly head out the Lexus window. In the branches of the huge banyan tree beyond the gate, Heston saw the flash of a paparazzo's camera.

"Cedric and I will be married! I'm going to marry a real artist, a genius, not a pop-culture hack like you," she bellowed. "You'll hear from *my* lawyer in the morning, Heston! I can't wait to be rid of you—and your brat!" Moments later, the car rolled out the opening gate and onto Galleon Drive. Hands on hips, Heston stood watching the vehicle disappear as the gate closed automatically behind it.

"Bite me,' he breathed heavily, with grim satisfaction.

By the following day, the news of his split from Maude was the lead story in the entertainment news. Maude's shrewish face, screaming at him out the window of the Lexus, became the major news photo of the day all over the Internet.

***

"Thanks for accepting our invitation, Poppy," said Heston loudly, two days later, on board *Windswept*. His sun-streaked hair was whipping in the sea wind, making him seem like the Greek god Poseidon, risen from the depths in some fanciful Hollywood film. Piloting the vessel, he stood at the wheel of his yacht. The ship's sails were raised and filled as she skimmed freely across the rhythmic waves of the aquamarine Gulf of Mexico.

The man in charge, Captain Demming sported a navy-striped sports jersey, off-white duck shorts, and bone-leather deck shoes. Captivated, Poppy sighed approvingly. Even his hairy legs were cute, bony, bald ankles and all.

His young daughter, Winston, was standing on the ship's bow, clinging to the handrail alongside one of the crew. Monitoring the child like a sentinel, Poppy had been sitting in the cockpit near Heston as he guided the sleek ship's course. Her limbs stiffening, Poppy stood to stretch her legs.

"It's good for Winnie to be aboard ship, sailing," Heston projected above the wind, as she moved in beside him. "Two nights ago she was traumatized. Even now, she's still in shock."

"I can well imagine," she said, using her fingers to push unruly hair from her eyes. Before setting sail, Heston had told her how he and Maude had parted ways in an ugly scene. Her heart bled for the little girl caught in the middle. She wanted to help.

So far, however, Winnie had been aloof to her overtures of friendship. She hoped to win the child over, not just because Winnie was part of Heston, but also because the child seemed in such pain. Thank goodness Heston's daughter had his abject love and devotion.

What a man he is. He admits his mistakes. Then he corrects them.

Incredulous, Poppy glanced adoringly at the object of her affection. The morning sun glinted in his silver-blue eyes as he caught her glance. He seemed so warm, yet so distant. Poppy could feel that he wanted and needed to share himself with her but was hesitant.

Who can blame him? He's been burned once too often. Haven't we all?

"Having a good time, Winner?" he called to his small daughter. Poppy looked towards the bow and saw Winnie, who was standing hand in hand with the crew member, shake her head. Her face unsmiling, Winnie wore a life vest—a regulation PDF, or Personal Flotation Device—at her father's insistence, over navy shorts, a white cotton shirt, and a billed ecru cap. Her fine blonde hair was pulled into a long ponytail, which protruded out the back of the cap, just above the adjustable strap. Her smooth skin swathed in sunblock, the child glistened in early morning sunlight like a fairy princess at dawn.

Such beauty. Poppy felt as though she were sailing the high seas with a family of Immortals. Gooseflesh rose on the skin of her arms. Again, she felt *enchantment.*

"I'd like us to anchor us somewhere. Winnie likes to snorkel," Heston said into Poppy's ear, injecting reality into her reverie.

"Sounds great!" agreed Poppy, holding on to her wide-brimmed straw hat, which kept trying to flap out to sea. The hat was an old standby of hers, its band a ring of sand-colored coquina shells. She hadn't had time to shop for new attire. Heston had phoned, inviting her to sail on the spur of the moment. At least she had possessed a decent swimsuit, a bikini of red-orange material with a large, white seashell print—which she now wore, beneath a long-sleeved, white-linen beach shirt, the buttons of which she had left open. She had had to make do with white sneakers. She was fresh out of deck shoes, not having been on a boat in years. Boats had always reminded her of Heston.

"Thanks for bringing the lunch," he beamed, his warm breath on her ear. She craved the nearness of him. She hated it when he pulled away and moved back to the wheel. His energy had filled the empty space around her. His presence made her feel protected.

"Still got your sea legs," he observed approvingly, smiling at her, his caps as white as those on the waves.

"Dramamine!" she responded into his ear. "An hour before I boarded. Plus...!" Poppy held up her wrist and shook the magnetic bracelet encircling it.

"Smart girl!" he grinned, cocking his head towards the bow. "Winner's like her old man—iron stomach!" Proudly, he patted his taut belly.

Rolling her eyes, Poppy patted Heston's flat midriff with the back of her hand. His abs were rock-hard. Looking up in surprise, she caught him staring down at her, his eyes filled with unmasked desire. Poppy's loins contracted. Her skin flushed. For an instant she was lost, alone with Heston in the wild bosom of nature.

"Daddy, I'm hungry!" she heard Winnie cry.

Looking around, she saw the child carefully making her way aft down the bouncing deck towards the cockpit. The crewman was holding Winnie's hand, shepherding her small steps.

"Take the wheel. We'll anchor off that key," Heston told the fellow, as Winnie jumped into her father's arms. "Come on," Heston said affectionately. "Let's go below and see what Miss Poppy brought us to nosh on."

Watching Heston and Winnie descend backwards down the stepladder into the hold, she turned and, with Heston's strong hands on her haunches, easily managed the descent into the ship's cabin.

"Thanks," she said sardonically, adjusting the hem of her shirt, once she was safely balanced on the cabin's clean floor. Taking off her hat, she tossed it onto the captain's chair.

"My pleasure," said Heston, tongue in cheek, lifting the hat and flinging it onto another chair.

"Here's the picnic basket, Daddy!" said Winnie, climbing onto one of two benches which ran the length of the varnished galley table. Poppy's picnic basket sat braced in the corner of the table. Challenge in his eyes, Heston sat back and let Poppy take charge of the luncheon gathering. Meeting his challenge, Poppy washed her hands and set to work.

"Your Daddy told me you like tuna fish. Is that true, Winnie?" she asked. Shyly, Winnie nodded. "Well, good, 'cause I made you a tuna salad sandwich," said Poppy, searching through the basket for plates and utensils. "And strawberry ice cream for dessert. Your daddy said it was your favorite. Will you help me set the table?" she asked. Somber-faced, Winnie nodded. With Poppy's help, Winnie washed her hands at the galley sink, and then laid the table, while Poppy brought out the more elegant fare she had prepared for Heston and herself.

"What about the crew?" she asked Heston, suddenly. "I brought enough for them, too."

"By all means–after we're done," said Heston. "Right now, I'm enjoying our little family gathering."

The word 'family' rang in Poppy's ears. He had said it on purpose. *He must have.*

"Will you eat tossed salad?" she said to Winnie, masking elation. Again, Winnie nodded. Heston raised his brow in surprise. Poppy shot a worried look at Heston. "It's all organic. I hope you don't mind."

"Mind?" croaked Heston. "I think it's great. Maude never fed her anything but dill pickles and diet soda pop. Please, carry on."

The intimate lunch came off pleasantly enough. Poppy encouraged Winnie to play hostess, and the little girl seemed to enjoy herself in the role. At one point, contemplating father and daughter across the galley table, she was struck anew by their uncanny resemblance–and it made her womb ache for the son she had lost. Did Noel resemble his father? Would she ever find out? She was on pins and needles waiting for the latest report from Rick DuBois.

After the meal, Heston tucked his sleepy daughter away for a nap in one of the cabin's snuggest berths. By now, the two crewmen had anchored the yacht not far from the site of Heston and Poppy's teenage tryst.

Exchanging places with the crew, she and Heston went topside, while the two workers went below for a midday meal, the bulk of which she had happily provided. Emerging from below deck, she realized she had forgotten her straw hat. About to descend after it, she caught sight of her surroundings and then gaped at Heston in astonishment.

"Heston!" she cried. "Is this...is it?"

"It is, indeed," said Heston, pleased with himself. "I thought you might like to revisit old haunts. Was I right?" He watched her from the corner of his eye.

"Oh, yes," she exclaimed. Spontaneously, she encircled Heston's trim waist with one arm. Before she knew what was happening, she felt Heston's arm go round her, slipping quickly beneath her unbuttoned beach robe. Awed, she felt the heavy heat of his hand searing the bare skin of her lower back. Mouth open, she uttered a little cry.

With expert ease, he swung her round to face him. Pressing himself against her, he placed a hand behind her head and, bending down, lifted her mouth to his, kissing her ravenously with pent-up force. As his tongue explored her mouth, his lower hand slipped beneath her bikini pants, cupping round her bottom cheek.

"Stop it!" Poppy gasped, wrenching herself away.

"Why?" he demanded, his countenance annoyed yet amused.

She was flummoxed. "Because we're not alone. Because your daughter is on board. Because I'm still married..." *So many reasons, every one of them valid, but none the true reason. I'm scared, Heston.*

Inhaling the heavy, warm Gulf air, she climbed out of the cockpit and moved to the fore section of the yacht. Clinging to the handrail, she glanced back at Heston, whose eyes were waiting for the truth. "Because I'm not ready yet," she half-confessed, turning towards the island. "There's too much uncertainty. It's all happening so fast."

"I can wait," said Heston, his voice deep and rich. "But I will have you."

His words rocked Poppy to the core of her being. She didn't argue with him. It would have been pointless. She only wanted time, and the courage to face what was happening between them. *And the possibility that you might leave me again.*

Following Poppy's lead, he mounted to the ship's deck, but stopped a few feet away from her. There, he held on to the mainsail mast, rotating his leonine head to scan the horizon. She looked around, too.

Vast turquoise waters outlined by distant patches of low-lying green foliage comprised their earthly domain. Gigantic, white cumulus clouds floating weightlessly in an azure sky filled their heavenly dome. From the oculus of the sun, far above the clouds, a relentless explosion of plat-inum-white heat poured down upon their lowly ship, now buoyant and shiny in hot, midday splendor.

"Look!" said Poppy, pointing to a dolphin's fin as it flashed momen-tarily above the water's sparkling surface.

"Maybe he remembers us," said Heston. "Well, more likely his parents would."

Poppy smiled shyly, her brow crinkling. "We have a lot to talk about, Seanie."

Bowing his head, Heston said, "I know."

Then, as she waited silently in the shade of the sails, he began to con-fide in her. Hesitant at first, he began pouring out his heart. He told her about his problems with Maude, about Maude's sexual perversions and about her wanton infidelity with Cedric Spicer. Head in hands, he revealed that divorce proceedings were underway, that Maude has moved to The Hideaway, the same hotel where Cedric Spicer and Montserrat Flynn still had rooms. Agonized, he showed her Winnie's drawing. Now she under-stood the depth of his emotional exhaustion.

Dropping onto a cushioned bench beneath the mast boom, he voiced his regrets about the past—how badly he had suffered his bouts with the bottle, and worse; how he wished he had had a wife whom he could have talked to, and confided in, someone who had cared about him as a human being, as a man, not just as a money-making machine or an arm adornment or a grand prize. Tenderly, Poppy stroked his thick brown hair as he rambled on.

Echoing his regret, once again, about Inez, he talked ashamedly about his role in his son, Franco's death. Ardently, she absorbed every word, every nuance. Without revealing a name, he mentioned his anonymous 'sponsor,' a man from a certain organization, who had helped him through detox a year ago. Although necessary, that relationship was not enough to satisfy his soul. What he needed, he told her, was his First Mate. When he clasped his hands around hers, she felt he might die of sheer need.

At last he broached the most tender subject of all—their illegitimate son. With quiet dignity, he informed her that Rick DuBois, the private eye, had disappeared two days ago, leaving word only that he had a new lead on their son's whereabouts. The news frightened her. Now it was she who clung to his hands.

Moved, he assured her that it would all right, no matter what the outcome. He had been calling DuBois day and night, but had received no answer at either number. Something was up. Of that, he was sure. They would have to wait it out and hope for the best. As he at last fell silent, Poppy found herself at a loss for words, too.

And, somehow, that was all right, she realized at her deepest level of being. Here and now, lulled by the hot sunshine and the lapping of waves against the ship's hull, Poppy accepted the fact that she and Heston were mere human beings, not immortals, rather just two confused, middle-aged adults with difficult, intertwined personal histories. As such, they were able to sit together in compassionate silence.

Each found comfort in that shared silence. The emotional bond between them was growing ever stronger and more resilient. Physical intimacy, when it finally happened between them, this time, would make that bond indelible. She knew it, and she sensed that he knew it, too.

That's why it's such a big step.

Sex with Heston Demming was not something to be treated lightly or casually. She had made that mistake in her youth. She had thought she could wipe away his memory from her mind, his love-making from her soul. How wrong she had been. Thinking back, she recalled how much she had loved him down through the years. Her love had begun a long time ago, when she and he had been mere children playing in the Lake Park schoolyard.

"Today is Valentine's Day," she informed him.

"Is it?" he queried, eyes sparkling.

Poppy eyed him warily. "I baked cookies for us all to share later."

"Win'll like that. Did you hear from your husband?"

"James sent roses. I didn't reply."

"Huh." Heston nodded his head.

"Do you remember the first valentine you ever gave me, Seanie H. Demming?" she teased, breaking the deep silence. "Mister XXOO."

Heston snorted, blushing. "Oh, yes. That big heart with the two kissing bumblebees. "Roses are red, Violets are blue; You bee my honey. I'll bee yourzzz, too. *Aaargh!*" he groaned, laughing. "How awful!"

"I loved it," said Poppy, chuckling in spite of herself. "I still have it."

"You don't?" said Heston, aghast. "Throw it away!"

"I'll never throw it away," Poppy countered, scandalized. "Shame on you, Sean. No, I'll keep that valentine until the day I die. Besides, you were only nine years old."

With a heavy sigh, Heston drew a small, oblong box from his pocket. "Well," he shrugged, "if you liked that, you probably won't like this." Opening the lid, he placed the box in her hands.

Poppy gasped. "Heston! I can't accept this." Daintily, regretfully, fearfully, she fingered the fine strand of diamonds and rubies. Awed, she gazed into his eyes.

"See, I knew you wouldn't like it," he quipped.

"Stop it!" she giggled helplessly, outraged and totally overwhelmed. "I love it! You know I do! Heston, thank you for the thought. It's beautiful. It's magnificent. You're wonderful. You're so generous. But I cannot accept it. I am *still married.*"

Heston's jaw went steely. "So you keep saying. Forget about it." Reluctantly retrieving the box from her hands, he snapped the lid shut, and dropped the box deeply into his pocket.

As though on cue, Winnie poked her pretty blonde head up from below deck. "Can we go snorkeling, now?" she asked her father sweetly. Her nap over, Winnie was filled with new vigor. Even her eyes looked brighter.

"You bet'cha we can, Ladybug!" he cried too merrily, jumping up and catching Winnie in his arms. She could not help but notice his rippling arm muscles. As he spun his daughter in circles, the little girl giggled riotously.

Ten minutes later, she, Heston, and Winnie were splashing in the salt water. After a peaceful, joy-filled half-hour of diving, swimming, and snorkeling, they were interrupted by a gaggle of boisterous tourists floating by on a canopied pontoon boat.

"Oh, my gosh, that's Heston Demming!" yelled one of the senior-citizen tourists, who was using binoculars to scour the anchored sailboat and its good-looking passengers.

"You don't mean it!" cried a matronly woman on board the tour boat, usurping the man's binoculars and ogling Heston's swim-suited derriere as he stood, magnificent, upon *Windswept's* broad bow. The male tourist whipped out his cell phone and dialed. Immediately, the tour boat pulled alongside, and the tourists swarmed to snap photographs of the international celebrity. Fifteen minutes after Heston began graciously posing for photos and signing autographs, the drone of a helicopter, coming closer and closer to the *Windswept,* sounded in the sky.

"*Uh oh,*" Heston said to Poppy as, shading his eyes with one hand, he located a growing speck beneath the clouds. "Damned paparazzi. I put to sea early, hoping to avoid these jokers. Now look." As the small helicopter began to circle the two boats, Heston excused himself and his shipboard party from the group of tourists. Staring up into the sky, Poppy could see a wily cameraman leaning out and filming from the side of the chopper. Taciturn, Heston piloted *Windswept* back to Naples Bay and Port Royal, as the sun dropped into the western sky. She left him alone. She knew better than to approach him in such a foul mood.

That night, as she lay alone and sunburned, in her queen-sized bed at Solamarina, her uneasy mind seethed with uncertainty. The nightly TV show biz news had reported their afternoon's excursion on the yacht. She had begun to realize what world-wide celebrity meant, and the magnitude of its implications for her future relationship with Heston.

Even on the remotest parts of the planet, Heston Demming could not escape his stardom. Unless she broke away now, she would become part of his public constellation. Her whole life would be exposed to public scrutiny. Perhaps it was already too late to break away. Today she had been filmed by a paparazzo. She had been photographed and videoed by every touristy Tom, Dick, and Harriet from Indiana to Michigan.

Tossing and turning, unable to sleep, she had a second realization, one that flashed repeatedly in her mind like an electric signboard. Of all the issues she and he had discussed that day, one issue had never arisen. He had never asked whether or not she was planning to ask James for a divorce. Next to the whereabouts of their son, this was the biggest question between them, and, she speculated, the one Heston was most loath to ask her.

Which is just as well, since it's the one I'm most afraid to answer.

What *was* the right answer? How could she leave James Talbot, the man she had vowed to love and honor, no matter what, *'til death do us part?*

An even worse thought occurred to her: What if Heston didn't want her to?

Chapter Fifteen

Sasha Bassett's cell phone rang, its ringtone the banter of a feisty, sea-going parrot. The squawking voice roused her from a torrid day-dream about Danny Vega's thighs. Rolling over on her beach towel, Sasha propped herself on one elbow and picked up the cell, not bothering to check out the number.

"Hello?" she said, brushing sand from her rose-lacquered nails.

"Rick DuBois, here, Little Miss Sasha. Remember me? The big, bad bayou PI? Well, I got some good news for you, pretty lady."

She bolted upright. The hair on the back of her neck rose.

"What news?" she gulped. With the dry end of the towel, she dabbed moisture from her sun-baked skin. She had come to Lowdermilk Park to-day instead of the city pier. She had needed a change of scene.

The private eye paused for effect, and then blurted out, "I found him."

The hot sun scorched the sand. Waves of heat were rising from the crowded beach. "What did you say?" she asked, disoriented.

"I said I found him. I found Heston Demming's bastard. You know, the boy you *hired* me to find two weeks ago?"

"Are you kidding me?" she said haltingly.

"I kid you not," DuBois replied happily.

"Where? How? Who?" The questions came tumbling out faster than she could think.

"Got a pencil? Boy's adopted name is Jacob Kieran McKendrick. Goes by Kieran. Started life as little Noel Demming. Navy brat. He was adopt-ed by a career military couple in Tampa, same year, same week as the birth of Demming's kid. Couple moved around a lot. Been tracing their move-ments over the years. Finally landed in Hawaii. Husband left the service and opened a bike shop on the island of Oahu. Kid went to public high school. He's tough but got a head on his shoulders, too. Kieran McKendrick is not in Hawaii at present, however."

"Well, where the heck is he?" barked Sasha, exasperated.

"Nashville, Tennessee. At Vanderbilt University. He's pre-med. Kid's gonna be a doctor. Smart as a whip. Good grades all through school. No juvie, here. The kid's a straight arrow. Leader of his church youth group.

Senior class salutatorian. Classmates call him Kipp."

"Are you joshing me?" Sasha repeated, thunderstruck.

"I already told you 'no,'" said Rick. "Kipp McKendrick. There's your boy. Wait 'til the world finds out about the Kippster."

"Does he...?"

"Look like Heston? Naw, not exactly. Good-looking young stud, though. A brown-eyed blondie. Tall, lanky, real athletic. Played quarter-back in high school. Track team. Runs like a deer. SCUBA. Bikes and surfs. Well, he would since his dad owned a bike shop. Adoptive dad, you know—Benjamin McKendrick. Benjy. Dad's deceased. Wife's Nancy. She's alive. Bought a pre-construction condo and moved to Kona, on The Big Island. She and Kipp are close."

"I don't believe this," said Sasha, lying down flat on her back. She threw a forearm over her eyes to block the sun's glare. In the background stood Lowdermilk's Polynesian-style deck.

"Believe it," said the P.I. proudly. "I said I'd do it—and I done it."

"Wait until I tell James," she whispered to herself. *Now he'll want to divorce her.*

"Eh? Whazzat?" said DuBois nosily. "Speak up, sugar muffin. Can't hear your sweet words."

"Never mind," she growled, picturing his toothy grin. Sitting up again, she asked, "Hey, Rick! Why did you call me with the news? Why not call Heston? I gave you his lawyer's card. Didn't you connect with him?"

"I did. I heard from The Star himself, too," he replied.

"Yeah? Then why call me with the news? I'm not paying your salary now," she said testily.

"Maybe not. But I'd rather sleep with you, sweet thang," he snorted. "I was trying to impress you with my prowess as a private investigator. Did I?"

She shuddered. *Why do I always get stuck with the cretins?* "Look, Rick, don't call me again, okay? Talk to Heston. Tell him your news. As for me, well, I've got other fish to fry, guy. Sorry. Matter of fact—you've just given me the ammunition I need to win the Shoot-Out at the Man Corral."

"Phooey on me."

"That's the way it goes."

"See you in the funny pa..."

She turned off the phone. *Good riddance.* Now she could bait the hook and reel in Big Jimbo. Her plan was coming together. She now had proof to show James, proof that his wife had lied to him from Day One. The on-ly thing she had to worry about now was Danny Vega. Tapping a mauve nail against her front teeth, she fretted. She had made a mistake–when she'd told Danny about hiring DuBois to find Heston's baby. Danny Vega was a wild card.

Quickly, she picked up the cell again and keyed in Rick's number.

"Yello, Little Miss," said DuBois with his signature twang. "Change your mind? Your place or mine? I'll bring the beer. You bring the pig's feet."

"Cut the crap, Rick. I need to know something."

"What?"

"Do you know a guy named Danny?" she asked, worried about showing her hand.

"Lots of 'em," said DuBois testily. "What's this about, kiddo? Time is money."

"Yeah, yeah. Danny Vega. Know him?" she queried.

There was a beat of silence. "Just got off the phone with him," he admitted.

"What?" she bleated.

"Vega got in touch with me a few days ago. Wanted to know the lay of the land. I'm in the money-business, sugar. You give me money, I give you the business."

"You told Danny? That you found Heston Demming's illegitimate son?"

"Now that's privileged information," he said, recoiling.

"What is? That you found the boy? Or that you told Danny Vega about it?" she flared. "Does Heston Demming know you told Danny about finding his kid? I'll bet he's paying you big bucks for your silence, Rick."

"Haven't broken it to the great Mr. Show-Biz yet. Calling him right now in a minute with the good news," he rejoined dismissively.

"Yeah, you're playing us all for suckers," she said. For a few seconds, all she heard was heavy breathing. Then DuBois spoke up.

"Danny Vega says he owes you one," he said in a low growl.

"And you sold him the information, anyhow?" she said, her flesh beginning to creep. "Thanks a lot, Rube."

"That's why I'm warning you. Consider it a freebie. I'd be careful if I was you, Little Missy," said the P.I, his tone now razor sharp. "Hell hath no fury like an old boyfriend scorned–unless it an old private dick scorned. I'd keep my mouth shut about all this if I was pretty little you."

She swallowed hard. "I guess I stand warned."

"Like I said–see you in the funny papers."

This time DuBois rang off first, and it was Sasha who was left holding a dead cell phone to her ear.

A Chance to Say Yes

***

Later that night, at Rainbow's coffee bar, Sasha found herself sitting at an outdoor table under the lights. Customers were clustered at other tables. A lone guitarist strummed his instrument under the evening spotlight. In stark contrast to the earlier heat of the day, the February evening was cool and crisp. Sasha felt she couldn't have asked for a better setting for her life-changing revelation.

Seated next to her, his chair pulled close, was James Talbot, a strained expression on his doughy face. His mood seemed as low as hers was high. Hands beneath the table, she crossed her fingers for luck. *No way does James Talbot expect the bombshell I'm about to drop...*

"What are you so happy about tonight? he asked her. Her lips spread into a cat-got-the canary smile. She knew she looked pretty. Tonight, she even felt pretty.

"You are so observant, Jamie," she gushed. "I was thinking about the sweet Valentine card you brought me tonight. Better late than never, I always say. Oh, by the way, did I mention that I have something to tell you?" she purred, pleased with herself.

"Lay it on me," he prompted, apparently only mildly interested.

She clasped her hand around his beefy forearm, which was lying on the tabletop. She needed to go slowly and carefully. Too much too fast would be bad. She wanted to convince him, not upset him." It's about...your wife," Sasha said, lowering her eyelids to indicate her reluctance to smear poor misguided Poppy.

"Poppy? What about her?"

She saw that James became instantly uncomfortable at the mention of his wife's name. *Darn it.* He was still so torn in his affections. Not to worry. This maneuver would push him over the edge of the fence.

"James, has Poppy ever given you any reason to doubt her?" she began nonchalantly.

"How do you mean?" he asked.

"Has Poppy ever lied to you—that you know of? Once you told me that her honesty was one of the things you valued most," said Sasha.

Indignant, he replied, "Well, does that sound like she ever lied to me?"

Sasha pressed forward ever so gently. "Well, what if you found out that Poppy hadn't been as truthful with you as you'd thought?" She felt his meaty arm stiffen under her grip. Behind the heavy eyeglasses, his eyes focused in on her. *Now I've got his attention.*

She continued on, choosing her words carefully. "What if you found out that Poppy had been lying to you about something really, really major. What would you do? Divorce her?"

James stalled. "I don't know. I doubt if that will ever happen, so it's not a problem."

"Yes, but suppose it did. I mean, suppose I told you something that I happen to know personally that she told you, that I know isn't true. Something that impacts you deep," she persisted.

"Like what? You're talking in riddles, Sasha. If you know something, just spit it out. I'm not saying I'll believe it. But I'll give it a fair hearing. Stop pussyfooting around. Let me in on whatever it is you think you know," he said.

She leaned in to James and spoke softly to intensify the blow. "What I know is..." Pausing, she looked around to make sure no one was eavesdropping. "What I know is, that your wife..."

"Poppy? Yeah?"

"Sweetums, your wife lied to you about never having kids." *There. It's out. Let him digest it for a few minutes.*

"Say what?" He looked skeptical.

She pressed her breasts against his biceps and spoke into his ear. "Your wife has a son. She gave him up for adoption. Her son's been located. He was raised in Hawaii. He's nineteen years old. His name is Kipp. He's a pre-med student at Vanderbilt." She sat back and let the axe fall. She watched as his expression changed from irritation to outrage.

"No way in hell," he scoffed.

"Way," she said, nodding her head knowingly. "Nineteen years ago, Penelope Susan Craft had a son out of wedlock. She kept it a secret. From you. From everyone. She never told a soul."

James looked shaken, his skin ashen in the evening light. He said nothing, but sat blinking steadily as he mentally examined the possibilities.

"You see what a bitch she was," said Sasha. "I hate to say it, but...Let's face it. She wasn't worried. She knew she already had a kid. She didn't care whether you had one. Why should she? All she cared about was herself. Probably wanted all your money for herself. How she could have lied to you all those years...and made you suffer. It just makes me so...*oooh*, so angry when I think about it," she insisted intimately. "Pretty cold, dumping a kid that way."

"Who's the father?"

"I'm not at liberty to say."

"So Poppy did lie to me?" whispered James. "Here I thought she was so honest and open."

Sympathetically, Sasha nodded. "I know, sweetums. I couldn't believe it either when I first found out," she said.

"How did you find out?" he asked.

Here comes the real test. "That's not really important, is it? Can't we just say I know, and leave it at that?" she reasoned, batting her lashes rapidly.

"No, Sasha. I need to know how you know such a thing," he said, pain scrawled across his face. "You're telling me my wife wasn't a virgin when we married. You're telling me she has a grown son, while refusing me any children at all. Those are serious charges. You better be able to back them up. If you're slandering my wife, I'll slap you silly."

She patted his forearm patiently. She had expected anger. "Now, now, Jamie. I know it's hard to realize you've been betrayed by the one person in the world you trusted with all your heart. For so many years. Yeah, I know how hard that can be. But I hope you don't think I would lie to you that way. Is that what you're saying? That you trust Poppy, but you don't trust me?" She pouted charmingly.

"No, of course not," he frowned.

"Then can't you just trust me when I tell you this painful truth–and know that I did it because I love you and don't want to hide anything from you. I only want the best for you, James, you know that, don't you?"

Sheepishly, hr capitulated. "Of course I do, cupcake."

"You see, there are other people involved. They might get hurt if I reveal too much. You can understand that, can't you, Jamie?"

"Of course. I hadn't thought of that."

Very pleased, she cuddled closer and rubbed his nose with hers. "I do love you so," she said sweetly. "I just hate it that she used you and humiliated you all those years. Laughing at you behind your back. Thinking she had duped you. You, the finest mind to ever come out of South Texas…"

"Yep," said James, his ire rising again. Sucking in too much air, he belched heavily.

"If it were me, I wouldn't stand for it," she said. "But if it's okay with you… If you want to let her walk all over you like that, and spoil your chances for ever having a family of your own, when she already has a kid…"

"Hell, no, it's not all right with me," he said, belching again.

"You mean you're not going to let her get away with it?" She asked, feigning shock.

"Absolutely not!" he bellowed, shaking off her hand. Startled, the guitarist missed a chord.

"What will you do about it?" asked Sasha, eyes wide.

"I'll divorce the slut. That's what I'll do. I'll divorce her. Hell, Sasha girl, this is the kick in the pants I've been needing. I'm going to start my whole life over again. With you! What say?" Clasping her hand in his, he fell onto one knee. Her mouth flew open.

"Sasha Bassett, will you marry me?" he pleaded earnestly. "Will you make me the happiest man in town? Will you bear me a whole passel of beautiful bambinos that look just like your sweet little ole self? With my smarts."

"Yes! I will!" she announced emphatically. Around them, the other patrons suddenly applauded. Elated, James smothered her with kisses, while the versatile guitarist strummed a recognizable version of The Wedding March.

Half an hour later, after James had ordered a round of lattes for the house and proposed a toast to honor in marriage, Sasha lovingly strolled arm in arm with him into the parking lot behind Rainbow's. The remote car lot was dark, lit only by streetlights at either end. As the newly engaged couple approached Sasha's VW, James, seeing that they were alone, clumsily caught her in a bear hug and kissed her with cowboy abandon.

She hated his kisses. It was all she could do to not gag, but she pretended to be excited and amorous. She *would* have his children. She *would* be his wife and live well—or die trying.

It could be worse, she consoled herself. *My fallback plan is Rick DuBois.*

***

In the shadow of the brick building, Danny Vega watched the couple embracing. Earlier, Danny had been cruising Fifth Avenue in a late-evening drive, trying to sort out his plans. He was plagued with problems—the death of his half-brother, his stepmother's breakdown, her illicit lust, and his break-up with Sasha. He missed Sasha *big time.*

Suddenly, there she was. She was sitting at a sidewalk table at Rainbow's outdoor cafe. Decked out like a floozy, she was cozying up to some gray-billed, middle-aged dude. He couldn't believe his eyes. On impulse, he swerved Rogelio's black Jaguar into Rainbow's back parking lot. Looking around, he spied Sasha's VW. It was her, all right. He decided to wait.

As he waited in darkness, he listened to the sounds of the night. It was the height of the tourist season in Naples. He heard car engines from the Avenue and music and occasional laughter from the sidewalk cafés. The faint strains of guitar strings wafted on the air. The guy was pretty good. *Isn't that The Wedding March?*

Bristlng, Danny spied Sasha and the old guy strolling into the parking lot, arm in arm. In cold fury, he watched the paunch take Sasha in his arms and ram his furry tongue down her throat. *His throat.* Rage welled up inside Danny. He *hated* this guy. If only he had a knife or a gun...

No, skin was better. What he really wanted was to pound the living shit out of the freakin' SOB. With his bare hands. Watching from the shadows, he couldn't believe his eyes. *This nerdy jerk is what she dumped me for? He must have a bundle in the bank.*

As the couple parted, he saw the man's features more clearly. *No! Not James Talbot! Poppy's husband? Unbelievable.*

Sneaking closer, hiding between cars, Danny continued to spy on the couple. Sasha climbed into her little VW. Talbot held the car door open for her. Then the *old fart* leaned in to give her a kiss. Danny was so close he could hear what she said to him. He could smell the sandalwood that saturated her hair and clothing. Crouching in the dark, Danny stilled his breathing to a minimum. The scent was making him crazy.

"Jamie, sweetums, do me a favor, please. Don't tell Poppy her son's been found. She'll find out soon enough. I don't want it to come from me," she begged Talbot.

"I'll tell her nothing," he said. "I don't care what happens to Poppy anymore. Let her find out the hard way. That'll plant a firecracker under her ass. She needs a good shakin' up." Patting his posterior, Talbot sensed something amiss. "My keys are missing," he said.

"I'll bet you left them on the table. You had them out when you were paying the check."

"Yeah, I did. You're a real cupcake." He leaned in and gave her a parting smooch.

"Want me to wait?" she asked? Danny knew that tone. She wanted to go home.

"Nah. Go on home. I'll see you in a couple of hours, Mrs. Talbot-to-be," he said.

"I'll be waiting, Mr. Talbot."

"Think about where you want to go on our honeymoon," he called, as her VW rolled out of the lot, red tail lights fading into the night.

Honeymoon?

Watching through slit eyes, Danny saw Talbot sidle back into Rainbow's. Waiting in the shadows, he improvised a quick plan. When Talbot, keys in hand, stepped out of Rainbow's gate, and made tracks for his SUV in the parking lot, Danny made his move.

As Talbot pressed the remote to unlock the Beamer door, Danny sprang at him. The body blow knocked Talbot to the ground with a heavy thud. Caught off guard, he flailed defensively on the asphalt, as Danny fell upon him, socking him, over and over, with stone-solid fists powered by jealous fury.

Thrilled, Danny felt the spongy tissue implode. He felt the sticky warm blood as it squirted out of James' flesh. He could smell it, too, and it fueled his rage, but, in the dark, he could not see it. All he knew was his superior strength destroying the potency of his sexual rival.

Delirious with power, he realized that Talbot had stopped flailing and was lying inert on the ground beneath him. Fear seized him by the throat. Springing to his feet, he felt the sticky warm blood on his hands. Wiping his hands on his shirt, he prodded Talbot with his foot. *Nothing.* The SOB was dead meat.

His breaths short and fast, Danny scanned the night for witnesses. There were none. Relieved, he stared down into the darkness at the mound of gutted flesh that was–or had been–Sasha's lover.

"Eat that, you..."

Talbot made no response. Danny stepped forward to bend down. His foot crunched the glass that had once been Talbot's lenses. His anger still hot, but cooling, he realized his predicament. Quickly, under cover of night, he ran for safety. *Shit! Where's the car?* Panicking, he found the black Jag, fumbled his way inside and drove away, leaving James Talbot a bloodied mess in the parking lot behind Rainbow's. Speeding north on Gulfshore Boulevard, he prayed that the lot wasn't videoed by a security camera.

***

In the dead of night, Danny steered the Jaguar into the drive of his father's Bay Colony home. From inside the car, he opened the automatic garage door, eased the vehicle into its customary spot, and lowered the garage door. Quietly, he shut the engine, stepped out, and closed the car door. An alarm bell went off in his head. Inez's car was missing.

As if I don't have enough trouble tonight.

Then again, perhaps his father was with her. Rogelio had said he'd watch over Inez. Concerned but preoccupied, Danny opened the trunk of the Jaguar. Doffing his father's spare windbreaker, he folded the garment neatly. Then he placed the windbreaker in the exact position he had found it, not ten minutes ago, in the trunk of the car. The jacket had done the trick. It had helped him get past the guard at the Bay Colony entry gate, no problem. Closing the trunk, stopped to take a few deep breaths. He would clean the jacket when he had a chance.

On the drive north, he had managed to remove the blood from his hands with bottled water and paper tissues already inside the car. Safely at home, he now stuffed the bloodied tissues into a brown-paper bag he had found stored on a shelf in the garage. Hopefully, he could sneak up to his room, without interference, and flush the bag and tissues down the toilet.

His body still felt ragged from the scrape. He had been really pumped. His hands and wrists ached now. His knuckles were bruised and swelling.

He'd have to get the car cleaned on the q.t. He knew some guys. He would look them up tomorrow. Right now, he needed to act as though nothing were amiss. Not a living soul knew he had done James Talbot. No one needed to know.

His panic had subsided during the past five minutes since he had made it through the guard gate unscathed. His mind was clearing. He was beginning to regret what he had done. But he had done it. There was no going back. Now he had to cover his ass.

Thankfully, he remembered the deal he had made earlier in the afternoon with *Everybody's Business*, the popular international tabloid newspaper. The money would be deposited in his account by tonight. It would be available first thing in the morning. He would cash out. He would flee to the Caribbean by tomorrow night.

Pick an island. Any island. Maybe he would invite Maude Winston to go with him. He'd heard she'd split with Heston. Maude was a babe. Skinny, but a babe. Mean as sin, he'd decided. Just the type he'd like to take down a few notches. A real challenge.

He didn't want Sasha anymore. Sasha was a two-timing slut. He would never forget the image of old man Talbot down her throat. *Yeah, it hurt.* Shaking his head to cast away the thought, he checked the inside of the car one more time for good measure. Everything checked out.

Now to go inside. Girding his loins, Danny padded though the garage-entry door and into the darkened house. Bag in hand, he tiptoed across the kitchen floor. Was his father at home or not? That was the big question.

A bright light suddenly illuminated the kitchen. Danny stopped short. Pupils adjusting, he saw his father blocking the kitchen doorway, hand on the wall at the light switch.

"Inez?" Rogelio said. Then added, "Oh, it's you, Daniel."

"Si, Popi," He stood paralyzed. It was only a matter of time before his father noticed.

"Have you seen your stepmother?" Rogelio asked. "I can't find her."

"You were supposed to watch her." Danny grasped the plastic bag to his chest and folded his arms.

"I fell asleep," said Rogelio, blinking. "Is that blood on your shirt?" he asked, realizing.

"Popi, I..." Danny began. "I need to go upstairs. I got to go to the bathroom, man." He tried to ease through the doorway, but Rogelio, now suddenly on guard, stood his ground.

"Let me see your hands, Daniel." His father jerked Danny's wrist from his chest. The plastic bag dropped to the tile floor. The bloody tissues spilled out. Quickly, Rogelio examined his son's hand and then looked sternly at him. "Who were you fighting?"

"Nobody, I…"

Rogelio slapped his cheek, hard. "Don't lie, Daniel. Who was it? What happened?"

"Some jerk," he replied, steely jawed, shrugging off his father's attack. "I was in a bar. Playing pool. He tried to cheat me. We had it out."

Rogelio watched his son's dark eyes. "I've known you all your life, son. I know who you are. Who did you fight?"

"I told you!" he cried. He did not want to hurt his father.

"You told me a lie! I want the truth! Who was it? Did you kill this man?"

"Get out of my way, old man," he snarled, pushing his father from the doorway. Stumbling momentarily, Rogelio recovered and, pursuing Danny, tackled him and wrestled him to the floor. "I'm older than you, but I'm not decrepit," said Rogelio, pinning Danny beneath him. "And I taught you everything you know. Whom did you fight?"

Exhausted and afraid, Danny had stopped fighting. Lying prone on the floor, he now let his muscles relax. The heart had gone out of him.

"You won't believe me if I tell you," he said wanly.

"Try me," said his father, looking down at him.

"James Talbot," he said on the exhale.

Rogelio cocked his head. "You mean Poppy's husband? The big accountant from Texas? Why?"

Danny nodded. "Let me up, Popi. I've got to wash up. In case the police come."

"The police?" echoed Rogelio, fully alert. "Did you win this fight?" His countenance darkened. "Where is Talbot now?"

Lying motionless on the tiles, Danny let his head roll to the side. He no longer cared what happened. "In the parking lot behind Rainbow's."

Loosening his grip, Rogelio slid off his son's body. "You left him lying injured? Is he alive?"

"I don't know," he confessed

Scrambling to his feet, Rogelio said, "I feared as much. Did you start it?" He was now hunting for his car keys. Resignedly, Danny pulled himself upright into a sitting position on the floor and, reaching into his pocket, tossed his father the keys to the Jaguar. He felt listless, disillusioned with himself, with his father, with Sasha, with life.

"Yes."

"Why?"

He licked his lips and looked away. "He was…Frenching Sasha."

Rogelio struggled to comprehend. "Your Sasha? Poppy's husband?" he asked, boggled, his interest piqued. Danny did not reply. "Did anyone see you?"

"No." Danny lolled his head.

"How many times, Danny? I thought you had yourself under control." Rogelio gazed at his son in deep sadness. "You left James Talbot to die?"

"He's still there. I am here."

"Ye gods." Rogelio glared at his son in consternation. As his son's eyes met his, his heart softened. "This is my fault. My fault. I have set a bad example for you all your life. I'm going to find him before the authorities do." Without another word, Rogelio strode to the garage and piled into the black Jaguar. Thirty minutes later, Danny emerged from an upstairs shower, wrapped a black velour bath towel around his waist, and answered his ringing cell phone.

"Talbot's gone," his father's voice said cryptically. "I'm heading for the emergency room. Find your stepmother. Daniel." Rogelio rang off.

Maybe, old man. Maybe not. Stripping off the wet towel, Danny Vega weighed his options in the full-length mirror of his bedroom-closet door.

Chapter Sixteen

L istening to love songs on the satellite radio, Poppy closed her eyes, but sleep would not come. Sitting up, she turned off the radio. Should she take something? Her insomnia problem was getting worse. All she could think of was Heston's fervent, penetrating kiss. She could still feel the heat of his arousal as he pressed her to his loins, his hot hand searing her bare flesh.

Enough. She looked at the digital clock on her nightstand. Only 9:25 p.m. Perhaps it was too early to sleep. Somehow, she had thought it was later. The bedside phone rang.

Heston? Reaching for the receiver, she held it to her ear. "Hello?"

"Are you sleeping?" said the unwelcome voice of Sasha Bassett.

"No," said Poppy, hostile, still seated on the bed.

"Can you meet me for a drink at the Starfish Grille? In, say, twenty minutes?" Sasha asked, her voice teasing, her attitude mysterious.

"Why should I?" said Poppy argumentatively.

"Because I have some news that will blow your socks off," said Sasha. "I want you to hear it from me first."

"Then tell me now."

"Oh, no. This news is too big for the phone. It's got to be in person or no go. Don't worry. I'm buying."

Again, Poppy glanced at the clock. "Okay," she said reluctantly. Hanging up, she immediately had second thoughts. It was like agreeing to meet a viper at the local pond.

Half an hour later, she found Sasha seated at the Starfish bar drinking a Singapore Sling. "Mineral water for me," she told the server, as she sat down across the table from Sasha and draped her shoulder bag over the back of the chair.

"Thanks for coming." Sasha's eyes were slanted, the corners of her mouth tilted. "This won't take long. I have to get home and feed Gabby."

"Good," said Poppy warily. "I don't have time to waste. Thanks," she said to the speedy server who places a bottle of mineral water in front of her, along with a cocktail glass filled with ice cubes. "I'll pour it, thanks," she said, dismissing the server.

Pouring the bottled water into the glass, she looked at Sasha. She had seen that look before. Sasha was gloating. The question was, *over what?*

"Out with it, Bassett," she said, sipping mineral water from the glass. "You've got something to say to me. Say it and let's go home."

"All right," said Sasha, her grim smile fading. "It's just this. I won't try to con you. I thought about it. I thought about giving you some song-and-dance routine, but I won't bother. We've known each other too long, Poppy. Here it is. I have been seeing your husband. We've been dating." Pausing, Sasha watched her closely. She said nothing, however, merely sipped her water, too stunned to react.

She felt as though she'd been socked in the stomach. Yet she had been expecting something dire and had steeled herself for it on the drive over.

"Dating?" she inquired at last.

"*AKA*, sleeping with," said Sasha, draining her cocktail glass. "And more."

"More?" Poppy said, unable to manage more than a one-word remark.

"Yeah, Poppy. We're making plans." The gloves were off. Sasha's expression was haughty and condescending. "I thought I should tell you. I thought I owed it to you. Why should you be the last to know?"

Standing, Poppy picked up her shoulder bag and hung it securely on her shoulder. Then she picked up the glass of icy water. "Here's what I owe you, girl friend," she said, slinging ice water into Sasha's smug little face.

Sputtering, her rival yelped, "You stupid bitch!"

"You're lucky I didn't stab you with the silverware," said Poppy, oblivious to the server, who had rushed over to table. "What a lying slut you are!"

"You want whole truth?" cried Sasha angrily, rising. "Here's the rest of it! The private detective found your bastard son. Chew on that, whore! You've got no business calling me a slut."

Stupefied, Poppy stood blinking. "I don't believe you!" she croaked.

"I don't care what you believe!" exclaimed Sasha, dabbing water from her face and chest.

"Where is he?" she whispered, realizing.

Throwing the wet napkin at her, Sasha cackled nastily and resumed her seat. "Stuff it, sister! If you want details, ask your precious movie star. He should know all about it by now. You and I are finished. As of now."

"Heston *knows?*" she breathed, incredulous.

"Have a nice day, ma'am," the server said wryly as Poppy turned suddenly and sprinted out the door of the Starfish Grille. Devastated, elated, irate, terrified, cut to the quick, she was blinded by jumbling emotions.

For a few moments, she could not even remember where she had parked her car. The parking lot at the Waterside Shops was not huge, but she didn't want to wander around, searching aimlessly. She wanted to escape *pronto. Try to think.*

Forcing herself into calmness, Poppy mentally retraced her steps and, at length, remembered where she had parked. Scurrying, in a bid to avoid encountering Sasha leaving the restaurant, she scrambled into the sedan and, after two screechy false starts, managed to fire the ignition. She couldn't remember the route home, but it didn't matter now. All she wanted to do was drive, drive, *drive.* Drive and cry and process.

They found Noel. They found my baby. Is it true? Can Sasha be trusted?

Amid traffic lights and violent tears, she steered the car east on Pine Ridge Road towards I-75. Swerving to avoid a crash with a white pickup, she frantically searched the glove box for tissues to wipe her eyes and nose. Her cell rang.

It better not be that gutter-slut Sasha again. Maybe Heston?

"Hello?" she said, wiping her drippy nose.

"Poppy?" It was a mature man's gravelly voice.

"Yes?" she sniffed.

"Rogelio Vega here. Poppy, I have some difficult news. Your husband, James, has been brought here to the emergency room. I'm at the Naples Central Hospital. You'd better come down here right away."

"Hospital?" she said, struggling to drive. "Why? What happened?"

"He's been injured."

"How? Is it serious?"

"I'm afraid so. They won't tell me anything more. I'm not family."

"I'm on my way," she promised.

"If I'm not here when you arrive, Poppy, I'll speak with you later on."

"Thanks, Rogelio," she mourned. *This couldn't be happening. What a bizarre night.*

Distraught, she made a sharp right turn onto Airport-Pulling Road and, recklessly sped south through traffic towards the Naples Central Hospital.

*   *   *

"Enjoy your purchase," the stout gun dealer said to Inez Vega. Smiling gaily, Inez patted the side of her leather purse and then zigzagged out the shop door. In the darkness of night, she stumbled over the curb, breaking a heel on her left shoe. Scooping both shoes from her feet, she opened the trunk of her car and tossed them inside. Barefoot in the smooth gravel, she wiggled her toes in pleasure, and then laughed out loud at herself.

Once inside the vehicle, she opened her purse and extracted her purchase, a .38-caliber revolver with matching bullets. *Like shopping for an ensemble at a boutique.* Again, she tittered at her own funny thought. Too bad others didn't recognize how clever she was. No one did, especially not Heston. Hess had never appreciated her style of humor.

Hess had never even *liked* her. He had been so cold when she had phoned him earlier in the day. All she wanted was to love him. That's what she had told him–plain and simple — but he wouldn't listen to her, even when she tried to explain. Again, he had rebuffed her. All he could talk about was that idiot Poppy Talbot and that stupid little daughter of his.

Inez felt flushed, humiliated, as she turned Heston's words over and over in her mind: *I realize now I've loved Poppy Craft all these years. I never really loved you, Inez, not the way I love Poppy. To be honest, with you and with myself, which I'm trying to be, I only married you on the rebound from Montserrat Flynn, when she abandoned me in Miami and flew off to Trinidad with that marine biologist. Please, please, leave me alone now, Inez. Please stop chasing me, honey. You're acting like one of my obsessed fans. If you need help, I'll get you help. I'm getting professional help for my daughter. The best that money can buy. Why not you, too? I'll do anything in the world for you, to help you, Inez. I'm desperately sorry for what I did to you and to Franco. But our getting back together is out of the question. You can see that, can't you?*

Inez cringed and buried her face in her hands. She wanted to die.

Reaching into her purse, she found a bottle of pills, opened it, and popped a few tablets into her mouth. She wasn't sure how many, maybe two, maybe three. It was too dark to be sure. Enough to help her forget the pain. While waiting for the drug to take effect, she lovingly stroked her sleek new gun and then placed it carefully inside the car's glove compartment.

"I need a gun," she said aloud to herself, too loudly. "I *need* it to protect myself from the man who killed my son. From Heston Demming. And from his whore, Poppy Craft. Hess hates me now. He wants to kill me," she muttered studying, her makeup in the car mirror. "He killed my son and got away with it, but he's not going to kill me, too. Oh, no. I'm going to protect myself. He'd like me to be out of the way. That's just what he wants, but I'm going to protect myself from Mr. High and Mighty." Her words were beginning to slur.

She smiled. *It was smart of me to buy that gun permit.*

Satisfied in her own mind, she started the car and drove the empty back streets of Naples, west of the Tamiami Trail. Wandering pleasantly in a drug-induced haze, she drove along Crayton Road, past lovely homes, manicured lawns, immaculate church yards. Turning onto Seagate Drive, she saw the lights from the multi-storied Naples Grande Hotel on her left, its copper roof asleep under the stars. Turning north, she drove past the Waterside Shops and past the Teutonic grandeur of the Naples Philharmonic and Art Museum. Then, giggling, she careened her car onto Pelican Bay Boulevard. She must be more careful. One couldn't drive too carefully in Naples. The police—or their cameras—were always lurking somewhere. They would stop you on any pretext. A haven for thieves, a town like this. The gluttonous place bulged with money and glitz, art and jewelry. And she loved every bit of it—except for that stupid Poppy Wallace Gallery. How she despised that red-headed, freckle-nosed strumpet. Vengeance in mind, she schemed as she drove along.

Pelican Bay Boulevard was free of traffic. Alone and aimless, Inez realized dimly that she did not want to go home. She did not want to see Rogelio. She did not want to see Danny. And Franco was gone. She couldn't go back to the graveyard. The guards had orders to call her husband if she showed up there unannounced.

She wanted to get lost. She wanted to lose herself, to be swallowed up and to disappear into nothingness. Was that death? It would come soon enough. What would it be like? Parking her car at the deserted north tram terminal of Pelican Bay Beach, she removed her steely new gun from the glove box and sauntered down the paved walkway leading into the private mangrove swamp preserve. Opening her purse, she sipped Scotch from a silver flask.

All night she could traipse the miles of wooden boardwalks. She could watch the sun rise from the private Pelican Bay beach. She wasn't frightened. She had her Pelican Bay ID card. She could hide in the bush if she had to. She had her gun. If any alligators charged at her, she would shoot them dead. She could shoot anyone or anything now. Suddenly, she was in control.

The thought seemed hilarious to her. Dropping to her knees, Inez laughed and laughed, all alone in the swampy wilderness at night. At her side, the ghost of Frankie laughed with her.

***

"I'm here to see my husband," Poppy said, rushing up to the emergency-room receptionist. "I was told he's been injured?"

"His name?"

"James Allen Talbot," she chattered, unnerved.

"One moment, please." While the male receptionist checked his computer screen, Poppy glanced around the ER waiting room. Small clusters of people occupied various seats within the rows of vacant chairs. "A doctor will be out to speak with you shortly," the receptionist said ominously. "Please have a seat in the waiting area."

"Thank you," said Poppy mechanically, but then persisted. "Do you know what's happened to my husband? Will he be all right?" Terrible scenarios of violent accidents were rumbling in her stressed mind.

The receptionist stared at her blankly. "The doctor will be out to see you shortly."

"You can't tell me anything more?" she asked.

"No, ma'am."

Exhaling loudly, she plopped, frustrated, into an empty chair next to a large extended family of migrant workers. Everyone in the group, from toddler to grandfather, was waiting for word of some beloved patient. Not so for James. She was the only person present on his behalf.

"Poppy Talbot?" said a man's voice behind her, a familiar voice of velvet gravel. Jerking around, expecting to see the doctor, she beheld instead the distinguished countenance of Rogelio Vega. "May I sit down?" he asked.

"Please do," she said, patting the seat of the adjacent chair. "Thanks for calling me, Rogelio."

"Have you seen him yet?" he asked.

"No. I'm waiting for the doctor now."

"Any word?"

"No, nothing. It sounds serious, doesn't it?" she chattered nervously.

Rogelio nodded. "Yes, it does."

"How did you know James was here?" she quizzed the courtly gent beside her. On the long drive to the hospital she had tried unsuccessfully to connect the dots.

"It's a long story, Poppy," he responded. "And not a pretty one. I am ashamed to tell you. I regret very much that I have anything to do with this matter, except that it allows me to be of service to you."

Flustered and confused, she cocked her head. "Why?" she asked. "Please, Rogelio. Tell me what you know."

"Please, Poppy," he said hesitantly. "I beg your indulgence. At this time, I cannot divulge what I may or may not know. For the moment, I must plead the Fifth Amendment."

"I don't understand," she said, brows knitted.

"Do you understand what it means to protect someone you love?" said Rogelio, his voice low. A whiff of cigar smoke clung to his clothes. Across

the room, a baby squealed. In the corner, a young couple studied the offerings in a candy machine. Suspended from the ceiling, a giant TV screen
carried a local golf match.

Oblivious, her eyes widened. "You mean that someone you love is
somehow involved in this?" Staring at the linoleum floor, Rogelio sat
mute.

"I see," she said. "Yes," she admitted reassuringly, "I know what it's
like to love someone so much you'd do anything for him—or her."

He winced at her words. "Do you? In a way, I'm sorry to hear it."

She looked askance. "What do you mean by that?"

"I was hoping against hope that you weren't in love. Ah, but such a
condition would defy human nature," he smiled sadly. "Whom do you
love, lovely flower? Not your boorish husband, surely?"

Her jaw dropped. "Rogelio!" she chided.

"Don't bother to spare my feelings," he said, eyelids drooping. "Tell
me. I am becoming reconciled to my fate."

"What fate is that?" she asked.

"An aging man who cannot have the thing he most truly wants in life,
a man who realizes, suddenly, that that precious thing will elude him
forever—into eternity."

Poppy blushed. "Are you talking about...?"

"You, Poppy," said Rogelio, his voice soft, his attitude gallant. "I'm
talking about you."

She stammered. "Rogelio, I'm sorry. If I've ever given you any cause to
believe, even for one moment, that I had any romantic feelings for you..."

"No! Stop, please!" He pressed his index finger to her lips, then removed it. "You never did. I swear it. I was only hoping, hoping against
hope, as I said. No," he said, blinking slowly. "I know now that I was only
dreaming." He seemed to be memorizing her face. "I've made mistakes,
Poppy. I set a bad example for my sons. I resented my wife. I did...bad
things."

"Oh, Rogelio!" she exclaimed, turning away from him and dropping
her head into her hands. *This is the most terrible night!*

"Oh, please. I did not mean to cause you distress. Your circum-stances
are serious enough. But I need to hear you say it, with your own lips. So I
will ask the question. Do you think...you could ever...love me, Poppy?"

Turning back to face him, she gathered her courage and all the dignity
she could muster. "No, Rogelio. I'm sorry. I could not ever love you that
way. My heart belongs to another man."

Slapping his hands to his knees in resignation, Rogelio stood up to his
full height. "And his name is not James Talbot, I'll warrant."

"Now really isn't the right time to..." she objected.

Rogelio interrupted her. "It's that blasted Heston Demming? Am I right? The daughters of men with the sons of gods," he mused unhappily. "I knew it, from the moment I saw the two of you together that night on the dock, at his housewarming party. There was something in the air, some electricity, some energy called up by the cosmos. Ah, yes. I knew that night I was undone."

Poppy shrank into her seat. "You could see that? Truly, Rogelio, I feel just awful about this."

"Don't," he said, patting her on the top of the head. "My fate is Inez. I know it now. And you—you'll have to tell James. I don't envy you that. At least, I'll never have to break someone's heart."

Mortified, she sat stone-silent. A woman in a white coat approached them suddenly. "Mrs. James Talbot?" she inquired of Poppy, who sat motionless.

"Yes," answered Rogelio. "This is Mrs. Talbot."

"Mrs. Talbot, I'm Dr. Janice Reese. I have some good news. Your husband has regained consciousness. But I also have some not-so-good news. We're admitting him to intensive care. He's not out of the woods yet."

Rogelio scowled. "Will he live?"

"Possibly," the doctor replied. "We'll do everything we can. But I can't make any promises."

"Oh, dear," moaned Poppy faintly. Then she clutched the lapel of the doctor's lab coat. "What happened to him, Doctor? I still don't know. Was it a car accident or what?" she pleaded. The doctor cast a look at Rogelio, then looked back at her and gently removed the hand from her lapel.

"Your husband was beaten within an inch of his life," said the female doctor matter-of-factly. "He's lucky to be alive."

Perturbed, Rogelio whistled faintly and glanced towards the exit door. Poppy merely gaped at the doctor. "Beaten? By whom?"

"We don't know yet," replied the doctor. "The police are with him now. I'm sure they'll be in to question you at some point, Mrs. Talbot—about your husband's movements."

"I don't' know anything about his movements," she cried. "We're separated."

"Oh, well," said the doctor, turning to leave. "They'll want to speak with you anyway, I'm sure. Routine. Maybe you don't know this, then. The guitarist from Rainbow's on Fifth Avenue found your husband bludgeoned in the parking lot. About an hour ago."

Dumbfounded, she stared at the gaunt woman.

Obtaining no response, the doctor continued. "The ER receptionist can direct you to intensive care, Mrs. Talbot, if you want to visit your husband later on. I'd give it a few minutes. Let us get him settled in," the doctor advised, walking away indifferently.

"Thank you, doctor," she said. Left standing alongside Rogelio, she turned to confront him. "You know who did this?" she whispered, her mind at work, calculating the possibilities.

Rogelio blanched. Again, he glanced towards the exit doors.

"*Adieu*, my flower," he said suddenly. swiveling on his heels and breezing out the exit door. Waving a courtly hand, he called a farewell. "*Vaya con Dios.*"

"And with you also," murmured Poppy, watching him go, her mind a whirlwind of speculation. There was only one obvious solution, one obvious culprit. *Can it be true?*

Her cell phone rang. She answered without thinking.

"Poppy?" the beloved voice said.

"Heston?"

"Yes."

"I was hoping you would call," she said dolefully.

"Can you meet me somewhere? Anywhere, I just need to see you, talk to you," he said. "I know it's late. Listen, I have some important news to share with you," he added tantalizingly. "It's really big news. I can't just blurt it out over the phone."

"I'm afraid you'll have to," she sighed woefully. "I'm in the emergency room. James has been beaten up. They're putting him in intensive care. He may not make it."

"What?!" He bellowed in her ear.

"It's true, Heston. Unbelievable, but true. I'm going in to see him in just a few minutes," she explained. "He's just regained consciousness. The police have been questioning him. Then they'll want to speak with me."

"Hell," he grumbled, at a loss. "Okay, look Poppy. This news can't wait. I don't want to tell you this way, but I will."

She cradled the phone. She heard her own shaky voice "I think I already know. I had a savage encounter with Sasha earlier tonight. She told me that our baby's been found. Is that it?"

"Sasha Bassett?" cried Heston, outraged. "How the devil does she know about it?"

"I don't know. I guess the private eye told her."

"Dammit! That means he betrayed my confidence," he seethed. "That means it's only a matter of time before…"

"Before what?" she asked, catching sight of two approaching uniformed policemen.

"Before the whole world knows," he growled. "Look, Poppy. Since you already know, I'll make this quick. I've taken steps. My lawyer's pulled some strings. We've contacted the adoptive mother and, with her permission, the boy himself. I'm flying him down here tomorrow from Nashville. He'll be here, at my place, by late afternoon. A limo is bringing him from the airport. I want you here with me, Poppy Sue. I want us to meet our son together. Will you be here?"

"Yes," she said, now staring dazedly at the two bulldog officers, who stood waiting for her to terminate the phone call. "We'll talk later, okay? The police are here and want to speak with me."

"Hey, do you want me to come up there?" Heston demanded. "Man, I'm an idiot! I'll be there in twenty minutes."

"No! Too much publicity!" she whispered cryptically. Nearby, the officers' trained ears were flapping.

"You're right, of course." said Heston. "See you tomorrow then, my heart. Call me immediately if you need anything. Anything at all, do you hear me? Poppy, are you happy with my arrangement?"

"I will be," she said softly, a lump in her throat.

"Good," he said abruptly, ringing off. Shutting down her cell phone, she faced the policemen directly. She could feel them sizing her up, as a witness and as a woman.

"Are you Mrs. Talbot, ma'am?" asked the taller of the two.

"Yes, Officer."

"What can you tell us about your husband's movements tonight?" asked the shorter one.

"Nothing," she replied. "My husband and I are separated. We live apart. We lead separate lives. Officers, please. You've talked to my husband. Tell me who did this to him." *Though I already know the answer...*

The two policemen exchanged glances. The shorter one took the lead.

"Ma'am, are you familiar with the name Daniel Vega?"

***

Early the next morning, Wallace Smythe sat working intently at his desktop computer in the gallery. Distracted, he picked up his ringing phone.

"Poppy Wallace Fine Art," he answered, focused on the screen. "How may I help you?"

"You can help me by clueing me in, asshole," said the strident voice of Cedric Spicer.

Snapping to attention, Wallace pushed his chair away from the desk and crossed his long legs in preparation. He grinned inwardly. *Here we go!*

"Clueing you in to what, Cedric, old buddy?" he sneered merrily, stroking his moustache with his index finger.

"Don't mess with me, Wally," Cedric spat. "I heard you've been buying up all my work. Every bit of it, for some anonymous buyer. Now I can't find a piece from my oeuvre anywhere. Where are my paintings? Who's got them? Who is your beastly client—as if I didn't know!"

"You don't know diddly, Ceddy," he said, shoulders shaking in silent laughter.

"I know you're going to tell me where my work is."

"Certainly. It's in storage. Permanently."

"How dare you! How dare he!" screamed Cedric.

Flinching, Wallace drew the phone away from his ear. "Please don't scream, my man. I get the message." *Oh, this is wonderful. Better than I'd hoped for.* He snickered silently.

"Well, you make sure Heston Demming gets the message. He can't take all my work off the market. He simply can't! My career will be ruined. I'll be lost to posterity."

"If not to posterior, eh?" Wallace joked gleefully.

"Shut up, you ice queen. I won't stand for it, hear me? You tell that to the great star Heston Dimwit. You tell him I won't stand for his ruining my career!" shouted Cedric.

"Ah, me, dear boy. You should have thought of that before you bonked his wife. Not that I have the slightest idea in the world what you're talking about. Heston who? Have a good day, twirp. And, please, *don't* keep in touch," Wallace smiled, about to hang up the phone.

"But my affair with Maude didn't mean anything!" Cedric insisted shrilly.

"Not to you, maybe," Wallace said.

"You've got this all wrong, Wallace."

"I know you two tried to screw me."

"No, I swear! Maude wasn't going hang you out to dry. Just Poppy."

"Tell it to your shrink, Cedric."

Bored, Wallace clicked off his phone and chunked it on the desk. Kicking his feet up on the desktop, he crossed his ankles and reclined in his chair, his arms behind his head. Proudly, he cherished his victory.

He had given Heston exactly the right advice. Cedric Spicer would never recover from this twist of fate. Spicer's life's work would rot in a hole. His puny career would swirl down the toilet drain to be lost forever. Thrilled, Wallace congratulated himself on a plot well conceived. He ruminated, a wicked smile twisting beneath his thick moustache.

Cedric, you creeping maggot! I know you too well. It was I who advised Heston not to harm you physically to extract his revenge. It was I who told him you would enjoy the beating too much. I'm the one who suggested he do something that would really hurt you. However, Heston himself came up with the idea of hoarding your life's work. The man's as resourceful as he is beautiful, eh, Ced? You back-stabbing charlatan...

Wallace Smythe's smile twisted into a thorny frown. His eyes glowered beneath a furrowed brow. *Screw me again, Cedric Spicer, and see what happens. Wait until Maude Winston finds out you were only using her. Perhaps there is justice after all.*

His frown twisted back into a smile. Savoring sweet vengeance, Wallace guffawed with malicious delight.

Chapter Seventeen

Rapaciously, Heston gnawed at the manicured nail of his left pinky finger. Queasy with anticipation, Poppy watched her man fidget. At the grand piano, little Winnie and her new nanny—Beryl Northgate, a fleshy, pug-nosed, blue-eyed Brit fresh from university—plucked the ivory keys to pass the time. The antique French clock on the mantelpiece read 4:37. Suddenly, Heston's personal assistant, dapper Andrew Upshaw, whisked into the living room unannounced. He was followed by the slow-moving Lissette, who was dressed in a maids' uniform.

"The driver just phoned me, Heston. Your son will be arriving in five minutes. The limousine just turned onto Gordon Drive."

Poppy and Heston looked at one another. Understanding flashed between them. The moment of truth was at hand. Would they be up to the challenge?

"*Oye,* Miss Winston!" smiled Lissette, chirpy as a lark. "Your new big brother will be here soon. Don't you want to meet him? Aren't you excited?"

Winnie banged the piano keys. "No!"

"Why not?" chided Lissette. "Eh?"

"Big brother died. Don't want a new one," Winnie pouted huffily.

"*Fea!*" chastised Lissette. "Why would such a pretty girl say such ugly things?" Lissette glanced at Poppy and shrugged.

"Perhaps Winnie's just a bit nervous," offered Beryl Northgate. "That's perfectly understandable under the circumstances."

Heston took the helm. "Winston's brother, Franco, loved her, but he wasn't always kind to her. Naturally, she expects all big brothers to be the same way. But, they're not, Winner," he said, bending down, hands on knees, to look Winnie in the face. "This big brother is a whole new person. He may be nothing at all like Franco. I think you should give him a chance. What do you think?"

Uncertain, Winnie looked to Poppy for direction. With a swift smile, Poppy nodded in the affirmative. Winston looked back at her father.

"Okay, Daddy," she said, lips set in a firm line.

"That's my girl," said Heston lovingly. He pulled the child into his arms and hugged her.

Again, Andrew peered into the living room. "The limo's entering the gate, sir. The young man will be arriving at any moment."

"Thank you, Andrew," said Heston, looking around at his motley crew. "Well, battle stations, everyone. Andy, tell Mrs. Palmer to send in the refreshments," he called.

"Oh, fine," said Poppy, rolling her eyes. "I'm afraid I'm all butterfingers today." *We'll be lucky if I don't throw up while playing hostess.*

"I'll do it," offered Winnie sincerely.

"You may have to, sweetheart." Flustered, Poppy walked forward, wobbling on her feet. "Seriously, Heston," she said, suddenly clutching his muscular forearms and swaying on her feet. "I'm not sure I can make it. Maybe I should leave. You see the boy. You meet him first and tell him all about me and –I'll catch you later." She was halfway across the foyer before he caught her and dragged her back into the living room.

"Forget about it, Craft," he said, pulling rank. "Our son has flown a thousand miles at the drop of a hat to meet us. You're meeting him. Now. If it doesn't work out, so be it. But you've been running away from this all your life. That ends here. Now. Today."

"Heston!"

"You're going to face it, at last, and you're going to face it with dignity. No matter how bad it is, it can't be any worse than all the dreadful scenarios you've been conjuring in your imagination for years. It can't be any worse than the hell you've put yourself through already."

Andrew Upshaw cleared his throat.

"Daddy," said Winston, tugging at the tail of Heston's sports jacket.

Near hysteria, Poppy bridled, "That's easy for you to say, Heston. You didn't even know our son existed all those years. You never spent one sleepless night over this child, but I did! For nineteen years!"

"You lost sleep over me?" a young, testosterone-laden baritone said unexpectedly. Wheeling around, Poppy and Heston caught sight of a tall, fair-haired, athletic young man hovering in the foyer. Clean-cut, clear-skinned, and outrageously handsome, he was wearing a navy-blue blazer, striped tie, and bone-colored trousers. If she hadn't known better, Poppy would have sworn she was staring at an old photo of her father as a young man—the same handsome young man who had provoked jealousy in his homely older brother, Melvin.

"That's what I was trying to tell you," sighed Winston, throwing her hands up in the air.

Standing behind Winnie, hands on the child's shoulders, Beryl smiled.

Next to her, Lissette tittered warmly as Heston strode forward to shake the hand of his first-born son and usher him into the parlor.

"Thank you for coming, Kieran," said Heston warmly, at his best under pressure. He turned and indicated Poppy. "And this is…"

Kieran stood unsmiling. "My mother, I presume?"

The room began to spin. Poppy felt Heston's strong arm grip round her. Taking up the slack, Heston said, "Yes, son. I'm your natural father, Heston Demming…"

"Everyone knows who you are," said Kieran caustically.

"…And this is Penelope Craft-Talbot, your mother," Heston finished hopefully.

"We call her 'Poppy'," chimed in Winston, "'cause she has red hair."

"Everyone calls me 'Kipp'," said Kieran.

"Do you prefer it?" asked Heston.

"Yes."

"Well, Kipp, this is your half-sister, Winston Demming, my daughter, and her nurse, Beryl Northgate, and Lissette Garcia, our domestic. Winnie's mother and I are estranged," Heston explained, extremely aware that Kipp's honey-brown eyes had never left Poppy's face. Nor had hers left Kipp.

"Can you shake hands?" Heston whispered to her.

Faltering in fear, she tried to raise her hand in a womanly handshake. His arm suddenly encircling her, Heston guided her hand to her son's. She felt the firm, sinewy grip of her grown son's warm hand. Tears stung her eyes.

Baby Noel…

"May I hug you?" she asked, barely audible.

"Certainly," said Kipp, obviously uncomfortable, but not adverse to a show of affection. As she placed her head tenderly upon his broad chest and wrapped her arms around his wasp-waisted torso, the young man placed his hands on her back noncommittally, without affection.

"In case anyone wants to know," he announced, "My name is Kipp McKendrick. Not Kipp Demming." Still in her embrace, he cast an amused but leery eye at little Winnie.

"We know who you are," said Winnie. "That's why you're here. Why do they call you Kipp?"

"Enough, *nina*," admonished Lissette, trotting out of the room towards the kitchen. With pale hands, Beryl squeezed Winnie's small shoulders.

"I don't know. They just do," the young man said flatly. Winnie rolled her eyes. Kipp patted Poppy's back uncomfortably, his face under rigid control.

"Please, everyone sit down," instructed Heston, as Lissette dutifully appeared with a richly laden tea service. "Perhaps you'd better serve..." he started to say, but Poppy drew herself away from Kipp and patted her hair in place.

"No, Heston. It's all right. I can do it," Poppy said serenely. Something had happened to her during that embrace, something that had fused the fractured elements of her distressed soul into a whole, functioning woman. At long last, in her own heart, she had claimed her lost child as her own.

"You will excuse me, then, please?" said Lissette. "So nice to have met you," she said, exiting the room, to Kipp.

"Likewise," said the young man stoically.

"Coffee, tea, lemonade?" Poppy asked Kipp graciously.

"Lemonade, please," said Kipp, joining the circle, at Heston's invitation, around the expansive coffee table. Skipping over to the couch, Winnie plopped down beside her father. She watched Kipp closely as he sank into the deep chair and then rose briefly to accept a glass of lemonade and plate of petit fours and gourmet cookies from Poppy.

"How was your flight, Kipp?" asked Heston politely, accepting a cup of coffee but waving away the goodies Poppy offered.

"I want them," said Winnie, accepting the plate. "And a cup of tea."

"What do we say?" Heston asked his daughter.

"Please," replied Winnie correctly.

"Very little tea with a lot of milk," Heston instructed Poppy, who complied in surprise. Again Heston turned his attention to Kipp. "Your flight. Was it satisfactory?"

"Oh, yes, sir," said Kipp, sipping his lemonade thirstily while balancing the small plate in his lap. "It was fine, thanks. Thank you for the ticket."

"No turbulence or anything?"

"No," said Kipp. Unobtrusively, his golden eyes scanned the elegant surroundings.

"Not 'til you got here, eh?" quipped Heston.

Cordially, Kipp cracked a smile. Poppy did, too. To be mannerly, she had poured herself a cup of tea but did not drink it. The knots in her stomach were relaxing. Still, she didn't want to push her luck.

"This is some place," observed Kipp, eyes roaming the room.

"Like it?" asked Heston genuinely.

Kipp shrugged. "Sure. What's not to like?"

"I just bought it," said Heston. "I had a vacation place in Aspen, and one in The Hamptons. Sold 'em both while I was filming my last picture.

Just settled on this one a couple of months ago. Not even that long. Right, Poppy?"

She nodded.

"What picture would that be, sir?" asked Kipp.

"*The Diary Key*," replied Heston. "It's a period piece. To be released next spring."

"Is Lennox Cordova in it?" Kipp raised his glass before sipping his lemonade. "A true babe," he toasted.

"Yes, she's very pretty, isn't she?" said Poppy. She hoped her tone didn't sound desperate. She wanted the boy to like her. Oh, how she wanted it. She ached for his approval. *Is that asking too much? After rejecting him for a lifetime?*

"Alas, no, she's not in *Diary Key*. But Lennox will be in my next picture, *Acapulco Moon*. After that, I fly to The Seychelles to do location work for a sci-fi comedy called *Stumble Bummer*." Heston shook his head but smiled abashedly. "I'm between pictures right now. It seemed like a good time to make the move back home to Naples," Heston elaborated.

Kipp's eyes were on him. In awe, Poppy watched the young man sizing up his real father. He had inherited the beauty of the Demming family.

"We're starting the new picture in a couple of weeks. In Mexico. Cancun. Know it? It's just across the Gulf from here."

"No," said Kipp. "I've never been there. I've traveled a lot though. We moved around a lot. My dad...I...I..."

"Don't worry," said Heston, pierced but stoic. "It's all right to refer to him as your dad. For all intents and purposes, Benjamin McKendrick was your father. Until now." Heston glanced affectionately at Poppy.

"He'll always be my father, one way or another," said Kipp defensively. "Benjy raised me. He broke his back providing for my mother and me." Guiltily, Kipp glanced at Poppy, whose face had fallen. "Just because I'm here, now, today, doesn't mean I've forgotten who raised me."

"Of course not, Kipp," Poppy admonished. "We know that." She glanced at Heston. "We realize how difficult this must be for you."

"It's difficult for us," said Heston.

"Not for me," said Winnie, nibbling on a tiny iced cake.

"Hush, child," said Beryl, smiling lamely at Kipp. Her chipmunk-like cheeks and prominent front teeth gave her an endearing smile. Her small blue eyes beamed brightly from behind black-framed lenses.

Kipp grinned, in spite of himself. Then his expression, once again, became stern. "I just don't want the two of you to have any false hopes. I'm not here to embrace you as my parents. I already have parents. I don't even know you people." Then Kipp reassessed. "Well, of course, I know who you are. Everybody in the world knows who you are..."

"Heston," said Heston, regarding the boy intensely. "Call me Heston. For now."

"Gee, I've even seen some of your movies. I even liked a couple of them," said Kipp.

"The ones with Lennox Cordova?" Heston grinned.

"Well, there's a start," injected Poppy hopefully.

"Then why did you agree to come here?" said Heston, his silver-blue eyes never leaving his son.

She felt strengthened. *He's mad about the boy.*

"Because...Gee, I don't know. Curious, I guess. Yesterday it seemed like the right thing to do. Now I'm not so sure." Kipp set down his glass and plate and folded back into the deep chair. "Maybe I should go. I don't feel right..."

"No, please, Kipp. Stay," she said, butterflies returning. "You're already here. Let's make the most of it. We were planning for you to stay overnight. We have a special dinner planned. And a sail, if you want it. Heston owns a yacht."

"A yacht?" Kipp asked.

"Uh huh," said Winnie, pointing. "Out back. *Windswept.* She's a beaut."

"So are you," said Kipp unexpectedly.

Winnie's jaw dropped. Pleased, she glanced from Poppy to Heston.

"If I have to have a kid sister, she might as well be a looker. As a matter of fact, you're a darned fine-looking bunch."

"Good looks run in the Demming family," said Poppy amiably, accepting the compliment with delight. "You resemble my father, too— your grandfather. He's passed on now, unfortunately."

Suddenly, emotion overcame Kipp. He stood up. "Do you have a bathroom?" he inquired nervously.

Heston stood and half-embraced the boy. "It's all right, son. Really. We understand what you're going through."

"Do you?" cried Kipp, shielding his eyes and pushing Heston away. "I don't think so. I don't think you know what it means to be tossed out like a piece of worthless garbage when you're just a week old. I don't think you could possibly know what that kind of rejection feels like. Well, I do. I've lived with it for nineteen years. I hate you people. You want me to love you, but I hate you. Don't you get it? Please, for Pete's sake, tell me where the bathroom is."

"I'll show you," said Poppy, rising, struggling valiantly to mask her devastation. Guiding the young man down the hallway, she returned, alone. In the long hallway, Lissette appeared suddenly, her face a beatific ray of hope.

"Don't worry, Miss Poppy. He'll come around," she said soothingly.

"Oh, Lissette, I hope you're right," she whispered.

"You'll see," said Lissette, on her way down the hall. "Just give the boy some time."

Bolstered, Poppy returned to the living room and resumed her seat in stark silence. Still worried, however, she glanced at Heston, who looked rocky himself

"Cookie, Daddy?" said Winnie, climbing onto Heston's lap as he crumbled back down onto the couch. Compassionately, the little girl held out her plate.

"No, thanks, Ladybug," he said, kissing her forehead affectionately. "But I do appreciate the thought."

His expression haggard, Heston stared for a moment at Poppy. He seemed about to weep.

Her heart flip-flopped in her breast. *It's all my fault, right from the very beginning.*

They waited a few moments in silence, until they heard footsteps approaching down the hallway. Reentering the living room, Kipp had collected himself. His macho demeanor had returned. He was once again the aloof young stranger.

"I don't hate you," he mumbled apologetically. "I'm just in shock. Understand?"

"Of course we do," said Heston urgently.

Dinner that night was a stilted affair. After Kipp had settled into one of the mansion's spacious guest suites, Heston presided at the dining-room table, with Poppy, on the opposite end, as his hostess. Kipp and Winnie sat on either side of the long, slender table. The conversation centered mainly on sports, as well as on Kipp's other interests and Heston's accomplishments.

The two men seemed to be searching each other out. Every now and then, however, Poppy caught her son watching her, his interest in her circumspect but tenacious. She would have to wait to speak with him alone, just the two of them.

Tonight was Heston's show. *Let him put it on.* Indeed, Heston's zeal took some of the pressure off her. At the table, her eyes roamed fondly over her long-lost son, much as her hands would have stroked him as an infant—lovingly and possessively.

Once or twice during dinner Kipp teased Winnie. Once, Winnie teased him right back. Once she threw a pea at him, much to her father's consternation.

That night Poppy slept fitfully in a guest room down the corridor from Kipp's. Heston had insisted she stay the night. When she walked into the breakfast room, early the next morning, she found the sideboard groaning with food, but herself alone at table.

"Where is everyone?" she asked Lissette, who finally appeared, distracted and agitated.

"In the media room, ma'am. Watching the big-screen TV," Lissette replied. "It's a scandal. That's what it is."

Alarmed, she asked Lissette to guide her to the media room. Arriving upstairs, she spotted Heston, Kipp, and Winnie, along with Beryl Northgate, all crowded in front of the screen, staring at it in apparent amazement. Listening to the announcer on screen, she at once under-stood why.

"Number-One Son was allegedly unaware, for all of nineteen years, that he was the progeny of one of the biggest film stars of our generation. Kipp Demming, shown here—down, gals and wannabes—is currently pre-med at Vanderbilt U. Will Medicine's loss be Hollywood's gain? With looks such as this youngster possesses, the sky may be the limit. Was Kipp the cause of the recent highly publicized break-up between Heston and his supermodel wife of five years, Maude Winston? Heston's earliest known mistress, Kipp's mom, Poppy, is a beauty in her own right, and, guess what, she's *baaack*." Transfixed, Poppy saw her own image suddenly flash onto the big screen. "*Yowza*," concluded the announcer with a gleam. "Score another point for our man, Heston."

"Slime ball," sneered Kipp. "Turn it off."

Beating Heston to the punch, Winnie grabbed the remote and shut the screen down. The group remained unaware of Poppy's presence behind them in the room. Dazed, Poppy noticed several tabloid newspapers draped over the back of the couch. The headlines screamed: STAR'S SON DISCOVERED; and HESTON'S TRAGEDY TURNS TO JOY.

Kipp's photograph was emblazoned beneath each headline, right next to her old high school yearbook picture.

"How did this happen?" she shouted, startling the others.

Jumping to his feet, Heston rushed over and pecked her cheek. "Good morning, Brown Eyes," he said, too jolly. "Did you have breakfast?"

"Yes, a bite. Heston, how did the media find out about Kipp? And me?"

"You heard the TV?"

She nodded. He sighed.

"You're not going to believe this, darling," he said, glancing at Kipp, Winnie, and Nanny Northgate, who, evidently, already knew the scoop. "My manager phoned me at 6:00 a.m., to tell me that the story had broken internationally. He said..." Pausing, Heston pressed the air with his hand to generate calmness within himself, "He said that—you won't believe this, Poppy—that our old friend *Danny Vega* had sold the story to one of the tabloids for $300,000. The rest, as they say, is his-tory. Unless I miss my guess, we owe this entire fiasco to Little Miss Sasha Blabbermouth Bassett, and to that seedy flatfoot, Rick DuBois."

"Why am I not surprised?" she murmured, heart palpitating. "I should have stayed in bed." Her first act upon arising had been to phone the hospital. From the nurse on duty, she'd learned James' condition had stabilized overnight. His doctors were planning to move him from the ICU to a regular room in the hospital. The nurse on the phone told her that, during sleep, James had been calling out the name 'Sasha.'

"Good morning?" said Kipp, who had been standing since becoming aware of her presence.

She sloughed off her stupor and cast her son a sad smile.

"Good morning, Kipp," she said, offering him her cheek. The young man kissed her, but sheepishly, his hands repeatedly rubbing the thighs of his tight jeans as he slumped back into his leather chair.

"Good morning, Miss Poppy!" cried Winnie, bouncing on the Scotch-plaid sofa. "You're a big star now, too. Everyone's a big star but me."

"Hold your horses, kiddo," warned Heston. "Your time's coming. Trust me."

Poppy knew he would shelter his daughter from the world as long as he could. Only recently she had learned that, since the child's birth, Winnie had graced nearly as many fan-magazine covers as her parents. The world couldn't seem to get enough of the little Winner Demming.

"You should sue the son of a gun who leaked this story," Kipp said to Heston. Standing side by side, the two Demming men were so alike. Alone inside herself, Poppy felt a new sensation, one she'd never before experienced.

Can it be pride? When I should be feeling shame?

Agreeing with Kipp's comment, Heston nodded. "I wish. But it's not that simple. I tried calling the Vega home, but there's no answer. A machine picks up. Can't get Inez. Can't get Danny. Or Rogelio. Most definitely can't get that little she-devil, Sasha or the gimmicky gumshoe."

"I'd be calling my lawyer," said Kipp.

"Trust me, it's the first thing I did," said Heston, trumped.

"My fiancée must be freaking out," said Kipp.

Poppy met Heston's eyes. "Fiancée?" she and Heston said in unison.

Beryl Northgate uttered a little cry.

"Yes. Marissa Neville," said Kipp, his cheeks glowing pink, as his parents turned to stare at him. "Marissa's at Vandy, too. She's a townie. A rich girl from Honolulu. We're both pre-med."

"Oh," said Heston, significantly, to Poppy, just as Winnie clamped Kipp by the hand and pulled him to his feet.

"I promised to show you *Windswept,*" the child said earnestly. "She's out back."

Shrugging her round shoulders at Poppy and Heston, Lissette waddled off behind the Demming children as they both exited through the sliding glass doors. Beryl clipped right behind her. As the doors slid shut behind the nanny, Poppy broke into a silly giggle.

"Who am I?" she said. "I can't seem to remember."

Heston drew her close and whispered in her ear. "I remember, Grandma. You're the love of my life. When I get hold of Danny Vega, I'll cut his heart out."

"Heston..." she whispered, her hand gently stroking his pulsing neck. "Be calm."

"I'll never be calm until I have you, safe and secure," he vowed hoarsely, his hot, scented breath in her ear. He brushed her cheekbone with his lips. "Not until you tell me you're free to be mine, and I can watch over you. At that precise instant, my life will begin anew."

Give me strength. "Oh, Heston. Have I learned nothing from abandoning my baby all those years ago?" She pressed her forehead to his collarbone. "How can I leave my husband now? When he's so badly injured? I couldn't walk out on him helpless. I just couldn't." Delicately, her fingers played with the chest hair peeking out from his V-necked tee.

"I know that," he said, his lips toying at her temple. "If you could, you wouldn't be the wonderful woman you've become." In sympathy and support, he intertwined his fingers with hers.

Andrew Upshaw rapped sharply at the media-room door. "I'm sorry to disturb you, Heston, but I felt you ought to know. Outside our gate, the reporters are descending. The media circus has found us. The neighbors are complaining."

"Blast it!" said Heston, tearing away from Poppy and dashing to a front window. "Andy, call the police," he commanded, peering out. "They'll take care of it. If they won't or can't, call the goon squad. I didn't pay ten million dollars to be hassled in my own home." A helicopter sounded over head. "And tell Kipp and Winnie to come inside," Heston added, aggravated. "Just when Winner was starting to come out of her shell," he muttered to Poppy, who now stood by his side at the window. Together they looked out at the encroaching world.

***

By late afternoon, the street in front of the Demming mansion had been cleared of interlopers. Cruising her car down Galleon Drive, Inez Vega saw only a quiet, banyan-lined street of costly and immaculately maintained homes. Heston's house number was 1708. It had been her listing. *It should be my home.*

She felt weary but the pills and alcohol sustained her. Since yesterday she had slept only at intervals, dozing in the car, on the beach, and, the previous night, on a bench in the mangrove preserve. Inez had never returned home to Bay Colony. She had lost her purse and cell phone somewhere in the mangroves. She was glad. She did not wish to see Rogelio ever again, and Danny would not admit his passion for her.

Screw him. This time, Danny hadn't even bothered to come looking for her. If he had, he'd have found her by now. Rogelio probably wanted her lost. Sulking, she watched the road.

Heston's mansion was at the tip-end of the bight. His lot fronted Naples Bay, which led directly out to the Gulf of Mexico, through Gordon Pass. She ought to know. She had sold him the place. As she drove along slowly, in the dimming sunlight, her eyes registered the number of each succeeding mailbox.

There it is. 1708 Galleon Drive.

The wrought-iron gate was closed to intruders. *Naturally.* Beyond the gate, through the iron bars, Inez could see the stately, yellow-stucco British Colonial. *Interesting.* A white limo was parked in front. A driver sat in the front seat, waiting.

Inez surveyed the property. It would be difficult to get inside, but she would do it. She would work out a plan. She patted the weapon in the holster strapped to her side.

It has to be done. If she did not do it, Heston would destroy her, the same way he had destroyed Frankie. Frankie had tried to warn her. He didn't like Heston. He told her Heston was dangerous. But she didn't listen. And now her dear boy was...

She trembled. She wouldn't let that happen to her. Franco was with her now. He would help her and protect her. Franco would guide her. Again, she patted the gun.

"Thank you, Frankie, dear," she said affectionately. Cocking her close-cropped head to the side, Inez listened. "Oh, yes, the redhead, too," she said aloud. "Don't worry, Frankie. I won't forget. She's the one who turned Heston against us. Everything was working until she poked her nose in."

In the rear-view mirror, she noticed a police car sneaking down the street towards her. Driving back up the street, she endeavored to remain inconspicuous. Twenty minutes later she cruised slowly back down Galleon Drive towards the same spot. The police car was absent.

Approaching Heston's gate, she slowed her car to a crawl. Between the bars, she saw the front door of the mansion swing open. A woman stepped out, with Heston following closely on her heels. Inside the car, Inez's skin prickled. Frigid air from the car's vents made the sensation unbearable. Automatically, she shut the AC off, her eyes still glued to the woman with Hess.

In the early evening light, she could not make out the details of the woman's appearance. She could see that the woman was wearing a man's cap and carrying a shoulder bag. Tripping lightly down the front steps, Hess was toting a large overnight bag, which he handed over to the limo driver. The driver placed the bag inside the limo's trunk, then walked around and opened the door for the woman, who had descended the steps also and now stood waiting.

It was Maude, of course. Or Heston's folly, Montserrat Flynn. What a witch that one was. Yet, as she looked more closely, Inez realized the woman was neither Maude Winston nor Montserrat Flynn. She felt a cold wave of dread wash over her.

Craning her neck, she watched through the bars as Hess engulfed the woman in a deep kiss. Then, beaming from ear to ear, he snatched the cap from the woman's head and slapped it onto his own tousled mop. The woman struggled for the cap, flirtatiously, but Heston won the bout. The woman's hair was *red.* Horrified, Inez realized the truth.

The woman was Poppy Craft-Talbot.

Flooring the gas pedal, Inez sped away down the darkening street. A few minutes later, as the white limo carrying Poppy Craft-Talbot rounded the corner onto Gordon Drive, the driver paid no mind to the headlights trailing far behind him. The headlights followed him all the way to the Naples Central Hospital.

Tailing the limo, Inez conceived a new plan. Heston's mansion was too secure to invade. She realized that now. There was only one place she could finish him and only one way to get there. She could do it. She was a good swimmer.

Frankie whispered conspiratorially, "Look for neighbors who are not at home, Mom."

"That's a good idea, Frankie," she said restlessly under her breath, eyes darting as she pondered. "I could sneak through their property and swim."

"You're a good swimmer, Mom," Frankie urged affectionately.

***

Poppy Craft-Talbot stood staring down at her husband. She couldn't comprehend what she was seeing. James was lying prone in a hospital bed. His distended face was a crazy quilt of cuts and bruises. Parts of his body were swollen and bandaged.

"I'm sorry I wasn't here earlier today," Poppy said, clearing her throat. "I…I couldn't get away. Circumstances. You know?"

"Yep. Sure," said James in a low voice that screamed of pain and heavy painkillers.

Poppy knew he didn't know why she hadn't been able to get away. How could she tell him? *What* would she tell him? That she had slept over at her movie-star lover's mansion. That the press had found out about their illegitimate son? That she couldn't escape the property until late in the afternoon because of the mob of paparazzi and reporters in the street out front?

"Why did Danny Vega do this to you, James?" she asked quietly, instead of explaining.

"Why does anybody do anything?" he said through new spaces where teeth once had been.

"Danny must have had a reason," she urged. "Is it—is it because you're d-dating Sasha?"

"I don't know," said James. He tilted his head towards the wall. "Yeah. Maybe."

She felt herself implode. "Danny was jealous?"

"He must have seen us making out. In the parking lot behind Rainbow's."

"I see."

"Do you see, Poppy? Some jealous maniac bashed my brains in because I was tonguing his honey-girl. How does that make *you* feel?" he rasped.

"Like you've moved on, for one thing," she ventured. "With my best friend."

"You already knew, didn't you?"

"Sasha told me last night that you guys were 'making plans'," she sniffed.

He grunted.

"Why? What's wrong?" she asked.

"All bets are off," he said.

Not sure she understood his meaning, Poppy weighed her options. "James, if you're having second thoughts about Sasha, there's something I need to tell you."

"Something bad, I'm sure. Let's have it."

"S-Sasha doesn't love you," she said.

He was silent. "She says she does," he said flatly.

"She's lying!" she cried. "She's using you. She's desperate to have a baby. She knows her biological clock is winding down. Tonya, her domineering mother, is pressuring her big-time to marry well and have kids. Her mom keeps Sasha pretty much under her thumb. She even owns the catering company Sasha works for, remember?"

"Yeah, I guess," said James.

"Sasha's trying to trap you. You can't trust her. She'll steal you blind. She'll betray you, the way she betrayed me by going to bed with you. She's head over heels in love with Danny Vega. She always has been. She always will be. Danny's the wild card in all this, that's for sure. It's not that I want to hurt you, Jimbo. I'm sorry. It's just that I don't want you to be hurt anymore than you already have been."

Again, he faced the wall. His voice was now even lower. She had to lean over him to catch his words. "Sasha told me one true thing. She told me about your bastard kid," he said. "You're the one who lied to me, Poppy."

Shocked, Poppy inched away from the bed. Befuddled, she struggled to respond. Of course, Sasha would have told him about the baby. It was a possibility that had escaped Poppy, caught up as she had been in recent events. Trapped, she pivoted towards the third-floor window and stared out, eyes brimming, at treetops and city lights.

"Did you hear me?" he asked.

"I heard you," she conceded. "What I hope you understand is this, James. I didn't lie only to you. I lied to Heston, too, by omission. And to my son. Worst of all, I lied to myself."

She heard a sharp intake of breath. "Heston Demming?" James rasped.

Closing her eyes, she nodded her head in acknowledgment. "I guess that's the part Sasha didn't tell you."

"My wife had Demming's bastard," James muttered in bestial distress.

Opening her eyes, Poppy rubbed her forearms for warmth and stared out into the night. "When I was seventeen, I bore Heston's son in secret. My uncle made me hide it from the world. Heston had been my high-school steady, not to mention my childhood playmate. He left me before I could tell him I was pregnant. It's too complicated to explain right now."

"Plus, I don't give a rat's ass," growled James with difficulty. "Any

252

way you cut it, Poppy, you lied to me and you screwed up my life by nearly ten years."

"Yes. You're right. I know that. I'm truly sorry."

"Sorry doesn't cut it. I want a divorce," said James, still facing away from her.

"Excuse me?" she said, too eagerly, again leaning across his prostrate body.

"I said, I want a divorce." He spoke slowly, deliberately.

She struggled for control of her emotions. "All right. If that's what you truly want."

"No, no! Don't protest so much," he quipped sarcastically. Then he groaned.

"Are you going to marry Sasha?" she asked too lightheartedly, suddenly desperate to find Heston. "And father her brood of baby foodies?"

"No way in hell," he said. "For your information, I've already broken off with Little Miss Sashay. She was here about an hour ago. I told her to get lost. She stormed out cussing me. There's lots of fish in the Gulf. No way am I marrying some chick with a psycho-thug boyfriend, who'd like nothing better than to bust my gut again. Or kill me, just for fun. Hell, no. Funny thing, Poppy. I don't love Sasha either. I just wanted a family of my own."

She heard the catch in his voice. "You can have that, Jim. You can find love."

"But not with you?"

"I...I..." The words caught in her throat.

"You're in love with Heston Demming," he said, his low voice cracking.

"All my life," she whispered to the sobbing man on the bed.

"I already knew," he blubbered ashamedly. "I saw you and Heston on TV this afternoon. I just wanted to hear it from your lips, Poppy." Gasping for air, he coughed uncontrollably.

Frantic, she pressed the call button for the nurse, who quieted James with an injection.

Ten minutes later, Poppy stood in a crowded elevator as it descended to the first floor. When the doors opened, she burst into the lobby and fled out into the barely lit parking lot. Spying the white limousine, she signaled the driver, who had spotted her in the headlights. The long sedan purred into position. Poppy scrambled into the back seat.

"Quick," she said to the surprised driver. "Take me back to the Demming home in Port Royal." What she wanted, more than anything in the world, right now, right at this very moment in the ever-expanding universe, was to make crazy, passionate love with the man of her dreams, and now of her reality. Desperately and deeply, she longed to lose herself in Heston's silver-blue eyes, to revel in his testosterone-rocketed, orange-myrrh scent. She yearned to feel him, inside and out, wrapped around her, running through her, melding into oneness with her very being, the way she had once felt, years ago. She ached to show him how he made her feel, then and *now*. How had he put it? *Like starlight on salt water.*

She slid the wedding band from her finger. Finally, she was free to love Heston the way he needed to be loved.

Chapter Eighteen

Heston was waiting for Poppy in the lamplight of the master-bedroom suite. She knew he expected her. Only minutes earlier, the limo driver had phoned him of their impending arrival. She had entered the dark mansion a whirlwind of desire. Now, seeing her heart's love, just as he had crawled out of bed—sleepy-eyed, thick hair disheveled, his body clad only in sweat pants, his naked chest exposed—she felt a warm tenderness clutch at her heart. She loved him so deeply and profoundly that it swept away every vestige of resistance.

"What happened? I thought you were going home," he said, advancing towards her.

"I am home," she said, running to him and throwing her arms around his neck. His confusion dying away, Heston seemed to absorb her aura. With heartfelt vigor, he folded her into his arms. Locked together, man and woman stood riveted, bound intimately by infinite gratitude.

Holding her fast, he asked, "What happened with James?" She felt a new knowledge in him.

"H-he asked me for a divorce," she said.

"And you said?"

"I agreed."

Her words rippled through the mass of muscle surrounding her, as an earthquake ripples through deep sea. How *much* her decision had meant to him. She loved him the more for it. Enmeshed, they clung to one another in burgeoning silence, until Heston spoke at last.

"Jesus, Mary, and Joseph," he uttered reverently. "Thank you." She nodded, ever so slightly.

"Did Kipp make his plane?" she asked, fingers cherishing his nape hair.

"Yes. He phoned from Atlanta. Photographers everywhere. Says he'll visit us again."

"Winnie?"

"Sleeping over at Lissette's house. With her playmate, Felicia. We smuggled Win and Nanny Northgate out in Lissette's Ford."

Poppy drew away and looked up into the silver-blues. "We're alone?"

Heston's mouth twitched in wry amusement. Boldly, he met her gaze. "Except for the housekeeper, who's watching game shows and curling her hair down the hall. Andy's gone out. The staff are gone home. The crew's gone. It's just you and me, Red."

He pulled her back to him, hard. "All alone...in this...great...big ...house..."

He kissed her forehead, her cheek, her nose, her chin, her neck. As his kisses cascaded onto her shoulders, her hands slid from his neck down to his bare waist. She could feel his ardor building. His hand found her breast. Her T-shirt was in the way.

"Raise your arms," he ordered. She lifted her arms over her head. Deftly, he stripped the T-shirt from her body, yanking the shirt quickly over her head and arms and then flinging it impatiently onto the carpet. His fire-ice eyes roamed her body. She felt her skin flush crimson. She wanted his eyes. She wanted his mouth. He knew what she wanted.

"Wait a minute," he said smoothly, running his hand down her arm. Striding to the door, he turned the bolt lock. Looking back at her with conquering eyes, he strode again to her, even more quickly, and grabbing her by the wrist, flung her across the king-size bed, dropped his sweat pants to his ankles, and crawled atop her hungrily Taking his head into her hands, she set her deepest need free, urging him closer, pressing him nearer. With his help, she slipped out of her slacks.

As Heston's mouth and hands took possession of her, Poppy felt the years of denial fall away from her like so many layers of outmoded clothing. Her life spark, her whole being, felt aflame in the present moment with Heston Demming, as he lovingly explored anew every inch of the wildly burning ocean he had traversed so many years ago. To Poppy, the past was what it was, but this moment was the culmination of all that ever was and all that ever would be. Flesh against flesh, blood pounding against blood, the whole sweaty pageant of human frailty coming alive in a glorious explosion of unleashed ecstasy.

For ecstasy it was, as Heston entered her at last, and the oneness became the completeness, over and over and over again, in a rhythmic organic soldering of man to woman, of woman to man. All the having, then the yearning, the fear, the not knowing, the not admitting, the regrets, the secrecy, the jealousy, the remorse, the adoring, the worshipping from afar, the companionship, the fun, the camaraderie, the gift of creation, all of it suddenly seemed to burst perpetually forth like an endless supernova star in a distant galaxy. Bestial ugliness or spiritual zenith, it all shimmered, spectacularly beautiful, because it was all part of the whole tremendous love she felt for Heston Demming, her natural mate, the man who had come home to her at last.

Lost within and without, Poppy cried out into the night, and, in the warmth of the lamplight, she saw her pleasure mirrored in Heston's eyes as he brought his face close to hers. Far from diminished, he seemed strengthened by her joy. Rolling over onto his back, he lifted her with him, in one sweeping, arching movement of masculine grace and shameless beauty. Riding the splendor of his desire, she knew no boundaries, no shame.

Then, lifting her and withdrawing, he rolled with her again, and this time came down on top of her and plowed into her, in a mind-blowing, heated final fury of passion. The cries Heston made were the cries in her dreams. Clinging to him, herself caught between two worlds, volcano and supernova, she felt the great shudder of his release, and felt herself being blasted out molten into the highest stratosphere, then, slowly, on gossamer threads, drifting back down to quiescent earth.

As Heston's rhythmic heat subsided, he fell across her, heavy, spent and breathless. How long they lay this way she did not know. Thought finally returned as she lay paralyzed beside him, but only one thought was worth thinking. *I love this man.* There was no need to say it. He knew. When he finally stirred, she stirred, too, each shifting position to accommodate the other's comfort. Words unspoken between them, Poppy and Heston drifted together into the bliss abyss of sleep.

Dawn was breaking when Poppy opened her eyes again. The lamp was still burning from the previous night. Heston was nowhere to be seen. Sitting up naked in bed, Poppy raised a hand to brush back red hair from her eyes. Her wrist glistened strangely. Thrilled, she realized that while she'd been sleeping, Heston had fastened his jeweled bracelet around her wrist in a final act of possession. Searching, she found him standing alone on the dock, staring up at the morning moon as it faded into the brightening sky, obscured by the light of the rising sun.

"Heston?" she said tentatively. He turned at the sound of her voice, his eyes twin stars of silver-blue. He opened his arms and she ran into the shelter of his love.

"Sleep well?" he asked, hugging her close.

"Uh-huh," she nodded cozily, snuggling into his virile warmth. "You?"

"Like the dead. I just woke Mrs. Palmer," he informed her. "Asked her to make us breakfast. She was a bit scandalized by your presence, but she'll get used to it. I called the crew. They're on the way over. I want to take the boat out—now. I want to be at sea—with you. Think you can handle that? At such an ungodly hour?"

"I'll get used to it," she giggled.

"Blasted right you will," he said. Biting down on his lower lip, he slapped her playfully on the behind. "Now get away from me before I get ideas."

Forty minutes later, *Windswept* was motoring her way through Gordon Pass towards the choppy Gulf of Mexico. Aboard and topside, Heston steered the wheel. Alive to the sea, Poppy stood at the ship's prow, hair whipping about her face. The salt spray stung her skin. Fascinated, she watched as, for a time, a yellow-tufted brown pelican flew low to the water's surface, parallel to the advancing yacht.

"Men, hoist the mainsail!" cried Heston into the wind. "Poppy! Go below and get me a bottled water. I'm thirsty as a camel this morning."

"Can't imagine why," she mumbled, obeying her lover's command. Backing down the stepladder into the cabin, she realized her own body was stiff and sore. It had been a while. Once descended into the cabin, she went to the refrigerator in the galley and extracted a individual-sized water bottle. Clutching the edge of the counter top, she steadied herself as the wave action increased.

BLAM!

She heard a loud report topside. *A shot?* Clattering up the steps, she emerged into the sunlight.

"Poppy, stay down!" yelled Heston on the wind.

She shrank down in alarm.

"Too late!" cried the voice of Inez Vega. "Please come up and join us, Penelope Sue."

With a frightened look at Heston, who still manned the wheel, Poppy followed Inez's command and emerged from below deck.

Standing in the cockpit, Inez held a small, ugly pistol. She was pointing the pistol directly at Heston's chest. Behind Heston stood his two crew members, shocked into silence by Inez's unexpected appearance and the discharge of her loaded firearm.

"Don't try anything, Poppy. He'll be dead before you reach him." Her dark eyes were frenzied, her lined face devoid of cosmetics. She wore only a sleek black one-piece swimsuit, which gave emphasis to her svelte figure. Her stringy tanned arms and legs were bare of gold bangles Her close-cropped dark hair was streaked with wild red-orange.

"Inez, what are you doing here?" said Poppy, struggling to take in the situation. She feigned calm, but fear was hurtling through her veins. How could she best help Heston?

"Keep your mouth shut." Inez swiveled the gun towards Poppy. "Just put down the water bottle and walk over there and stand with the other three."

"Why?" She played for time. Perhaps one of the crew would act.

"Shut up." Again, Inez swiveled the gun. "Move."

The look in the madwoman's eyes prompted Poppy to step forward. Setting down the bottle, she clung to faint hope as she moved to Heston's side.

"Stop," said Inez, following her with the gun.

"Inez, this is nuts. Why are you doing this?" Heston demanded.

"Self-protection," she replied, staring down her four hostages. As Heston steered, the sailboat motored its way through Gordon Pass, its sails not yet raised. Poppy could feel Heston's every cell vibrating. The wave action of the gulf jarred the boat spasmodically. She felt nauseated with fear. Her mind was in a tailspin. A million bad ideas crossed her mind.

"She's going green at the gills," Heston advised, aware of Poppy's every vibration.

"Don't vomit on me, Poppy," warned Inez. "I don't want to have to wade through your mess—you and your damned women," she snarled at Heston. She held the gun steady, still aimed at his taut belly.

"I'm all right," said Poppy, gaining control.

"You men!" Inez barked at the two crewmen behind Heston and Poppy. "Time to walk the plank."

Heston cried out in protest, "Inez, in the name of all that's sacred...!"

"Shut up, Hess! I'm not talking to you." She zeroed in on the two wary crewmen, who reluctantly did her bidding by walking to the port side of the yacht.

"Jump in," she commanded them.

"Skipper...?" Terrified, the two men teetered on the edge of indecision.

"Do it. I'll come back for you," Heston ordered. Poppy guessed he was thinking what she was thinking—that the crewmen's chances would be better in the water than onboard ship with a gun-wielding madwoman.

"Poppy, go with them," Heston said.

"No!" Inez shrieked wildly. "Poppy stays here. Frankie wants her here."

Poppy and Heston exchanged glances.

Inez aimed menacingly at her ex-husband. "My gun is loaded. I *will* shoot. If you jump, Poppy, I'll blow Hess away. Instantly!"

"No, don't! I won't jump!" shouted Poppy.

"Go on, then," Inez said to the crewmen, one of whom patted his back pocket in a silent message to Heston. Then, as the yacht motored out to sea, her two crewmen exchanged glances, clasped hands, and then, whooping loudly, hurtled themselves into the brine. Appalled, Poppy longed to look back, to make sure the men had surfaced in the yacht's wake, but she dared not turn away from Inez. If startled, Inez might shoot Heston. Obviously, this was to be Inez's ultimate act of violence. *How to forestall it?*

"At least throw them a life raft," Heston said, infuriated.

"No," said Inez, waving the gun. "Let's go below."

Suddenly, Heston cocked his head.

"Where did she come from?" Poppy whispered to Heston, turning to follow Inez's command. Hand on the wheel, he stood still, listening. Then Poppy heard it, too—the drone of a helicopter. Heston winked at her.

"She was hiding under the tarp on deck," he said in a loud voice.

"Why did she shoot?" Poppy asked loudly.

"I tried to take her gun away."

"How did she get here?"

"I swam!" Inez screamed, waving the gun under Poppy's nose. Then she, too, heard the drone of the approaching aircraft. Looking up into the sky, she gasped, her plan thwarted.

Heston lunged for her pistol.

"*Heston!*" Poppy screamed at the top of her lungs, as Inez looked down. Inez's black-suited body flew backwards onto the floor of the cockpit. Heston forced his ex-wife's gun-arm towards the sky and the gun went off in a terrific blast.

His strength superior, he wrested the smoking gun from his ex-wife's hand.

"Help us!" cried Poppy to the cameraman in the helicopter. The noise was loud now, as the chopper hovered above them. The wind from the whirling blades blasted downward.

"Don't waste your breath!" shouted Heston, hair flying. Staring down at Inez, he secured the gun in the waistband of his shorts. "If we die, he makes more money!"

"You're not hurt?" Poppy shouted, bouncing to Heston's side.

"No!" he shouted into her ear. "The bullet fired out to sea. Missed us both." He indicated Inez, who now lay sobbing pathetically on the floor of the cockpit.

It's all under control," he wheezed tensely. "Are you all right?"

Numb, she nodded and said loudly, "Yes. Thanks to you."

"I'm shutting *Windswept* down," he shouted, glaring up at the noisy chopper. "Radio the Coast Guard. Tell them what's happening. Tell them to pick up my crew first. They may have already. They had a cell phone, but I think we're too far out. Tell the Coast Guard to contact Rogelio Vega. Tell him we're coming in with his wife, to meet us at the Coast Guard station. Don't bother to hide the facts." He pointed up at the paparazzi chopper. "The jigs up."

"Aye-aye, sir," said Poppy admiringly.

Huddled, Inez sobbed inconsolably on the floor.

Following orders, Poppy turned her attention to the task at hand. Minutes later, her mission completed, she realized that *Windswept* was now adrift at sea. Looking around, she saw that Heston and Inez now were entwined on the floor, Inez's head resting on his chest.

The helicopter had moved away to the east. She assumed the cameraman was filming with a zoom lens. Dropping to her knees beside Heston, she sat back on her heels and eyed him with tender concern. His brimming eyes met Poppy's.

"Damn and blast," he muttered, a tear spilling out as he smoothed Inez's cropped head. "The last thing I need right now is more bad publicity."

"You were wonderful, Heston," said Poppy. "You *are* wonderful."

"No play-acting, for once," he sighed, adding, "Inez, you've seen too many of my movies. But you're no killer, honey."

"You're the killer, Heston!" Inez howled. "You killed my Frankie. You killed me. You killed me, Hess." Inez pounded her bony fists against his hard flesh. "I *need* to kill you—you and that witch! Poppy Craft turned you against me. Against Franco. She made you kill him, so she could take you away from me!"

Breaking free, Inez lashed out at Poppy, who stumbled out of reach just in the nick of time. Grasping Inez's arms, Heston locked her again in a stationary hold and lowered her back onto the deck.

"I need Frankie. I need Frankie," Inez sobbed into his broad chest.

"I know. And I'm so sorry, Inez. I am so sorry. I am so very, very sorry," he chanted hoarsely, softly rocking the deranged woman in his arms. His perfect face was contorted in agony.

Poppy knew the hideous thoughts running through his mind. In memory, he was reliving the day his mother had found his father hanging by the neck in their Lake Park backyard. Poppy averted her gaze to the horizon.

A beautiful night. A horrendous morning after. What will become of us all?

Chapter Nineteen

On the nearly deserted beach, on private Keewadin Island south of the Port Royal Club, the warm, March day was balmy and glorious. The high tide had just begun to recede. White-capped waves dotted the surface of the Gulf. Standing in the strong, gusty breeze that danced across the shimmering sand, Poppy clung to her new white-billed cap. Into her lungs, she drew the heady, seaweed-scented air.

Feeling particularly snazzy, she was sporting her latest clothing purchase, one paid for by Heston—a teal-colored bikini with a matching mesh jacket and gold-lame thong sandals. Not far from her feet, beneath a big, yellow-and-white-striped sun umbrella, sat little Winston Demming, who was happily patting the cool, crunchy sand. The girl's broad-brimmed, pink-straw sun hat was strapped in place beneath her chin with a baby-blue, gros-grain ribbon. Wisps of fine blonde hair protruded from beneath the hat and jostled on the breeze.

That morning, at the drugstore, Poppy had purchased two long, skinny, lavender Wacky Noodles, and an inexpensive blue-plastic pail, one filled with red, blue, and yellow plastic spades, shovels. When presented with the simple gifts, Winnie had been overjoyed. The swim-suited child had kerplunked herself down onto the sand and immediately set to work with a spade. Lost in her construction project, Winnie was now oblivious to the sight of her father and her half-brother, Kipp, who were tossing a Frisbee back and forth, just down the beach from where she sat. Poppy watched the rambunctious match in awe.

What fit and strong men. Really, Kipp is a grown man, underage still, but physically a man. My baby is a man. His father is a stud. Can this amazing thing really be my life?

Both of her men were attired in beach wear. Her son was wearing black trucks with a khaki T-shirt and reflective sunglasses. The love of her life was wearing electric-blue trunks with a white tank top and black designer shades. Kipp's limbs and hair were pale compared to his father's. Fortunately—from Poppy's point of view—her son had not inherited her tendency to freckle. Still, Kipp had just flown in from Nashville and shouldn't get too much sun too fast. Three weeks had passed since his first visit to Naples. Reaching into the cooler, which sat in the shade of the umbrella, she dislodged two cold, dripping bottles from the ice.

"You fellows want a drink?" she called to them. She held the soft-drink bottles aloft, wiggling them in her hands.

Wheeling around to catch an elusive Frisbee, Kipp crashed gracelessly to the sand.

"Yes!" cried Heston, laughing. Jogging over to Kipp, Heston extended a hand to his chuckling son and jerked the youth to his feet. Wiping gritty sand from his body, Kipp jogged southward to retrieve the Frisbee, then turned and followed Heston's path back to where Poppy and Winnie waited. Hot and sweaty, the two men collapsed onto the beach towels she had spread earlier on the ground beneath the cooler. Kipp pushed his sunglasses to the top of his blonde head. Heston tossed his shades onto the beach towel. With thumb and forefinger, he massaged his own closed eyelids.

"Kipp, you better rest in the shade." She pointed to a spot beside Winnie, beneath the big umbrella. "Are you hurt?" she added, concerned.

"Nah," said Kipp. Licking his bee-stung lips, Kipp exchanged a grin with his father. Springing up, he relocated to the shady spot his mother had indicated. Pleased, she handed him a bottle of soda pop, and then handed a similar one to Heston, whose eyes were teasing her mercilessly.

"What's so funny?"

"Nothing." He exchanged a second grin with Kipp. Snickering, both men drank thirstily from their pop bottles.

"Stop it, you two! Want some juice, honey?" Poppy asked Winnie, who was busily patting sand into a mound.

"No, thank you, Miss Poppy." Winnie's small, sweet voice carried on the wind.

"Did I tell you I went on the Internet and looked at your website?" Kipp's honey-brown eyes teased Heston as he drank from the soft-drink bottle.

"Cool, huh?" Poppy beamed, sinking into one of folding beach chairs they had brought along for comfort. *Naturally, these men choose to "rough it" on the hard ground.*

"What did you think?" Heston's silver-blues met his son's challenge.

"It was great. I liked the way you explained everything that happened," admitted Kipp. "I was kind of surprised to see my own face though."

Heston relaxed. "We—meaning your mother and I" he said, indicating her, "and my business group wanted to make sure my fans heard my side of recent events—you know, Franco's death, the public revelation about your existence, my divorce from Maude, and Inez's arrest. A lot of stuff had happened with me lately. We addressed those issues. Other sordid details we've been able to keep from the public."

"Like what?" asked Kipp

"We'll fill you in," said Poppy defensively. "Down the line." She wasn't ready yet to reveal Maude's evil scheme to frame her for art fraud or Heston's lifelong penchant for Montserrat Flynn.

"How's your fan base taking it, Dad?" asked Kipp. He tossed off the word casually, but his honey-browns found the Gulf horizon.

Poppy and Heston exchanged tender glances.

"Pretty well, son, according to the feedback we've received. Sixty-two percent of the emails have been favorable. That's good in anybody's book. My movie rentals are still high; sales, higher in some cases." In good spirits, he nodded his head casually. Pleased with life, he finished off his soda pop. "Hey, Winner!" he cried, jumping up, all at once full of pep. "How about a dip?" Bending down, Heston grabbed his shades from the towel and donned them.

Delighted, Winnie nodded and ceased her play. Hopping up, she brushed the sand from her small body. Scooping Winnie into his bronzed, muscular arms, Heston carried his little girl towards the breaking waves.

"Noodles, Daddy!" Winnie paddled her feet in the air and pointed towards the swim toys.

"I've got 'em," said Kipp, scooping up the plastic noodles and handing them to Winnie.

"What do you say, Winner?" said Heston.

"Thank you, big brother."

"You're welcome, sis."

Chuckling, Heston carried Winnie and the flailing purple noodles into the water. The wind had died down incrementally, but the waves were still marvelous swells. Kipp walked over and stood next to Poppy. She hoped Heston would be careful with Winnie in the water.

"No fans or stalkers on this private island," observed Kipp.

Poppy shook her head. "Your father wanted today to be strictly family."

"Oh."

"The waves usually aren't this big here."

Kipp pursed his lips. "I grew up on the North Shore of Oahu," he explained. "In my book, these puny swells don't even count as waves."

Cocking her head, she looked at her son. "Want to take a stroll up the beach?" she asked him. Her heart thudded. *Suppose he says no?*

"Certainly," he answered, after a moment's hesitation. Disappointed, Poppy noticed that he had not called her 'Mom.' Her eyes sought and found Heston's and Winnie's heads bobbing above the water's surface. Could she blame him? *I certainly haven't earned the title.*

Standing up, mother and son began a slow amble northward along the sandy shoreline.

"We'd better not stay out too much longer," she observed. "You don't want to get too much sun straightaway. I can't take much sun either."

"Yeah," Kipp nodded, his reflective shades still resting atop his golden head. "This year is the first time I haven't had a tan since I was eleven or twelve. Since moving to Oahu."

"My dad was a blond. So was his brother." Poppy's legs strode idly along in the wet sand. On her left, Kipp was closer to the water. He seemed so tall. His long, lean arms and legs were graced with golden-blond fuzz. The water sloshed over his strong ankles.

"Tell me about him." He strolled beside her slowly so as not to outpace her.

"There's so much to tell you. I don't know where to begin," she said. "He was young when he died. So was my mom. I have only childhood memories of them. But I have lots of photos to share with you. Is this all too strange for you, Kipp? To find a new family all of a sudden?"

"Yes," he confessed candidly. "It's really weird. A movie star's family to boot."

Neither mother nor son looked at one another. Both pairs of eyes scanned surf and sand.

"You seem to be handling it better now."

"I've gotten used to the idea. My...I mean, Nancy seems okay with it. You know, my..."

"Adoptive mother. The woman in Hawaii who raised you."

"Right."

"Well, that's good. I'm glad to hear it. Heston and I would like to have Nancy come and stay with us for a while. With you here, naturally. That way, maybe, we could all get to know each other." Her gut wrenched. She was terrified at the thought of meeting the woman who had raised her son. But it would be sometime in the distant future. Time would, perhaps, help her to face the inevitable.

"That's awesome," breathed Kipp. His relief was tangible. "Nancy's just knocked out that Heston is my real father. She was more excited about it than I was." He smiled affectionately. "My girlfriend, Marissa, is afraid I will become an actor now."

"A dream come true?" she said, almost under her breath.

"It's what every orphan dreams about, except me," he confessed. "I don't admire entertainers. I admire doctors and healers. I want to live a life of service to others. I want to save people's lives, not play-act for a living. I don't want to create junk for people to consume. I want to nourish them, physically and spiritually."

Poppy heard the passion in her son's resonant voice. Stopping in her tracks, she turned and looked up at him, as he, too, stopped and turned to face her. The sea wind brushed her cheeks like soft feathers

"Have you told this to Heston?"

"No. But I will."

"You can say it in a way that doesn't hurt him," she advised, squinting up at her son's handsome face.

Kipp looked around guiltily. "Okay. You love him a lot, eh?" Softly, in the outdoor glare, her son was squinting down at her.

Somehow, her eyes flooded, Poppy sank into his arms. "I'm sorry I hurt you, Kipp. All those *years* of hurt. There's nothing I can do, nothing I can say, to make up for the pain I caused you."

Kipp hugged her tightly, earnest as a cub finding his way home to the cave.

"I was mad at first," he said. "But I've had time to think about it now. I know you were a kid, younger than I am now. It must have been hard. With your uncle pressuring you. Heston gone to the big city. I get it. I get what you were up against."

"That doesn't excuse what I did." His khaki-colored T-shirt was wet from her tears.

"Gee, no, it doesn't. But it means you and I can find a way through," he said warmly, hugging her, while stifling his own tears.

"What's going on here?" came Heston's voice from down the beach. Breaking free, Poppy saw Heston strutting towards them, hand-in-hand with little Winnie.

"Hi," Poppy said, sniffling, yet smiling. She wiped the wet from her eyes.

"Everything okay?" asked Heston, looking from mother to son and back again.

"Fine," she said.

"Great," acknowledged Kipp. He exchanged a glance with her. "Mother and I were just having a moment."

Her heart took wings. It soared out over the waves and into the clouds and beyond, circling the sun ecstatically, and infiltrating the stars beyond, before it sailed back, at last, and nestled deeply within her maternal breast.

"Well, fine," said Heston, turning away, his eyes searching the white caps. "*Excellente.*"

"Did you have a good swim, Winnie?" she asked the child.

Winnie nodded. The little beauty had donned her father's sunglasses, which were too big for her delicate face and head. The sunglasses bobbled comically as Winnie nodded. "Why are you crying?" she asked, shades askew, glaring upwards at her new brother.

"I'm not crying, you little scamp," he said, grabbing out for Winnie, who squealed delightedly. Letting go of her father's hand, Winnie zipped down the beach, with Kipp hot in pursuit. Within seconds, he had collected his half-sister in his arms and, dropping onto the sand, was tickling her into wild gales of laughter.

***

Lying in Heston's bed, sunlight flooding the master suite, Poppy treasured the feeling of Heston's body weight on top of her. Inexplicably, the pressure of his weighty muscular mass intensified her afterglow. Satiated, he lay paralyzed, his face flattened, right cheek down, between her breasts, only his hands moving, as he sensuously, if absentmindedly, kneaded the meaty flesh of her haunches. Nearly a month had passed since she and Heston had resumed their bouts of unrestrained passion. They truly were lovers now, in every sense of the word.

As they lay lost in serenity, morning was advancing towards midday. Trays of unwashed breakfast dishes sat forgotten on the dresser, right beside Poppy's elegant little assemblage of sea things. Heston had refused to let Lissette back into the master suite to collect them. He and Poppy had been awake for hours. He had not wanted their orgiastic revels interrupted by mundane housekeeping chores. They were now finishing the morning's lovemaking, lying adrift in each other's arms. Half-comatose, Heston lay enraptured and quiescent, hardly recognizable as the man who, only a short while earlier, had been savage in his quest for satisfaction.

Nestling close, Poppy lay smug and secure in her ability to please him. She had loved him now in every way there was to love a man—and yet, somehow she knew their future still held the boundless promise of discovery. She counted herself as the luckiest woman in the world. She was the bedmate, the lover, the mistress, and, indeed, the intimate worshipper of the most desirable man on the planet—or, rather, as Heston himself would have joked, had he heard her secret thoughts, the second-most desirable. All the bad publicity had sent his box-office draw to the next level. Intoxicated by love-lust, she now lay saturated in Heston Demming-ness. His male essence permeated every fiber of her being.

Her life was no longer her own. Her life now belonged to him, to her new family. She was part of his bigger world now. The tabloids, the glossy rags, the TV gossip shows, all had found her. Her privacy was forever gone. Her image was emblazoned daily, around the globe, as the woman who had won Heston Demming as a bedmate, a dubious, yet fantastic distinction, one she could not—would not—ever deny, for she belonged in Heston's bed. It was what she had been born for. She knew that now with a fearsome certainty. Not even the old tapes in her head of Uncle Mel's shaming harangues and violent assaults could shake her from the conviction that she was Heston Demming's natural wife.

Her fingers skimmed through her man's thick hair, curved around his broad shoulders, and pressed into the smooth, spongy muscle of his upper back. Groaning with pleasure, she felt the heavy heat of his chest pressing against her belly. Sleepily, he stirred. Tenderly, she again stroked his hair and pressed his head to her breast. She did not want him to move—ever.

But he did.

Slowly, he repositioned himself. Now, propped up on one elbow, he stared down lovingly into her face, the warm glow of possession in his eyes. His pride of ownership took her breath away. *Oh, no. There is no escape from this. And I don't want to escape from this—not now, not ever.*

"Poppy?" he inquired throatily. Idly, she stroked the thick stubble that covered his square jaw and upper lip. Her finger traced the corner of his lips.

"What, love?" Eyelids languid, she was half-dozing in bliss.

"Will you marry me?"

Coming awake, she opened her eyes wide. She dropped her hand from his cheek.

"Heston!" Fear gripped her heart. All the old daunting trepidation surged within her. Seeming to sense her fear, he bent and softly kissed her trembling lips.

"I love you more than my life's measure," he whispered. "Please, Poppy—this time—will you marry me? Don't deny me again."

She wanted to cry 'yes,' to shout it to the angels on high, but the word choked in her gullet. As before, in that time long ago, she was shackled by a secret knowledge, one she had not yet shared with him. True, there was no sign of Montserrat Flynn, nor did she believe there ever would be again, although she felt less secure about the X factor, Lennox Cordova. As the wife of a movie idol, Poppy was learning that there always would be competition for her prize. However, the life growing within her could not be denied.

"H-Heston," she stammered.

"Yes?" His finger gently pushed a strand of unruly hair from her forehead.

"I have to tell you something."

Still balanced on one elbow, he inched closer. "What? Tell me."

Now or never. Her soul stared straight into his. "I'm going to have a baby."

"What, again?" he joked, not batting an eyelash

"Silly," she chided, tapping his shoulder with her hand to offset her anxiety. But she had seen the wild, bestial glory flare in his eyes. His face was suddenly radiant, luminous as the life-giving sun itself. Could he tell she was frozen with fright?

"I'm going to have a baby, so maybe you don't want..."

Taking her by the upper arms, he sat her upright in the bed.

"You listen to me," he said, stalwart. "That's where you're wrong. This time WE are going to have a baby. Poppy, marry me! Marry me!" His hands wrenched her upper arms. "Poppy Craft, will you marry me at last? Say 'yes'," he commanded urgently, shaking her firmly, but gently. "In the name of Heaven, let me be a father to our child. And you be the mother you were meant to be." He took her face between his hands. "Penelope Susan Craft, will you marry me?"

"Y-yes, Heston," Poppy whispered, melting. "I will marry you. *Yes! Yes! Yes!* I don't want there to be any confusion this ti—"

Heston's mouth clamped down upon hers before she could emit another syllable. Her arms went round his neck. He was right, so very, very right. Their union was meant to be. Like starlight on salt water, their love was, and always had been, generative in nature.

Epilogue

In pre-dawn darkness, Heston Demming stood over Franco's grave. Overhead, a wide, brightening sky sang the promise of hope. Staring down at his young son's grave, Heston's heart knew only despair. *Why had this happened? What possible end could it serve?* Blinking back the tears, he thought about his own father—the drinking bouts, the physical attacks, the emotional abuse, the anger, the abject grief of shame and failure, the gruesome suicide.

Thirty-years ago, his father, Sean Douglas Demming, had been a prominent doctor in Chicago. Doug had joined a practice and married Heston's mother, Kay MacCormack, a nurse from Kansas City. Kay had produced a son, whom, in an inspired compromise, she had named after both her husband and her favorite movie actor. Then something had gone terribly wrong in Dr. Douglas Demming's career.

Heston had never revealed to the public the exact circumstances of his father's disgrace. He had paid handsomely to keep the secret. Nor had he yet told his son, Kipp, the future doctor. He knew the facts would be devastating. He had been devastated upon learning them himself.

His parents had hidden the facts from him during his childhood. His father, Douglas, had been accused of malpractice, that was all they had told him. His father had lost his medical license. Penniless and shamed, the Demmings had fled far away, to the southernmost tip of the United States.

Trying to put his life back together, Douglas Demming had worked odd jobs but had never recovered from the blow. Finally, humiliated beyond rescue or redemption, he had hanged himself one night, in the backyard of his small, flat-roofed home in Lake Park.

Kay had found her husband's body there in the early morning, during a summer downpour. Heston remembered waking to his mother's screams when she ran in, drenched and hysterical, to wake him. He remembered the police, his father's dangling body, the funeral, the nightmare of Kay's grief and his own torment. He remembered how desperate his mother had seemed ever after.

Prior to Doug's death, Kay had kept up a stoic front, probably for his sake. Once the awful deed had been done, she fell apart. Not long after, his mother had started abusing prescription drugs. In her various jobs as a nurse, she had had access to the pills and other medications. At first, he had thought his mom was drunk, as his dad had been, when—coming home from school, or from his afternoon and evening job as a supermarket bag-boy—Heston had found her lying unconscious, barely breathing.

Then had come that terrible day—not long after high-school graduation—when he had found his mother's own dead body lying face down on her mattress, her hair matted with sweat, her soft skin still warm. He had turned her body over. Heston shuddered and shoved the picture from his mind. He focused instead on the mound of green grass lying atop Franco's grave.

Now they are both lying here, next to Franco—the grandson they never knew, the one who had never known them. He contemplated the three adjacent memorial plaques and, at last, he wept openly, unable to stem the tide of his despair. *It's all my fault. It must be my fault. I'm the only constant in the whole scenario.*

If only I had listened to my father when he tried to talk to me. Instead, I pushed him away, shouted him down, wouldn't hear him. I treated him as my enemy instead of as the hurting soul he was. If only I had paid attention to my mother's pain, instead of trying to drink away my own, as I did even then, as a kid, a teenager, an adolescent.

If only I had found a place in my heart for Franco, my little son whom I ignored until he hated me with all the emotion which should have come to me as love.

Closing his eyes, Heston mouthed a prayer to his Maker. He promised his Maker that things would be different from now on. Freely, he relinquished his own arrogance, admitting that his righteous anger and egomania had caused him to bring harm to others. He thanked his Maker that he did not need drink anymore, that he had been able to control his cravings for alcohol, and that he had found the love of the woman intended for him since the beginning of time. He thanked his Maker for Kipp and Winnie and for giving him another chance to correct his behavior, unbelievably, with another fine son or daughter on the way.

Why have I been given such blessings in my life? Why me? Why the money, the fame? Why couldn't my parents have lived to have seen my success?

At least he had Poppy. He didn't know the answers to the questions he asked. His only aim in life now was to prove his worthiness for such blessings by safeguarding and caring for the loved ones with whom he had been blessed. He even decided, on the spot, to give Maude a decent divorce settlement, instead of the paltry sum agreed to in their prenuptial agreement. A model's career was even shorter lived than a leading man's. Maude *was* the mother of his daughter. He would give Rogelio money for the care of Inez, too, and he would find some meaningful way to honor his son Franco's life—and his own mother's and father's lives.

Money is the one thing I have plenty of to give. It's a good place to start.

He drew a cotton handkerchief from his pocket and wiped his damp face dry. Even now, it was all about making amends. As a recovering alcoholic, he had started down that path thinking that it would be difficult, but he hadn't realized just how long and arduous the path would be, nor how far back into the past he would have to tread in his quest for redemption and restitution.

Now, bowing his head, he prayed to his Maker and asked for guidance as well as forgiveness. This time he vowed to make amends to the dead, as well as to the living, for all he had done wrong. It would never be enough, but it was all he could do now.

In spite of what the world thought, he knew himself to be far from perfect. With Poppy's love, and guidance from above, he might even be able to accept that inescapable fact of life—and be okay with it. The world would find out soon enough. He was aging daily.

He knew his career would not last forever. He vowed to make the most of the years he had left—with his beautiful, amazing wife-to-be and his phenomenal and precious children. He saw now that it was his job to protect them all. From now on, he would do his job. At long last, he had been given the presence and the power to be a real man, not just an actor playing a role, not just an action hero in some screenwriter's digital fantasy.

I am a real man.

"Heston?" He heard her soft voice calling him from the car. "Is everything okay?"

He turned slightly, so that Poppy could hear his voice but could not see his face directly.

"Yes, love," he croaked in his worst stage voice. "I'm finished here. For now."

He heard the clip-clop of high heels on the nearby paved roadway. Then she was by his side, hooking her small arm around his elbow.

"Please don't blame yourself anymore, darling. Be kind to yourself. Forgive yourself. That's the only course that leads back to life. Haven't you learned yet? Everything happens the way it's supposed to. Otherwise, it would have happened another way. That's my philosophy, anyhow. So far, it's kept me sane."

"You're a real woman, you know that?" They ambled towards the waiting car.

"So they tell me," she nodded, squeezing his bicep and forearm with her strong, little hands. Gently, she led him towards the car. "I'm looking forward to our trip to Mexico tomorrow," she said to steady him. "I've never been on a movie set before."

"Thanks for helping me learn my lines," he said genuinely. Dawn was breaking as they approached his Ferrari.

"I enjoyed it."

He paused in his stroll and turned to her. "Did I tell you that my agent wants to represent Kipp? He thinks Kipp Demming could be the next big thing in the entertainment industry."

"Really? How does Kipp feel about it?" Poppy's face reflected his feelings.

He felt torn—proud, but apprehensive. *What does Kipp want?* His son had told him he wanted a career in medicine, not show business. Would he still feel that way when he learned the truth?

"I don't know," he replied. "I haven't told him yet. She wants to represent Winner, too. As soon as I give the word." He mimicked his agent's voice: "The kid's a natural. Gorgeous, sensitive, well-connected."

"Good heavens."

"No kidding."

"She wants to start a Demming-family acting dynasty?" Poppy marveled.

"*Uh-huh*," he nodded.

"How do you feel about it?" she asked him.

"Well, I'll admit I'm intrigued by the idea. I've decided to form my own production company, anyway. Why not make it a family affair? Of course, Winston is too young, yet. Still too fragile, too emotionally vulnerable. But the play therapy is helping her, and so is the art therapy. And you're good for her. So good. So when she's older, stronger...why not? If she wants to. As for Kipp, all I can do is ask. I'll present him with the opportunity—and the facts. Let him decide."

Standing on tiptoe, Poppy pulled his face down to hers and kissed his cheek.

"I love you, Heston," she whispered.

"Likewise," he said. "Get in the car."

Willingly, she obeyed. Her easy acquiescence to his need pleased him. It was one of the qualities he loved most about her. "Where to?" she asked.

"Home. Bed," he replied, slipping behind the wheel.

COMING SOON!

TINA MURRAY

A WILD DREAM OF LOVE
A HESTON DEMMING MYSTERY BOOK 2

**"Romance, revenge, redemption—and a
rock-music legend to die for."**

Kipp Demming rides the wave of fame and debauchery that rock-n-roll offers until he can take no more.

Imagine a lead singer's surprise to learn that a plain girl looking for her next step in life could hold his happy ever after...

Will old secrets be unearthed and lives destroyed? Or will unseen forces guide the destiny of the Demming family's entertainment dynasty?

**For more information
visit:** www.SpeakingVolumes.us

On Sale Now!

ANNE ARGULA
QUINN MYSTERIES

For more information
visit: www.SpeakingVolumes.us

On Sale Now!

BETH GROUNDWATER
CLAIRE HANOVER MYSTERIES

On Sale Now!

AWARD-WINNING AUTHOR
BARBARA D'AMATO
MYSTERIES

For more information
visit: www.SpeakingVolumes.us